RETRIBUTION

RETRIBUTION

RETRIBUTION

BOOK THREE IN THE RECUSAL SERIES

DONALD CATALANO

coffeetownpress

Kenmore, WA

coffeetown**press**

A Coffeetown Press book published by Epicenter Press

Epicenter Press
6524 NE 181st St.
Suite 2
Kenmore, WA 98028

For more information go to:
www.Camelpress.com
www.Coffeetownpress.com
www.Epicenterpress.com
www.donaldcatalano-author.com

This is a work of fiction. Names, characters, places, brands, media, and incidents are either the product of the author's imagination or are used fictitiously.

Cover design by Scott Book
Design by Melissa Vail Coffman

Retribution
Copyright © 2023 by Donald Catalano

Library of Congress Control Number: 2023935572

ISBN: 978-1-68492-113-3 (Trade Paper)
ISBN: 978-1-68492-114-0 (eBook)

Printed in the United States of America

To the preservation of liberal democracy
and social freedom.

ACKNOWLEDGMENTS

MANY THANKS TO MY LITERARY AGENT, Barbara Hogenson. Much appreciation to my editors and publishers at Coffeetown Press. Gratitude to my friends Pat Fullam, Molly Johnson, Keith Stolte, Mary Francis Patston, and Ben Massarella whose love and support made this series possible.

CHAPTER 1

Tʜᴇ Wʜɪᴛᴇ Hᴏᴜsᴇ ᴡᴀs sᴛɪʟʟ ᴀ ᴄʜᴀᴏᴛɪᴄ sᴄᴇɴᴇ two days after the attempt on President Andrew Cochran's life.

"Howard, what are you still doing here? You can go back to the Naval Observatory if you like," Stuart Prentice stated to his long-time political adversary just outside of the Oval Office.

"What are you talking about, I belong here," former Vice-President Howard Mason objected to his colleague across the political aisle.

"Howard, you resigned from the Vice-Presidency two days ago before the attempt on the President's life. The following morning, once all of the details came to light, I promptly resigned as Speaker of the House and as a Representative in Congress. I was sworn in as Acting President yesterday, remember?" Stuart Prentice chided the former Vice-President with a sly grin.

"Yes, of course I remember but there is work to be done. I am fully aware of the President's agenda and protocols," Howard Mason interjected.

"I appreciate that Howard, I sincerely do. But the President is still in intensive care. Even though the prognosis is seemingly improved for his full recovery, until he is capable of resuming his duties as President, I am in charge of dispensing the duties of the Office of the Presidency. It's all delineated in 3 U.S.C. Subsection 19 of the 20th Amendment, under the Presidential Succession Act of 1947, as you are well aware. I am honored that you want to help, but right now, I need to get a handle on things.

When I need your advice and guidance, I will certainly let you know. But in the meantime, go to the hospital and be with your friend or go home and get some rest," Stuart Prentice advised as he ran his right hand through his thick dark brown hair, his deep blue eyes sparkling.

Stuart Prentice was well known for being someone who would "cut to the chase." Stuart didn't countenance the ineffectiveness and indecision of others. Never had, never would. He had a clear-cut focus on the task at hand. And at that time, the task at hand was to listen to the morning security briefings from senior advisors to the President and attempt to grasp the magnitude of the job ahead of him. As the liberal leader of the Democrats in the House of Representatives, Stuart Prentice was a fifty-one-year-old political progressive ideologue who was fully embracing the imperative need of understanding the challenges ahead of the country and keeping the nation safe and stable during a time of tumult and unease due to an assassination attempt on the President.

As Speaker of the House, Stuart Prentice, along with the liberal lions of the Senate, such as Henry Fitzsimmons and Perry Douglas, forged an alliance that allowed the President to remain politically intact as he shifted to far more moderate and even liberal domestic policies. Legislation was passed, judicial appointments were made and confirmed by the Senate, all as part of a gentleman's agreement between the Democratic leaders of the House and Senate and the politically-damaged-by-scandal Republican President who saw the salvation of his administration and his legacy through political bargaining and taking far less strident Conservative stances than he had previously professed on most domestic issues. The Democrats in Congress approved of the President's moderate approach, as the President's own party shuddered in horror and denounced any compromise as treason to the Conservative cause. Republican leaders such as Cletus Sawyer demanded retribution against the person who they perceived to be their treacherous and treasonous leader. Other Republican leaders such as then Vice-President Howard Mason were less strident in their expressed views but still kept more than an arms-length from fully supporting President Cochran.

Speaker of the House, and now Acting President Stuart Prentice, saw far more advantage in his negotiated truce with Andrew Cochran than he saw in any use of Howard Mason. Howard wasn't Vice-President, he wasn't even the popular Republican Senator from Ohio anymore.

With ten months left in the Cochran administration, Stuart saw count-less opportunities to seize on and achieve some major legislative policy victories working hand-in-hand with a cooperative Andrew Cochran. Howard Mason had resigned hours too early. Though no charges had been brought as of yet by the FBI, Howard Mason was still under inves-tigation given his proximity to the President and the poisoned bourbon. Howard Mason was politically damaged goods. The sooner you clear the rot out of a situation, the sooner you can preserve the healthy remain-ders of a politically convenient administration.

POSY BRANCH HAD NOT TRULY SLEPT in more than 60 hours. She believed that she was already asleep and in the midst of a horrible nightmare, and that the only way to rectify this tragic wrong was to finally awaken from this terror, go to work, and give a big welcoming hug to her close friend and co-business partner Chiffon LaBelle. To fall asleep and then wake up with Chiffon no longer alive in this world was something her fragile being could not countenance. Chiffon had become a very important part of Posy's life. Her business partner in French Tips, as well as a dear and trusted friend. Posy ferociously fought every temptation to fall asleep. She would not have it, despite the encouragement of her friend and col-league Michael Crowley, who attempted to convince Posy that she was only hurting herself, something that Chiffon would never want under any circumstances. Michael was Posy's rock, both in her business, as her star bartender, but also as a confidant and friend. Yet, Posy was incon-solable. All she could do was stare out the window of her apartment and imagine the most heinous image of "Strange Fruit." She would mumble in her incoherent withered state about wanting to "cut all of the trees down." Michael sat by her side as he waited for the doctor to arrive. Posy needed help, and Michael was going to see to it that that was precisely what she got. Help!

THE EARLY MARCH BREEZE LEVITATED the supple branches of the large willow tree as its leaves and boughs sang a hauntingly beautiful dirge. Aaron Rose and Clay Grover sat in the shadows under the hanging limbs of the magnificent tree located in a public park in the Marigny neighbor-hood of New Orleans. The couple ate their lunch during a break from their work at Caleb Butler's small law firm.

"Three days after Chiffon's murder and I still can't believe that she is gone. It's like a nightmare that I can't wake up from," Clay solemnly stated as he sat back against the rough bark of the willow tree.

"I'm sorry, I can't talk about it without breaking down in tears," Aaron softly confessed.

"I understand," Clay acknowledged. "It's as if the world is spinning out of control. At least the little bit of positive news is that the President is now in somewhat stable condition. Apparently, he did not ingest enough of the digitalis poison that was mixed into the bottle of bourbon."

"As the FBI pointed out in their news conference, the President took a couple of small sips of the bourbon, as opposed to Kate Wilson gulping down almost an entire bottle of spring water or Justice Martin drinking a half of a glass of tap water," Aaron added. "One usually doesn't chug bourbon, so the President was lucky enough not to ingest a fatal amount of the poison. And, with time and proper care, the President will recover from his digestive tract and heart issues, which would be great news."

"The best news for Andrew Cochran may be that the sympathy that he has received after the attempt on his life has unquestionably altered the Republican primaries. After losing four states in a row to open the primary and caucus season, it now looks like in the latest polls that Cochran will take a good number of the Presidential Election Super Tuesday states that had been up for grabs. Meanwhile, the momentum that Vice-President Mason had after his announcement of seeking the party's nomination for President has all but collapsed. It looks like his campaign is over before it actually had a chance to flourish," Clay noted.

"It all makes me so extremely sad," Aaron lamented. "Nothing is as it should be or even as it appears. It's all shadows on the wall, and you have no idea what's their actual size or origin. Or even more importantly, who is casting these shadows?

"Big secrets cannot remain secrets for very long, too many people need to be involved," Clay stated.

The door of Bessie Collin's small voodoo shop on north Rampart Street remained bolted shut for the third day in a row. The "Closed" sign hung from the window of the rickety old door. A few potential customers peered through the window attempting to discern why the place of business was not open during the normal business hours. No one knew that answer, except for Bessie Collins. And Bessie was in her kitchen at home, with her apron on as she prepared and baked over two dozen pies in the last day or so. She did little else but bake. Bessie was afraid of what she might do if she didn't fully invest herself physically and mentally into the preparation of assorted pies. She had no desire to find out what she might do. She was living in fear of what she might do.

STANFORD WINCHESTER SAT ON THE BALCONY of his Royal Street home in New Orleans as he rocked in his chair while reading the morning Times-Picayune newspaper. His head shook and he sighed as he read the accounts of the attempted murder of President Cochran and he also read about the tragic local news about the hanging death of Chiffon LaBelle. Recently retired Judge Stanford Winchester and his fiancée Judge Whitlee Hammond had met Chiffon a number of times at French Tips, Juleps & Jazz. He was horrified to read the grizzly details of her murder. He was fond of Chiffon and was saddened by her death.

"Horrible, horrible news," Stanford repeated as he was joined on the balcony by Whitlee.

"Ms. LaBelle was so full of life, what an absolute tragedy," Whitlee agreed in a somber tone. "Just when you think we've moved forward in this country, then we are confronted with this despicable type of hate crime just proving there is still so much work to be done. And then the attempted assassination of the President, what is this world coming to?"

"People who feel as if they are losing the strings of power will do whatever they deem is necessary to keep and control that power," Stanford stated solemnly.

"You don't believe that Howard Mason had anything to do with the attempted poisoning of the President, do you?" Whitlee asked.

"Of course not," Stanford quickly replied. "I've met Howard Mason a couple of times, including during my time in Washington being considered for the Supreme Court vacancy. He did not seem to be a man who would have the ability to knowingly poison another man. It just isn't part of his make-up. No, Howard Mason is not an attempted murderer. He is the dupe for a plot fashioned by men far more ruthless and cold-hearted than Howard Mason could ever be. I know men who are capable of this type of planned treachery, and they are far different people than the former Vice-President."

"It couldn't possibly be . . ." Whitlee began before quickly ending her inquiry.

"Anything is possible, my love, when it comes to the pursuit of power. Anything is possible, especially among ruthless men."

SENATOR PERRY DOUGLAS AND HIS PRESIDENTIAL campaign manager Carolyn Barnes sat chatting on his campaign bus while stuck in traffic heading into Denver, Colorado.

"Well Carolyn, a week ago I would never have anticipated that my old friend Stuart Prentice would be Acting President of the United States. But here we are with a liberal President and control of both the House and Senate," Perry Douglas stated with a sly smile.

"Yes, but this honeymoon is going to be especially short. It sounds like President Cochran is out of immediate danger and is on his way to recovering from the attempt on his life. There is nothing that Stuart can practically achieve other than to maintain the status quo and engender the American people with a sense of stability and security," Carolyn responded.

"Truly, but it portends well for the future, I think. It allows the nation to see the leadership and even hand of a liberal Democrat in the White House. Stuart will not act as a political opportunist. He understands that the advantage here is one of promotion and appearances more than the attempt at a fast political policy grab. Could we be so sure that that wouldn't happen if in a similar situation the Republicans had taken temporary control of the Presidency and both the House and Senate? My guess is that they would be attempting to stack the Federal courts with Conservative jurists and taking advantage of the situation to push their right-wing agenda."

"I'm sure that's not far from the truth," Carolyn asserted. "But, only an irrational mad man would seize on the power of the office and take political advantage while the country is reeling from an attempt on the life of their elected leader."

"That is just one difference between us and them. We put the good of the country ahead of our own ideological imperative in times of unrest. The best thing that Stuart can do is to keep things as stable as possible both internationally and domestically. Reassure the American people that our nation is strong because our institutions and laws are solidly at work, the way they were designed to by the Founding Fathers."

"Speaking of solidly at work, our campaign folks on the ground here in Colorado have done a great job at getting the apparatus set-up for a solid get-out-the-vote ground game on Super Tuesday. We are looking good for a solid victory," Carolyn stated with a short smile.

"Excellent! We badly need Colorado on Tuesday," Perry Douglas responded optimistically. "Hellen Raymond will clean up in Alaska, Alabama, Arkansas, Georgia, and Oklahoma. If we can counter with primary victories in Massachusetts, Minnesota, Vermont, Virginia, and here in Colorado we will be just fine. Texas and Tennessee are toss-ups, so if we can split those contests we're on our way. Of course, a supportive word from Acting President Stuart Prentice wouldn't hurt either," Perry said with a smile.

"I'll see what I can do," Carolyn, a smart and savvy African American political operative replied. "I'm pretty sure that his folks would be receptive to a gentle nod in our direction. After all, what are friends for?"

"Yes, indeed Carolyn," Perry Douglas eagerly agreed.

MARK BACKUS PATIENTLY LISTENED TO HIS FRIEND, former Vice-President Howard Mason, as he ranted into the telephone from his living room at the Naval Observatory.

"That ass made it seem like it was a pronounced privilege that I could stay in my house for the time being," Howard snarled into the telephone.

"Well, after all Howard, you did resign the Vice-Presidency, and eventually there will be another Vice-President appointed once Andrew Cochran is physically and mentally capable of resuming his duties as President. In the meantime, we are stuck with Acting President Prentice," Mark calmly responded.

"He shooed me away like I was a swarm of annoying gnats. No one is more familiar with the day-to-day workings of the White House than I am," Howard challenged.

"If the shoe were on the other foot, we wouldn't be acting much differently," Mark stated.

"And the humiliation of still being questioned by the FBI is unbearable. I'm not a stupid man. I wouldn't give the man that I've just announced I'm challenging for the Presidency a bottle of poison for Christ's sake!" Howard exclaimed. "Yet, here I am being viewed like a criminal by law enforcement, and being treated like an uninvited house guest by that pompous ass Stuart Prentice!"

"Howard you should take this time to hit the campaign trail. We still have a few days before Super Tuesday. You still have a shot at the Republican nomination for President," Mark said as he attempted to calm his old friend down.

"Really Mark? My polling numbers have cratered in the last two days as the suspicion of my possible role in the attempted assassination of the President hangs over my head like the Sword of Damocles. And then I am publicly humiliated and shunted aside by Speaker Prentice and his ilk. You really think this is a good time to hit the campaign trail?" Howard asked with a piqued tone to his voice.

"Yes Howard, I do, unless you are planning to quit the race before it's really even begun," Mark rebutted. "Look, things are not going well, I grant you that. But you still have an opportunity to pick-up Vermont, Minnesota, Massachusetts, and possibly Virginia on Super Tuesday. We are within striking distance in each of those states. But we need to get on the air quickly with campaign ads, and get you out making appearances. If you can take two of those states while Cochran, Wilson and Cletus Sawyer each take two to four states, we are still right there in the fight. No one has an upper hand."

"Oh, you don't think that death-bed boy is making significant inroads? Brian showed me just this morning how his numbers are soaring," Howard snarled in return.

"Yes, public sympathy is on his side right now, but that can change quickly. The incumbent President finished second in four primaries and caucuses before the attempt on his life. He is not that well loved by Republican primary voters. They are just waiting for a time and reason to shun him once again," Mark offered his unnerved friend.

"Perhaps you're right, Mark, but I am truly skeptical," Howard replied. "Perhaps after the FBI uncovers who was behind the plot to poison the President and fully exonerates me that we can make some headway again. Our caucus results in Nevada were very promising."

"That's all I'm saying Howard. Don't fold up the tent just yet. We still have a chance to get into this race as a serious contender. Don't let your aggravation at the current situation dissuade you from making a full-fledged run at the nomination. It's not over, my friend, and in fact

I don't even see a fat lady in the room, yet," Mark offered with a small chortle.

"Screw the fat lady, we need law enforcement to quickly find out who tried to kill that asshole Cochran and soon," Howard Mason reiterated over the phone.

THE DEEP SOUTHERN VOICE ON ONE end of the telephone conversation was none too pleased at the current circumstances in Washington D.C.

"How the hell did things get so screwed up? Who the fuck tried to kill Cochran and frame that idiot Mason for the attempt?" The low and belligerent voice questioned.

"We're looking into it sir, we think we may have a few leads," the other voice responded.

"Well, we know who it wasn't, even though nothing would please me more than to see Andrew Cochran residing in Arlington National Cemetery instead of 1600 Pennsylvania Avenue."

"Cochran has many enemies on the right wing of the Republican Party. There are several well-heeled individuals that share your sentiments, but few who would take the calculated risks involved with an attempt on the life of the President of the United States," the somber reasoned voice stated into the phone.

"Find out which idiot took that ill-advised risk and soon. Three days ago, Andrew Cochran was an incumbent unable to win a single contest. Now, while he lies in a hospital bed, his poll numbers have skyrocketed. Whoever, made this stupid move against him did nothing but put him right back in the race and even in the fucking lead!" The Southern voice harangued. "Get me some answers fast, so we can attempt to mitigate this disaster!"

CHAPTER 2

It was the Monday before the Super Tuesday Presidentail primaries were to be held in twelve states. The biggest one-day prize in the early primary election season. President Andrew Cochran finally had been released from the hospital. He had suffered some digestive tract and kidney issues due to his poisoning, but overall he had come through the ordeal in fairly good physical condition. His political condition was also markedly better. Recent polling showed him in the lead in seven of the twelve states up for grabs in the primaries. He was on his way to a landslide victory in his native Georgia and had sizable leads in Colorado and Massachusetts. President Cochran maintained small leads in the polling in Minnesota, Vermont, Virginia, and Tennessee. Senator Cletus Sawyer was expectedly ahead in his home state of Alabama, and Jedediah Wilson had clear leads in Arkansas, Texas and Oklahoma. Howard Mason was within striking range in Minnesota, Vermont and Virginia. Only Alaska was seen as an absolute toss-up state.

On the Democratic side of the nomination contest, it appeared as if Senator Hellen Raymond of North Carolina would prevail in five states and Senator Perry Douglas of Illinois, would also claim victories in five states with two states up for grabs among the Democratic nominees left in the race. It was early March, but politically things were beginning to heat-up in the Presidential race. Rapidly.

FBI DIRECTOR JAMES TURNER SAT BEHIND his office desk thinking about everything that had just been reported to him by the FBI agents directly involved in investigating the assassination attempt on the President of the United States. He re-reviewed the notes that he had taken during the course of his debrief from the agents. He slowly shook his head as he continued his review of his notes. Something just didn't add up. How did poison get into the bottle of bourbon presented earlier that day to Andrew Cochran by his Vice-President upon his resignation? The forensic studies done on the bottle, the seal, and even the box did not indicate that the bottle had been tampered with at all. The fingerprints were consistent with those taken from Andrew Cochran, Howard Mason, and Mason's aide, who had purchased the bottle from a Capitol Hill liquor store. Nothing appeared to be untoward, no evidence of tampering. So how did the poison get into the bottle and thereby be ingested by the President. None of the facts were adding up.

THE SMALL BAPTIST CHURCH IN THE Bywater neighborhood of New Orleans was packed on that Monday morning in early March. People of all colors, genders, sexual preferences, and religious beliefs or not, took a seat on the old rickety pews as they awaited the commencement of the memorial service for their friend and colleague Chiffon LaBelle. The pastor waited until all of the guests could make their way into the narrow entry way and find a seat in the crowded pews. Posy Branch, Michael and all of the staff and musicians from French Tips, Juleps & Jazz sat together in one row. Caleb Butler, Aaron Rose, Clay Grover, Emily DuBois, and the entire staff of Caleb Butler's law office occupied a second row in the old church. Further in the back of the church sat Stanford Winchester and Whitlee Hammond.

Pastor Clarence Mayhew had known Chiffon LaBelle for several years. When possible, Chiffon would sing with the church choir on Sunday mornings. They had become close friends, so it was with a very heavy heart that Pastor Mayhew began his comments.

"She had the voice of an angel and occasionally, when necessary, the vocabulary of a truck driver. Chiffon LaBelle possessed a heart of gold and the inner strength and fortitude of fire-forged steel. She was the best friend to the most vulnerable of us and the tireless foe of those who take advantage and oppress those who cannot stand for themselves. Her moral compass was always pointed to the true and righteous center. She asked for nothing more than simple acceptance and respect, yet she gave everything she could for a friend in need. Chiffon lived her life in the pursuit of happiness and justice. That is all she ever asked for from this, at times, very cruel world. She deserved better and far more than our judgmental and intolerant society could ever dole out to her. All she ever truly wanted was love. She did not deserve to be subjected to the hate and scorn that often came with her decision to live her life as the person she believed herself to be. Sympathy and acceptance lost one of their greatest allies. We all loved her wholly. We will all miss her greatly."

Others stood and spoke of their great friend and colleague. Michael told a lovely story that characterized Chiffon's sense of humor and quick wit. Posy was unable to speak. Still weak and fatigued, though under a doctor's care, she could not muster the stamina or inner strength to eulogize her great friend. She valiantly tried to stifle her cries of anguish, but there hadn't been enough time to heal her wounds. Posy was damaged. It would take considerable time and effort to regain any sense of normalcy in her life. Her cherished friend, Chiffon's light had been cruelly extinguished, and Posy's life had been changed forever.

After the memorial service, the assemblage of Chiffon's co-workers, friends, and neighbors were invited by Posy and Michael to a luncheon in honor of Chiffon that was held at French Tips, Juleps & Jazz. Catered food from local restaurants filled long tables at the back of the large room. Beautiful splays of white roses adorned the tables. The clubs band played the jazz standards that Chiffon often sang, as guests milled about exchanging comments and shared stories about their friend Chiffon LaBelle.

Posy found it difficult to share happy and funny stories of her friend, though there were many. Her grief was all consuming. Though she knew that life had to go on and that she needed to channel her anguish and sorrow into an acknowledgement and acceptance of the facts of Chiffon's death, she could not bring herself to do it. Not now, not until Chiffon's murderer was found and received the full extent of judicially sanctioned retribution for the heinous hate crime committed. Instead, Posy stood quietly in a corner of the room, watching the guests mingle and share stories about Chiffon. Michael looked on with great concern, as he witnessed the pure joy and love of life siphoned from his boss, his mentor, and more importantly his dear friend.

Clay Grover and Aaron Rose were gathered in a small circle with Caleb Butler, Stanford Winchester and Whitlee Hammond discussing the tragic loss of someone they had come to know and cherish.

"Nothing brought her down, not after Katrina," Caleb Butler, Chiffon's attorney for the Katrina lawsuit, stated to the group. "She had been through hell during Katrina. Chiffon would often remind me, 'Caleb, when you're walking through hell you've got to keep on walking, otherwise you will get stuck there. There is light on the other side, but only if you keep moving positively forward each and every day. You can't let adversity slow or stop your personal growth and movement to a better life.' She truly believed that as she fought to get out of her own personal hell and become the loving and caring woman that we all knew."

"All she ever wanted was the same respect and dignity that she freely afforded to others," Aaron quickly added.

"A kind and loving soul occupying a conflicted body. But Chiffon discovered who she was and joyfully embraced her transformation. That takes more guts and courage than most of us could ever hope to display," Clay said while brushing his blonde hair from his eyes.

"My encounters with Ms. LaBelle were limited, but I could not help but be impressed with the spirit and enthusiasm with which she seemingly embraced life," Stanford Winchester responded. "She always had a smile on her face and greeted everyone as if they were part of her large expanded family."

The kind words and tributes extended far into the late afternoon. A tragic and senseless death is heavily felt by the community of friends and associates for quite a while. It is not taken casually or without the profound sense of loss. Chiffon LaBelle's death was profound. You need not look any farther than the pained and empty stare in Posy Branch's eyes to fully understand the meaning of loss.

BESSIE COLLINS HAD NOT LEFT HER HOUSE in days. She occupied most of her time in the preparation and baking of pies. In fact, her refrigerator and kitchen table and counters were filled with dozens of freshly made and untouched pies of several assorted varieties and flavors. Yet, once one pie was completed, Bessie almost mechanically went through the process of creating yet another.

"Bessie, my love, you've got to stop," her husband Lucius softly stated as he looked into his wife's forlorn eyes. Iffin' this is your way of punishing yourself, God knows that you is a good woman who'd never hurt nobody."

"It's my fault Lucius. It's my fault. Thank Jesus that the President is recovering cuz if he died, I'd never be able to live with myself," Bessie replied barely above a whisper.

"My sweet girl, you had nothing to do with that. You only guessing that Esther was involved. You ain't got no proof. And besides, how would Esther Francois be able to poison the President of the United States. It don't make no kind of sense," Lucius insisted.

"Same way that my auntie, Queen Rita done help with the poisoning of them two folk in Washington, including a Supreme Court Justice. God rest their souls. Esther be conspiring with powerful people and using black magic."

"You don't know that. No sense punishing yourself for something ain't been proved. Them FBI folk they is investigating and they surely will find out who done this terrible deed. But, you got to get back to your life. People been calling the house wanting to know when the shop is gonna open again. Papa Levi stopped by to see how you is," Lucius stated.

"I can't see Papa Levi right now. I'm afraid of what I might say. But I am mostly angry with myself, tho Papa Levi done brought Esther into my shop. But I said yes, it surely is my guilt to bear," Bessie answered.

"You can't keep yourself locked up in this house like it's some kind of prison. You got to move on, girl. There's too many people that need the old Bessie back. They need to see that smile of yours and the light and happiness in your eyes. And I surely count myself as first in that line," Lucius said with a warm smile.

"You is a good man, Lucius Collins. You is a good husband that always done right by me. But I ain't ready just yet to move on. I got me some thinking and praying that I need to do before I can get back to my old ways. Too much damage been done at that voodoo shop. Too much."

"GOOD AFTERNOON BOULDER!" ROBERT DOUGLAS, the charismatic son of Presidentil candidate Perry Douglas, enthusiastically greeted the large crowd that filled the auditorium at the University of Colorado. "My father has been keeping me locked in the proverbial campaign closet lately, but I am so excited and happy to be back in front of my peeps. As you all know, I'm out and very proud. They can't keep us in the closet for long can they?" Robert challenged to the resounding delight of his audience of young college students.

"If you've been following me on Facebook and Twitter, you know that I've not been happy about being off the campaign trail. But I begged and pleaded with my dad's campaign team to let me come to Boulder, this Monday afternoon before tomorrow's Super Tuesday primary. One of my dad's aides asked me why I was so emphatic about making the trip out here. I looked him straight in the eye, and simply said, 'Dude, I need me some Rocky Mountain High, Colorado,'" Robert announced with a huge grin on his face as the crowd exploded into laughter, cheers and sustained applause.

"Step one, get out and vote tomorrow. Step two, through your support ensure that Senator Perry Douglas is the next President of the United States. Step three, we will make marijuana legal in all fifty states! If out-of-time old men can't put down their bourbon bottles, why the hell should we put down our joints? Alcohol kills, weed chills!" The crowd followed Robert's lead and joined in a joyous chant, "Alcohol kills, weed chills."

Robert Douglas, the popular and provocative son of Senator Perry Douglas continued his speech for forty minutes. By the time he was finished with his address, the crowd was ready to elect Robert as President. He strode off the stage filled with confidence and pleased to be back in front of adoring college crowds.

ONE HOUR LATER, CAROLYN BARNES, the campaign manager for Perry Douglas' Presidential campaign was waiting backstage in an Aspen auditorium where her candidate was concluding his remarks before a large crowd.

"Nice crowd, good people. I felt like we really connected," Perry Douglas said to Carolyn with a smile, moments after he left the stage.

"Well then, you are the second Douglas to really connect with a crowd this afternoon," Carolyn stated.

"Oh, did Robert have a good speech on his return to the campaign trail to help his dear old dad?" Perry asked with a satisfied grin.

"You might very well think that, I couldn't possibly comment," Carolyn sarcastically replied.

"Oh no, what's wrong?" Perry asked with an anxious look on his face.

"Let's just say that after a couple of weeks off of the campaign trail, young Robert was feeling his oats."

"This doesn't sound good. What did he do?" Perry asked, grimacing before he even heard the answer.

"Robert started his speech by pretty much accusing you and the campaign of locking him in the 'closet.' Later in his comments, he basically promised the crowd that a vote for you for President equated to a vote for nationally legalized marijuana. By the end of his address he had the entire college crowd chanting, 'Alcohol kills, weed chills.' Congratulations, you and your son are now the Cheech and Chong of Presidential politics," Carolyn announced to her candidate. Perry Douglas remained silent for several moments after hearing what Carolyn had to report about Robert's campaign appearance. He then began to laugh. Whole-hearted robust guffaws. The kind of laughter that makes you start to cry.

"That's my boy!" Perry enthused. "You've got to give it to him, the boy has some flamboyance and flair to him! I'm not surprised that he had his say about his fatherly-imposed exile from the campaign trail. Frankly, I would have been shocked if he didn't get a little dig in at me about that, he was none too pleased. But the weed comments in front of a college crowd in Boulder, Colorado, well, that's just inspired!"

"You're not concerned about being equated as the legalized marijuana candidate?" Carolyn questioned.

"Not too much, no," Perry stated without hesitation. "I'm more concerned about the anti-liquor stance that he took. I really don't need distilleries running campaign ads against me. Look, I'm a progressive liberal, there is no hiding that fact. I can easily say that Robert was expressing his own views not mine, but I will not run away from my position of believing that there are no harmful effects of legalizing small amounts of marijuana for recreational adult usage. I've said that for years. Hell, on his twenty-first birthday, Robert and I smoked a joint together. Robert might have been a bit more hyperbolic in his statements than I would have been, but the truth of the matter is that I agree with the overall sentiment of his statements. It's time to stop aggrandizing alcohol every five minutes on television, yet we treat weed like some treacherous life stealing substance. It's not. Time for politics to catch-up with science."

"If you're comfortable with his statements, then we have no problems," Carolyn responded.

"I'm getting the sense that you're not," Perry said.

"I have a brother who had a drug problem. He went to prison because of it. So, I'm a little wary about jumping on the legalized weed bandwagon."

"Was his problem with weed?"

"No, not really. He became addicted to crack, but he also smoked some weed."

"I get it. I understand. But the scientific research done over the years has pretty much debunked the notion that marijuana is a portal drug that leads to harder drug use. It simply isn't true. That said, I'm not telling you that we should make this campaign about legalizing weed. That's not what our campaign is about. But, Robert's comments, I believe are generally harmless. I've got this one," Perry Douglas reassured his campaign manager with a fulsome smile. "Everything gonna be alright," Perry began to sing to Carolyn in his best Bob Marley impersonation. Carolyn could only smile.

REPUBLICAN SENATOR CLETUS SAWYER SAT IN the back booth of a barbecue restaurant in Dallas, Texas with his campaign advisor, Lamont Basemore, going over the most recent polling results on the eve of the Super Tuesday primaries. Cletus took a meaty bite from his sauced spare ribs.

"Hell Lamont, I hope to God that someone poisoned these damn ribs, cuz it looks like that's the best way to get votes from these idiot primary voters," Cletus huffed between bites. "Check and see if Howard Mason is back in the kitchen." Cletus smirked to his aide, his face smeared with an orange-brown sauce.

Lamont motioned toward his candidate attempting to pantomime with his hand the fact that Cletus' face was covered with barbecue sauce.

"What in blue blazes are you trying to do? Cletus asked with an irritated tone.

"You've got sauce on your face," Lamont said barely above a whisper.

"Jesus Christ, Lamont, I'm elbow deep in ribs, we're miles from the nearest TV camera, what the hell are you worried about?" Cletus roared.

"I'm worried that we are slipping perilously behind Andrew Cochran in these latest polls. The jump he's had in the polls is nothing short of astonishing," Lamont confessed.

"Well then, pull out that pearl-handled 38-revolver you carry and shoot me in the foot!" Cletus chided. "I can't do one damn thing to mitigate the overwrought sympathy that that Georgian scoundrel has elicited from the stupid sheep who vote in this country. What do you want me to do?"

"A bigger TV ad buy in the battleground states would probably be helpful? Lamont meekly responded.

"So, in other words you are telling me to go beg Jim Bob McCallum for more campaign money? Cletus asked.

"It wouldn't hurt."

"It certainly won't hurt your self-respect Lamont, but that man already thinks that he owns me. I am a three term Senator from Alabama and he treats me like a slow-witted adopted red-headed stepchild who he barely tolerates. He may be a friend, but he is a friend with plenty of baggage who routinely over stays his welcome," Cletus stated with contempt.

"We aren't going anywhere without his help," Lamont reminded Cletus.

"I know that, I'm mostly just blowing off some steam. But truly, I ain't so sure anymore that ol' Jim Bob and I are on the same page with the same agenda," Cletus confessed. "But his money is as green as it comes, so we smile and just ask for more. Now, pass me them collard greens and splash some hot sauce on them, will ya?"

Sergeant Norris Coaltree sat in the back of French Tips, Juleps & Jazz after the crowd had left following the memorial luncheon for Chiffon LaBelle. Michael had just returned from making sure that Posy Branch was safely at her home.

"It's not him Michael, Olivier Bellevue did not commit the murder of Chiffon LaBelle. The late night/early morning of Chiffon's murder, Olivier was at the Midtowne Spa in Houston, Texas. It's a gay bath house. Several of the patrons and staff recognized his photo. Some knew him from previous visits. His alibi is pretty much air tight," Norris told his friend.

"Then he arranged it. You listened to the security tapes, he threatened us right before he left. And he considered Chiffon his enemy, who he swore to get back at," Michael argued.

"I understand, but right now we've got nothing on him."

"What about those redneck boys I told you about?" Michael queried.

"We're looking for them now. We've got a pretty good idea about who they are. Not surprisingly, they've been in trouble before. Both have rap sheets as long as your arm, but it's all petty theft and the like. Nothing this serious before," Norris responded.

"I'm happy to come down to the precinct and identify them whenever you need me," Michael offered.

"Will do," Norris replied. "Look, I know how much this means to you. How much you loved Chiffon. We will find her killers. I promise you. But for the time being, steer clear of Olivier Bellevue. He was none too pleased to be questioned about a murder. He doesn't have a lot of good things to say about you and Posy right now. Best not to stir anything up, it would only muddy the waters."

"I understand," Michael solemnly nodded.

"Be safe, my friend."

CHAPTER 3

IT WAS THE EARLY EVENING OF THE SUPER TUESDAY primaries and some of the east coast states were beginning to report their voting tallies. President Andrew Cochran watched the results on television while lying in bed with monitors still hooked up to his body monitoring his vital signs and renal functions. His wife Sue Lynn sat in a chair near his bedside.

"It's far too early to get over our skis, but so far it appears that the tide has turned," the President stated to the First Lady. "Georgia was always a given but not by 25 points. We're up by 12 points in Massachusetts, 9 points in Virginia, 10 points in Tennessee, and 7 points in Vermont. So far, Cletus is only ahead in his home state of Alabama, and Jedediah Wilson ain't even hit the board yet."

"Yes, dear, it looks promising, but as you yourself warned it's way too early to get excited," Sue Lynn replied with a slight smile.

"What do the damn doctors say about me being able to resume my duties as President?" Andrew Cochran questioned.

"Not until at least the end of this week," Sue Lynn responded. "Maybe not even then. You were just released from the hospital yesterday. Don't try to rush your recovery Andy. Stuart Prentice is not doing anything to ruin the country. He's taking advice from your staff and maintaining a steady course while you recuperate. He's actually been very sweet and supportive of me," Sue Lynn added.

"It's funny that in a time of crisis, it's the Democrats who have come to our aid, as our Republican colleagues turn their backs on us. Not to mention my Vice-President jumping ship at the first sign of trouble and then challenging me for the nomination," Andrew Cochran allowed.

"It's unfortunate but true. You know who your friends are when the going gets tough," Sue Lynn added.

"Speaking of friends, have you heard anything from Nathan while I've been recovering?" Andrew asked his wife.

"Daily. He spent the first three days when you were in intensive care camped out in the hospital waiting room. He has sent floral arrangements, he called twice daily to check on your health status and progress, he even sent you a bottle of bourbon," Sue Lynn said with a gentle smile.

"Leave it to Nathan to find a way to insert levity into a grave situation," Andrew grinned in return.

"He loves you Andy. I had lost sight of that fact when he was embroiled in his own legal problems. I was so angry and resentful of him for the last three years. He caused you so much political harm. But it is true, you know who your friends are when times are tough. Everyone is your friend for the good times, but it's during the low moments when you truly find out who has your back. I've finally come to the realization that Nathan has your back," Sue Lynn confessed.

"I'm so glad to hear you say that Sue Lynn. I'll never be able to cut Nathan out of my life. It would be like cutting off an arm. So, it helps immensely to know that you understand he's always going to be a part of me, a part of our lives," Andrew confirmed.

"Look Andy," Sue Lynn said while pointing at the television set in the room, "NBC News has just declared you the winner in Tennessee."

"There you go!" Andrew exclaimed. "My first primary win is my home state of Georgia, and my second win is Nathan's home state of Tennessee. It's kismet. It's a new beginning, a new start for all of us."

CLETUS SAWYER SAT IN HIS HOTEL SUITE in Mobile, Alabama watching the Super Tuesday election results on television much like most of the nation. He stared at his cellphone several times before finally scrolling down his contacts list and selecting a number. The number of Jim Bob McCallum, the billionare fiancier of Senator Sawyer's presidential bid.

"Evening Jim Bob, this is Cletus," he haltingly said into the phone. "How are you?"

"Well Cletus, I'm watching my money circling the drain, that's how I am," Jim Bob smugly replied.

"It's early Jim Bob, the networks have declared winners in only three states, and we had a great night in Alabama," Cletus stated with confidence.

"It's your damn home state Cletus!" Jim Bob snarled. "You better be able to win more than the place where you were born and raised for Christ's sake."

"Oh, we will, we most surely will," Cletus replied enthusiastically.

"Cletus, switch over to ABC News, they just declared Massachusetts and Vermont for Cochran. Now, as you were saying?" Jim Bob asked his voice dripping with sarcasm.

"I'm not worried, it's still early."

"Said the man condemned to death as he was strapped down to the gurney at 11:58 p.m., with the warden counting down to midnight." Jim Bob responded. "What was it that you called me about anyway? I sure hope it wasn't to crow about your precious victory in Alabama," Jim Bob questioned.

"No, of course not," Cletus meekly stated. "It's just that we could use some additional monetary help for the next few weeks of primary contests. You know, buying some TV commercial time and getting the staff paid in the upcoming states."

"So, you need money to help win your race for the nomination, eh?" Jim Bob asked.

"Yes, precisely."

"Well Cletus, I ain't in the business of betting on dead horses. It's been my experience at Fairgrounds Racetrack that dead horses don't tend to win races. Why on God's green earth would I want to watch more of my money circle the drain?

"We've still got a real chance here, Jim Bob," Cletus implored.

"Whoops! There goes Virginia into Cochran's win column," Jim Bob said with a devilish chuckle while watching TV. "Cletus, right now you are surely looking like a dead horse. As I said before, I ain't in the business of betting on dead animals. If by tomorrow morning, the veterinarians can find a pulse in your carcass, perhaps I will reconsider. But for right now, I'd be going for my hunting rifle and a merciful and humane ending." With that Jim Bob hung up the telephone.

"Hello? Hello?" Cletus shouted into the phone until the flat electronic sound of the dial tone sounded the final shot.

SENATOR PERRY DOUGLAS HAD ONE EYE on the television screen in his hotel suite in Minneapolis, Minnesota, while he also quickly glanced at polling data being given to him by a campaign consultant.

"Carolyn, what's the count so far?" Perry questioned his campaign manager from across the room.

"We've won Massachusetts and Vermont. Hellen Raymond has won Alabama and Georgia. Things are looking good for us here in Minnesota according to the early vote counts. Virginia, and Texas are still up for grabs," Carolyn Barnes shouted in response.

"I take it that Raymond will take Arkansas, Tennessee, Oklahoma, and Alaska, right?"

"Yeah, we never had much of a chance in those states. You're not exactly the best friend of Evangelical voters," Carolyn replied.

"And is my pot-head son going to deliver Colorado for us?" Perry queried with a smirk.

"It's still early, but it looks like it," Carolyn stated.

"Then it looks like a sage decision to allow Robert back on the campaign trail despite my trepidations, eh?" Perry asked.

"The boy can charm the pants off of anyone," Carolyn replied without thinking.

"Do we really want to use the term 'charm the pants off' with respect to my gay son?" Perry challenged his campaign manager with a hearty laugh.

"Point taken," Carolyn chuckled in response.

"If we can take Texas tonight, that's the big enchilada. I know we'll get good results out of Austin, Dallas, Houston, and San Antonio, it's just a matter of whether that will be enough to offset the bath we'll take in west Texas," Perry surmised.

"It all boils down to turnout in the cities. Hellen Raymond can't touch you with the black and Hispanic metropolitan vote."

"Have you seen my wife? Where is Katherine?" Perry Douglas inquired.

"Yes, she's down the hall watching the Bulls and Timberwolves basketball game on television with a couple of our pollsters," Carolyn replied.

"Nice to see she cares so much about one of the biggest nights of my political career," Perry smirked.

"Hey, I'd be right there with her, except for the fact that somebody's got to hold your hand," Carolyn chuckled in return.

"Thanks, so very reassuring," Perry sarcastically scoffed with a grin.

HOWARD MASON PLOPPED HIMSELF DOWN into an overstuffed upholstered chair while taking in the election results from his hotel suite in Minneapolis.

"Mark, we better take Minnesota otherwise we're going to get shut-out on Super Tuesday. Jedediah Wilson just scored wins in Arkansas, Oklahoma, and Texas," Howard Mason said to his longtime political advisor Mark Backus.

"We're in a dogfight here in Minnesota with Cochran but we've got a shot to pull this out," Mark replied.

"I wish that I had poisoned that son-of-a-bitch Cochran. If I did it, I would've made sure that it was a lethal dose," Howard said with a menacing grin.

"The American people have a big heart. Every President that has survived an assassination attempt tends to get a big bump in their favorability ratings for a few weeks. People rally around their leader even if they couldn't stand the asshole beforehand," Mark stated.

"Then why didn't Kissinger shoot Nixon in the leg when Watergate was bringing down his Presidency?" Howard joked.

"By that time, Henry probably should have shot him in the head and saved the American people from that Memorex nightmare," Mark laughed.

"I don't get it. I mean, ok, feel sorry for Cochran because of the attempt on his life, but don't vote for him if you weren't going to do so before he got poisoned. If not for that, I may have won Massachusetts, Vermont, Virginia, and possibly Colorado," Howard lamented.

"So, who do you think tried to poison Cochran?" Mark asked.

"I don't have a clue. Granted there are many people in the party, especially on the far right, who would have paid to buy a lottery ticket for the opportunity to take a crack at taking out the S.O.B., but not many would have the guts to actually try," Howard offered.

"Sort of odd that the FBI hasn't released information about any concrete leads isn't it?" Mark asked.

"Who knows? They keep things close to the vest until they are absolutely sure of their facts. Hell, they still haven't fully exonerated me! All I got was that I was no longer the main subject of their investigation," Howard said with disgust.

"No one thinks that you did it, Howard. Everyone knows that someone set you up to be a suspect," Mark stated.

"Yeah, well, all the good that that is doing me. I'm fighting for my political life to get a win in Minnesota so that I don't get completely shutout on Super Tuesday. How come Cochran drinks the poison, but I'm the one who is dying?"

AARON ROSE WAS IN THE KITCHEN of their Marigny neighborhood home cooking marinated chicken breasts in a grill pan while Clay Grover tossed a field greens salad and opened a bottle of Sancerre wine. The small television in their kitchen displayed the latest polling and results on the night of the Super Tuesday primaries.

"So, are we excited yet?" Aaron asked Clay with a playful smile.

"About eating dinner? Of course I am," Clay replied, full well knowing that wasn't what Aaron was asking him about.

"Go ahead and play coy, but you know what I'm talking about," Aaron challenged his husband. "Why can't you just admit that the possibility of being Senator Douglas' White House Chief of Staff is becoming more of a potential reality? It looks like he will have a pretty good night and will be the Democratic frontrunner tomorrow morning."

"I just don't think about it as much as you do. That prospect does not thrill and titillate me like it does you," Clay responded with a shrug.

"Seriously, you aren't at all excited over the prospect of being the person running the White House?" Aaron questioned, as he used his spatula to finally cook the opposite side of the chicken breasts.

"Of course, I am, but we are very different people in that respect. You want to talk about it all the time and get giddy with excitement. I internalize far more and don't show my emotions very often. I suppose it's part of my Southern upbringing. Public displays of affection and emotion were not something that we did very often in my family. It's that Southern reserve and dignity, I guess. Plus, as kids we were taught to be pragmatic and not hope and wish for things that may not be attainable. We were more focused on the here and now, as opposed to some nebulous future hopes," Clay offered.

"That makes me kind of sad," Aaron said. "Kids are supposed to dream about what their lives can be. Reality is tough enough when you become an adult. Hope and inspiration is what childhood should be about."

"I guess," Clay shrugged.

"Turn up the sound on the television will ya?" Aaron asked. "Senator Perry is about to make his victory speech from Minnesota."

"THANK YOU, MINNESOTA!" PERRY DOUGLAS ROARED from the lectern on the campaign headquarters hotel stage in Minneapolis.

"When I started this campaign over a year ago, it was with a shoestring budget, a few staffers, and the belief that America can do better. That the American people deserved better. Republicans have always taken care of big business, the wealthy, and the influential. But what about the rest of America? Why should a majority of our people have to wait and hope for a trickle down from the wealthy and privileged class? Why should we put up with the crumbs off the tables of the fat cats who care little about the average family and citizen? The time has come to invest in the middle and working class. The time has come to level the playing field so that all Americans can aspire to and achieve a better life for themselves and their children. The system is broken, my friends, and I have no intention to apply small inconsequential Band-Aid solutions. We need to cut out the rot and influence peddling in government, and once again make government work for the people it is supposed to serve. My Republican colleagues are always haranguing about the evils of big government. They are not interested in a government that works for the average citizen. Well, if that's the case, let's make sure that we remove them from government in November. If you don't like big government, then don't run for office. Let the men and women who care about making government work for everyone take over. I want to be the Democratic voice leading that charge. I want to represent all of you. I hear you, now let's make Washington hear all of us. Thank you for your support. You are my strength. You are my courage. Now, let's finish the job and finally give to the people of this nation the government that they deserve. God bless you Minnesota, and God bless these United States of America."

THE SUPER TUESDAY PRIMARIES INDICATED A strong shift in the political winds for the Republican Party. It was an extremely good night for President Cochran. Of the twelve state contests that were fought for that night, Andrew Cochran won half of them. A clear and resounding departure from his 0-4 start. And in many instances the margin of his victory wasn't even close. Jedediah Wilson picked up four states. Cletus Sawyer and Howard Mason each garnered one state. But in Cletus Sawyer's case, the only state that he won was his home state of Alabama.

Meanwhile, on the Democratic side of the primary races, Perry Douglas was able to capture six of the twelve contests, including the largest delegate haul so far by winning Texas. Hellen Raymond remained competitive, but it was clear that Perry Douglas was now the clear front-runner for the Democratic nomination for President of the United States.

WEDNESDAY MORNING AND PRESIDENT COCHRAN RECEIVED a phone call from his old and dear friend, Nathan Whitaker.

"Good morning Mr. President and congratulations on a wonderful evening," Nathan enthusiastically chirped into the telephone.

"Thank you, my friend. It was a pretty good night, wasn't it?" Andrew Cochran replied.

"It most certainly was, but how are you? How are you feeling?" Nathan questioned his friend.

"Better every day," Andrew pronounced. "There are some renal issues that the doctors are monitoring, but they've told me that I should make a full recovery."

"That's excellent news," Nathan added.

"Look Nathan, Sue Lynn has told me about how you were basically living in the waiting room of the hospital for three days while I was in intensive care. She informed me about the flowers, and daily well-being calls and everything else. And I just want to express how much that means to me, old friend. You've always been there for me. Since we were a couple of wet-behind-the-ears college freshman at Vanderbilt. As Sue Lynn said just last night, 'you've always had my back.' And we both know that my political resurrection last night would not have been remotely possible without your counsel and strategic vision. You are in large part the reason that I still have a fighting chance to win the nomination. So, thank you from the bottom of my heart."

"You are welcome sir. Whether I am in government or not, I serve at the pleasure of the President of the United States."

"Yes, I wish I could do something about that. You know if I could, I would love to bring you back as part of my administration, but unfortunately that is not possible for several reasons. And I cannot hire you as a member of my official campaign staff. But we might be able to get you a position with one of our super pacs, but of course, it would have to be somewhat under the table and out of the view of the press and the public at large," Andrew Cochran informed his former White House Chief of Staff.

"I'm not worried about that," Nathan replied. "I just want to do all I can, in whatever capacity, to ensure that you win the party's nomination. If that role is nothing more than a few strategic conversations, that is fine with me."

"We can do better than that. Let me have a word with a few people and see what we can come up with. I need you Nathan. That's been true for most of my adult life and continues to be true today," Andrew Cochran said with full sincerity.

"Thank you," Nathan responded with great sincerity.

"Now, let's not get too emotional my friend, there's plenty of work still to do," Andrew added. "Oh, and Sue Lynn told me about you sending me a bottle of bourbon. You are one sick bastard, Nathan. Leave it to you to do something so perfectly inappropriate, yet hysterical."

"Well, that was just sort of my quiet nod to our prior conversations and to The Police song, 'Message in a Bottle,'" Nathan said softly with a small laugh.

"We certainly did send an "S.O.S. to the World" didn't we my friend? We most certainly did," Andrew Cochran agreed.

CHAPTER 4

ONE WEEK LATER, AND NOT MUCH HAD CHANGED with respect to Posy Branch's health and outlook on life. She had become a shell of her former vibrant self. She spent most of her days at French Tips, Juleps & Jazz, in the back room of the establishment, sitting all alone. Her past penchant for 'working the crowds', mingling with customers and laughing and singing her way through the days had quickly vanished with the loss of her friend and partner Chiffon LaBelle. She had lost ten pounds and her zest for life. Michael did the best he could to attempt to brighten her spirits, but nothing was working.

"Posy you can't continue like this," Michael admonished his friend. "You're not eating properly, you're not getting enough rest, and it shows. If Chiffon knew you weren't taking care of yourself she'd be reading you the riot act. This is the very last thing she'd ever want to see happen to her dear friend."

"I can't help myself. I don't care if I live or die," Posy softly replied with her head bowed.

"Stop that! Stop it right now!" Michael insisted. "You're breaking my heart and you are disrespecting the memory of Chiffon. She'd whoop your behind if she heard you say that. There's a room full of customers and your hand-picked staff of employees on the other side of this door who rely on you. Who need you. Who love you. It was unimaginable what happened to Chiffon. I cry every morning when I wake up and think about what she must have gone through. But then I wipe my tears away, shave and shower and come here to work because I love it here. Because I loved her. And because I love you, Posy. You took a tired old nail salon and made this a place of joy and laughter. People flock here because they want to share in the fun and loving atmosphere that you created. If you let all that go, you're not doing any service to the memory of our beloved friend. In fact, you're letting Olivier and those redneck boys, and anyone else who chooses hate over love win. I'm not going to let that happen. So, get out of that chair and get out there and live your life robustly the way you always have. If you don't do it for yourself, at least do it for Chiffon. That girl was so full of love and life, you've got to continue on for her."

"You're right sugar, you are, but I'm not sure that I can do it," Posy replied while looking into Michael's kind blue eyes.

"I'm not saying that you have to go out there and be the life of the party right now. But at least mingle with people, talk with them, it's a start. C'mon, I'll help you. Grab hold of my arm. Let's go out there together. 'Life is so worth living, and if you're going to live it, live it all the way. Full tilt. No regrets.' You told me that just days after I started working here. You were right then, and you're still right now. Lean on me. We'll do this together."

Michael opened the office door and he and Posy walked arm-in-arm out into the crowd, the bustle, the boisterous noise, and the laughter. Posy cracked a slight smile as people wished her well and paid their respects. It may have actually been only a few steps, but it was miles down a progressive, restorative road paved with love. As Chiffon often sang during karaoke nights, her favorite song from the musical "The Wiz", "Come on and ease on down, ease on down the road. Don't you carry nothing that might be a load. Come on ease on down, ease on down the road."

THE NEXT REPUBLICAN DEBATE THAT WAS TO BE HELD prior to the primaries in Idaho, Hawaii, Mississippi, and Michigan had been postponed to allow additional time for President Cochran to heal and rest. Not all of the candidates were thrilled with that change in scheduling.

"It was scheduled Mark, they can't just change it willy-nilly like that," Howard Mason protested to his senior advisor.

"And normally they wouldn't, but they consider an attempt on the life of the incumbent President as an extenuating circumstance," Mark calmly replied.

"But this was my first chance to be part of the debates since I announced my intentions to seek the nomination," Howard rebutted. "And, I would have had the stage without Cochran there and could have taken advantage of the situation to make some hay."

"I understand Howard, but we have no control here. The Republican Party chairman and the RNC made this decision and we just have to abide by it."

"I could be out of the race before I even get a chance to talk to the American people from a debate stage," Howard pressed on. "Five more states had their primary contests a couple of days ago and I didn't win a single one. Louisiana went to Cletus Sawyer. Jedidiah Wilson took Nebraska, and the too ill to debate Andrew Cochran wound up winning Maine, Kansas, and Kentucky. Kentucky, Mark, Kentucky! I was the very popular Senator from Ohio, Kentucky is basically a suburb of Cincinnati, for Christ's sake. I couldn't win Kentucky because I can't get on a stage with that asshole Cochran and show the American people what a fraud and traitor he is to Conservative values."

"I know Howard, I know, but it's out of our hands," Mark replied with a loud sigh.

"What about our backers? Are we still getting their financial support?" Howard anxiously asked.

"That's another issue, I'm sorry to say," Mark answered.

"God damn it, Mark! You told me before we went down this road that we'd have some very influential people flocking to give us money and support. You promised that well-heeled Republican donors were encouraging me to challenge Cochran," Howard ranted.

"That was then, this is now," Mark retorted a bit miffed by Howard's tone. "Everything I said then was true. But the suspicion of your possible involvement in the attempt on the President's life, sure didn't help matters. And neither did your showing at the polls on Super Tuesday. Money backs winners and right now, we desperately need a win to keep going. You've got to win Michigan, Howard. It's our firewall. Otherwise, the support and the money will go elsewhere."

"Well, isn't that just great!" Howard sarcastically spat out. "If I had remained in my position as Vice-President, I'd be Acting President right now instead of Stuart Prentice. I took a risk based on political advice, and now I look like a fool without the advantages and gravitas of a government position and I'm bleeding out political support and financial backing daily. Isn't that just swell!"

"It's not over yet Howard, but you absolutely need to win Michigan next week. If you can do that, and the debates get rescheduled before the next big round of states which will include Florida, Illinois, Missouri, North Carolina, and your home state of Ohio, you could be right back in the race. If not, well . . ." Mark said as his voice trailed off and a disgruntled Howard turned his back and walked away.

PRESIDENT COCHRAN WAS OUT OF BED and walking around, albeit rather slowly and gingerly. His doctors had removed him from the machines monitoring his vital signs. He was beginning to eat regular food and his normal skin tones were rapidly replacing his bedridden white pallor. It was just a matter of days before he would be able to resume his duties and responsibilities as President of the United States. In the meantime, he was attending short meetings and briefings along with Acting President Stuart Prentice.

"Stuart, I have to thank you," Andrew Cochran began. "The way you have stepped into the breach and kept the ship of state afloat without incidence or issue has been so very reassuring to me. I'm afforded the ability to slowly get my sea legs back under me without having to worry about anything going on in the Oval Office that immediately requires my attention. My Chief of Staff, Sam Brainard informs me that you are doing an excellent job of keeping all of the balls in the air. That's one thing I never anticipated before I became President, how many different things land on your desk every single day. Nancy absolutely adores you, and Sue Lynn tells me about how very kind and thoughtful you've been to her. I'm so grateful for all you've done. So, very simply, thank you Stuart."

"You are welcome, Mr. President, it's been my honor to serve," Stuart stated with a twinkle in his eyes and a gentle smile. "Sometimes being Speaker of the House is akin to attempting to herd cats. Just as you think you have one corralled, two or three more are skirting out of line and another is attempting to gouge your eyes out. So, I'm pleased to have a different kind of challenge for a little while."

"Come now, wrangling Democratic members of the House surely can't be as difficult as dealing with the 'Animal Farm' on my side of the aisle, can it?" President Cochran asked with a short laugh.

"Oh you'd be surprised, we certainly have our fair share of stubbornness and idiocy to go around," Stuart replied.

"Well, that's reassuring to know. Though on second thought, I guess it is just as distressing," Andrew Cochran related. "You know Stuart, I once considered you to be the virulent enemy that needed to be defeated at all costs. And, then my administration became embroiled in the scandal involving my former Chief of Staff, and everything changed. Now, it's my own party that views me as an egregious enemy against Conservatism, and I've been embraced and supported by the Democrats ever since."

"What is the old adage? 'Politics make strange bedfellows,' that seems apropos here doesn't it?" Stuart asked.

"Indeed it does," Andrew responded. "Once again, thank you Stuart for all you've done for our country and all that you've done for me."

"You are welcome, Mr. President."

"DO YOU WANT TO BE PRESIDENT OR DON'T YOU, it's a simple question?" The deep Southern voice asked over the phone.

"Of course I do, but at what price?" The other voice on the telephone call questioned.

"At my price, that is not negotiable. It never has been," the deep Southern voice replied.

"But there are no guarantees for success," the other voice stated.

"You want a guarantee go buy a toaster. I'm offering you a chance at the pinnacle of power in this world. Take it or leave it."

"I need a little more time to think and study about it," the other participant stated.

"You study long, you study wrong," the deep Southern voice interjected. "I need an answer tomorrow. There's other fish in the sea, and you're just another guppy, ya hear?"

The other caller took the phone away from his ear, as the dial tone monotonously droned on.

THE STROBING BLUE LIGHTS OF THE POLICE VEHICLES parried with the red strobe lights of the EMT vans as they sat parked at the edge of the murky and swampy shores of the bayou about 150 miles west of New Orleans near Lafayette, Louisiana. The lights splashed off of the large cypress trees overgrown with heavy Spanish moss. The remains of the two bodies were carefully removed from the intertwined boughs and moss. The nutria lumbered to get out of the way of the emergency workers as they set about the task of extracting the human remains. It soon became clear that the bodies had been there for several days. Gators and raccoons had their way with portions of the legs and torsos. Once the two bodies were taken from the swamp, they were examined and the initial details of each body were photographed, described and documented. The remains of both of the bodies were male, Caucasian, and in their mid-twenties. One had red hair, the other had a shaved head.

CHAPTER 5

"**W**HERE DID YOU GO LAST NIGHT?**" Aaron Rose asked his husband Clay Grover as he wiped the sleep from his eyes. "I woke up about 3:00 a.m. and you were gone."

"Couldn't sleep. I started to toss and turn but I didn't want to wake you, so I got up and went to the couch for a little while. When I realized that I wasn't going to get back to sleep, I went for a run to burn off some of my nervous energy," Clay responded.

"What are you so nervous about, dear?" Aaron asked.

"I'm not sure I know. It seems to be a combination of things. I suppose that you're right and I'm thinking about the possibility of working in a President Douglas administration if that were to come to fruition. I'm a little bored at work and longing for another major case to tackle. And, I still think about what happened to poor Chiffon. She had been through so much in her life, and had finally turned the corner and got the respect she yearned for and the money she needed to buy part of a business. She was looking to buy a house and complete her sexual transition, but in the blink of an eye, she's gone. Just like that, everything that she fought so hard to achieve is inconsequential. To be honest, that scares me," Clay confessed.

"Life is transient. We never know how or when the end will come. But we can't focus on that. We have to focus on living in the present and make the most we can of each day," Aaron replied while rubbing the back of Clay's neck. "Do you want me to help you relax?"

"Not right now, I think I'm going to try to get back to sleep. I don't have much on my plate at work today so I might go in a little later. I'll see you later at the office, ok? Clay asked.

"Sure, of course," Aaron responded. "Try to get back to sleep. I'm going to jump in the shower and get ready for work. I'll see you later."

The couple gently kissed and Aaron headed into the bathroom. Clay laid back on the bed, but there would be no going back to sleep. Not that day.

Jim Bob McCallum sat in his luxurious office in Baton Rouge, Louisiana. His assistant Culbert Smiley sat across the large ornate desk from his boss and twitched nervously.

"What in Sam Hill are you doing Culbert? You look like you're having an epileptic seizure," Jim Bob asked his nervous assistant.

"No, sir, I'm fine, just a little nervous twitch," Culbert meekly replied.

"Do I make you nervous son?" Jim Bob challenged the young man.

"Uh, well . . ." Culbert began.

"Good!" Jim Bob roared with a hearty laugh. "Fear is a very important tool to have in one's arsenal. Fear can earn you respect. Fear can give you a true competitive advantage. You ain't gonna get far in this dog-eat-dog world unless your competitor's fear what you can do to them. You understand me boy?"

"Yes, sir," Culbert squeaked out barely above a whisper.

"Alright then, tell me what our investigators uncovered," Jim Bob demanded. "Who is the money man behind that mealy-mouthed simpleton Howard Mason?"

"It appears that it's Race Casserly," Culbert answered.

"Dagnabbit!" Jim Bob exclaimed. "I knew that old horse thief was behind Mason. We been going back and forth against each other in business and politics for going on twenty years now. I can't stand that son-of-a-bitch, and he thinks even less of me. We've been fighting like cats and dogs to wrest away control of the Republican Party from one another for years. Race's pappy was old Texas oil money going back to the 1930's. He cheated and swindled his way to the top, and Race is a chip off that old block of horse dung. Race backed Senator Conway Sturgeon for the Republican nomination for President four years ago.

But I picked the winning horse with Andrew Cochran. Ol' Race was apoplectic when Cochran won. One of the happiest days of my life. But then, as we found out, Cochran couldn't cut the mustard when things got a little dicey with Nathan Whitaker and sold his soul to them damn, godless Democrats. Now, I've got Cletus Sawyer and Race done hitched his wagon to Howard Mason. Mind you, neither are the thoroughbred I once thought Cochran to be. They're both pretty much useless plow horses, but you can't win the race if you ain't got a horse. Damn! And I was about to put old Cletus out to pasture. I threatened to cut off his funding the other day, but now I'm stuck with him. Hell, if I'm gonna take the chance of letting Race Casserly run this country or even the Republican Party. I'd as soon swallow poison than to let that scoundrel beat me at a game of tiddlywinks."

"Yes, sir," Culbert mumbled.

"Alright, get Culbert, but leave me the investigator's file," Jim Bob stated as Culbert awkwardly raised out of his chair, handed the file to Jim Bob with his trembling right hand, and proceeded to walk towards the door. "One more thing boy," Jim Bob bellowed, "grow yourself a set of balls!"

"WHAT'S UP HOWARD?" MARK BACKUS ASKED, clearing his throat and shaking the cobwebs from his sleep deprived mind as he spoke into the telephone. "It's 1:30 in the morning."

"Mark, we need to do a one-million-dollar air buy in Michigan starting tomorrow. Split the money between our pro-Mason thirty second television and radio commercials and the negative ads against Cochran that we have racked up and ready to go," Howard Mason emphatically told his top campaign advisor over the phone.

"Howard, we don't have a million dollars to spend on electronic media in Michigan. At tops we have two hundred thousand," Mark wearily replied.

"We do now," Howard proclaimed. "We've got a week to get our message across and win the Michigan primary. Time is wasting, we need to move today."

"Where's the money coming from?" Mark asked.

"Let me worry about that. We've got it, that's all that matters. I also want to change my campaign schedule. I want to live in Michigan for the next week. As you told me just the other day, if we win Michigan we're still alive to fight another day. Let's go win Michigan!" Howard enthusiastically exclaimed.

"Alright Howard, I'll contact our media and communications manager in a few hours once daybreaks," Mark stated. "Get some sleep, you're going to need it."

"Let's fuck that asshole Cochran!" Howard proclaimed.

"Eight hours later, Cletus Sawyer was taking a telephone call from his most prominent primary campaign fundraiser, Jim Bob McCallum.

"Jim Bob, I'm honored that you've had a change of heart and decided to continue funding my campaign," Cletus joyfully stated.

"Well, Cletus we're old and dear friends the two of us. We've done some good work together, why would you think I wouldn't support my old friend? Jim Bob asked with a heavy drawl.

"The other night you said I was a dead horse . . ." Cletus began.

"Now Cletus, you know me well enough to know that after I get a snoot full, I'm prone to some downright bombastic bluster. Hell, everyone south of the Mason-Dixon Line knows that I can be a cantankerous old coot. Truth be told, I think that you would make one fine President, otherwise I wouldn't be so willing to fund your excellent campaign," Jim Bob said almost choking on his false sincerity.

"Gosh, Jim Bob, I don't know what to say," Cletus tentatively responded.

"You don't need to say anything. You just need to put my money to good use and start winning some state primaries. Next week is Mississippi. They like you down there. Hell, Alabama is their kissing cousin, in some cases quite literally. Have your campaign folks put a good chunk of my money into winning Mississippi. Then a couple weeks down the line, I think you got a real chance to win Florida, North Carolina, and Missouri. If you can pull that off, you're right back in the thick of it," Jim Bob encouraged.

"You're right as rain, Jim Bob, you surely are," Cletus said his voice soaring with confidence. "That's a fine game plan for success. Bear Bryant would be right proud!"

"Roll Tide!" Jim Bob loudly pronounced.

"Yes, sir, yee haw!" Cletus over excitedly screamed into the phone.

"Simmer down Cletus, simmer down," Jim Bob advised. "We got to keep our focus on the ball. We got to make sure that that no account treasonous liar Cochran wishes he done died from that poison. You need to bring your "A" game for the next debate. They can't keep coddling and protecting Cochran forever. He's gonna have to show his face sooner than later, and when he does you'll expose him for the fraud that he is."

"I can do it. We can do it. I know that to be the God's honest truth," Cletus said. "I ain't gonna let you down."

"That's fine. That's real good Cletus. One last thing, I'm going to send my boy Culbert to your campaign office in Alabama on my private plane later today. He's going to give your folks a videotape that y'all will find very enlightening. I leave it up to you and your people as to how to make the best use and advantage of it. You understand?" Jim Bob pointedly asked.

"Yes, yes, Jim Bob, and thank you once again for your support and your confidence in me," Cletus sincerely replied.

"So long Cletus," Jim Bob said as he hung up the phone. Moments later, Jim Bob shook his head and muttered to himself, "The things I have to do to prop up the village idiots I require to achieve power."

CHAPTER 6

Stanford Winchester, Whitlee Hammond, and Naomi and Virgil Cutler all took their places around the table at Arnaud's restaurant in the French Quarter. The jazz band softly played in the background as the friends settled in. Naomi Cutler dabbed away her tears of joy over seeing her former boss and good friend.

"You know Stanford, Naomi cries when she sees me too, it's just for a completely different reason," Virgil Cutler laughed.

"Well, I don't believe that for one minute. You two lovebirds could be a national advertisement campaign for a happy marriage," Stanford chuckled in return.

"Speaking of marriage, y'all got a date for your nuptials yet?" Naomi asked turning towards Whitlee.

"Yes. It's going to be on Saturday, June 11th. I surely hope that both of you will be able to make it," Whitlee responded.

"With bells on" Naomi replied with a small giggle.

Moments later, Lucius Collins approached Stanford Winchester's regular table at Arnaud's with a huge smile on his face.

"A gracious good evening to this outstanding table of fine people, I see we's gonna have a good time this lovely night," Lucius proclaimed.

"Good to see you again, my dear friend," Stanford Winchester warmly stated as he rose from his seat to shake Lucius' hand. Since becoming engaged to Whitlee, and his retirement from the Fifth Circuit, Stanford's normal weekly tradition of his solitary Wednesday night dinner at Arnaud's had become far less frequent. In fact, Stanford had not been to Arnaud's and seen Lucius for almost two months. A fact not lost on the two friends as they looked into each other's eyes, shook each other's hands a little longer, and squeezed their hands together a little tighter. "I've missed you," Stanford softly said before the two men relinquished their fulsome grip of friendship.

"May I offer this esteemed table a pre-dinner cocktail?" Lucius asked awaiting Stanford's anticipated response.

"Do birds have beaks?" Stanford chirped in reply, not wanting to disappoint his friend and desiring to perpetuate at least some time-honored traditions.

"They surely do, sir, they surely do," Lucius replied on cue with a hearty laugh.

After taking cocktail orders, Lucius went to the bar to place the order with Stanford just steps behind him on his way to the men's room.

"How is your beautiful wife?" Stanford asked as he placed his hand on Lucius' shoulder.

"Things a bit strange these days," Lucius quietly offered with his head bowed.

"I did hear that Bessie's shop's been closed for a bit, is she alright?" Stanford asked with concern in his voice.

"Truth be told, I ain't so sure," Lucius said reluctantly.

"Lucius, we're old friends. You know how much I cherish my friendship with both you and Bessie. Is there anything I can do?" Stanford asked.

"Ever since the attempt on the life of President Cochran, Bessie done locked herself in the house. She don't go out but to shop for baking goods, and she ain't spoke to no one but me," Lucius confessed.

"My word, why is that?" Stanford questioned.

"Well sir, Bessie thinks she had some role to play in the unfortunate poisoning of the President. She convinced herself that her business partner, Esther Francois, be responsible for the poison and doing some black magic. After what went on with her auntie, Queen Rita, and them poor folks in Washington a few years back, she done got it into her head that Esther somehow had a role in the President drinking that poison."

"Why I can't believe that for one minute," Stanford replied.

"I done tried to tell her that, but she don't pay me no mind, sir," Lucius responded while shaking his head.

"Do you think it would help if I stopped by the house and talked to her tomorrow?" Stanford asked.

"Oh, I do know how much Bessie looks up to and respects you Justice Winchester," Lucius responded.

"Then I will do just that. See if I can reason with her, and make her understand that she had nothing to do with that horrible event," Stanford said with great conviction.

"Thank you, sir. If there is anyone on God's green earth that Bessie would listen to it would be you, sir," Lucius stated.

"I'll see what I can do. It breaks my heart to think that Bessie is blaming herself for something that could not possibly be her responsibility," Stanford stated.

"I best be getting these here drinks to the table," Lucius said while taking hold of the tray full of cocktails.

"Don't you worry, my friend. I'll have a talk with Bessie tomorrow," Stanford responded with an encouraging smile.

SERGEANT NORRIS COALTREE STOPPED BY FRENCH TIPS, Juleps & Jazz to have a word with his friend Michael about the murder investigation concerning Chiffon LaBelle.

"Michael, I've got some unfortunate news about those two Cajun boys that you told me were harassing Chiffon a while back," Norris said quietly. "The Lafayette police fished two male Caucasian bodies out of the bayou. They fit the description of the two men you had identified as threatening Chiffon. They sent me a couple of pictures, would you mind taking a look?"

Michael looked at the photographs that Norris handed to him.

"Yep, that's them," Michael confirmed. "Do the police have any idea what happened?"

"It appears that they were drugged and then drowned in the swamp and left there for the gators," Norris answered.

"Where does that leave the investigation?" Michael questioned.

"Well, we're looking into their friends and acquaintances, but right now we're not getting much cooperation."

"Do me a favor?" Michael asked. "Don't say anything to Posy about this. She's just starting to get back into a normal routine. If she knew that the investigation into Chiffon's murder had hit a roadblock, it could send her back into a tailspin."

"Sure, I will leave providing information to Posy about the murder to you, for the time being. I certainly wouldn't want to do or say anything that would cause Posy any further pain," Norris responded.

"Thanks for stopping by and keeping me posted," Michael stated while reaching out and shaking Norris' hand.

"Whatever I can do to help," Norris responded.

RACE CASSERLY SAT IN HIS LARGE OFFICE in a high rise in Houston, Texas. His lanky 6'3" body extended back in a comfortable leather chair as his alligator boots pressed up against the mahogany desk. His graying dark hair accentuated his slender face and pointed chin. His white teeth offset his green eyes. Race's attractive face became the portal for his booming deep voice when his lips parted to speak.

"Jim Bob McCallum had his chance with Andrew Cochran, he blew it. His boy didn't have the stones to take the heat of scandal and went running to the Democrats to cut deals at the first sign of trouble. Jim Bob quickly dumped his sellout, and now thinks he can make some headway with that Alabama fool, Cletus Sawyer?" Race inquired to his business aide Carlisle Buchanan in his deep Southern drawl.

"That appears to be the old boy's strategy. He just pumped a few extra million into Sawyer's campaign," Carlisle responded.

"A fool's errand. Good money after bad," Race huffed. "Mind you, Howard Mason ain't gonna conjure up any memories of Ronald Reagan, but at least Howard ain't afraid of his shadow and can sound half intelligible, which is more than you can say about dumb as a rock Cletus Sawyer."

"Intelligence ain't something that the American people seem to care much about in their politicians," Carlisle stated with a smirk.

"Ain't that the truth? I had some good say and influence in the White House when the last moron from the Lone Star state pulled off the trick of portraying himself as someone you'd want to have a beer with. People are clueless sheep. You got to tell them what they want, and then give it to them," Race summarized.

"Why do you have to back anyone in this race? It ain't exactly an august field, and Cochran seems to be gaining momentum after the assassination attempt," Carlisle questioned.

"Yeah, well, I got people out there still trying to find out which fool made that attempt on Cochran's life. Howard Mason was only able to remain standing after that frame job because it was handled so badly and it was quite evident that even Howard wasn't stupid enough to poison the man he resigned the Vice-Presidency from the same day. With a little bit more smarts and precision they could have pulled that off and sunk Howard for good. Now, thankfully Howard is getting a little sympathy bump in the polls for being the unknowing dupe and scapegoat of a Presidential assassination attempt," Race stated.

"But not nearly the sympathy vote that Cochran is getting. I agree Howard was able to handle the initial drop in the polls once the investigation and the media basically exonerated him from blame. But Cochran is riding high, while Sawyer and Howard still are running behind Jedediah Wilson," Carlisle interjected.

"That won't be for long, even Jim Bob is well aware of that fact," Race replied.

"So what is the story about your and McCallum's battles for control of the Republican Party?" Carlisle asked.

"Oh, that is a long tale for another time," Race said with a wry smile while using his boots to push away from his desk.

President Andrew Cochran sat in his chair in the Oval Office for the first time since he had ingested digitalis poison. He had resumed the duties and responsibilities of the Presidency. Stuart Prentice was back in his position as Speaker of the House. The country and the Cochran administration had survived the assassination attempt on the President, and the American system of succession of power had worked flawlessly. But now, Andrew Cochran had to select a new Vice-President to serve out the remainder of his first term. He met with his Chief of Staff, Sam Brainard and other senior advisers to discuss just that topic.

"Well, the list of names of folks interested in the Vice-Presidency has certainly grown since the attempt on your life, sir," Sam Brainard began. "Now that you are doing well in the polls, there are several candidates who have expressed genuine interest."

"So, no one wanted the job when I was 0-4 after the first four primary contests, but now that I'm near the top again, everyone wants the job?" Andrew Cochran quizzed Sam.

"I wouldn't say everyone, there are still several influential people in the party who have expressed disdain about the job, but we have a more robust list now than when it looked like they would be serving as an inconsequential placeholder for a lame duck President," Sam responded.

"Whoever we pick will be my running mate going into the fall general election, if we get there, so the pick has to help us in the general, right?" Andrew Cochran asked his advisors.

"We still have to get to the general election. We are in much better position now, but we still trail Jedediah Wilson in the delegate tallies. And frankly, we're not that far ahead of Cletus Sawyer," Sam added.

"So, do we go with a more moderate pick for the general election or for a more conservative choice to try to appeal to the primary voters?" Andrew Cochran questioned.

"You could see if Cletus wants to delay his Presidential aspirations for four years and offer him V.P. for his supporters and delegates," Sam offered.

"Oh, hell no!" Andrew Cochran bellowed. "The V.P. doesn't have to be someone I like, hell, the choice of Howard four years ago proved that point, but it can't be someone who I have absolutely no respect for. And that would be Cletus Sawyer."

"Howard Mason round two?" Sam asked with a devilish grin.

"I don't think that Howard is that good of a contortionist to be able to explain that one," President Cochran chuckled. "Besides, how would it look for me to offer the job to the same guy who scorned me just a couple of weeks ago?"

"We've got a few days, but we need to come up with a V.P. choice fairly soon," Sam stated.

"Alright, everyone put your thinking caps on, we need some concrete choices to consider. Let's reassemble tomorrow afternoon. Everyone be ready with a name to put forth. Got it?" President Cochran inquired.

"Yes sir."

AN HOUR LATER, PRESIDENT COCHRAN FISHED his smartphone from his pants pocket and chose a name from his contacts list. Moments later the call was received.

"Hey Nathan, I need your help with something. Let me pick your brain on a suitable replacement for Howard Mason as my new Vice-President and running mate."

"I anticipated your call, sir. I've made a short list of some very credible options," Nathan replied.

"Excellent!" Andrew Cochran exclaimed. "Let me hear it."

THE NEXT MORNING, STANFORD WINCHESTER was at the door of Lucius and Bessie Collins house. Stanford knew that Lucius would be at work and Bessie would be home alone. He knocked on the front door, and within a few seconds he was being greeted by his longtime friend.

"Justice Winchester, what a great honor," Bessie Collins stated as she took off her apron and attempted to fix her hair.

"Bessie don't go frettin' over the likes of me, and please call me Stanford."

"Yes, of course, Stanford please come in," Bessie welcomed her guest.

"Why it smells downright wonderful in here," Stanford said smelling the fresh baked pies.

"Can I get you a slice?" Bessie asked. "I've got pretty much every variety of pie you could think of."

"No, not right now, but thank you kindly," Stanford responded. "Bessie I've heard that you been keeping to yourself lately. That you haven't opened your business in over two weeks now. Is everything alright?"

Bessie looked down at her shoes and then slowly raised her gaze to meet the concerned warm eyes of her friend. "I'm afraid of what I may have done," Bessie quietly confessed.

"Bessie, my dear friend, you are not capable of doing anything wrong. I've known you for all these years, and I do tell that a kinder, more generous, and warm-hearted person does not walk on this earth. Your every instinct is to be helpful and full of empathy."

"You don't understand, Stanford. I turned my back on black magic and wrongful things cuz I was making good money."

"I surely know that is not true," Stanford forcefully replied. "Lucius told me that you are blaming yourself for the poisoning of President Cochran. That is absolutely not possible."

"Black magic and the foxglove done killed that Supreme Court Justice and that young clerk three years ago. The poison done come from my auntie, Queen Rita's voodoo shop. It was the same poison that the President done drank. It ain't coincidence. I knows it in my bones," Bessie adamantly stated. "I took Esther Francois into my shop cuz she was bringing in good money. I turned my back when I suspected that she was doing black magic. You got to see that this is my fault."

"My dear Bessie, the FBI is hard at work investigating the attempt on the President's life. They will not stop until they have uncovered all of the facts. If they suspected that the poison came from your shop, they would have contacted you as part of their investigation. I'm wholly confident that it is simply coincidental. Have you spoken to Esther about this?" Stanford inquired.

"Only the night that it happened. I ain't seen nor spoke to her since," Bessie answered.

"Bessie you are a wonderful businesswoman. I'd hate to see you give up your business over an unsubstantiated feeling without knowing all of the facts," Stanford allowed. "If you truly believe that Esther played a role in the attempt on the President's life, you should talk to the authorities. I know people in the Federal government and the FBI that I can put you in touch with if you'd like to speak to them. I'm quite sure that they could help put your mind to rest and quash your fears."

"Maybe you is right. Maybe I should talk to someone from the government and tell them what I know."

"I'm happy to make those arrangements, if you like. I want to put your mind to rest, so that you can put this all behind you and move on with your life," Stanford said with a reassuring smile as he reached out and took Bessie's hand into his own.

"Yes, I should talk to the officials, let them know what I know and see if they could use that information," Bessie agreed.

"Excellent! I'll make the arrangements and I'd be more than happy to accompany you when you go see them," Stanford acknowledged.

"Thank you, Stanford, thank you. My mind is feeling freer already."

"Happy to do so, it's what friends are for," Stanford stated with a big smile and a nod.

The results from the Idaho, Hawaii, Mississippi, and Michigan primaries, once again, rearranged the pieces in the nomination puzzle. On the Republican side of the contest, Jedediah Wilson won in the state of Idaho. Cletus Sawyer won in Mississippi, and Howard Mason won the states of Michigan and Hawaii. For the first time since before Super Tuesday, President Cochran was shutout from the win column.

On the Democratic side of the ledger, Hellen Raymond took Idaho and Mississippi, while Perry Douglas was able to secure victory in Hawaii, and Michigan. The Presidential nomination race was now in full gallop.

CHAPTER 7

DEEP WOUNDS HEAL SLOWLY. THEY REQUIRE TIME, patience, attention and care. And, so was the case with Posy Branch. One week, then another and yet another, but slowly Michael and the rest of the staff at French Tips, Juleps & Jazz witnessed the emotional and psychological healing of Posy. No longer the silent morose recluse shuttered behind her office door, Posy was now back out front chatting and smiling with her customers. Of course, she had her occasional relapses but slow and steady progress was being made, and that is all anyone who knew and loved her could ask for. Posy's mother Charlotte Branch was in New Orleans for an extended visit. Charlotte had come to the Big Easy when she sensed that her daughter desperately needed her love and support soon after the horrific murder of her dear friend Chiffon LaBelle. Charlotte had helped coax and nurture her daughter out of her long depression. Emily Dickinson wrote, "A mother is one to whom you hurry when you are troubled." Posy Branch hurried into her mother's arms when she felt her entire world come crashing down upon her. And, Charlotte Branch was the one person who was instrumental in pulling her daughter from the depths of despair and helping her chart her way back to that ever elusive happiness.

"Come on mama, let Song Ye do your nails. She's got a new pretty peach color that would look real nice on you," Posy encouraged her mother.

"Honey, I done had my nails done two days ago, they still look nice," Charlotte Branch sweetly responded to her daughter.

"Well, then how about a pedicure, you haven't had one since last week," Posy added.

"Sweetie, that's right kind of you, but I ain't no beauty queen that needs to be pampered, your nail gals got real customers to attend to," Charlotte stated with a gentle smile.

"Well, then how about if Michael makes you a nice mango julep?" Posy asked.

"I just peeled a dozen mangos, couldn't be no fresher," Michael added from behind the bar. "How about it Mrs. Branch?"

"Michael, sugar, I mentioned two weeks ago, please just call me Charlotte, no need for formality here."

"Alright Charlotte, how about I fix you up a real nice mango julep?" Michael asked with a big smile on his handsome face.

"Lands sake, y'all just spoiling me to death. Y'all been so nice to me, it's making it hard for me to leave," Charlotte said with a short giggle.

"Then don't," Posy said quickly and emphatically. "Stay here in New Orleans with me and Michael. Help us run the business."

"Oh my sweet girl, that is a lovely offer, but you know I can't," Charlotte replied. "I got my home in Savannah. And you well know, that I've been helping out your Uncle Delmar down at the Dollar Store since he had his hip surgery. He called just the other day asking when I'd be coming back home. My older brother surely did help me out when I was younger, least I could do is help him now that he is getting on in years."

"But what am I going to do when you leave?" Posy implored her mother.

"You're gonna go on with your life and be happy and successful, just like you been before," Charlotte stated as she reached out and gently touched Posy's cheek. "You're a fighter and fierce competitor Posy. Always have been since you was old enough to walk and talk. Sure, life can bring you down from time to time, but you always sprung right back up and landed on your feet. And you going to do it again."

"I only got better cuz you was here to bring me back to life," Posy quietly replied.

"No sugar, you done that, not me. I was here to witness your determination not to let Chiffon's death be in vain. You got yourself back together for her memory, and because you are surrounded by real fine people here who love you and need you in their lives. Michael helped bring you back, I was here just observing his love and commitment to you," Charlotte said just above a whisper.

"Sure would be nice to have you around for a bit longer," Michael interjected.

"Why thank you darlin', that's kind of you to say. But I got to get myself back to Savannah in a couple of days. I got my life to live there like y'all got your place here in New Orleans."

"Well, we still got two days until you leave, and we gonna make the most of it," Posy declared. "So, sit down at the bar. Michael is gonna make you a nice julep, and we gonna dance when the band gets here in a bit. I know you can shimmy and shake. I do recall you and daddy shaking on the dance floor when I was just a little girl."

"That was many years ago, I ain't so sure I got that shimmy anymore," Charlotte confessed with a slight blush of her cheeks.

"Well, then we're gonna find out," Michael said with a wide smile.

"You are one fine specimen of a man, Michael. And as sweet as any sweet tea on this here planet. I may be old, and these bones is getting brittle, but ain't no way I could turn down the opportunity to dance with such a good-looking man!" Charlotte exclaimed with a big laugh.

"Then we gonna party tonight," Posy proclaimed with a twinkle in her eyes.

The deep wounds had healed over. It was time to remove the stitches and get on with a limitless life well-lived. Chiffon would have wanted nothing more.

"COME ON CAROLYN, DANCE WITH ME," Robert Douglas implored his father's campaign manager, Carolyn Barnes. The DJ at the Douglas for President fundraising party at Paris Nightclub in Chicago had begun playing Motown. Smokey Robinson's, "You've Really Got a Hold on Me," had faded into the upbeat Supremes song, "You Can't Hurry Love." Robert took Carolyn by the hand as he mouthed the opening lyrics of the song to her.

"I need love, love, to ease my mind. I need to find, find someone to call mine. But mama said, You can't hurry love. No, you've just got to wait. She said love don't come easy. It's a game of give and take."

Carolyn finally relented and followed the playful son of her candidate out onto the dance floor. They danced very well together. Then, Robert spun and effortlessly moved in circles around a laughing Carolyn as the song ended.

"That was fun, thank you Robert," Carolyn giggled as the couple returned to the bar area. "I don't think I knew before what a wonderful dancer you are. Why is it that gay men always seem to be better dancers than straight guys?" Carolyn asked.

"I don't know. I think we are just less uptight about, well, everything, including dancing," Robert responded.

"Well, whatever it is, it works," Carolyn said with a gentle smile. "And speaking of working, are you happy to be back on the campaign trail?"

"I love it!" Robert said gleefully. "I never thought much about public speaking. I mean, I certainly do my fair share of talking to customers and clients at the art gallery. But, getting up in front of hundreds or even thousands of people, I had never done that before or even given it much thought. But, I have to tell you, it can get pretty addictive. The adoration from the crowd washes over you and you feel reborn."

"Yes, and speaking of addictive, I assume that your dad talked to you about endorsing weed?" Carolyn inquired.

"Oh God, not you too, Carolyn," Robert responded. "I got it, I'll tone it down. Heck, I was just having some fun."

"Your father and I are all about you having fun out there on the campaign trail doing events, but we also have a message we need to impart to the crowds. And your pot advocacy can distract from our overall message," Carolyn stated.

"Ok, I get it," Robert answered with a sigh. "No more advocating weed."

"Thank you," Carolyn replied.

"Why was I pulled from events for a few weeks in February?" Robert asked. "Dad never gave me much of an answer."

"I can't really say. That's something you should talk to your father about," Carolyn responded with a sheepish expression on her face.

"Can't say or won't say?" Robert challenged with a sly smile.

"You can't hurry love. No, you've just got to wait. She said love don't come easy. It's a game of give and take," Carolyn sang in response to Robert's question with a big grin etched across her face.

AARON ROSE AND CLAY GROVER BEGAN BOUNCING up and down with their hands in the air, as if they just didn't care, as the chorus line from the Weather Girl's massive hit disco song, "It's Raining Men" exploded from the sound system at the French Quarter gay nightclub, OZ.

"We should do this more often," Clay said after the couple departed the dance floor.

"It sure is fun to get out and dance every now and then, but I'm pretty fond of snuggling on the couch with a glass of wine and watching a good movie as well," Aaron replied.

"But we're too young to be stuck at home all the time," Clay replied.

"I never considered it being stuck," Aaron said slightly annoyed by Clay's comment. "I love our time at home, just the two of us."

"I do as well, but isn't it great when we can go out and just let loose a little bit?" Clay asked his husband.

"Well, it's never been a secret that I'm more of a homebody than you are, but I thought that we had struck a nice balance between going out and staying home," Aaron responded, feeling defensive.

"And we have, my darling, for the most part. I guess I'd like to see us be a little more active in the community. You know, try out some new things," Clay stated.

"Like try what new things?" Aaron asked his voice full of apprehension.

"Never mind, drop it," Clay huffed in response. "I'm sorry I said anything at all. Let's just go home. You clearly would rather be there than out having fun with me."

"You know, we can have plenty of fun at home as well," Aaron replied seductively, attempting to lighten the heavy mood that had overtaken the conversation.

"Yeah, sure," Clay said somewhat dismissively. "Let's go."

The couple left OZ and walked home in silence. Neither wanted to say a thing for fear of turning a slight crack into a massive crater.

CHAPTER 8

It was late March and just days away from the first Republican debate since the attempt on the life of President Cochran. It was also merely days prior to the primaries in Florida, Illinois, Missouri, North Carolina, and Ohio which would have a profound impact on the race for the White House. But President Cochran and his advisors were focused on their choice for Vice-President.

"I think we need a placeholder. Someone who will serve through the remainder of the first term, but then you can choose a different running mate at the convention to be your Vice-President for the general election," Landon Hamilton, Andrew Cochran's campaign manager stated.

"Who is willing to do that?" The President queried. "Why would someone want to be Vice-President for eight months well-knowing I won't pick them to be my running mate for the general election?"

"Oh sir, you'd be surprised," Landon replied. "For example, Senator Markus Cavanaugh, from Montana. He is one of the few Republican Senators who still has a slightly moderate, libertarian bent to him. However, he's getting primaried out by his Tea Party opponent. He is down double digits. He will lose his primary and his Senate career. Wouldn't you rather end your political career as Vice-President of the United States rather than a one term Senator from Montana? And there are others in similar positions."

"But why not just pick someone who I intend to run with in the fall now? Perhaps get a bit of a bump in the polls from announcing it as well?" The President questioned.

"From a strategic point of view, if it is a brokered convention, and right now there is a very good chance that none of the candidates will have the 1,237 delegates necessary to win the nomination on the first ballot, you lose the ability to use the Vice-Presidency as a bargaining chip if you choose your running mate now," Landon pointed out.

"I get that Landon, but I can tell you definitively that I have no desire to have either Cletus Sawyer or Jedediah Wilson as my Vice-President. None. I'd consider bringing Howard back, but I'm pretty sure that ship has sailed," Andrew Cochran responded.

"Well, Mr. President, if you want to choose your fall running mate now and make him your current Vice-President, it should be someone with Conservative bonafides to shore up what little support you have from the party base," Landon asserted.

"Like it or not, I am not the staunch Conservative that I ran as four years ago. I've moderated my views and my policies, much to the chagrin of our party's base of right-wing zealots. While he served as Acting President, Stuart Prentice and I had some fascinating and enjoyable conversations together. I have to admit, at times, I agreed more with Stuart on domestic policy positions moving forward than I do with many in my own party. I can't go back to being an intractable Conservative. I'm not that man, and I'm not sure that I ever was. I ran as a Conservative firebrand four years ago and it got me elected. But deep down I often questioned some of the principles I espoused for the sake of political expediency. I'm through with pretending to be something that I'm not. I'm running as a moderate Republican. Who says we can't offer the Republican Party primary voters a real choice?"

"Because you won't win," Landon quickly interjected.

"Then, so be it," the President forcefully replied. "I'd rather run a principled campaign offering a real choice to the voters, than to tow the party line and behave as an irrational ideologue."

"Do you have in mind the name of the man you'd consider making your current Vice-President and future running mate?"

"Who said anything about it being a man?" Andrew Cochran retorted. "I've got a call into Congresswoman Cynthia Bridgman of New Hampshire."

"A woman, a moderate from New England, and one of three elected Republicans who are pro-choice! That Mr. President is political suicide!" Landon bluntly stated. "I cannot make that into a winning ticket in a Republican primary."

"People are known to recover from and thrive after suicide attempts, Landon. I've already recovered from being poisoned, I'm just moving on to my second political life," Andrew Cochran offered with a sly smile.

Later that March day, second lives and second chances abounded. Landon Hamilton tendered his resignation letter as campaign manager to Andrew Cochran. The resignation was accepted by the President and hours later, Nathan Whitaker was being asked to be the Cochran campaign's new senior advisor, strategist, and manager.

"Mr. President this is a highly risky move," Nathan Whitaker cautioned his old friend.

"Frankly, my dear, I don't give a damn," Andrew said mimicking his best Clark Gable impersonation. "You are a free citizen of this country. You have been fully exonerated by a trial of your peers. You have been found guilty of nothing. You have every right, same as any other citizen. If I choose to make you my campaign manager that is my prerogative. If it costs me some votes or supporter dollars, it is a price that I'm willing to pay. I want someone I trust completely running my campaign. This is how it was always supposed to be. I'd rather lose with you by my side, than to win without you in my life. It's just that simple, Nathan," Andrew sincerely stated.

"I am overwhelmed with gratitude and appreciation for the honor and trust that you've imparted to me, sir," Nathan softly replied.

"It wasn't going to be enough having you stashed in the background of some super pac providing me with your advice and counsel on a sporadic basis," Andrew Cochran allowed. "If we're going to reinvent my Presidency and my campaign, I need you by my side every step of the way. It's time that the Republican Party joins the 21st century. It's time that Republican voters get a choice between myopic obstructionism and Conservative dogma, and pragmatic and moderate problem solving. We may very well lose the nomination, but at least we will do so in a principled and constructive way. Remember how as young Republicans we use to sing the praises of Howard Baker? You idolized him as your Senator from Tennessee, Nathan."

"A great man of values and moderation who believed in and chose his country's best interests over partisan party politics," Nathan added.

"Precisely!" Andrew exclaimed. "Let's run a campaign that would make Howard Baker proud. Let's try to take the Republican Party back from the right wing zealots. Are you with me?"

"Always and forever," Nathan answered without hesitation.

"I'm meeting with Congresswoman Cynthia Bridgman tomorrow morning, I'd like you with me," Andrew stated.

"Cindy is a brilliant choice for Vice-President. She will garner a lot of support from the suburban Republican women voters who are tired of the Party's closeted bigotry, misogyny, and racism. Her pro-choice stance will alienate some, but appeal to many others," Nathan stated.

"I figured you'd say that since she was at the top of the short list that you provided to me last week," Andrew laughed. "We are of one mind, you and I, we always have been. You aided in saving my chances to win the nomination. Now, that we have a second chance, let's go win this nomination and save the Party," Andrew Cochran stated.

"Count me in, sir."

DAYS LATER, THE FIRST REPUBLICAN PRESIDENTIAL debate since the attempt on President Cochran's life was taking place in Manchester, New Hampshire. Four lecterns were equally spaced across the large stage in the auditorium. The candidates filed onto the stage to the applause of the viewing assemblage. The Fox News moderator began the proceedings by welcoming the four candidates and the large crowd. The scheduled policy focus for the debate was jobs, taxes, and the economy. However, good intentions and tentative agendas did not constrain the candidates as they quickly broached other topics and challenged each other's fitness to be President of the United States. President Cochran took advantage of the debate and its large television audience to make a major announcement to the country.

"Tomorrow morning, I intend to nominate Congresswoman Cynthia Bridgman of New Hampshire as the new Vice-President of the United States replacing former Vice-President Howard Mason. It is my hope that Congress will move swiftly to confirm her nomination. Additionally, Congresswoman Bridgman has graciously agreed to be my running mate if I am lucky enough to win the Republican Party nomination," President Cochran announced to gasps of surprise by the crowd.

"This is a cheap political stunt done before a New Hampshire audience for optimal effect," Cletus Sawyer asserted.

"Oh, there is nothing cheap about it," President Cochran responded with a playful smirk to laughter from the assembled audience. "I am merely making the American people aware of my nominee to replace Howard Mason as Vice-President, and at the same time making my proposed running mate known to the public at large. Back in Georgia we would call that, 'killing two birds with one stone.' I like to consider it as a useful expenditure of time for informational purposes."

"Congresswoman Bridgman should never be within a heartbeat of the Presidency given her appalling and immoral stance against protecting the lives of the unborn," Jedediah Wilson vehemently accused.

"Gentlemen, please," the moderator beseeched the four participating nominees. "This is not a debate on the merits of any Vice-Presidential nominee, it is a debate on your stated economic policies and proposals."

The debate waged on more or less focused on economic policies, until a very odd non sequitur was verbally released by Cletus Sawyer.

"Reverend Wilson, you have repeatedly stated in the past that you would not fund AIDS research because you believe that AIDS is God's punishment on the immoral behavior of homosexuals, isn't that correct?" Cletus Sawyer challenged his opponent.

"That is partly true," Jedediah Wilson replied looking askance at Cletus Sawyer.

"The Bible tells us that homosexuality is an abomination, vile, and a moral plague against God's law, wouldn't you agree?" Cletus continued to press his questioning.

"What does this have to do with economic policies?" Jedediah Wilson asked in response, clearly annoyed by Senator Sawyer's line of inquiry.

"I'm just asking to ascertain what programs a Wilson administration would and would not seek funding for, since you clearly agree that homosexuality is a grave offense against God and cannot be promoted, tolerated, or funded by the Federal government. Do you concur?" Cletus questioned.

"I do not seek to punish the sinner only the sin," Jedediah Wilson conceded. "But I would like to take this opportunity to declare that a Wilson administration would not allow one penny of Federal tax money to be spent in the funding of Planned Parenthood. There is a special place in hell for abortion murders."

Andrew Cochran and Howard Mason looked at each other and shrugged their shoulders unable to grasp the significance or purpose of Cletus Sawyer's odd diversion into his questioning. Thirty minutes later the debate ended with the major headline being the surprise announcement of President Cochran's nominee to fill the Vice-President vacancy and be his new campaign running mate. Everything else from the debate faded into the background much like the sound of Muzak in an elevator.

"UH-OH," CAROLYN BARNES SAID AS SHE WATCHED the Republican debate on television from a hotel suite in Cleveland, Ohio with her candidate, Senator Perry Douglas. "If Cochran can win the Republican nomination, he has just made himself a far more formidable candidate in the general election."

"I agree," Perry Douglas stated. "Though he might have set him-self on fire with respect to his Republican base. I like Cindy Bridgman, she is a thoughtful and articulate woman. She is a suitable choice for Vice-President. Since we control the Senate, the Democrats will give the President the support he needs to get the simple majority required for confirmation. I bet we can count the number of Republicans who will vote for her confirmation using just our fingers. No toes required. And, you well know the right wing Conservative voters will condemn Cochran for his pick. He might as well have chosen Gloria Steinem for Vice-President. I don't see how he gets the nomination."

"I'm not so sure," Carolyn responded. "He's still got a bit of bounce in the polls from the assassination attempt."

"He expunged that tonight with his announcement of Cindy Bridgman as his choice for Vice-President. I truly thought he'd go in the exact opposite direction. I thought he'd go with a white male Conservative to attempt to woo back the far right of his party. They were apoplectic when the President was seen as being polite, respectful and thankful to Stuart Prentice," Perry Douglas countered.

"I'm not convinced that this wasn't a shrewd well-planned politi-cal calculation," Carolyn stated. "You know Landon Hamilton is out as Cochran's campaign manager, right?"

"No, I wasn't aware. Who replaced him?" Perry Douglas asked.

"Nathan Whitaker," Carolyn answered.

"What? Cochran brought a man indicted for a double murder in to be his campaign manager!" Perry exclaimed in disbelief.

"Whitaker was found guilty of nothing in a court of law."

"Still the stigma, the immense baggage Whitaker brings with him. I can't help but see this as a huge detriment to his campaign," Perry stated.

"Nathan Whitaker has proven himself to be a very skilled political operative willing to take unorthodox chances. Thing is, he is generally right about the chances he takes on behalf of his life-long friend and candidate. He's already gotten him elected President once before against high odds," Carolyn added.

"Wow! That amazes me that Cochran would go back to Nathan Whitaker after the fact that he almost brought down his administration before it even got started."

"Don't overlook the power and influence of a lengthy deep and abid-ing friendship. Plus, Cochran had lost four state contests in a row. He was going nowhere. His Presidency was being viewed as failed, and he was being treated like a lame duck by his own party. He was even chal-lenged by his Vice-President for the party's nomination. In fact, Mason was quickly viewed by many as the heir apparent. Then, there was an assassination attempt on the President's life involving digitalis poison. The nature of the assassination attempt shadowed Howard Mason due to the surrounding circumstances, and his polling numbers and repu-tation soon took a severe hit. The country, as it always does during times of crisis, rallied around its fallen leader. In the next two weeks, the President's polling numbers skyrocketed and he began to pick off one state primary after the other. He has claimed a slew of delegates and is either tied or leading in the most recent polls. His campaign went from being on life support, nearly pronounced dead, to now pick-ing a running mate with an eye not on the sprint that is the Republican primary season, but rather glaring straight ahead to the marathon that is the general election. Do you think that Nathan Whitaker just started to advise and strategize for the President a day or two ago?" Carolyn asked with a glint in her eye.

"No!" Perry exclaimed after taking a few moments to mull over all of the implications of Carolyn's statement.

CHAPTER 9

T HE ROAD TO RECOVERY CONTINUED FOR POSY BRANCH, even though her supportive mom Charlotte had left New Orleans to go back home to Savannah. Michael was the bedrock of support and encouragement on which Posy began to rebuild her confidence and love of life. Tragedy can bring you down, but love can build you back up. Posy was ready to move forward. Her infectious smile and her hearty laugh had returned. She began singing again with the band. She continued to mill with the customers, warmly greeting old friends. Michael no longer needed to remind her to eat properly and get her rest. She was sleeping through the nights. The nightmares had not completely left her, yet they were now few and far between. Loyal customers had returned to French Tips, Juleps & Jazz to witness the resurrection of someone who had brought so much fun and entertainment into their lives. Among those loyal customers were Stanford Winchester and Whitlee Hammond.

"It is so sweet that y'all stopped by to see me," Posy enthusiastically said to Stanford and Whitlee.

"I could not be happier to see you smiling and laughing again," Stanford replied.

"And so am I," Whitlee added. "Plus, I could certainly use a manicure, my nails are an absolute disaster."

"Well, Song Ye has an opening, and I'm sure that Michael can keep

Stanford entertained with a nicely crafted Sazerac while you have your nails done," Posy offered with a gentle smile.

While Whitlee took a seat at Song Ye's nail station, Stanford sat at the bar and Michael prepared his cocktail.

"Posy seems to be getting along just fine now," Stanford acknowledged.

"I think she's turned the corner. I was so worried the first weeks after Chiffon's murder. She seemed to lose her will to live. But then her mother came down from Savannah, and she's been getting progressively better each day," Michael afforded with a nod.

"Nothing heals like the loving touch of a devoted mother," Stanford stated, and then asked, "And what of the investigation into Chiffon's murder?"

"I'm afraid there's not much progress being made on that front. Olivier Bellevue seems to have an airtight alibi, and the two young Cajun men who had harassed and threatened Chiffon were found dead in a swamp just outside of Lafayette," Michael answered.

"Does Posy know that?" Stanford inquired.

"I'm trying to keep knowledge of the murder investigation away from her at this time. I fear that if she knows there isn't much progress being made that that might send her back into a crushing depression. She's still so fragile," Michael responded.

"That's probably for the best for the time being," Stanford agreed. "I have several friends in law enforcement both on the state and federal level. I'll make some inquiries and see if I can ascertain what they may be thinking."

"Thank you," Michael stated. "It won't be long before Posy will want to know what progress is being made in the murder investigation. She won't rest until Chiffon has her rightful retribution in a court of law."

"I'll do whatever I can Michael, you have my word."

AARON ROSE AND HIS CO-WORKER, EMILY DUBOIS were having lunch at the Who Dat Coffee Cafe in the Marigny neighborhood of New Orleans. Emily just shook her head as she watched Aaron take an enormous bite of his double beef patty Who Dat burger.

"Everything ok with the two of you?" Emily hesitantly inquired.

"Why do you ask?" Aaron questioned with a furrowed brow.

"There's a tension between the two of you that is filling the office. It's a small firm, we can all feel it," Emily stated.

"I'm not sure," Aaron quietly responded. "Clay's got a lot on his mind right now. There's something that I can't really talk about that is weighing on him. He isn't sleeping very well. Some nights I wake up in the early morning and he's gone. He goes running at 2am. It's crazy."

"Ok, I didn't mean to pry," Emily said with a smile. "It's just that you guys are so great together. You both give off this amazing energy and happy vibe. It just seems to be missing lately, so I was concerned."

"Well, thank you for that. I'm sure that we'll be fine. Truth be told, I probably have been pushing him too much to make up his mind. He's got to figure it out for himself and come to a decision about what he truly wants in life," Aaron responded.

"Shouldn't it be that you both work it out since your lives are shared with one another?" Emily asked.

"Yeah, of course. I was just saying I shouldn't pressure him into a decision that he might not want to make," Aaron replied.

"It all sounds a bit mysterious."

"I'm sorry, I can't tell you anything more at this time. All I can say is that it is definitely a life altering decision for both of us if it actually comes to fruition," Aaron coyly answered.

"Got it. The prosecution rests," Emily stated with a grin as she watched Aaron attack his burger.

Bessie Collins' hand slightly trembled as she reached out and put the key into the door lock and turned it to the left. The dead bolt slid open, and she tentatively pushed open the door to the voodoo shop that she had left locked and shuttered for almost four weeks. As Bessie entered, the old tiny bell above the doorway acknowledged her return. She turned on the lights and illuminated the darkened store. Bessie walked towards the back room and sighed deeply as she stared at the chair, table, and small area from which Esther Francois had conducted business in her shop. Her old friend, Stanford Winchester had convinced her that the time had come to confront her inner demons. Bessie was determined to get on with her life and re-establish what was once a small but thriving business. Everything looked the same, though Bessie was not wholly convinced that everything could ever be the same. The gentle knock on the door signified Bessie's first test.

"Miss Bessie, you in there?" Papa Levi softly called out before he entered the shop.

"I'm in the back," Bessie said attempting to brace herself emotionally for her first physical meeting with Papa Levi in a few weeks. Papa Levi walked to the back room of the shop and peaked his head through the beaded curtain.

"Surely is good to have you back Miss Bessie," Papa Levi offered with his head bowed. "Folk been asking after you. Wonderin' if you gonna reopen. Some of the clients done gone over to Marie Laveau's or some of them other places for readings and the such."

"Well, I don't rightly know what we gonna do here anymore," Bessie responded.

"We?" Papa Levi asked with surprise in his voice. "You still want me 'round here?"

"Why, of course, I do," Bessie answered with a warm smile. "I can't run this place without you. And iffin' we gonna get this business back up and runnin' we got to figure out a plan goin' forward. Figure out what we wanna be and what services we be offering."

"Them is good words to hear. I surely do appreciate it," Papa Levi replied with a crooked grin. Bessie walked over and gave Papa Levi a proper hug. His body slightly trembled as he felt the love and support of his friend.

"Alright then, where is the broom? We got some cleaning up to do," Bessie cheerfully stated.

"Right here in the corner. I'm fixin' to get to sweeping this old place real good," Papa Levi chuckled. Bessie grabbed a rag and began dusting off the counter tops. She hesitated for a minute before saying another word.

"Where's Esther?" She asked.

"She be spending a goodly amount of her time down at Jackson Square doing tarot cards and palm readings," Papa Levi replied with his eyes downcast at the old wooden floor.

"She say anything about me? About how things was left?" Bessie sheepishly inquired.

"Not to me, Miss Bessie," Papa Levi answered. "I wouldn't go worrying about such things. What is done is done. You said what you felt you needed to say."

"Well, Justice Winchester took me to talk to some local FBI folk. They done told me that they ain't got no cause to think that the poison that President Cochran done drank came from New Orleans. They still investigating, but they don't see no connection to my shop," Bessie told Papa Levi.

"Yes, ma'am," Papa Levi muttered.

"With all the bad that been done over three years ago and the connection with my auntie, Queen Rita, I just figured that might be the same thing all over again," Bessie confessed making her case.

"Yes ma'am, surely is understandable, it surely is," Papa Levi repeated.

"We can't be living in the past, can we Papa Levi? We need to move on and get this business up and running again. I just ain't sure how we should proceed. I need to think long and hard on that," Bessie stated.

"You is back, and that is all that matters right here and now," Papa Levi replied while sweeping the floor as Bessie began to hum as she wiped the dust off of the display cases of amulets and charms. Bessie tried her best to relegate the past to the past. No telling what the future might hold.

AMONG THE SKETCH ARTISTS, JUGGLERS, MIMES, and musicians scattered throughout Jackson Square, there are a number of small booths or folding tables inhabited by spiritualists and fortune tellers offering their services to the passing local public and tourists. Esther Francois sat behind a folding table with her arms folded as she leaned back in her chair letting the warm sun caress her aged and creased face. She opened her eyes as she heard footsteps of someone approaching her small corner of the Square.

"You done heard?" The visitor asked Esther. "After weeks, Bessie Collins done opened up her shop again."

"Folk gonna do what they gonna do," Esther replied with her eyes barely opened in the bright sunshine.

"You ain't interested?" The visitor asked.

"Ain't no business of mine," Esther softly responded.

"You still doin' the sacrifice down by Lake Pontchartrain tomorrow night?" The visitor persisted in his inquiry.

"Nothin' changed, has it?" Esther replied, now shielding the sun from her eyes with her hand so that she could look directly into the eyes of her visitor. "Important people still want things done, and they got money to get what they want. Dat the simple truth of life," Esther stated while she closed her eyes and moved her head upwards to the heavens.

CHAPTER 10

JIM BOB MCCALLUM GENTLY ROCKED BACK AND FORTH in his large leather office chair. He cradled his cellphone next to his right ear.

"Cletus, perhaps you should consider announcing a Vice-Presidential pick as well prior to the convention. Make the primary voters aware of the fact that you alone are the true proud Conservative in this coon hunt," Jim Bob drawled.

"I'm not so sure about that Jim Bob," Cletus Sawyer responded. "It would take my leverage away prior to the convention in case I need to offer it to one of my opponents."

"Cletus, who the hell you going to offer VP to that is currently in the race?" Jim Bob angrily questioned. "We both know that it ain't gonna be Jedediah Wilson. And, over my dead body, it sure as hell ain't gonna be Howard Mason! Mason is the hand-picked fool of Race Casserly. I'd as soon you chose my no account brother-in-law Chauncey, and that boy ain't been right in the head since he was twenty-four years old and got himself arrested for huffing glue and trying to hold up a bank using a ham and cheese submarine sandwich like it was a gun."

"Now, Jim Bob, I know what I'm doing," Cletus mildly objected.

"Then what in blue blazes was that bizarre line of questioning about homosexuals in the last debate? Folks just figured you was fixated on homosexuals. Came right out of the blue, and you left it unfinished. Just seemed weird watching on television," Jim Bob stated.

"I was setting him up for what's to come next," Cletus asserted.

"Don't mess this up, Cletus," Jim Bob warned. "I paid a pretty penny for them investigators. If you're gonna take a swing, you better not swing and miss. You best knock the son-of-a-bitch out."

"I know what I'm doing," Cletus firmly reasserted.

"You keep telling me that but so far I ain't seen no evidence or proof. I got a lot riding on this here race. I've invested a lot of time and money in you, Cletus. Don't let me down," Jim Bob bluntly stated.

"You got nothing . . ." Cletus began to say before he heard the monotone drone of the dial tone on the other end of the phone.

"I THINK YOU CAN EASE UP A LINK OR TWO off of the dog collar you got on Howard Mason," Race Casserly instructed his business associate, Carlisle Buchanan, in a deep booming Southern drawl. "The boy was afraid to say anything during the last debate. We want a candidate we can control not choke the life out of."

"The assassination attempt still has some doubting Howard, we don't want him to say anything that might drop his polling numbers," Carlisle responded.

"I get it, but Howard ain't retarded like Cletus Sawyer. We can trust him not to say too many impolitic things at a debate. Hell, the boy's got to be able to defend himself and seem like a knowledgeable, likable candidate, not some speechless frightened toad jumping into the oncoming headlights," Race pronounced before taking a long sip of whiskey.

"Yeah, that's true."

"In some respects, I wish I had reached out to Cochran five years ago. Unlike Jim Bob I would have stuck with him even after the scandal and his jump to moderate politics. What the hell do I care if my politician sounds reasonable and compromises as long as there is no compromising on the few interests that I want protected. Pay all the lip service you want to climate change and green energy just as long as I'm still getting at least $75 for a barrel of crude oil, and I ain't jumping through all them blasted EPA regulations to get it out of the ground," Race stated. "I'm a businessman, I couldn't give a rats ass about who gay men fuck or whether a woman decides to kill her three-month-old fetus or not. As long as it don't interfere with oil production and costs, makes no never mind to me."

"Why didn't you get Cochran years ago?" Carlisle asked.

"Cuz Ol'Jim Bob had already stuck his tongue in the ear of the very ambitious Nathan Whitaker, before I could get myself ensconced in the world of then Governor Cochran. I got to give it to him, Jim Bob's got an eye for political talent. He heavily invested in his relationship with Nathan Whitaker before anyone was paying attention to Cochran as Presidential material. Most folks on the inside saw Cochran as a light-weight with a good sob story and not much else. A lot of us missed see-ing the forest for the trees. We were all watching Cochran, and none of us had an eye on Whitaker. Except, Jim Bob. He saw the political power and relentless ambition of the man behind the curtain," Race replied with a shake of his head.

"And now Cochran has replaced Landon Hamilton with his old friend, Nathan Whitaker for the home stretch of the nomination process."

"Andrew Cochran ain't stupid like most of his opponents. He is smart enough to realize that you gotta dance with the one who brung ya. Cochran is still Governor of Georgia without Nathan Whitaker. If that. And he sure as hell wasn't going to smell the nomination this time around without him. You think it's just coincidence that after his campaign fortunes took a 180 degree turn for the better and he is now looking like the leader in the clubhouse that he names Whitaker his cam-paign manager? You think Landon Hamilton had anything to do with his good fortune to be poisoned and recover? Please, Nathan Whitaker is why Cochran became President, and he is why despite all of the odds he may be going back to Pennsylvania Avenue. The choice of a moderate woman from New Hampshire as his running mate was viewed by many in our party as political suicide. They couldn't be more wrong, which is why they are all losers. It was a political masterstroke, undoubtedly wholly planned out by Nathan Whitaker. Cochran was going nowhere pretending to be a strict Conservative. We got more of them idiots than we can use. Instead he charted out a compromised moderate position with the Democratic majorities in Congress. And guess what? He got things done. Infrastructure spending has led to job growth. Even die-hard Evangelicals can look the other way on some social policies as long as they got good paying jobs. Cochran is taking a page from the play-book of the old moderate Republicans, who use to roam this political earth. And he's winning because of it not in spite of it," Race summed up.

"But times have changed, things are different now," Carlisle challenged.

"Not really. Not as long as you're a good ol' boy. Cochran ain't a Harvard law professor with a funny name who seems too "different" and aloof for common folks to understand and appreciate. He's still got that rags to riches, raised from the ashes background story and an aw-shucks demeanor. He doesn't threaten people with his intellect or make them feel inferior, even though they are. As long as the country is doing well and there's good jobs to be had, people don't care if you're a right wing zealot or a down the line moderate. The Republicans, as a party, put too much stock in protecting social issues from the 1950's. It's the 21st century, things change. Time that we all grew up and realized that the coalitions we thought were rock solid, ain't so solid anymore. Cochran is succeeding cuz Nathan Whitaker understands that better than anyone else in the Republican party. My only regret is that I didn't get my hands on him before Jim Bob McCallum did," Race Casserly lamented.

IT WAS WHAT THE PUNDITS REFERRED TO AS "Second Super Tuesday." The late March primary elections held in the states of Florida, North Carolina, Ohio, Missouri, and Illinois. A large number of delegates were at stake. In a close race, these contests could swing momentum for any of the remaining candidates. However, the Republican primary voters were muddled and befuddled. Deeply held policy positions were shifting seemingly daily. President Andrew Cochran elected to his first term as a rock-ribbed Southern Constitutional Conservative was sounding and acting more like a moderate independent. And with a female Vice-President and running mate, he was becoming more progressive every day. The Republican voters who had yearned for decades for a more populist less strident and dogmatic approach to politics flocked to his side. Independent voters in states whose primaries were not restricted to only registered Republicans also joined the Cochran bandwagon. Yet, President Cochran's initial sympathy polling bounce in the first couple of weeks since the aftermath of the assassination attempt had begun to wane. Conservative base voters who wanted war against and not compromise with the Democrats in Congress began to recoil from the President's outreach and rhetoric. And the naming of moderate New Englander Cynthia Bridgman as his running mate was seen by some as the very last straw. Andrew Cochran had abandoned his Conservative bonafides. He was dead to them. They were left with choosing between Senator Cletus Sawyer, former Vice-President Howard Mason, and Reverend Jedediah Wilson. Each of the three had their own pockets of support among the party faithful. But none had the ability to form a coalition strong enough to unseat Cochran. This was the Republican Party landscape moving into a critical series of primary elections.

Meanwhile, things were far more tranquil and easily understood on the Democratic side of the political ledger. Senator Perry Douglas was slightly ahead of his opponent Senator Hellen Raymond in the delegate count tallies and also in the recent state polls. Unlike the rancor and vitriol of the Republican debates, the Democratic debates were rather sedate, even boring. One moderate and one progressive Democrat don't tend to set the stage on fire like firebrand Conservatives going up against a newly-minted Howard Baker-like moderate Republican. Shifts were afoot, as the policy positions once lit by the bright sunlight of transparency were becoming increasingly lost in the shadows. In the light of that day, how does one differentiate the character of a man or woman from the reputation?

STANFORD WINCHESTER JUST SHOOK HIS HEAD as he watched cable news. With his fiancée next to his side, Stanford had reached a tipping point with respect to his tolerance of his Republican party's suicide mission.

"You cannot say such heinous things about a sitting President. And when it comes from members of your own party, it's simply intolerable. I just cannot countenance this kind of talk," Stanford stated with a look of intense displeasure on his face.

"It's just election year politics, my dear," Whitlee replied.

"No, no it's not," Stanford declared. "A so-called man of the cloth, a man who has supposedly pledged his life to serving God, is accusing President Cochran of promoting infanticide and declaring that the President is having a homosexual affair with his campaign manager while they practice voodoo in the White House. There is not one scintilla worth of fact supporting those claims. When did it become acceptable to live in an alternate universe where facts are meaningless? I spent most of my adult life in search of provable facts and applying the law to validate well-reasoned judgments based on facts and the law."

"It's baseless rhetoric, there's no sense getting upset about it," Whitlee offered attempting to calm Stanford.

"Not getting upset about it, is what allows these despicable lies to propagate and demean public discourse. The Republican Party is speaking from a position fully lacking objective reality. That is frightening," Stanford explained. "Untruths fester and lessen us all if we don't quash them with the bright light of facts. I see now how once you allow politics to write its own rules and establish its own set of facts, you create a true threat to democracy. Opinions and differences in the approach to the country's problems is one thing. It is what the founding fathers saw as the strength of a party system of governance. You are allowed your own opinions, but you are not allowed your own set of facts. Once that occurs, anarchy cannot be far behind," Stanford forcefully stated.

"I've not seen you so agitated like this before," Whitlee responded.

"You see my dear, I've been hiding my head in the sand for the past couple of decades. I've been a partisan participant in this name calling witch hunt which is what contemporary politics has devolved into. I too played the game. I am as guilty as the rest. But no more. I cannot sit idly by while I watch our country lose its moral balance and ethical certitude in fairness. The democratic institutions of this country are far too important to remain silent," Stanford confessed.

"What do you purport to do?" Whitley questioned.

"I'm renouncing my membership with the Republican Party. Each and every debate performance by the nominees of that Party only sickens me and makes me understand that I have not left the Party, the Party has left me and millions others like me," Stanford said.

"Are the Democrats any better?"

"This year, yes, yes they are. Their two candidates are thoughtful, honest, sensible and professional people. They conduct themselves with dignity and respect for each other. But that aside, I'm not joining the Democratic Party. Instead I plan on registering as an Independent. I will choose the candidates who I believe conduct themselves in a gentile manner and who do their best to present factually-based arguments, not this wild-eyed baseless hyperbole," Stanford concluded.

"I'm not there yet. I'm not ready to renounce my Republican Party affiliation," Whitlee stated. "Don't get me wrong, I agree with most everything you said. But I'm not ready to take that step."

"And, you don't need to my dear," Stanford assured Whitlee. "I am doing this for myself, and I don't intend to make any demands on you in this regard. I just cannot continue to support something I find wholly indefensible. My time has come. There must be a reckoning. And for better or worse, it appears that that is exactly what this election is setting up to be."

It was the Wednesday morning after the "Second Super Tuesday" primaries. President Cochran re-established his leading position in the Republican nomination process by securing victories in Illinois and Florida. Howard Mason easily won his home state of Ohio. Jedediah Wilson claimed the state of Missouri, and Senator Cletus Sawyer pulled out a close win in North Carolina. Predictably, Senator Perry Douglas won his home state of Illinois in a landslide. He also added Florida and Ohio to his win column. Likewise, Senator Hellen Raymond won by a landslide in her home state of North Carolina. She also added Missouri to her victory total.

The front runners gained slight advantage, but nothing definitive had been determined. There was no clear light at the end of the nomination tunnel. Everything and everyone was still lingering in the political shadows

CHAPTER 11

"**A**RE YOU NOT FEELING WELL?" Clay Grover questioned his husband Aaron Rose as the two men jogged together past the enormous oak trees in Audubon Park in New Orleans.

"I'm fine, I'm great. What are you talking about?" Aaron responded.

"It's been a couple days since the results of the primary elections in five major states were announced and you haven't said a word about it. Especially since, Senator Douglas is now without a doubt in the lead for the Democratic Party nomination," Clay stated.

"Oh that," Aaron stated coyly. "It is what it is. You're a big boy, you are aware of the possible implications, you don't need me reminding you after every contest."

"Whoa, this is new!" Clay exclaimed, as he and Aaron were in perfect sync with their running gait as they passed the Grand Fountain in the park.

"I'm not going to nag you," Aaron responded. "You've got a lot on your mind, and you don't need me constantly reminding you of that fact."

"I appreciate that," Clay said as he turned towards Aaron and gave him a nod and smile.

"I can't want for you something that you don't wholly want for yourself. It's ultimately your decision, and I am perfectly fine with whatever you decide," Aaron summed up.

"We're a team, you and I. It is our decision not just mine, in that it will determine where we live for the next four or eight years."

"I will be happy regardless of where we are as long as we are there together," Aaron added.

"It is glorious here though, isn't it? The weather in early April is ideal. And this park has come alive in the past week or two," Clay observed as he looked around at the flora and fauna surrounding them on their late afternoon run.

"Truly, but there's nothing wrong with a jog around the Tidal Basin in Washington this time of year either," Aaron asserted.

"Subtle, my love, subtle," Clay laughed as he jogged along. "C'mon, I'll race you to the rookery," Clay said as he began to pick up his pace.

"Oh jeez, those great egrets scare the crap out of me!" Aaron complained.

"I'll protect you, we're a team," Clay called out as he raced ahead.

"We're a team, always have been," Andrew Cochran stated to his campaign manager and life-long friend Nathan Whitaker from a hotel suite at the Pfister Hotel in downtown Milwaukee, Wisconsin.

"I am thrilled to be back in the thick of it, that's for sure," Nathan replied with a big grin. "The fundraiser tonight is sold out. We are picking up steam here in Wisconsin, and are tied with Howard Mason in the latest polling."

"I've gone from losing the first four contests of the primary season to being in the lead and it's mostly due to your counsel and strategic advice," Andrew Cochran praised his friend.

"We're barely 100 delegates ahead of Jedediah Wilson, and Howard and Cletus are not that far behind. We've still got a lot of work to do," Nathan conceded.

"The fact that I am in the lead is a major accomplishment," Andrew responded with a smile.

"Frankly, I never thought that I would ever again be in this role, managing your campaign," Nathan confessed. "I was told that you wouldn't even accept my letters. So to me, I am reborn. A new lease on life I never imagined I'd get the opportunity to have."

"Well, the letters were Sam and Sue Lynn wrongly attempting to determine what they thought was best for me. Once I discovered what they were doing, I put an immediate stop to it. That, of course, led to our meeting at Camp David just prior to your trial," Andrew stated.

"That meeting meant so much to me. It helped me get through some pretty rough patches," Nathan allowed.

"You've been through a lot, there is no denying that. But, we've come full circle, old chum. It's you and me back on the road, pressing the flesh and planning our campaign together. Even Sue Lynn is thankful for what you've done for me. For my campaign," Andrew said with a nod.

"She doesn't know . . ." Nathan began.

"No, of course not." Andrew quickly and emphatically replied. "Only you and I, and it's always got to remain so."

"Yes, of course. You can trust me."

"I know I can. In fact, I trusted you with my life," Andrew responded. "Now, let's get down to the ballroom and raise some money for this victory campaign."

HOWARD MASON AND HIS CHIEF POLITICAL STRATEGIST Mark Backus went for a late afternoon run prior to a campaign event in Madison, Wisconsin later that evening. The duo jogged past the majestic white granite Wisconsin State Capital building as they discussed the state of the Republican Party nomination race. It was early April and a pronounced chill lingered in the air, yet signs of spring abounded on the newly budding trees surrounding the Capitol building.

"If we can win Wisconsin and then follow it up with a victory in New York a couple weeks hence we will be right back in the thick of it," Mark Backus mentioned to his friend and candidate.

"Where are we in the polls?" Howard inquired.

"We're virtually tied with Cochran in both states while Sawyer and Wilson lag far behind. Neither has much chance in northern moderate states," Mark answered. "In fact the map is in our favor. Most of the Southern states have already voted. After New York; Maryland, Pennsylvania, New Jersey, and California are the last big delegate states left, and we've got a fighter's chance in each of them."

"So, if not for the assassination attempt on the President, I might be leading right now," Howard asserted.

"It would be very close, Wilson built up a pretty good delegate lead in some of the Southern states, but yeah, I'd say so," Mark responded.

"Speaking of that Howard, I've meant to ask you, whose idea was it for you to bring the bottle of bourbon the morning you resigned the Vice-Presidency?"

"It was Cochran, who first suggested it when I was going to resign a week earlier. He asked me to think about my resignation for a week and if I still wanted to pursue it, to bring a bottle of good bourbon so that we could toast each other and say goodbye properly," Howard allowed.

"Cochran asked you to bring the bourbon?" Mark clarified.

"Yeah. He offered me a drink, but it was the morning, so neither of us partook at that time. In fact, when I gave him the bottle, he said he was only joking about the bourbon and told me to take it and enjoy it myself."

"But of course you didn't. You left the bottle with Cochran, who then had a glass late that afternoon," Mark stated.

"Yes. Why the questions?" Howard asked, nearly stumbling after taking a wrong step during his jog.

"Just curious," Mark replied. "How did you procure the bottle of bourbon?"

"I asked one of my staff go to a DC liquor store and buy it. The bottle was in a sealed wooden box when I gave it to Cochran."

"To your knowledge, no one had opened the bottle or even the box it came in prior to you giving it to the President, correct?" Mark asked.

"That's right, it was sealed when I handed it to him," Howard confirmed. "Look, the FBI asked me about all of this for three days straight after Cochran's poisoning. I told them several times exactly what I'm telling you now."

"So, how did the poison get into the bottle? And who would have had access to that bottle from the time that you gave it to Cochran to the time he took those first few sips?" Mark inquired.

"I don't know. I have no idea who was in the President's office during the course of the day. It was several hours from when I presented it to him until the time he opened it and drank it," Howard explained.

"It seems curious doesn't it?" Mark questioned. "Every visitor to the Oval Office is logged in, correct?"

"Yes, of course. But there's still the President's staff, his secretary Nancy, and the Secret Service detail who may come and go," Howard responded.

"We're now well over a month from the day of the poisoning and yet the FBI has not announced any developments in their investigation. I'm sure they've talked several times to everyone who had access to the Oval Office, so why the delay in finding a suspect?" Mark asked.

"I don't have a clue," Howard stated.

"Maybe because there are no clues," Mark asserted. Howard stopped dead in his tracks. He took a deep breath and looked directly at his friend.

"Cochran isn't stupid or devious enough to poison himself," Howard firmly countered.

"Who said anything about being stupid?" Mark asked.

CHAPTER 12

POSY BRANCH WEAVED HER WAY IN AND OUT of the large crowd at her establishment French Tips, Juleps & Jazz. A large smile adorned her pretty face as she stopped to chat with some of her regular customers. Michael beamed from behind the bar pleased to see the Posy he so loved back to being her typical energetic self. Playful charisma was always Posy's top playing card, and it once again was part of her deck.

"It took me a while, but I finally realized that I was disrespecting the memory of Chiffon by not keeping this place, a place of fun, music, and happiness. That is the greatest legacy for her, for this place to remain exactly what it was when she was working the room," Posy said. "Speaking of Chiffon, have you heard anything about the investigation of her murder from your friend Sergeant Coaltree?"

"This isn't the time to talk about that, we're flush with customers," Michael said attempting to side-step the question.

"Alright baby, but don't hide nothin' from me Michael, I'm a big girl," Posy reassured her friend.

"Song Ye is trying to get your attention," Michael mentioned.

"Yeah, I see her waving, I should go check out what all the commotion is about." Posy walked over to that far side of the room where Song Ye's nail station was located. It was too crowded to clearly see it from the bar area. As Posy approached the partitioned nail station she recognized the back of the person sitting at the nail station with his hands on the work station counter.

"What the hell do you want here, Olivier?" Posy dismissively asked Olivier Bellevue as he sat there smiling at Posy.

"Why, to get my nails done, of course," Olivier said with a smarmy tone. "Best nail salon in all of New Orleans from what I been told."

"There's plenty of other places you can go to," Posy answered, clearly irritated by his presence. "You got a lot of nerve showing up here."

"Well, I thought I was doing you a favor. Bringing you some business. I had heard that things weren't going that well. That your clients were drifting away. But clearly that was a false rumor. You seem to be doing just fine," Olivier responded surveying the packed crowd.

"You are not welcome here, why don't you just get up and go," Posy said, her anger growing at just seeing him sitting there like he owned the place.

"I'm not looking for trouble. I came to lend support to an old friend in a time of need," Olivier stated with a sly grin.

"I don't need or want your support or your money. We are not friends. I just want you to leave," Posy demanded.

"That's not good business practice, turning away paying customers," Olivier replied with an unctuous smile.

"I asked you nicely to please leave my establishment," Posy reiterated as Olivier reclined farther back in the chair at Song Ye's work station.

"Ms. Branch asked you to leave," Michael said as he loomed over Olivier at the work station with his baseball bat held securely in his left hand.

"Well, I know when I am not welcomed," Olivier said while rising to his feet. "Look for my scathing review of this inappropriate behavior on Yelp. This is no way to treat a paying customer." Olivier walked out the door and into the crowd outside in the French Market area.

"What was that all about?" Michael asked Posy.

"I ain't exactly sure. I think he was just trying to get my goat," Posy replied. "Whatever Olivier is up to it surely ain't good."

STANFORD WINCHESTER HAD MADE IT OFFICIAL. He had changed his party affiliation from Republican to Independent. This was not just a mere formality. This was an action that bespoke of a true identity shift within Stanford Winchester. He was born into a family where his grandfather was the Governor of the state of Louisiana. A blue-dog Democrat but a Southern Conservative in many ways. His father was a die-hard Republican. Every year of his life since childhood, Stanford had identified himself as a Republican. That fact only became more entrenched when he went to college and became enamored by the Conservative intellectuals such as William F. Buckley who rallied around Barry Goldwater. So, this change was consequential. This act had deep meaning for a man who did not take political labels lightly. For Stanford, being a Republican wasn't just a party affiliation, it was a way of life. A philosophy that was at the very core of who he was as a white man of means living in the South. Stanford did not celebrate his change of party allegiance but rather mourned it as he sat on a stool at Fritzel's having a Sazerac in the late afternoon, waiting to meet his fiancée Whitlee Hammond on her way to their house after she completed her day of work at the Federal Court building. Seated next to Stanford at the bar was his old friend, Calvin Putnam.

"Don't you think that you are taking all of this out of context and making too much of some ridiculous political rhetoric?" Calvin asked his friend.

"It's more than the rhetoric, Calvin, it is the indignity of it and the lack of respect for time-honored political civility and institutions," Stanford answered while shaking his head. "It is a clear and present threat to democracy itself, if you ask me."

"The Democrats are just as bad. Except they utilize the media elites to do their dirty work. As Mercutio uttered as he was dying, "A pox on both their houses."

"Hell, I know you've had enough to drink Calvin, when you're quoting 'Romeo and Juliet' to me," Stanford chuckled. "And besides, it ain't the same. The Democrats aren't accusing each other of crimes against God and humanity. The Democrats are not attempting to erode faith in American democracy. There's a very big difference. But I'm not joining the Democrats, I'm just saying in my own way that I no longer want to affiliate myself with the Republican Party."

"Your beloved father and even your grandfather, the Governor, are rolling in their graves."

"My grandfather had his own legacy of less than democratic actions at times in office, but he and his cohorts never disgraced themselves by questioning the moral integrity of the President of the United States. He never told tales that were wholly made up fiction. He might have fudged on the truth from time to time, but he never attempted to create his own truth in a parallel universe of distortion. Trust me, if he were alive today, he'd be quitting this Party as well," Stanford argued.

"Well, you're a grown man," Calvin allowed. "But I think that you are over-reacting. I'm a proud Republican and I will die that way."

"I respect your opinion, Calvin, I just can't countenance what I see and hear on a daily basis from men who purport to represent family values. We should not be teaching our children the art of deceitful beguilement."

"Now Stanford, you know as well as I do that Southern mendacity has long been seen as part of the charm of politics in Louisiana. We've got a long and not so illustrious history on that account," Calvin replied.

"Never practiced by me," Stanford firmly countered. "Not to toot my own horn, but I have always put a premium on dealing with facts and attempting to parse out the half-truths and downright lies. I'm too old to change now. Besides, I'm not renouncing my Republican friends, if I did that I'd be spending a lot of time alone. All I'm saying is that I do not appreciate or even recognize the Republican Party now."

"Well, I've got to admit that this comes as a real kick in the head," Calvin stated. "But you're a good man Stanford, you always have been. You live your life by your own moral and ethical principles, and it's hard to argue with that."

"Thank you, Calvin, them is fine words to hear. But clearly, it's time to cut you off. That is way too much liquor talking," Stanford laughed as he gently slapped his friend on the back.

CYNTHIA BRIDGMAN TOOK A SEAT IN THE OVAL OFFICE as she awaited the arrival of President Cochran. It was not her only time in the Oval Office, but it certainly was one of a very few. Cynthia smoothed out her pants suit as she sat quietly with her hands in her lap. Cynthia was an attractive woman of forty-eight years old. With dark hair and brown eyes, she looked every bit the part of an elegant, intelligent woman of Congress. She was born and lived in New Hampshire for most of her life. She was the valedictorian when she graduated at the top of her class from the University of New Hampshire. She attended Yale Law School, where she was chief editor of the Law Review. Cynthia glanced around the impressive office of the President, taking in the paintings and photographs on the walls and on the President's desk.

"May I get you some coffee or tea," Nancy, the President's secretary offered.

"Thank you, that is so very kind, but I'm fine," Cynthia replied.

"I've been told the President will be with you momentarily," Nancy stated. And, several moments later, President Cochran walked into the Oval Office.

"Good morning, Mr. President," Cynthia said as she rose to her feet to greet the Commander-In-Chief.

"Cynthia, thank you so much for coming this morning. I am delighted to see you," Andrew Cochran greeted his Vice-Presidential nominee with a warm smile.

"Thank you, Mr. President for bestowing me with the high honor of selecting me as your Vice-President and running mate."

"I've been informed by the Speaker of the House and the Senate Majority Leader that you should receive a very timely up or down vote in the next few days. The Democrats have little incentive to dawdle on your confirmation. You are well liked," Andrew Cochran stated.

"Well, I'm afraid that there are several members of our Party that are not as enthused by my choice," Cynthia acknowledged.

"Oh, I'm very aware. They have voiced their displeasure," Andrew responded. "Sometimes I have to check my Party affiliation just to make sure I know which Party I'm supposed to be the leader of. Honestly, I don't know what the problem is with some of our members."

"It's my pro-choice stance, which as I stated at our first vetting meeting, I have no intention of walking back or hedging on sir," Cynthia stated.

"And I have no intent on asking you to," Andrew replied. "I ran for the Presidency as a rock-ribbed Conservative. I checked all of the social issues boxes. I was against marriage equality, I was against equal pay for women, and I was against legalized abortion. But my thinking on each of those issues is evolving to the point that I don't believe that we have any major philosophical differences. When you serve as President you quickly come to realize that you represent the entire nation, not just your ideological constituency. The office makes you reassess your perspective on social policies that impact so many American citizens that may not share your perspectives. You begin to question what right you and your party have to impose their own social mores on a vast swath of fellow citizens. All of this is simply to say that I would not have chosen you if I believed that my ideology would be in conflict with your firmly held beliefs."

"I am heartened by your response, sir. I did have some doubts about how you would handle the inevitable question about our differences on a woman's right to choose," Cynthia stated.

"I have no doubt that my position on squaring your pro-choice advocacy with my previous record of running as a pro-life Conservative will be raised at the Party debate next week. I am prepared to unequivocally state that there is no distance between the two of us on the issue. Instead of the top of the ticket requiring the Vice-President to acquiesce to the Presidential candidate's ideology, I am going to do the opposite. This administration is going to support a woman's right to choose. I'm sure that a goodly number of delegates from the Southern states we have already garnered in our column will threaten to change their choice for President. However, Nathan has looked into this and the State Republican Party rules for most of the states involved, the delegates are bound to me on the first ballot. Expressing my views on women's rights should only increase our delegate possibilities in upcoming states like New York, New Jersey, and California," Andrew Cochran summarized.

"I deeply appreciate your support and expressions of solidarity, sir, but I would not want you to reverse your stance on long-held religious and moral beliefs for the sake of my inclusion on the ticket," Cynthia responded.

"That's just the thing. I'm not so sure that my beliefs on the topic were ever that strongly held. I must confess that my public rhetoric had not always matched what I actually felt in my heart," Andrew began. "I was raised, for the most part, by my Grandma Blanche. Grandma Blanche was a practical woman. Oh, we went to church every Sunday, but she taught me to think for myself and not just embrace every tenant of Christian dogma. Though the topic didn't come up much Grandma Blanche was very much in favor of women's rights. It was only after I became heavily involved in Republican Party politics that I began to espouse a hard line ideology on reproductive rights. A fair portion of that was for political expediency. It's hard to get elected to anything in Georgia as a Republican unless you fall in line and parrot the Party rhetoric. So, I did. I'm not proud to say it, but it was a means to an end. But, did I truly believe in a lot of the social positions of the Party? No. Therefore, this reversal on social policy positions is not as difficult for me as an individual as it is as a Republican candidate."

"Thank you for sharing that with me, sir. That allays some of my trepidations," Cynthia confirmed.

"Fear not, we are a united team. And that fact makes me infinitely happy. We are going to turn this Grand Old Party on its head, Cindy. We may not succeed, but it's time this Party was dragged into the 21st century by the scruff of its neck. Teddy Roosevelt was a progressive Republican. There have been many progressive Republicans throughout the history of the Party. They just don't exist anymore because mutually beneficial political alliances eschewed them from the ranks. Well, it's time to resurrect the Republican progressive. And you and I are going to do exactly that in this election. Are you with me?" Andrew Cochran asked his running mate with a glint in his eye.

"Most certainly!"

"Po-lit-ical Su-i-cide," Cletus Sawyer dramatically stated into the phone over pronouncing every syllable.

"I ain't so sure," Jim Bob McCallum replied with a dismissive huff. "Populism ain't dead in the Republican Party, we just induced it into a nice long Rip Van Winkle like coma with the aid of the Evangelical moral majority and the Tea Party over the years. The libertarians within our ranks are viewing us as a big government party as well. Except we use government to restrict the social agendas we don't cotton to such as abortion, immigration, weed, and fags. It's a mistake to think that populist views wouldn't resonate with part of the Republican electorate. And though we've tortured most of the moderates out of Party leadership, that don't mean they don't exist in the voting rank-and-file."

"I do hear what you're saying, Jim Bob, but ain't no way Cochran's selection of that Bridgman woman is gonna do anything but piss-off the base," Cletus retorted.

"Cletus, you own a map and a calendar?" Jim Bob asked with a smarmy tone in his voice. "The South has already voted in this nomination circus. The delegates Cochran got in the South, are bound to him on the first ballot. What's left are mostly northern states. You don't think that Republican moderates in California and New York ain't gonna take a shine to Cochran and his moderate woman? Hell, she's from New England. New England Republicans are more rare than three dollar bills. You know how many delegates are up for grabs in just New York and California alone? I wouldn't get too cocky if I was you, Cletus."

"Now, don't you go worrying Jim Bob, we gonna do just fine," Cletus said attempting to calm the fears of his largest benefactor.

"Christ help me!" Jim Bob exclaimed. "Cletus, do the damn math! You're trailing Wilson and Cochran in delegates. Your best states to pick up big chunks of delegates are long over. You don't got a lot of appeal in the North. As long as it stays a four man race, you ain't going nowhere. You got to get rid of Jedediah Wilson and be the lone Conservative in the race. This thing ain't gonna be over before the convention. But if Cochran wins on the first ballot, then it's over. So you got to make sure that don't happen. Good thing is that Cochran is turning into more of a blue dog Democrat every day. By the next debate he's gonna be one of them damn Smurfs! Howard Mason is trying to straddle the line between base pandering Conservative and pragmatic moderate. Only you and Wilson are the true Conservatives in the race. And, there just ain't enough time left. There's no more room at the inn, Jesus gotta go. I gave you what you need to turn him out to the stables. What you waiting for?"

"Strategy," Cletus confidently replied. "I got this. I'm just stringing him along trying to make him look like a real untenable hypocrite."

"I've done warned you before, Cletus, don't you mess this up. Wilson has got to go, and you need to make sure that his delegates see no other alternative than to support you. Once you get that done, you should be either in the lead or at the least tied. Then Cochran and Mason can cancel each other out for the moderate votes, and you clean up with the base," Jim Bob clearly stated.

"That surely is the plan. Step one is to . . ." Cletus began to outline before he was abruptly cut off by Jim Bob.

"Get'er done boy!" Jim Bob emphatically said into the phone and then quickly ended the call.

CHAPTER 13

IT WAS LATE MAY. THE MAJORITY OF THE STATE nominating prima-ries and caucuses had taken place. All eyes were focused on the last Republican and Democratic debates to be held prior to the final major states holding their nominating elections. Still up for grabs were the del-egates from the states of California, New Jersey, Montana, New Mexico, and South Dakota. The magic number to win the nomination for the Republicans was 1237 delegates. None of the four Republican candi-dates for President had over 1000 delegates. There were a total of 303 delegates left to be won in the five remaining state contests. The chances of any candidate going into the Republican Convention with the 1237 delegates required to win the nomination was remote, at best. An open convention seemed the most likely scenario.

Meanwhile, the Democratic nomination would be won with 2382 total delegates. A total of 694 delegates were up for grabs in the last five primaries with a massive 475 of those delegates to be determined by the California primary. Senator Perry Douglas had amassed 2001 delegates prior to the June 7th final state primaries. He needed 381 of the 694 remaining delegates to win the Democratic nomination for President. The weather was warming up all over the nation and the bright late spring sun was forcing winter's shadows into a hasty retreat.

STANFORD WINCHESTER STOOD ON THE BALCONY of his Royal Street home in New Orleans surveying the pedestrian traffic below. He smiled as he sipped at his glass of sweet tea. In less than one month's time he would no longer be relegated to life as a bachelor. And he could not have been happier about that change in his marital status.

"Look at you, you look lit up like a Christmas tree," Whitlee commented as she joined a happily smiling and humming Stanford on the balcony.

"Why, that is because you are the string of lights that has illuminated this tired old spruce tree," Stanford chuckled in response.

"Are you content in retirement, my love?" Whitlee asked.

"Most days, yes," Stanford answered. "Though I have to admit, I get bored from time to time. But if you are asking me if I miss the bench, the answer is no. I accomplished everything I could as a judge. Another case wasn't going to float my boat."

"And, what of teaching law at Tulane?"

"Well, I just might do that in the fall semester," Stanford responded.

"And what of writing a book?" Whitlee pressed.

"I've scribbled a few notes, but I have not committed to it as of yet," Stanford stated. "Besides, I'm preoccupied with politics right now. Or rather I should say, that I am disgusted with politics right now."

"Do you have any second thoughts about changing your party affiliation to Independent?" Whitlee questioned.

"Not for a single moment. Though some of the old antiques I have an occasional cocktail with are the first to call me a traitor and a sellout," Stanford confessed with a satisfied smile.

"That doesn't bother you?" Whitlee inquired.

"Ha! I enjoy it. It gives me an opportunity to remind them about how wrong they are about most things. We engage in lively banter and good debate. It allows me to take this old wit out for a vigorous jog from time to time."

"And these are the same people who will be attending our wedding?" Whitlee asked.

"Yes, most are my dear. But they cherish you, it's just me that they are annoyed with at the moment. Everyone knows that weddings are all about the bride, the attendance of the groom though mandatory, is at best ignored and at times treated with disdain. You can always hear the whispers in the back of the church, 'oh, she could have done much better than him,'" Stanford chortled.

"Now, you're just exaggerating. Your old friends still adore you," Whitlee pronounced.

"Have you been to Fritzel's lately?" Stanford questioned with a sly grin and a hearty laugh.

CAROLYN BARNES SAT AT THE BACK of the auditorium as she listened to her candidate finish up his preparation session for the last Democratic Party debate prior to the critical primaries in California and New Jersey.

"How was it?" Perry Douglas asked as he stepped off the stage and walked towards his campaign manager.

"Good," Carolyn assessed. "You made all your main points. The 'empowerment through respect and acceptance' line was a nice touch."

"That's a line that Robert has been using lately. I thought the symmetry of both of us using the line would be effective," Perry replied.

"Yes, he was speaking at Berkley yesterday, they treated him like a king," Carolyn related.

"He's making a real difference," Perry contended. "Seldom do campaign surrogates have the type of influence that Robert is displaying from one event to the next."

"There is no doubt, he's very popular with his generation, and certainly getting our message across. But, his security detail told me that he stopped to smoke a joint with some students after a rally in San Francisco the other day. Sometimes he just won't be constrained by the orthodoxy of political campaigning," Carolyn lamented.

"If taking a couple of tokes with a few students is the most egregious thing Robert does on the campaign trail, we can certainly live with that," Perry responded.

"I'm just afraid that, at times, some of his flamboyance can be a distraction from our message," Carolyn asserted.

"If you think he's doing harm . . ." Perry began before being quickly interrupted by Carolyn.

"Oh no," Carolyn interjected. "He's doing far more good than he is distracting with some of his antics. Young voters are listening to him. They relate to him. They believe in Robert."

"The boy keeps telling me that he has no interest in public service, yet he is more of a natural politician than his three term Senatorial father,"

Perry stated. "He has the charm and charisma of a young Bobby Kennedy when it comes to outreach to younger voters."

"And it all ended for Bobby in California," Carolyn added.

"That's a rather maudlin thought. It had not occurred to me, but you're right," Perry replied. "And how are we doing in the polls in California?"

"We're doing very well in the urban areas, but getting our butt kicked in the rural and eastern part of the state. It's going to be close. But if we can get some tremendous turnout in the metropolitan areas we could squeak out enough delegates to perhaps clinch on the first ballot, if not win outright before the convention," Carolyn answered.

"Good, that is very good news. It would be great if we can sow this up before the convention. The Republicans are clearly moving towards an open convention. What a free-for-all that should be!" Perry exclaimed.

"A good debate performance could be what we need for that extra excitement and push for a big win in California," Carolyn said.

"I'll do what I can. Have security keep a close eye on Robert during his California rallies," Perry asked.

"Any reason you expect issues?"

"Nope, just chalk it up to a nervous and over-protective father. Nothing more," Perry responded with a grin.

THE SECRET SERVICE JOGGED ALONG WITH the President and his campaign manager Nathan Whitaker, as they ran through some of the beautiful grounds of Princeton University. Andrew looked confident and contented while discussing debate strategy with Nathan as both men picked up their pace and extended their running gait.

"Keep positive in the messaging. Express how things are good and only going to get better in a second term of a Cochran administration. Jedediah and Cletus are pushing this doom and gloom scenario that is turning off the public," Nathan stated.

"How are we doing in New Jersey in the polls?" Andrew asked.

"Pretty much tied with Howard. As the primaries have moved to Northern states, you and Howard have taken over because Wilson and Sawyer cannot gain any traction this side of the Mason-Dixon Line," Nathan replied. "As long as Wilson and Sawyer both remain in the race, they keep splitting the ideological base voters. You and Howard are splitting the moderate Republican vote and we are all headed to an open convention."

"So, there's no way to gain a stranglehold on the primary election at this late date?" Andrew asked his top advisor.

"Even if we have a landslide win in California and do very well here in New Jersey, there's little chance to sew things up. I'm afraid that we are going back to backroom negotiating for delegate votes. Our best chance is to call for party unity behind the incumbent President and the only candidate who can present a moderate agenda more likely to win in the general election," Nathan summed up.

"The base will never go along, they hate me," Andrew contended.

"Yes, yes they do," Nathan conceded. "But as flawed as they may see you, as traitorous to Conservative values they may claim you to be, in the long run you are still a Republican. And when it comes right down to winning national elections, I think the allure of holding onto the White House, will ultimately make the base fall in line. They will hold their collective noses, and vote for the incumbent Republican instead of taking a chance at losing by double digits to the Democrats by nominating a Conservative firebrand who cannot win in the general."

"That seems like sound reasoning, but when have you known our base to be reasonable?" Andrew Cochran inquired with a sly smile.

"Well, it's coming very close to being time for that come-to-Jesus moment. Neither Jedediah or Cletus could win a general election. The choice is between Howard and you, if the Party actually wants to win. You are the first Republican President in twelve years, does the base want to go wandering out in the desert for another twelve years? I think not," Nathan assured his candidate.

"We'll soon see, my friend."

CHAPTER 14

I T WAS JUNE AND THE COUNTRY WAS READY for warm temperatures
and a revival of spirits. The malaise of winter was over and a new
energized optimism was taking effect during a summer that would be
witness to the Summer Olympics and the nominations for President
of the United States. In San Francisco, the two Democratic candidates were scheduled to debate, while across the country at Princeton
University in New Jersey, the four Republican Party nominees were
ready to square off.

PRESIDENT ANDREW COCHRAN HAD HAD ENOUGH. He stood patiently
behind his podium at the Republican Presidential Debate at Princeton
University as his three opponents decried what a traitor he was to the
Republican Party and Conservative ideology for the better part of an
hour. His loyalty, his patriotism, and even his sexual identity, had been
challenged by the other three candidates.

"There has never been a bigger flip-flopper on all substantive issues
that Republican voters care about than Andrew Cochran," Cletus
Sawyer summed up. "Andrew Cochran ran four years ago as a staunch
Conservative and fierce supporter of the Constitution. And at that
time, everyone up here on this stage gave him our full-throated support. But months into his new administration, Andrew Cochran began
to waver on the issues he clearly stood for prior to his election. He

began to compromise with the Democratic Congress, basically siding with their tax and spend ways. He nominated to the Supreme Court a justice who has sided more with the Democratic members of the Court than he has with the Republican members in the last two years. We did not elect a Republican President with the expectation that he would turn around and spit in the face of the Constitution. What kind of man, purports to be one thing and then acts and does things wholly to the contrary of his previously espoused views? What kind of man turns his back on his Party and his supporters without a second thought? What kind of man selects a woman who promotes the killing of inno-cent life as his Vice-President? A man with no dignity, a man with no conscience, a traitor to everything that Conservative Republicans hold dear. This man does not deserve to be President for one more minute let alone for four more years."

The moderator of the debate turned to President Cochran and informed him, "Mr. President, you have two minutes to respond."

"Not only this evening, but during the course of this entire campaign, I have listened to my opponents define what a Republican is, and how I am no longer someone who can represent the Grand Old Party. They oft refer to me as a traitor. So, I'd like to take a moment to remind my fellow candidates exactly what the Republican Party stands for and of the amaz-ing men who have proudly represented this party over the last century and a half. The Republican Party was formed in 1854 by several former anti-slavery members of the Whig Party. In 1860, the Republican Party nominated Abraham Lincoln as their Presidential candidate. Six weeks after Lincoln's election, South Carolina was the first state to secede from the Union, with several others following not far behind. We were the Party standing up against slavery. Protecting the rights of all men. And today, due to the myopic and bigoted views and policy positions of far too many in the Republican base, we mightily struggle during national elections to garner even ten percent of the African-American vote. The Party of Lincoln has turned its back on the very constituency that it fought to protect from its inception. I am ashamed that it has come to this. So, forgive me if I don't support or condone the shouts of hatred and bigotry that I hear at the campaign events of my fellow nominees. This is not who we are. This is no longer the Party of Lincoln," Andrew Cochran passionately stated before pausing for a moment.

"President William McKinley supported the middle-class and small businesses. He was the first president to promote pluralism. He argued that prosperity should be 'shared by all ethnic and religious groups.' Yet in our party today, many espouse a philosophy that promotes intolerance and the exclusion of those of the Muslim faith. Hispanics are viewed as unwanted infringers unworthy of citizenship. This is no longer the Party of McKinley. President Theodore Roosevelt ushered in the Progressive Era in the United States in the early 20th century. Roosevelt championed his 'Square Deal' domestic policies, promising the average citizen fairness, breaking of large trusts, government regulation of the railroads, and pure food and drugs. Land conservation was also key to Roosevelt's domestic policies. Some of our party leaders, including the gentlemen on this very stage view government regulation as a war on business, instead of protection for the average citizen. They demand private oil drilling on sacred government held lands. I am the only candidate on this stage who has not called for the abolition of the Environmental Protection Agency. My opponents list this as something they would do on day one of their Presidency. This is not in keeping with our heritage. This is no longer the party of Theodore Roosevelt. In fact, even the term 'progressive' has become an unspeakable term that requires nothing but condemnation. President Dwight Eisenhower fought for his country and was one of the principal architects of the Allied Forces victory in World War II. He authorized the establishment of NASA. He launched the Interstate Highway System. He fiercely advocated for strong science education with the establishment of the National Defense Education Act. Eisenhower warned of the dangers of the military industrial complex, and made sure that under his watch Social Security was expanded. Today's Republican Party denies science and climate change. We are more than willing to snuggle up with large industrial war marketeers. We are quick to defund NASA and push space exploration into the private marketplace. And we are the Party that continues the fight to do away with the safety net for the elderly that is Social Security. No, my friends, this modern Republican Party is no longer the party of Eisenhower. President Ronald Reagan was embraced by Conservative Republicans for his stances on social issues, but let us not forget that it was Reagan, who in a bipartisan way, resolved the Social Security financial crisis, providing enough additional funding to keep Social Security financially fiscal for 25 additional years. It was also President Reagan who signed an immigration bill that gave, what today is described as amnesty, to millions of undocumented immigrant workers. You need only listen to the unrepentant loathing of our undocumented residents that is expressed by my opponents in this campaign to understand that no, this is no longer the Party of Reagan. I ask, where are the Rockefeller Republicans? Where are the fervent supporters of Charles Percy, Lowell Weicker, and Howard Baker? All outstanding Republican statesmen who would not recognize their Party today." President Cochran paused briefly as he surveyed the large auditorium.

"My fellow Americans, and specifically my fellow Republicans, if you are tired of gridlock in Washington, if you are tired of the ugliness and animosity of modern politics, if you want an even playing field where all Americans can get a leg up instead of just the wealthy, I am not here to offer you a new Republican Party. Rather I am here to attempt to restore the Republican Party of our glorious past. The Party of Lincoln which had enormous African-American support and cherished the humanity of all men. The Party of McKinley which promoted pluralism and shunned religious or ethnic intolerance. The Party of Teddy Roosevelt that did not see fault in practical government regulations. The Party of Eisenhower which embraced science and space exploration. The Party of Reagan which understood that bipartisan support across the aisle was far preferred to partisan bickering and legislative inactivity. And the party of countless good men of high moral character who did not see pure evil in progressive domestic policies that aid all of the American people, but rather saw opportunity to compromise and work together for a better United States. If you want to return to the days when the Republican Party was more than the Party of intolerance and partisan gridlock, then I am the only candidate on this stage who is offering you a return to our Republican roots in order to achieve a better American future. It's just that simple. Let's once again find our true heart and love of all of the citizens of this great and wonderful land."

The auditorium broke into loud applause and wild cheers for the President of the United States. Andrew Cochran had defined Republicanism for those who had lost sight of its progressive and inclusive past. Andrew Cochran shamed intolerance and inactivity and reinstated the principle of moderate political compromise. And Nathan Whitaker who was off to the side of the stage could only applaud his old friend and smile.

THE FOLLOWING DAY, NATHAN WHITAKER MET in a hotel suite with Vice-President Cynthia Bridgman prior to a campaign event in Newark, New Jersey.

"Well, that was some speech that President Cochran gave last night towards the end of the debate. It was filled with passion and hope," Cynthia Bridgman offered.

"Indeed it was, Madame Vice-President," Nathan responded.

"Nathan, please, just call me Cindy. After all, it is my understanding that I would not be Vice-President if not for your enthusiastic support of my nomination to the President," Cynthia Bridgman asked.

"You were the best person for the position and a true asset to the ticket," Nathan replied with a smile.

"Nevertheless, I want to thank you for your support. I believe that we can do a great number of good things in a second term of a Cochran administration."

"Cindy, you are one of the few Republicans left in Congress who don't view compromise as a four letter word, and you don't reflexively eschew working with Democrats for unwavering political dogma. You made our choice easy, once we determined that we were going to try to resurrect moderate Republicanism. The Neoconservatives have had their day. And what we have to show for it is decades of a broken legislative system and rampant partisanship," Nathan stated.

"Being from New Hampshire, you're born with a vibrant independent streak. I never believed that either party had all the answers and that working together to solve problems was the only way to ensure progress," Cindy replied while staring directly into Nathan's eyes.

"Does your family share your independent views?" Nathan inquired.

"What is left of my family, yes. I have been divorced from my former husband for ten years now. Regrettably, our relationship has become somewhat estranged. My two grown girls, Samantha and Claire certainly share my views. It was actually my daughter Claire who persuaded me to embrace a pro-choice platform when I first ran for Congress twelve years ago. As you are well aware, being a pro-choice Republican is not something one does lightly," Cindy answered.

"And your parents?" Nathan questioned.

"Both are gone now, but they were both registered Republicans. Yet they voted for Jack Kennedy in 1960. They didn't allow party affiliation to sway them for voting for a candidate who they truly believed in. Someone they thought would be good for the country."

"How proud they would be to see their daughter as Vice-President of the United States," Nathan offered.

"Yes, I think of that daily. None of my achievements could have been possible without their loving support and pragmatic guidance," Cindy replied.

"I'm so pleased that you agreed to join the Cochran administration. It's a delight to have an intelligent, successful, strong-minded, and beautiful woman gracing the White House," Nathan stated with a sly grin.

"You mean other than the First Lady, of course," Cindy quickly reminded Nathan.

"Yes, of course," Nathan blushed. "I hope that we become wonderful friends," Nathan added.

"We already are, Nathan," Cindy smiled in return.

THE FINAL FIVE PRIMARY AND CAUCUS STATES held their elections. Once the results were tallied, Senator Perry Douglas was less than 50 delegates from clinching the Democratic nomination for President on the first ballot. Democratic Super-delegates were being pressed for their support. The campaign of Senator Hellen Raymond pledged to continue their fight for the nomination to the Democratic convention in late July.

Meanwhile, President Andrew Cochran led in delegates for the nomination, but he was approximately 200 delegates shy of winning the Republican nomination for President on the first ballot. Howard Mason, Cletus Sawyer, and Jedediah Wilson were not far behind. It would be virtually impossible for Andrew Cochran to win the nomination without siphoning off delegate votes from one or two of his opponents. The temperatures were rising across the country as were the political machinations.

CHAPTER 15

Posy Branch hummed to herself as she stared into her full length bedroom mirror appraising her appearance. She moved her right hand down the front of her knee length royal blue dress brushing out any small creases. The string of white pearls around her slender neck accentuated her beautiful smile and her flawless complexion. Posy's teenaged beauty queen past was long gone, but she had matured into a lovely and successful woman. She had created a business that was the envy of many New Orleans merchants. She was surrounded by loving friends and co-workers who did their best to protect her, to help her thrive with continued success. Posy understood all of this as she continued her reflective gaze. Her front door bell rang interrupting her trance-like state. She slid on her high-heeled pumps and walked to the door.

"Look at you!" Posy exclaimed as her eyes flashed up and down the silhouette of her friend and co-worker Michael. "Ain't you Prince Charming looking so handsome in your gorgeous light gray Armani suit! Damn Michael, if you wasn't gay, we might not be making this here wedding!"

"Oh go on now Posy, you say that to all the boys," Michael joked back with a slight blush on his cheeks. "You look stunning," he quickly added.

"We're pretty enough to be on top the wedding cake, that's for sure," Posy laughed in return. "Speaking of, we best be going. You know how prompt Justice Winchester is, that preacher gonna start right on time. Where is it again that we's going?"

"Race and Religious," Michael answered. "It's a lovely 1830s two story Creole cottage, plus a three story townhouse and another two story slave quarters at the corner of Race and Religious streets nestled along the Lower Garden District riverfront."

"Been here for a good piece now, and I still don't know too much about the Big Easy," Posy lamented.

"You need to get out more," Michael stated. "You spend too much time at work. It's time that we brought on someone else to help manage the place."

"I know sugar, you speaking the truth. But if I hire someone to replace Chiffon, well . . ." Posy stated as her voice trailed off.

"It's time Posy, you can't do it alone, and I've got to be behind the bar," Michael affirmed.

"Next week I'll start looking. I promise," Posy replied. "But right now we best skedaddle and get us to Race and Religious."

AARON ROSE ADJUSTED THE WINDSOR KNOT in the blue and red striped tie that hung around the neck of Clay Grover. He took a step backwards, examined his work, and then moved forward a step to readjust the tie.

"We're going to be late," Clay chastised his husband.

"I want my husband to look perfect," Aaron said with a giggle.

"I thought I already did," Clay replied matter-of-factly.

"Hmm, arrogance. I suppose the White House Chief of Staff needs to demonstrate abundant self-confidence and a soupçon of arrogance," Aaron remarked with a wry grin.

"You mean the type of arrogance the leads one to use French terms in casual conversation?" Clay chuckled.

"Touché!" Aaron exclaimed, followed by a laugh.

"You realize that we can't say anything to anyone at the wedding about Senator Douglas' offer, right?" Clay queried.

"Of course, and I wouldn't. It's your news to relay, but it's kind of getting real now," Aaron replied.

"Senator Douglas doesn't have the nomination yet, and then there's that small hurdle better known as the general election," Clay stated with a touch of sarcasm.

"The nomination is merely a formality at this point," Aaron interjected.

"Nothing is done until it's done. Plus, if Cochran gets the Republican nomination he will be a difficult foe in the general election especially after adding Congresswoman Bridgman to the ticket," Clay said.

"You mean Vice-President Bridgman," Aaron corrected.

"Yeah, that's right, she is now the VP. Amazing how quickly the Democrats confirmed an appointee of a Republican President."

"Stuart Prentice respects Cochran. He was treated with respect and heartily thanked when he served as Acting President," Aaron added. "Still, the prospect is getting closer than ever."

"Perhaps, but right now we've got to jet. We don't want to be late," Clay stated.

BESSIE COLLINS AWKWARDLY REACHED AROUND to the back of her head attempting to use a pin to secure her lovely hat to her hair.

"Let me help you with that," Lucius said with a gentle smile. "I know you got eyes in the back of your head, you just don't got an extra pair of hands there."

"I'm just so nervous," Bessie admitted. "I've been praying for this day ever since Stanford done lost LeeAnn all them years ago. That man been so sad and lonely for all them many years. Now, finally, he gonna have someone to share his life with again. You look at him now and he seems twenty years younger. Finding love is such a wonderful thing."

"Oh, I surely do know that," Lucius said as he gently pinned Bessie's hat to her hair. "Speaking of happy, it surely is nice to see you all chipper and smiling again."

"It took me a piece to get it out of my head that I may have had something to do with President Cochran's poisoning," Bessie stated. "But once Stanford took me to see them FBI fellas and they told me that there wasn't a connection between my shop and the poison, I knew it wasn't my fault."

"You seen Esther?" Lucius asked.

"Not a once. Not since the night in Jackson Square," Bessie answered.

"You miss her and the business she brought?" Lucius inquired.

"You know, truth be told, not much at all. Well, I surely do miss the money she brought in, but I never trusted Esther. I always had suspicions about her. Ain't good to be in business with someone you don't trust."

"And everything back to normal between you and Papa Levi?"

"Heck ya. We two peas in a pod. I never truly blamed him for what I believed Esther did. I blamed myself. Business ain't what it use to be, but we still getting along and making decent money," Bessie related to Lucius.

"Well, my darling girl, we oughta get. Don't want to miss seeing Whitlee walking down that aisle and watch as Stanford busts his buttons he be so proud and happy," Lucius said with a smile.

"You right about that, you surely right about that."

JIM BOB MCCALLUM SAT ON THE PORCH of his large mansion in the Garden District of New Orleans in a rocking chair by his side was his wife Mabel. Jim Bob carefully lifted a glass of sweet tea to Mabel's lips as she took a short sip from a straw and silently stared off into the distance.

"It just ain't right. It's so damn disrespectful!" Jim Bob snapped. "LeeAnn deserved far better than to have her memory tarnished this way. The fact that that man claimed to love her so much, yet here he is getting married this very afternoon to another woman just galls me. I know you agree with me, my love, because we were both such good and loyal friends to LeeAnn." Jim Bob took a long sip of bourbon as he pushed his rocking chair into a slow rock with his cowboy boots.

"And frankly, I got no idea what that Whitlee woman sees in that treacherous scoundrel anyway. He ain't got no loyalty to no one but himself. He called me friend for decades, but then he turned on me, telling all sorts of horrible lies. On this very day, he stands before God and takes another woman as his wife, desecrating the memory of my beloved LeeAnn. Well, I tell you true, his day will come. God will have his way with that egregious sinner. Righteous retribution will rain down on his head. And that day, I cannot wait to see."

IT WAS A GORGEOUS SUN-FILLED LATE SATURDAY afternoon on June 11th. It was warm, of course, but not oppressively so. The two resplendent fountains and the lush courtyard at Race and Religious were decorated with dozens of hanging lights. The guests arrived and were seated in wicker cane chairs in rows fronted by a simple floral decorated archway. From the street, the assemblage could hear a small marching jazz band approaching. In traditional New Orleans style, the bridal party walked the street towards the courtyard proceeded by a band of jazz musicians and several men carrying colorful parasols to protect the bride from the heat and celebrate the forthcoming nuptials. The band played Stanford's favorite song, "When the Saints Go Marching In." A few moments later Stanford was standing in the courtyard at the archway. He looked dapper in a navy blue suit, white shirt, and bold red and yellow striped bowtie. A single small white calla lily graced his label. At his side were his older brother Malcolm and his longtime friend Calvin Putnam. Once the groom was in position, the band began to play "Here Comes the Bride," as Whitlee Hammond slowly walked down the aisle of the courtyard proceeded by her sister Meg, and her dear friend Alice. Whitlee wore a knee length off white dress and carried a gorgeous bouquet of white roses and vibrant greenery. A friend of the couple, and judge from the Fifth Circuit Court of Appeals, presided over the wedding ceremony.

Immediately following the twenty-minute wedding ceremony, tuxedoed waiters circulated among the wedding guests with trays of champagne flutes. As the afternoon sun gave way to the evening dusk, the dinner reception for the married couple commenced within the confines of the lush courtyard where the staff had set-up round tables with gleaming white table clothes adorned with splays of fresh cut flowers. A candied pecan and smoked peach salad was followed by red snapper stuffed with crabmeat, and bananas foster for dessert. The champagne and the bourbon flowed as the jazz band played with gusto. Stanford took his bride by the hand as they headed to the dance floor for their first dance as a couple. The band played Gershwin's "Embraceable You" as Stanford twirled Whitlee into his arms.

"We first danced together to this song at Posy's establishment," Stanford whispered into Whitlee's ear.

"Yes, I remember that she nearly had to shame you into dancing with me," Whitlee chuckled in response.

"Well, we were working together at the time, and I certainly didn't want it to be construed that we were dating," Stanford allowed.

"You and your sense of measured decorum and proper conduct," Whitlee sweetly stated.

"It all worked out to this glorious day, didn't it?" Stanford asked.

"Indeed. And I could not possibly be happier," Whitlee replied.

"Get ready, spin, twirl, dip," Stanford coached as the music was reaching its ending stanzas. He effortlessly spun Whitlee into his arms, then dipped her to nearly the ground before bringing her back to his chest in one precise movement. As the music ended the couple engaged in a long and loving kiss to the loud applause of their assembled guests.

"I do declare, Stanford is a regular Fred Astaire," Posy Branch chortled to Michael, Aaron, and Clay from the side of the courtyard.

"I wish I could dance like that," Aaron lamented to Clay as he watched the happy couple.

"We should take lessons. It's one thing to bump and grind to 1980s disco at OZ, but twirling and dipping like that is simply elegant," Clay stated with an envious grin.

"That's an outstanding idea. There could be an inaugural ball in our not too distant future," Aaron enthused.

"Perhaps," Clay smiled between sips of his champagne.

As was his custom, Stanford made it a point to dance with most of his female friends. Both Bessie and Posy were delighted to take the dance floor with their dear friend. They squealed and laughed as he twirled them across the courtyard. Later in the evening, when the Whiskey Sours and Sazeracs began to replace the champagne and pinot noir as the liquor of choice, the jazz band moved from classic jazz standards to soul, funk, and rhythm and blues. As the opening stanzas of LaBelle's classic New Orleans hit song "Lady Marmalade" filled the air, Posy, Michael, Aaron, and Clay raced to the dance floor. They all bumped and shimmied their way across the courtyard in unison. Then, Michael danced with Clay as Aaron and Posy danced together. Clay smiled broadly as Michael wrapped his large muscular arms around Clay's waist and torso. As the song ended, a few tears streamed down Posy's cheek.

"What's wrong? Did I step on your toes?" Aaron asked as he looked at Posy wipe her tears away.

"Oh no sugar, it wasn't nothing you did," Posy explained. "It's just that Chiffon and I use to sing the hell out of that song. The girl had some serious pipes."

"Yes, I recall, she was a very talented singer," Aaron interjected.

"I miss her so much," Posy stated while dabbing away her tears. "But she'd be the first one kicking my butt if she saw me crying at this happy event. Her spirit is within me, I truly believe that. So, come on Aaron,

let's get that beautiful tight behind of yours back out on the dance floor
and shake what your mama gave you for the pure joy of living!"

"Amen to that Sister Posy!" Aaron boisterously declared.

CHAPTER 16

THE MONTH OF JUNE SOON FADED into distant memory as the heat of July came on as subtle as a blowtorch. Each political party's Presidential nominating convention was to be held later in the month. Humidity was on the rise as was the political wrangling of the candidates who bartered for delegates and party platform positions favorable to their beliefs. However, heated passion was not restricted to only politics.

"I HAD NO IDEA THAT YOU WERE BORN AND LIVED most of your life in Cleveland. I thought you were from New Orleans," Clay Grover said to Michael as he sat across the bar at French Tips, Juleps & Jazz, sipping a peach julep.

"I get that a lot," Michael replied. "I've been living and working down here for almost six years now. I think I've started to talk with a slight accent. Being around Posy all the time, you pick things up she says and then you start to repeat them. Six years ago, I had no idea what the term meant and had never heard it before, but now if something happens that doesn't seem right or just doesn't add up I say, 'that dog don't hunt.' I picked that one up from her along with several others. I like it. It's just a more colorful way of speaking."

"Oh, you don't have to explain that to me," Clay chuckled. "Born and raised in South Carolina. I've got a Master's degree in Southern colloquialisms."

"Funny, you don't have much of an accent and I don't hear you use Southern terms much," Michael noted.

"Law school and eight years on the staff of a U.S. Senator will disabuse you from using common Southern slang. You become very formal in your word usage and cognizant of any regional accents. I cringe when I hear someone use the word 'ain't' at times," Clay confessed.

"Then you shouldn't spend too much time around here, Posy says it in virtually every sentence," Michael laughed.

"I can adapt. And besides I like it around here. It's a whole lot of fun, filled with energy. And filled with really good people," Clay added with a smirk on his handsome face.

"Where's Aaron?" Michael inquired. "The last couple of times that I've seen you in here you've been alone."

"He's at a family reunion in Chicago for a week," Clay answered. "I was invited, but you know how it is being around someone's family. All the old stories and jokes that you don't know or don't find terribly interesting. They're all so close, I feel like an outsider. Besides, it's a reunion for his entire extended family. There's dozens and dozens of them all congregating together for days on end. I come from a relatively small family, it's all so foreign to me."

"Yeah, I get it. I was an only child. When I was young, I use to feel so lonely all the time. I wanted a brother or sister. Now, I love my independence. I only have to be accountable to myself," Michael responded.

"Surely, you've got a significant other?" Clay asked.

"Nope. I'm kind of a loner, I guess. I've had boyfriends before but it just doesn't seem to work out for me. Plus, to be frank, I don't understand monogamy. I don't get why you would only want to have sex with the same person for the rest of your life," Michael stated without hesitation.

"I'm probably not the best person in the world to offer up a compelling defense of monogamy," Clay admitted. "Before Aaron and I decided to become a couple, I was quite the slut. I loved having sex with different men and experimenting with various things."

"It's part of the coming out process for gay men, I think," Michael added. "But then you met Aaron and fell in love and decided to be monogamous, right?"

"Well, yeah, I mean, of course," Clay hesitated and affirmed. "I love

Aaron with all my heart. But the eye wanders from time to time. I mean a good looking man is a good looking man."

"Oh really," Michael said as his voice raised slightly. Moments later, Posy emerged from the back room of the establishment and strolled over to the bar.

"So, what are you two beautiful men talking about?" She asked.

"Nothing," Clay interjected quickly, "nothing at all."

CAROLYN BARNES WAS SITTING AT THE HOTEL BAR in Philadelphia having a cocktail after a long business day. She was in the Democratic convention city meeting with members of the Democratic platform committee leading up to the convention. She wanted to make sure that her candidate's views and positions on key domestic and foreign policy issues were aptly represented in the party platform. After twelve hours of political haggling with party operatives, a cocktail or six, was imperative. Carolyn sat alone at the bar taking her first sip of a peach Cosmopolitan.

"Nirvana," Carolyn moaned to herself.

"I've heard Philadelphia referred to as many things but never nirvana," the male voice behind Carolyn stated. Carolyn turned her head and smiled.

"Riley Banks, I wasn't sure that they would even allow you in the City of Brotherly Love," Carolyn said as she acknowledged her competitor.

"I snuck in," Riley replied with a wide grin. "You're here a bit early, the platform committee fight isn't supposed to commence until tomorrow afternoon. But I suppose that's just your style, attempting to get a jump on the competition."

"I do what I do," Carolyn said light-heartedly. "I see Senator Raymond saw fit to send her senior political advisor to the platform fray."

"And, Senator Douglas has countered with his campaign manager. The stakes are high," Riley stated while flashing his brilliant white smile and staring directly at Carolyn. "May I join you?" He asked.

"It's a free country and the bartender is pretty good," Carolyn grinned.

"I could discern that from the audible gasp you uttered after sipping your cocktail," Riley joshed.

"A girl's got to find pleasure where she can," Carolyn coyly replied.

"Really?" Riley inquired with gleeful hope.

"You've spent far too many years in the company of college frat boys," Carolyn jokingly admonished. "Speaking of, how did a renowned Political Science professor from Chapel Hill become entangled in the unseemly wrestling match that is modern politics?"

"I suppose after years of teaching politics it was time to actually indulge in the practice of politics. I met Hellen a few years ago at a North Carolina Democratic Party function and was quite impressed by her. She convinced me that I needed to do some practical field work if I truly wanted to understand politics. So, for three years now, I've been on her advisory staff."

"Hellen Raymond has always had an eye for talent," Carolyn responded.

"That is an excellent pick-up line," Riley cooed with a sly grin.

"There's that horny frat boy again!" Carolyn exclaimed with a hearty laugh.

"And you? Are you happy working with Senator Douglas?"

"Immensely. He is such a good and decent man. He treats everyone around him with such respect. I've been in politics for a number of years now, and have worked with some folks who, well, let's just say I would never want to go back and work for ever again. But, with Perry, I am so comfortable with him. We work well together," Carolyn answered.

"I'm glad to hear it. Sounds like he would make a wonderful running mate on the Raymond Presidential ticket," Riley stated.

"Uh, let me remind you that Senator Douglas is fifty delegates away from winning the Democratic nomination on the first ballot. I plan to leave here in three days with commitments from super delegates for at least that much. If anything, it would be Senator Douglas offering Senator Raymond the Vice-President's slot on the ticket," Carolyn corrected Riley.

"Is that an offer?" Riley questioned.

"I don't know. Is there interest?" Carolyn replied a bit taken aback by the blunt inquiry.

"Maybe," Riley confessed.

"Did we just turn this highly contentious and argumentative Democratic convention into a love fest?" Carolyn asked still somewhat perplexed at what had just occurred.

"Oh, I do hope so on so many levels," Riley responded with a seductive glance.

"Oh my!" Carolyn exclaimed. Quickly followed by, "Hmmm, well now . . ." she murmured.

POSY BRANCH WALKED INTO THE NEW ORLEANS Police Department precinct and approached the front desk.

"Excuse me officer, is Sergeant Norris Coaltree in?" Posy asked.

"Yes ma'am, may I please have your name?"

"Posy Branch. Please tell him that I am the proprietor of French Tips, Juleps & Jazz," Posy responded. A few minutes later, Posy was escorted to Sergeant Coaltree's office.

"Ms. Branch, to what do I owe this distinct pleasure?" Norris Coaltree asked.

"Please call me Posy. I don't cotton to needless formality. Sergeant Coaltree, I've come here today to inquire about the progress of the investigation into the murder of my dear friend and business partner, Chiffon LaBelle," Posy stated.

"Has Michael mentioned anything to you in this respect?" Norris questioned Posy.

"Michael as you very well know is trying to protect me from the truth. He won't say anything that he thinks will upset me. And I love him for the way he looks out for me. But I ain't a china doll no more. I just want to make sure that justice is done and those who killed my sweet Chiffon are caught and tried in a court of law," Posy responded.

"Well, there were some developments in the case a few weeks ago. The two men who pushed and verbally assaulted Chiffon were found dead in a swamp outside of LaFayette. We had been searching for them after we realized that Olivier Bellevue had an airtight alibi for where he was the night Ms. LaBelle was murdered," Norris Coaltree stated.

"I know in my heart that Olivier had something to do with Chiffon's murder. He may have not committed the murder himself, but he surely was involved," Posy fervently claimed.

"We're keeping an eye on him," Norris replied.

"Did you know that he came to my business the other day?" Posy questioned.

"No, no, I wasn't aware," Norris answered. "What did he say? What did he do?"

"He didn't say nothing. He told me he was there just to get a manicure. But, I know he was just toying with me. He was trying to rile me up, and show me that he could get away with murdering Chiffon," Posy said while shaking her head.

"Well, if he comes back be sure to give me a call right quick," Norris said. "He didn't threaten you at all?"

"Not a few days ago, but he threatened all of us, Chiffon, Michael, and me when we were about to expose his lying and cheating ways if he didn't sign off his share of the business to Chiffon," Posy explained.

"If you are ever in a situation where you don't feel safe, please give me a call. Here's my card," Norris stated as he handed his business card to Posy. "Does your husband escort you to and from work?"

"Shoot! I divorced that scoundrel years ago, I ain't married no more," Posy said with a chuckle.

"Your boyfriend then?"

"I'm a single woman. Still looking for the right man to settle down with," Posy related.

"Really?" Norris asked with a tad of excitement in his voice.

"I don't see no picture of Mrs. Coaltree on your desk," Posy stated rather bluntly.

"There is no Mrs. Coaltree, well, other than my mama," Norris responded.

"Oh yeah, that's right, you're a friend of Michael's," Posy said with a knowing smile.

"Michael and I go back aways. I met him when he first got to New Orleans. He was a young kid from Cleveland. But Michael and I are just friends. We play hoops together and play cards from time to time. But I'm not gay," Norris confessed.

"Well, the world is an interesting place, ain't it?" Posy said with a grin.

CHAPTER 17

THE REPUBLICAN PARTY NOMINATING CONVENTION was one week away as Race Casserly boarded his Gulfstream jet for his trip to Cleveland. His business associate Carlisle Buchanan sat in a cream-colored leather chair sipping a glass of bourbon.

"Just got a text from Mark Backus, he's gonna meet us at the hotel in Cleveland," Carlisle read from his iPhone.

"Yeah, that's fine," Race replied in his deep Texan accent. "Mark's a good man, but I ain't sure he's got the killer mentality needed to work some of these delegates. You got to play hardball and I'm just not sure he's got that in him."

"He's kind of like Howard," Carlisle added.

"Exactly!" Race exclaimed. "They're both decent men, mostly. But neither of them got that pit bull dog instinct. It's probably why they been friends for so long. Neither of them is alphas, just a couple of betas."

"If you play to win, you need snakes," Carlisle offered.

"Precisely, that's why we are headed to Cleveland. I've got some west Texas snakes and some New Jersey pit bulls joining us for some serious delegate wrangling. I'm sure Jim Bob is gonna have Cletus drop his bomb on Jeremiah Wilson any day now, so when that bomb hits, you got to be ready to scurry to collect as many of the Wilson delegates that will be fleeing from that sinking ship," Race confirmed.

"I hear tell Nathan Whitaker is already in Cleveland," Carlisle stated.

"Now, that's the kind of ruthless killer you need on your side. Nathan will stop at nothing to make sure that Andrew Cochran wins the Party nomination. I'd rest a whole lot easier if Nathan was working for Howard. But he ain't, so I'd rather not have him working for anyone. That's just the simple truth of it," Race stated with a steely glint in his eyes.

"What's that line from the bible, something like, 'And you will know the truth, and the truth will set you free,'" Carlisle interjected.

"Yeah, that sounds right. Let's make sure that Nathan Whitaker sees some 'truth' and that that 'truth' sets him free," Race confirmed.

CAROLYN BARNES WAS BACK IN CHICAGO meeting with Senator Douglas at his downtown Senatorial office in the Dirksen Building.

"So how was Philadelphia?" Perry Doulas asked of his campaign manager.

"Interesting to say the least," Carolyn related to her boss. "Riley Banks was there on behalf of the Raymond campaign."

"Riley is an interesting guy. Brilliant political science professor turned strategic guru. What did old Riley have to say?" Perry inquired with a grin.

"I think the nomination is ours if we ask Hellen Raymond to be our Veep," Carolyn bluntly replied.

"Truly?" Perry asked a bit surprised by the announcement. "She has pledged to take the fight to the convention floor."

"I think they realize that they don't have a path to garner enough super delegates. They understand that we are close to winning on the first ballot. They've made the political calculation that they'd like to be a part of a winning ticket," Carolyn surmised.

"And this is coming straight from Hellen? Perry asked.

"Pretty sure," Carolyn admitted.

"We could do a lot worse than Hellen Raymond as our Vice-President. Hellen balances the ticket in a lot of different ways. And we sure could use her popularity in the state to turn North Carolina blue," Perry Douglas rationalized.

"If not for the encounter with Riley Banks, I still would have suggested we put Senator Raymond on our VP short list," Carolyn stated. "But we should poll test it. Offer up another couple of names for VP and see who poll tests the best."

"When does the Raymond campaign want a response?" Perry questioned.

"Riley didn't put an expiration date on the offer. We have two weeks before our convention week begins. I assume we have until at least the middle of next week. We can do our poll data studies and fully vet Hellen in about 10 days," Carolyn explained.

"If Cochran gets elected we'll have dueling female Vice-Presidential nominees on each ticket for the first time in American history," Perry stated.

"That's not a bad thing," Carolyn allowed. "I think it would energize the election."

"I think so as well. So, you're on board with Hellen as Veep?" Perry inquired of his campaign manager.

"Most def," Carolyn responded with a big grin.

"Well, if Hellen and Riley are willing to wait for an answer for ten days, let's do our due diligence and put Hellen's name on the top of our list," Perry instructed.

"Leave Riley Banks to me. I've got him covered," Carolyn stated with a sly smile.

JIM BOB MCCALLUM PACED BACK AND FORTH in his plush and expansive office with his cellphone next to his left ear.

"Cletus, you do understand that the nominating convention is next week, don't you?" Jim Bob asked, his voice dripping with sarcasm.

"You got no worries, we are prepared," Cletus confidently responded.

"Are you prepared to lose, cuz that is what is going to happen," Jim Bob snapped back. "You cannot win as long as Jedediah Wilson is in this race, and a week from the convention, here he sits with as many delegates as you got. Neither of you can beat Cochran if you both split the base voters. What part of that don't you understand?" Jim Bob challenged.

"Jim Bob, I've been setting him up. It's all been a well-planned trap," Cletus crowed.

"You mean the ridiculous non-sequitur comments and questions about homosexuality during the debates that no one outside of you understood are some part of a brilliant plan?" Jim Bob asked, his voice now doing back strokes in a pool of sarcasm.

"We got him right where we want him," Cletus repeated ignoring Jim Bob's tone.

"I've been hunting all my life, Cletus. And here's the thing. If you set a bear trap, and the bear sniffs around the trap but never steps into it, you ain't caught a damn thing. Time is running out, and I surely don't see no bear pelt on your wall," Jim Bob snarled.

"It's all part of a delicate strategy," Cletus replied.

"If your delicate strategy is to lose the nomination fight, and waste millions of dollars of my money, so far it's been an excellent strategy!" Jim Bob yelped into the phone. "Spring the god-damn trap and get Jedediah Wilson out of the race. And do it in a way that assures his delegates have no choice but to vote for you at the convention."

"Jim Bob, you worry too much. You just wait and see, I'm gonna . . ." Cletus began to say before he realized he was speaking to a dial tone. "Jim Bob? Hello? Hello?"

IT WAS THE SATURDAY BEFORE THE REPUBLICAN National Convention week in Cleveland. President Andrew Cochran and Nathan Whitaker were sitting together inside the Aspen lodge at Camp David plotting convention week strategy and relaxing a bit before the storm to come.

"It's like old times, the two of us hunkering down together and plotting and planning for every eventuality," Andrew Cochran relayed with a smile.

"We used to do this when we were preparing for finals at Vanderbilt. Just going over every conceivable topic that could be included on the test. Questioning and analyzing the best possible responses. Then years later, we did the same thing prior to my campaign for Governor of Georgia. And when I ran for the White House, there we were shoulder to shoulder mapping out an overall strategy for victory. And now, here we are again doing the same thing. This is how it was always supposed to be. I couldn't have succeeded on those tests or won those elections without you. That is still the case."

"This is all I ever wanted. The two of us working to achieve the same goal like we always did," Nathan heartily agreed.

"We've always been a team. I bring a more cautious approach and a realistic pragmatism to the table, and you were always the dreamer. You added the flamboyance, theatrics, and risk and reward analysis that I'm just not wired to handle competently," Andrew said while glancing at his friend.

"Yeah, I remember you always use to tell me not to go too far in the risks I was willing to take. 'Don't go jumping off of cliffs without looking first Nathan,' you use to say, 'you never know if it's gonna be a soft landing.' Well, some of those landings I didn't stick. That's for sure. But still, here we are preparing for the re-election of the President of the United States," Nathan said wistfully.

"Let's have some bourbon, shall we?" Andrew Cochran suggested as he walked to the bar and poured a couple glasses of bourbon. He handed one glass to Nathan. Nathan looked at the glass of bourbon and took a cautious sniff.

"Hell, I ain't gonna poison my best friend," Andrew laughed as he watched Nathan's hesitation.

"Chalk it up to reflexive conditioning," Nathan chuckled in response.

"Cheers, my friend, you taught me how to be less cautious and at least eye those cliffs," Andrew said as he toasted his friend. "This bourbon is testament to that fact."

"How are you getting along with Cindy Bridgman?" Nathan asked.

"Oh, Cindy's great, we're getting along fine. The question is how are you getting along with Cindy?" Andrew asked with a sly grin.

"What are you up to?" Nathan asked with a cautious stare at his friend.

"Cindy told me that the two of you had a nice time in Newark," Andrew remarked.

"Andy, no one has a good time in Newark. It was a pleasant get-to-know-you conversation, that's all," Nathan bluntly responded.

OK, OK, I didn't realize I was stepping on toes," Andrew apologized. "Cindy may not be beauty queen glamorous like Posy, but she's an attractive woman, who is single much like yourself."

"Put your bow and arrow away Cupid. I didn't push Cindy for the Vice-Presidency because I was attempting to turn your White House into my personal dating service," Nathan joshed. "I just thought she was the best person for an expansive Republican ticket. An attempt to tack back to the moderate side of the Party."

"If a moderate side still exists," Andrew Cochran added.

"Well, we'll find that out in less than a week, I reckon."

"So, you've got no designs on Cindy Bridgman?" Andrew asked with a wicked grin.

"Right now, I've only got designs on lighting up this here joint," Nathan said as he pulled a marijuana cigarette out of his jeans jacket pocket.

"Oh hell, now you're talking!" Andrew enthusiastically replied.

CHAPTER 18

"WELL, HELLO STRANGER," MICHAEL SAID with a smile as he watched Clay Grover saunter up to the bar at French Tips, Juleps & Jazz. "Three nights in a row, you must really be missing Aaron. Don't you like being home alone?"

"Not really, I'm not much of a homebody, that's more Aaron's thing," Clay confessed. "Besides, why would I want to stay home alone when I can have a lovely conversation with an insightful and interesting friend?"

"Not to mention several cocktails," Michael offered with a smile.

"Only adds to the pleasure equation," Clay affirmed. "Speaking of pleasure, how do you keep your chest so glistening and clean shaven?"

"Huh? Thanks, I guess. I'm not a really hairy guy to begin with. I'm pretty smooth naturally, so it's just a quick daily shave while I'm shaving my face and then I oil up when I get here. My shirts would be an oily mess if I did that at home," Michael responded. "Why the interest?"

"You've got great pecs and impressive abs, and you keep them so smooth. Just thought I'd compliment you that's all," Clay stated with a grin.

"I wish Posy would let me wear a shirt from time to time, I get a little embarrassed always parading around here shirtless."

"It suits you, I wouldn't change a thing," Clay offered.

"I'm not a natural exhibitionist. I'm actually fairly shy by nature. But when I moved down to New Orleans from Cleveland, the only jobs I could get for a while was as a dancer at OZ and Bourbon Pub," Michael confessed.

"Really!" Clay exclaimed. "I never knew that you were a go-go boy. Of course, I've only known you from French Tips."

"Yeah, Posy saw me dance at OZ one night, and asked me if I wanted a job. She was just opening her new business and she was looking for someone to help draw in her female clientele. The shirtless thing was part of our deal. But sometimes, it's just awkward, you know? Trust me, even strippers can get embarrassed and feel self-conscious," Michael related to Clay.

"You've got no reason to be self-conscious, you've got a great body," Clay stated.

"No one wants to be seen as just a piece of meat. I've got a brain too. I might not be an attorney, but I can carry on a thoughtful conversation," Michael responded a bit defensively.

"Oh crap, I'm so sorry," Clay quickly replied. "I didn't mean to infer that you only have a nice body. I mean, you do, but there is so much more to you than just that. You're kind and generous, and I respect the hell out of how you protect and promote Posy. You are such a great friend to her."

"It's fine, thank you for the kind words. I just get a little annoyed when the only thing people see in me is my body. I didn't mean to get all pissy with you. We're friends and I know you weren't trying to come on to me," Michael stated. "I admire the loving relationship that you and Aaron have together. Hopefully, someday I can find someone like Aaron to settle down with."

"You will," Clay softly answered. Clay then looked at the ground and sighed.

BESSIE COLLINS HAD FINISHED PUTTING THE DAY'S REVENUE into the small safe at her voodoo shop. She had made up her mind after thinking about it for a good long time, that it was time to make amends. She locked the front door behind her and turned to Papa Levi and sighed.

"What's wrong Miss Bessie?" Papa Levi asked.

"I knows what I got to do, but it surely would be nice to have a smiling friendly face with me," Bessie said as sweetly as possible.

"I ain't got nowhere I needs to be," Papa Levi replied. "I'll walk with you, iffin' you want."

"Thank you. That would be real nice. Thank you," Bessie repeated as she took Papa Levi by the arm and they slowly made their way to Jackson Square. There, sitting in her accustomed corner of the square, was Esther Francois. Her arms folded and her eyes closed as she gently rocked back and forth in her folding chair.

"Esther," Bessie said softly.

"Who dat?" Esther snapped without opening her eyes.

"It's Bessie Collins, Esther."

Esther slowly opened her eyes and glanced directly at Bessie for several moments.

"You need a reading?" Esther asked.

"No, no, I need an audience for about two minutes," Bessie responded. "Esther, I'm sorry. I was wrong to accuse you of something I now know you didn't do. It's just that with the history of my shop and what my auntie, Queen Rita done did to them folks in Washington a few years ago. When I heard the news, well, I over-reacted. I came down here and called you out for something you didn't do. So, once again, I'm sorry."

"What is done is done. You cannot carry the past around your neck like an anchor stone. You can't move forward and are forever rooted in the past. Much behind, but even more ahead. If you have come here to remove your stone, so be it. I walk in my shoes, so I have no idea what it is like to walk in your shoes," Esther responded.

"Thank you, Esther for understanding," Bessie said with a warm smile.

"Thank me not, for I have done nothing. What you brought to my table you will take away with you. You owe me nothing. Nothing is all I know," Esther stated. She then closed her eyes and sat quietly as Bessie and Papa Levi walked off into the shadows of Jackson Square.

POSY BRANCH STOOD IN FRONT OF THE FLOOR LENGTH MIRROR on her bedroom closet door. She surveyed her tight jeans, snake skin boots, and pretty blue blouse. It had been a while since Posy was last on a date with a man. She felt like a teenaged girl waiting to be picked up at her house by the captain of the football team. Which was not far from the truth. Norris Coaltree was once a captain on his high school football team. Born and raised in rural Louisiana, Norris went to college at the University of New Orleans majoring in criminal justice. After graduation, he joined the New Orleans Police Department where he eventually raised to the rank of Sergeant. With dark brown hair and deep set blue eyes and a good athletic build, Norris was a nice looking man. He had never married, though there were a couple of women he had been committed to over the years. But he never found anyone who he had clicked with completely.

Posy heard a knock on her door. She took one last glance in the mirror and exhaled. It was time to get back in the dating saddle and go for a ride.

"Hello, there, please come in," Posy stated as Norris stood outside her front door, grinning ear-to-ear.

"Thank you, you look lovely," Norris, a tad awkwardly, blurted out. Posy smiled feeling her whole body slightly tingle.

"Look, I ain't real diplomatic about these things. It's been a while since I've gone out on a date. But we both too grown to be acting like jittery teenagers so let's just relax and enjoy ourselves. What do you say?" Posy challenged with a sweet grin.

"Sounds real good to me," Norris replied. "I got to admit, it's been some time since I've been out on a date as well, so I'm glad we can get that behind us."

"How about a drink before we head out to dinner?" Posy offered. "Where was it that you said we was going?"

"Dick and Jenny's. It ain't much to look at, kinda quirky. But they've got an outstanding gumbo and some of the best oysters in the Big Easy. Plus, it's just down the street from Tipitina's. I thought we could go there after dinner. I've got tickets to see Dr. John and the Nite Trippers," Norris stated.

"Get out!" Posy shouted. "I love me some Dr. John. I can sashay all day to 'Iko'. And 'Right Place Wrong Time', please child! You kidding me, right?"

"No, here's the tickets," Norris said pulling out his wallet, a tad taken aback by Posy's energetic response. "We're going."

"You don't know. Norris Coaltree, you don't know!" Posy exclaimed. "The Doctor's music takes me way back. I grew up listening to Dr. John. There's a whole lot of happiness I get when I listen to his music. So, this is special for me. It truly is."

"Wow, I'm so thrilled that you're looking forward to it. I knew from the way you always sing and dance around French Tips that you liked music, but I had no idea about your connection with Dr. John," Norris responded shaking his head.

"This is going to be special. This here is a real treat for me. You got no idea," Posy excitedly confirmed. "Now what can I get you to drink to get this night started off right proper?"

"A little bourbon on the rocks would be great, if you have it," Norris asked.

"Honey child, I run a bar, there ain't much that I don't have in the way of liquor. You good with Buffalo Trace Elmer T. Lee Single Barrel Bourbon over ice?"

"I'm so good with that," Norris contentedly answered.

"This surely gonna be a fun night, it surely is," Posy cheerfully proclaimed as she turned and sashayed into the kitchen singing "Iko Iko".

AARON ROSE AND HIS COUSIN WILLIAM stood on the street corner in the Hyde Park neighborhood of Chicago waiting for their Uber car. They were headed to Boystown and for the two cousins, it was not soon enough.

"I love being around my family for days on end, but there comes a time that you've just got to get away," Aaron matter-of-factly stated.

"You're absolutely right," William confirmed. "I love playing with the kids, and rubbing Margret's baby bump, and the rest of it, but after three days I feel like I'm drowning in the heterosexuality of it all. It's just not my life. I'm a young proud and out gay man, who has no desire to ever have children."

"You're still so young, you don't know yet," Aaron counseled his cousin.

"You're only eight years older than me. I don't see you with kids, either," William stated.

"Clay and I haven't decided yet if we're going to have a family. There's a lot going on right now that has our immediate future up in the air. I'm not quite sure where we will be living in about six months," Aaron explained.

"That doesn't sound like you're very committed to having someone calling you 'pops'", William countered.

"I certainly wouldn't mind it, but Clay and I haven't discussed it to any great length," Aaron said. "I'm not so sure Clay wants kids."

"They're very expensive and once they grow up they will blame you for all of their problems and issues," William responded with a chuckle.

"Spoken like a young gay man more interested in partying and acting irresponsibly than thinking about the future," Aaron stated with a grin.

"Yeah, go on grandpa!" William chided his cousin. "We're the only two out members of the whole family. We got to stick together. Though I got no idea what cousin Tina is waiting on. You pull up to a family reunion driving a pick-up truck and wearing a flannel shirt in July and your hair is shorter than mine and you don't think people are gonna wonder when you will be uttering the 'L' word?"

"Leave Tina alone, she's good folk," Aaron chuckled in response.

"Yeah, queer as folk," William said with a sly smile. "But what's going on with you and Clay? You barely mentioned him these last few days."

"We're fine. Just going through a little distance right now. Nothing serious. As I mentioned before, there's just a lot going on that has Clay in a more contemplative, distant mood," Aaron explained.

"You sure that's all there is? He's a fine specimen of a man. Plenty of boys would want to jump on that," William stated bluntly.

"Yes! It's just a stressful time right now," Aaron countered.

"Which is why you are spending six days at a family reunion in Chicago instead of the two days you would spend here when you were single and living in Washington?" William asked with a smirk.

"That was a different time in my life. I had certain responsibilities that I couldn't shirk," Aaron insisted.

"Now, it's just a husband that you can shirk?" William asked. "Look, I'm just busting your balls a little bit. Truth be told, I'm a little envious that you have a gorgeous, smart guy like Clay in your life. But, my gay-dar is sensing that there might be more going on than just a little stress, that's all."

"I appreciate the concern, but we're fine. Truly. Let's go get a drink and have some fun. It's Broadway show tunes night at Sidetracks," Aaron announced.

"Thank God, I need this after days of family breeder conversation. Pretty boys singing along to 'West Side Story', count me in!" William exclaimed.

CHAPTER 19

T HE HEAT AND HUMIDITY IN CLEVELAND ramped up as the Republicans came to town. The wrangling for party platform positions was only succeeded by the arm twisting for delegates. Political maneuverings were dominating most waking hours of the day leading up to the Monday of an open convention. Seldom do party conventions act as anything other than a rubber stamp for the leading candidate. But when you have four candidates all within a few hundred committed delegates of one another nothing is usual. However, while the political operatives of most of the candidate's campaigns spent that opening Monday morning, wooing delegates, Nathan Whitaker was standing in front of the British Invasion exhibit at the Rock & Roll Hall of Fame while texting his friend, who just happened to be the President of the United States.

"Guess where I'm at?" Nathan texted Andrew Cochran. "I'm standing in front of John Lennon's Gibson 160-E guitar that he used to record 'Give Peace a Chance.' How cool is that?"

"Very cool. But I'm meeting the Israeli Prime Minister in five minutes, and then taking Air Force One to Cleveland later tonight. Perhaps, we can discuss this later," Andrew Cochran texted in response.

"Ok, I'll get you a post card," Nathan texted back. "This is far more interesting than Middle East diplomacy."

Meanwhile, at the White House, Sam Brainard, the President's Chief of Staff, patiently waited while he watched the President reading and replying to text messages. "Mr. President, I've been informed that the Prime Minister of Israel has just arrived at the White House. Do you need additional time?"

"No, Sam, I'm ready to roll. Nathan was just texting me from the Rock & Roll Hall of Fame," President Cochran casually stated.

"Pardon me, sir?" Sam asked, unsure that he had heard the President clearly.

"He's admiring John Lennon's Gibson guitar," Andrew Cochran said.

"I'm sorry, Nathan is not at the Convention center or courting delegates?" Sam asked completely bewildered.

"Nope, he's sight-seeing. He told me that we've got this locked up," Andrew Cochran responded.

"But, we don't sir. It's going to be an open convention," Sam reiterated.

"Sam, I understand your hesitancy. But Nathan has run my campaigns ever since I first took on a two term incumbent in the Republican primary for Governor of Georgia. When Nathan says something about a campaign, I've learned that you can take it to the bank. He's never been wrong, and never not delivered for me. I'm not about to question his judgment now," the President stated with a confident smile and the wink of an eye.

"But, sir," Sam began before being interrupted by the President.

"Come on Sam, we've got the Middle East to fix," Andrew Cochran said to his Chief of Staff as he turned to walk out of the Oval Office and greet his guest.

SENATOR CLETUS SAWYER SAT IN A BOOTH at a downtown Cleveland restaurant having breakfast with his campaign advisor Lamont Basemore.

"Lamont, have you reached out to Jedediah Wilson's folks to set-up a meeting?" Cletus inquired.

"I made an entreaty to them a couple of days ago, but Wilson refuses to sit down with us without knowing what the meeting is about," Lamont answered.

"Hell, it's about the end of his political life!" Cletus stated with a big grin. "Did you inform them that it is in their best interest to listen to what we have to say?"

"Yes, in a way, I did. I certainly didn't want to divulge any specifics, but I told them that they would be very interested in what we had to say,"

Lamont confirmed. "Yet, they declined. They want to know the specific reason and purpose of the meeting."

"I'd like to do this the easy way, without causing Jedediah too much embarrassment and shame. But, bottom line, he's toast. We've got the goods on him. And his delegates will align with the true Conservative in this race when the truth comes to light. Now, that can be in a private meeting or a release to the major news agencies. It's his choice," Cletus stated.

"But he doesn't know that. I've not provided any specifics about the reason for the meeting per your request," Lamont argued.

"Well then, go back to his people, let them know we have something very incriminating about their candidate that we are prepared to share with them but it has to be in a private face-to-face meeting between me and Jedediah. Present them with an ultimatum that we will release what we have to the press if they do not deign to meet with us. Give them 24 hours. If we don't meet before noon tomorrow, they can find out what we have on the noon cable news shows," Cletus told his advisor.

"But don't we risk alienating his delegates if we go directly to the press?" Lamont questioned.

"Where they gonna go? They won't be able to support his sinful hypocrisy. They ain't going to that neo-liberal Cochran. Sure we might lose a few to Howard Mason, but most will see him as a Conservative pretender. There's only one alternative, and that's me," Cletus said with a contented grin as he snaked a piece of bacon into this open mouth.

"Perhaps, if they refuse a meeting, we send a copy of the tape to them. I'm sure they'd be willing to meet if they understood the context of our request for a meeting," Lamont raised.

"They get one chance. Meet with us before noon tomorrow or else we go public. That's all they need to know," Cletus stated with conviction.

"Are you sure, you don't want to give them a little more wiggle room and keep this as amicable as possible?" Lamont persisted.

"Ain't nothing amicable about political extortion. They're getting their chance right now. Ball's in their court," Cletus insisted. "Look Lamont, this is big boy politics. As we say back home, 'if you can't run with the big dogs, you best stay on the porch.'"

HOWARD MASON SAT IN HIS HOTEL SUITE in Cleveland having coffee with his chief political advisor, Mark Backus. Howard restlessly thumbed through a tabulation of delegates by state.

"Where's our path to the nomination?" Howard asked with a dumb-founded expression on his face.

"It's going to be tough, there is no doubt about that," Mark replied. "But there is a path if everything falls our way. The first step though is to make sure that Andrew Cochran does not secure enough delegates to win on first ballot. As things drag on past the first ballot, and delegates are no longer tied to their candidate anything can happen."

"But there are four of us all within striking range and no one seems willing to acquiesce one iota," Howard asserted.

"That may change rather quickly," Mark said with a knowing nod of his head.

"How so?"

"I received a call from Race Casserly last night. He assured me that Jedediah Wilson's delegates would be looking for another candidate to support in the next day or two," Mark allowed.

"How does he know that?" Howard questioned.

"Race did not get into specifics other than to say that he is aware of the fact that Jim Bob McCallum dug up some dirt on Wilson and has handed it over to Cletus Sawyer's campaign," Mark answered.

"That's got to be some juicy stuff if Race is confident enough to say that it will make Wilson drop out of the race," Howard replied. "Though if so, what the hell is Cletus Sawyer waiting for?"

"That's the one million dollar or rather 400 delegate question."

"More importantly, what can we be doing to insure that the Wilson delegates find a home in our campaign?" Howard asked.

"I've got some of our political operatives wining and dining some of the state chairs of the Wilson delegations. A lot of them see Cletus Sawyer as an old fool. Many cannot stomach the insincere political makeover of Andrew Cochran. They want a Conservative firebrand not a 1980's like moderate facilitator as their next President. We can provide a happy home for those wayward Wilson delegates," Mark stated.

"But Cochran needs about 125 delegates to get the nomination on the first ballot. I need close to 300 delegates to clinch the nomination. My understanding from some of our folks is that Nathan Whitaker is making all sorts of promises and has gained a sizable cache of delegate support in just the last few days," Howard stated with apprehension.

"That's true. Whitaker has made some very impressive inroads. There is a lot to be said about the power and cache of the Presidency from the perspective of what you can offer people for their support. There aren't many people who wouldn't want to be the ambassador to France. So, we've got to bank on the fact that the Wilson delegates truly believe in their Conservative convictions more than they want an invitation to a State dinner," Mark allowed.

"Well, conviction never filled anyone's belly or lined their pockets," Howard sadly replied.

CAROLYN BARNES WAITED AT A TABLE at a restaurant just off Capitol Hill for Senator Perry Douglas to arrive for a lunch meeting. She glanced at her tablet to note certain data points. She was ready.

"Greetings! I assume that the vetting process went well and all concerns were satisfied?" Perry asked as he took a seat.

"There is nothing in Hellen Raymond's vetting report that would point to any problems whatsoever. And, she appears willing to allow some of her personal beliefs to take a back seat to the positions of the leader of the ticket."

"This is the best possible VP, am I right?"

"Absolutely," Carolyn enthusiastically proclaimed. "Hellen balances out the ticket perfectly."

"So, when can we make this a done deal and go into the convention as a united front?" Perry inquired.

"I'm working out the logistics with her people now. We're thinking a rather public meeting tomorrow between the two of you at some trendy DC restaurant, just to get the media buzzing, and then declare your intentions to be a united ticket on Friday after the Republican Convention ends," Carolyn summarized.

"Excellent," Perry declared.

NATHAN WHITAKER WAS MAKING THE BEST of a few hours of downtime from the campaign in the last couple of weeks. He sat patiently in his hotel room suite in Cleveland waiting on the arrival of a fairly expensive call girl. She was a 'gift' from a fellow political operative who was seeking to curry favor with the Cochran administration. Highly recommended and pretty kinky, she was the one token of respect and fealty that Nathan was willing to accept. The following two hours were mostly a hazy blur of a sexual smorgasbord. After the young woman left, Nathan finished off the glass of bourbon that had been sitting on his bedside table. After a few minutes, Nathan experienced a very rapid and irregular heartbeat. His vision became blurred and an overwhelming feeling of nausea and confusion were overtaking his senses. Nathan tried to lie down on the bed, but his breathing quickly became labored. Nathan immediately dialed 911 while he was still conscious. Nathan Whitaker even in his weakened and addled state was fairly certain of what had happened to him. He had done his research. He attempted to induce his own vomiting and then remain aware and awake.

"I believe that I've been poisoned, please come quickly," Nathan garbled into the phone as he felt himself begin to slowly lose consciousness.

CHAPTER 20

THE HOTEL SUITE IN CLEVELAND was filled with people. Mostly operatives and managers, but also the Presidential candidate. The candidate sat in a large upholstered chair in the corner and surveyed the mess in the room. He stared at the unmade bed and sighed deeply.

"Can I get the room, please? I need to make a call and would rather that it didn't sound like a God-damned three ring circus in here," Senator Cletus Sawyer clearly stated to his entourage. Slowly, the assembled moved out of the bedroom and into the living room area of the large suite. Cletus closed the door and dialed the phone number he had been given just moments earlier.

"May I please speak with Jedediah Wilson, this is Senator Cletus Sawyer calling." Cletus fidgeted in his chair as he waited for the call to be conveyed to his primary opponent. Moments later he heard Jedediah Wilson intone a deep and somber "Hello" into the phone.

"Jedediah, this is Cletus Sawyer here, I won't take up much of your time but I've got something very important to relay to you," Cletus began. "Ain't no good way to say this so I'm just gonna be blunt. My folks been trying to convince you for days now to have a meeting with us. But nary a word have we heard. So, bottom line is that I have a videotape of you in a hotel room about two years ago. You were not alone. My guess is that you know exactly what is on that video. I'd like to strike a bargain with you." There was a delay where nothing was said followed by a dial tone indicating the ending of the call.

"Tarnation!" Cletus ranted as he began to re-dial the phone number. A different voice answered the call, "hello."

"Cletus Sawyer again for Jedediah Wilson," Cletus forcefully stated into the phone, only to be met with yet another dial tone and ended call. Cletus yet again dialed the phone number and waited for an answer.

"Look here, I'm not playing," Cletus angrily spat into the phone before being hung-up on for the third time. Cletus Sawyer sat silently in his large chair simmering like a very full metal pot on a hot wood burning stove. Boiling over was inevitable, it was just a matter of when.

PERRY DOUGLAS HELD THE CHAIR for his campaign opponent as they prepared to share a meal together at a tony Washington DC restaurant. As Hellen Raymond sat down, Perry Douglas gently pushed the chair towards the white table-clothed square table.

"It is a true pleasure that we can share this meal and hopefully many more together Hellen," Perry offered. "You know that I have always admired and respected you as a colleague in the Senate. We've done some good work together on the Senate Judiciary Committee. We are friends. So, it is only fitting that we join together as friends and partners in an attempt to gain the White House."

"Well, thank you Perry. As you very well know the feeling is mutual. You have provided exemplary leadership on the Judiciary Committee. I think that we could make a rather formidable pair if the nation decides so in November. I am truly honored that you have considered adding me to the ticket," Hellen replied in her lilting North Carolinian accent.

"Oh, it's not a consideration it is a whole-hearted offer. I thought that was made clear. If not, let me clarify right now. Hellen Raymond would you please consent to joining my campaign and together we will take back the White House for the Democratic Party and for the country?" Perry Douglas asked with clear eyes and good intent.

"Yes, of course, it would be my pleasure," Hellen responded with a nod of the head and a friendly smile.

"You campaigned very well, I am lucky to be on the verge of the Party nomination," Perry offered. "We will be very formidable allies together. My wife is a big fan of yours. She often informs me that she would be happy voting for you instead of me."

"That's kind. Please give my best to Katherine," Hellen responded. "Though I suppose we should address the elephant in the room. I have always been inclined to be measured when it comes to a woman's choice. I abhor abortion on a personal level, but that is my choice. It is not up to me to make personal life decisions for other women."

"And that is all I need to hear. You have your own ideological and moral beliefs, yet you stand for the right of other women to make their own decisions, correct?"

"Correct," Helen answered.

"Then we have no divergence in our opinions. And I feel good about our prospects of defeating whoever our Republican foe may be in the fall," Perry cheerfully smiled.

"Andrew Cochran is doing whatever he can to moderate his Party," Hellen stated. "Cindy Bridgman was an excellent choice."

"I agree, Congresswoman Bridgman was an outstanding choice for a Republican Party with moderate and even some progressive views circa 1975. That Party doesn't exist anymore," Perry said while shaking his head. "I give Cochran credit for the effort. But the Republicans have become so narrow-minded and myopic, drifting so far to the right fringes of political discourse, can they reverse the ship that quickly? I doubt it."

"It's what elections and political conventions are all about. We will see in the next few days," Hellen said with a smile.

POSY BRANCH COULD NOT CONTAIN the broad and happy smile that creased her attractive face. She spent her days at French Tips, Juleps & Jazz singing and laughing with her customers. The change of mood and behavior were in stark difference to the sullen and introspection of six months prior. And, no one was happier about the return of the boisterous and fun-loving Posy than Michael.

"Somebody's got that glow about them these days," Michael joshed with his friend and employer. "One might think that love was in the air."

"Go on now Michael!" Posy exclaimed. "Can't a girl be happy without everyone saying she's in love?"

"So, you're not in love then. Perhaps I should say something to Norris," Michael teased in return.

"You mind your juleps and your own business," Posy laughed.

"Speaking of juleps, when you gonna bring them pineapple ginger juleps back? Them tasty delights is real popular with the ladies."

"I wasn't speaking about juleps, I was talking about love," Michael smirked.

"Michael, I love you with all my heart. Every day I thank the Lord for putting you in my life. But don't be messing with me on this," Posy said through a crooked grin.

"I'm not the one messing with you," Michael chortled. "Look, for the record, I think it's great. I love you both, and it just feels right. I've never seen Norris quite this discombobulated. That boy don't know up from down. He's way beyond the moon!"

"Truly?" Posy asked with a bit of anxiety in her voice. "I ain't sure what a respectable police Sergeant would see in a nail salon owner barkeep?"

"Posy, you do own a mirror, right? You are a stunning looking woman. You are a beauty queen with just a couple of character building crow's feet. But that's just where it starts. You blew into this town and started a business that is the envy of every French Quarter merchant. You brought life, love, and music to a city that has a three century tradition of life and music. There's not a straight man within five hundred miles that wouldn't fall all over themselves to spend some time with you," Michael insisted.

"Damn, if you ain't more than that gorgeous smile and those jaw-dropping pecs. Thank you, sweetie, for saying that. Sometimes a girl could stand a little pep talk. You really think that Norris wants to spend some time with me? Posy asked.

"How many times are you fishing your cellphone out of your jeans pocket over the course of a day and see that you got a call from Sergeant Coaltree?" Michael inquired well knowing the answer. "The boy can't believe that he gets to spend time with someone as wonderful and beautiful as you, Posy Branch."

"He sure is a good man," Posy stated happily.

"And you sure are a good woman. Now, from my perspective, good people belong together," Michael stated.

"We'll see sugar, we will see. But I surely hope you is right."

Jim Bob McCallum watched the breaking news report on CNN from his opulent office. He grabbed a book and hurled it against the wall. The book slammed against the plasterboard surface and created a loud thud.

"Stupid is as stupid does!" Jim Bob ranted. "I knew he would fuck this up. I knew it! Culbert, get your ass in here."

"Sir," Culbert Smiley meekly offered as he stood in the doorway of Jim Bob's office.

"Get that jackass Cletus Sawyer on the phone," Jim Bob roared. "Did you see what he did? Did you see?"

"No sir," Culbert replied.

"I gave Cletus all the ammunition that he needed to get Jedediah Wilson out of the Presidential race and grab a substantial number of delegates for himself once the rats began leaving Jebediah's sinking ship. Instead of skillfully negotiating a face-saving arrangement with Wilson in return for Wilson's commitment to have his delegates support Cletus, he completely fucked it up! One of his Alabama in-bred idiots leaked to the Associated Press the videotape of Jedediah Wilson caught with two rent boys in a hotel room, which of course led Wilson to denounce Cletus. Wilson's supporters will now look for any alternative other than Cletus to back. Looks like Howard Mason will gain the greatest advantage from this strategic debacle."

"Excuse me sir, what's a rent boy?" Culbert asked.

"For the love of God Culbert, grow-up and move out of your mama's house. You're a 33-year-old man for Christ's sake! It's what it sounds like. They're male prostitutes. And personally, I couldn't give a rat's ass who anyone has sex with. But then again, if you're a holier-than-thou preacher who has built his entire career on condemning the scourge of homosexuality in America, and your political cache is claiming that the President and his campaign manager are homosexual lovers having anal sex during Satanic worship ceremonies in the Oval office, then you probably shouldn't be seen in a videotape with some twenty-four-year-old blonde boy's dick in your mouth," Jim Bob explained.

"Oh, ok," Culbert timidly replied.

"Alright then, get that moron Cletus on the line. I need to cut him off before he further embarrasses me. What a disaster he's turn out to be! Then get me Nathan Whitaker. Time for some fence mending. I'll be damned if I'm going to sit out a Presidential race just because my horse went lame and I had to put him down. Nathan and I danced real nice together for a while, no reason we can't do the cha-cha again," Jim Bob allowed with a wicked smile.

"But I thought that you were opposed to President Cochran's more moderate political stances? You're always calling him a yellow-dog traitor to the Conservative cause," Culbert asked.

"I am, and he is. But, Culbert, when you boil down the political stew, you soon find out that the only ingredients left that are worth a hill of beans are influence and power, and their ability to enhance one's wealth and prestige. I am a Conservative Republican mostly because it best suits my financial well-being and my religious beliefs. But when the rubber meets the road, I'll support a baby-killing liberal if he will protect my financial interests and provide me with a cache of influence and reputational power," Jim Bob responded. "Beliefs are cheap and expendable when money and power are concerned."

THE SECRET SERVICE AGENTS WERE PRESENT and highly visible when President Cochran arrived at St. Vincent Charity Medical Center in Cleveland, Ohio. However, when Andrew Cochran entered the hospital room of his friend Nathan Whitaker he asked the agents that they be left alone.

"How are you doing buddy?" Andrew Cochran softly whispered as he sat in a chair next to Nathan's hospital bed.

"Well, you should know from first-hand experience how I'm doing," Nathan replied with a grin. "I'm ok, though my stomach and intestines feel as if they've been put through a meat grinder."

"What do the doctors say?"

"I've ingested poison. My blood pressure was through the roof when I was admitted. The poison shocked my heart, but luckily my heart was strong enough to sustain the initial after effects. They pumped my stomach. They're going to monitor my vital signs and keep me here for a couple of days. But they think I should make a full recovery."

"It wasn't an accident was it?" Andrew asked quietly.

"No. I'm not completely certain, but my guess is that the poison was put into my drink by the prostitute I was with," Nathan explained. "Not to worry, I didn't mention anything about the prostitute to the police who questioned me here at the hospital."

"Then how do you explain being poisoned?" Andrew inquired.

"How did you explain being poisoned?" Nathan responded with a wink. "That's the beauty of it. You don't have to explain it. Someone else who means you harm did it to you. In fact, this little episode could work to our advantage. Just further proof that enemies of the President and the American public are at large and continue to plot against the President and his closest associates."

"Nathan, I'm not looking for political advantage, I'm just concerned about the well-being of my friend who had an attempt made on his life."

"I'm going to be fine, Andy. The young woman didn't know enough about what she was doing. She clearly didn't put enough poison into my drink and I only took a short sip. I knew fairly quickly what was happening because, well, I know," Nathan responded.

"But the fact remains that someone was attempting to kill you," Andrew stated with grave concern.

"It's Presidential politics prior to an open convention. I'm surprised it took them this long to try to take me out," Nathan conceded with a small laugh.

"But who?" Andrew questioned.

"Sawyer and Mason don't have the balls to try something like this. But the money men behind them do. My guess is that it was at least planned and financed by Race Casserly or Jim Bob McCallum. I don't think that Wilson and his people are smart enough to pull this off," Nathan stated.

"That's right, you haven't heard," Andrew stated. "Someone anonymously left a copy of a videotape at the office of the Associated Press. The video was of Jedediah Wilson and two male prostitutes in, let's just say, compromising positions. Wilson withdrew from the race this morning and has instructed his delegates not to support Cletus Sawyer. Clearly, Wilson thinks that Sawyer is behind the videotape release."

"That is outstanding news!" Nathan exclaimed. "You've all but got the nomination now, Andy. We only needed around 50 more delegates to win the nomination on the first ballot. My guess is that you will get that much from just the Wilson defectors."

"Easy buddy. Your job right now is to just get some rest and get better. We've got plenty of folks on staff who can do delegate wrangling. The nomination vote is tomorrow night. You got me to this point, Nathan. I wouldn't be sniffing the nomination if not for you. But, we've got great people, most of whom you hired, who can get us across the finish line from here," Andrew instructed his friend.

"OK, but can you at least hand me my phone? I can make a couple of calls, can't I?" Nathan asked. "It's over on that table."

"Here you go," Andrew stated while handing the smartphone to Nathan. Nathan stared at the list of missed calls.

"I have two missed calls from Jim Bob McCallum. He is either checking to see if I'm dead because he ordered the attempt on my life or Race Casserly wants me dead. If that's the case, and with both Wilson and Sawyer no longer viable as candidates, then Jim Bob is looking for a candidate to support," Nathan bluntly laid out.

"No! We don't need Jim Bob McCallum's money," Andrew firmly pronounced.

"You're right, we probably don't. Though Perry Douglas and the Democrats will have an enormous war chest. I'm not saying that we jump off any cliffs without looking, but we will need all the friends we can muster for the general election. I'm just saying . . ." Nathan replied with a sly smile.

CHAPTER 21

POLITICAL CONVENTIONS CAN BE LIKE CHAPTERS in a book. The story can traverse through scene changes and various unexpected plot twists, but invariably a hero will emerge. There will be disappointment, regret and anger felt by all but the winner. The winner gets the happy ending. The winner gets to be the focal point for the remainder of the book. From the convention rises the hero. Oft times, the hero is usually evident from the very beginning of the story but not without having to face conflict, adversity, and numerous plot shifts and treacherous machinations. President Andrew Cochran withstood denunciations from his own party. He shifted his political focus due to very real threats to his nascent administration. He made bedfellows with his most virulent opposition. President Andrew Cochran took on all comers and prevailed. Bloodied and battered, yet he still stood with Rocky-like conviction. He had against all odds become the victor. The 'Prince' fought for his political survival. Rules may have been broken. Truths may have become convoluted. Actions may have been morally questionable. But the name of the game is winning. And Andrew Cochran was able to pull off a stunning political comeback and won his Party's nomination for President of the United States. Somewhere Niccolo Machiavelli was beaming with pride.

Less dramatic, less filled with treachery and in-fighting, the Democratic Convention also produced its hero. Divergent stories, but a similar outcome. The Democrats had anointed Senator Perry Douglas as their shining star.

"Well, I'll be," Stanford Winchester muttered to himself as he read the Wall Street Journal while sipping sweet tea on the balcony of his New Orleans home.

"What's that dear?" His wife Whitlee asked from just inside the screen door leading out to the balcony.

"I would have bet you dollars to donuts that Andrew Cochran could not possibly win the Republican Party nomination for President," Stanford responded.

"There is something to be said about the influence and cache of a sitting President," Whitlee offered.

"True, but this is a President who ran opposed to most of the major issues prescribed by his party's base constituency. You've got to remember, he was loathed by a majority of the right-wing of the party. And frankly, I'm not sure that there is much left of the Republican Party other than the Conservative far right-wing. But he survived an attempt on his life, which allowed a good number of the rank and file to view the man, the leader of this country, and not just a traitor to a policy issue," Stanford stated.

"Clearly, there is still a moderate vein that runs through the Republican Party," Whitlee observed.

"Or just a lack of will to surrender the White House to the Democrats by backing a candidate most of the general electorate would not countenance," Stanford countered. "Cletus Sawyer always struck me as someone who was a cup or two short of a full gallon. He was my advocate during the Judiciary Committee hearings and the man said some things to me that were just lacking common sense. And, Jedediah Wilson is one of the reasons I no longer call myself a Republican. Those who claim to be so very pious and have the ear of God often prove to be ungodly in so many ways. Don't get me wrong, who a man or woman chooses to lie with is their decision. But it tends to be the ones who protest the loudest against a certain sexual identity who are the ones who have the most to hide."

"Still a shocking development, nonetheless. I don't think that many envisioned that a man who was so focused on the sexual conduct of others, would have the lack of clarity to get caught in his own sexual dalliances," Whitlee added. "And what of Howard Mason?"

"Politically, Howard Mason is the medicine that you take only when you are truly sick. It's got a weird color and aroma to it, and it just tastes nasty when you swallow it. But it does ultimately make you feel better if you give it a chance. But clearly the Republican convention delegates felt that the Party wasn't sick enough to give itself a dose of Howard Mason," Stanford answered with a chuckle.

"So, here we are at the end of July, and Andrew Cochran is the incumbent seeking reelection with Nathan Whitaker back pulling all the right strings as his campaign manager. That scenario seemed ridiculous just six short months ago. The question, tho, is whether Cochran's conversion to moderate Republicanism is real or just a campaign stunt to get reelected?" Whitlee inquired.

"I'm not sure, to tell you the truth," Stanford replied. "What I can tell you is that Nathan Whitaker is a savvy political savant. I have met a good many people in politics during my several decades on the bench and few have impressed me as much as Nathan Whitaker did when I met with him a few times during my nomination to the Supreme Court and through the vetting process. He is highly intelligent, wellspoken, gracious and charming." Stanford paused for a moment and sighed. "I'm just not sure that the man has a moral conscience. I truly don't think that there is anything at all that he wouldn't do to support, promote and protect his life-long friend. And that my dear, scares me a little bit. Blind devotion is rare in politics, and it's rarely a good thing."

THE JAM-PACKED ARENA IN PHILADELPHIA QUICKLY FILLED with balloons and streamers as Perry Douglas and his running mate Hellen Raymond stood center stage waving to the assemblage of Democratic leaders and delegates. Soon, the families of both candidates joined them on stage. A loud roar from the crowd greeted Robert Douglas as he waved and smiled his way to center stage. Robert bowed deeply to the crowd which only ignited an even heartier ovation. Perry Douglas looked at his son and smiled broadly as he gave him a parental wink. After several more minutes of wild cheering, balloon drops and confetti cannons the candidates and their families departed the stage. Backstage Carolyn Barnes joined her candidate and the two engaged in a robust and loving hug.

"This could not have been remotely possible if not for your herculean efforts," Perry Douglas said to Carolyn Barnes. "Thank you from the bottom of my heart. I'm not sure what I can ever do to repay you."

"Let's start with winning the general election," Carolyn replied with a big laugh. "So many people are part of this victory, I'm only one of them."

"And here's the rock star in the family," Perry said with a proud smile as Robert joined the two backstage. "Did you hear that applause, those chants? You're a natural, I'm the one who struggles with being comfortable in my own skin," Perry stated to his son.

"I have to admit, it's pretty heady stuff," Robert giddily responded. "The adrenaline rush you get from a large crowd is intoxicating."

"So, two years hence we will be running your campaign for the Illinois 9th Congressional District?" Carolyn inquired with a grin.

"Oh no, no!" Robert exclaimed. "This has been great and I'm really enjoying myself," Robert answered. "But I'm not a politician. I'm happy to help my dad any way I can in the general election. But once this is over, I will be more than content to return to my placid life as an art gallery curator."

"My guess is that there aren't many occasions at the art gallery where 15,000 people are cheering and chanting your name," Carolyn joshed.

"True dat," Robert grinned in return. "It will take a little time to adjust to the serenity and anonymity of art gallery life, but I'm looking forward to it."

"In the meantime, can we book you for some campaign appearances in August?" Carolyn asked.

"Absolutely, wherever you need me," Robert responded. Carolyn smiled and walked away. Robert then put his arm around his father.

"I am so proud of you, Pops. You've connected with millions of Americans in a way that gives them hope for their future. I can't thank you enough for letting me be just a little part of this wild ride," Robert said sincerely to his father.

"Robert, I'm the one who should be thanking you. Your entire life you've been honest and open about who you are. It took me a while to realize that even when we were living under the same roof. Yet, you can go out on the campaign trail and share your story with thousands of strangers. That takes a lot of guts, trust me. I'm not sure I would have had a modicum of success wrangling the youth vote and the LGBTQ vote without your assistance. So, thank you son, from a very grateful father."

"Yeah, the Douglas men make a pretty good team," Robert affirmed with a sheepish grin.

"Oh hell yes!" Perry exclaimed.

AARON ROSE AND CLAY GROVER SAT NEXT to each other on the couch in the living room of their yellow shotgun house in New Orleans. They watched the images on television as the balloons and confetti rained down on Perry Douglas and Hellen Raymond at the Democratic Party convention.

"Wow!" Aaron exclaimed. "That was quite a different convention than the free-for-all the Republicans held in Cleveland a week earlier."

"Pretty much the difference between unity and civil war," Clay concurred. "The Democrats are united while the Republicans still have fissures in their party. Cochran barely squeaked by on the first ballot. For an incumbent President that's not good. There are still Republican voters who will not support him. They see him as selling out on their core issues. They'd rather sit at home or vote for the Libertarian Party candidate."

"So, what you're saying is that a Douglas win is looking pretty good?" Aaron questioned with a smile.

"Please, don't go there Aaron," Clay entreated. "I really don't want to talk about whether I'm excited about a job I'm not sure I want to take."

"Sure, cool. I was just being playful," Aaron replied a bit perplexed by Clay's tone. Both men sat quietly for several moments just staring at the television screen.

"Are we ok?" Aaron finally mustered himself to ask. "When I was in Chicago for my family reunion, even my cousin William was asking me if there was a problem between the two of us?"

"What did you tell him?" Clay inquired.

"No, of course. I just said that there was something afoot that made our ability to plan where we will be living in the next 6 months difficult. That there was a bit of stress right now, but that everything between us was fine," Aaron plainly stated. "William did ask me if we were planning on having a family. We were in the midst of all these kids at the reunion and the topic came up. I told him we hadn't really discussed it much and that we needed to sort out where and what we would be doing first."

"Do you really think that adopting kids is a good idea?" Clay asked, his tone less than welcoming to the idea.

"I'm not sure, we never really broached the topic. Would you like to talk about it now?" Aaron offered.

"No Aaron, not really," Clay curtly responded. "I mean, come on. You keep pushing me to take the Chief of Staff Job if Senator Douglas wins the Presidency, and you think we should plan on having a family? Are we making decisions as a fully equalized partnership or are you just going to make all of the decisions for both of us and I need to sit back and accept all of your decisions and just say, yes dear?"

"Whoa! Where is this coming from?" Aaron asked, now a bit defensive. "I never said that I should make all of the decisions. Whether you decide to accept Senator Douglas' offer is entirely up to you. In fact, if we move back to DC I have no idea what I'll do for a job. But I'm happy to do so to further your career. And as to children, we've never discussed it. And maybe, we haven't discussed it because neither of us is that keen on the idea. I don't know, Clay. But I'm not sure where you're getting this notion that I'm trying to control everything in our lives, because I'm not."

"Why are we always stuck at home? We're still young. We should be going out more, trying different things, being more adventurous in our lives. The idea that working all day, coming home and cooking dinner, and then watching TV and then going to sleep constitutes a life well lived is anathema to me," Clay stated with conviction.

"Truly? Is this all about the fact that I don't like to go out every night of the week? That I don't want to have threesomes with guys we pick up in a bar? Do risky and unsavory things? Is that the problem here? Because if it is, we need to get this straight between us," a clearly frustrated Aaron demanded.

"This conversation is ridiculous," Clay countered. "I suggest that we drop it right now, before either of says something we might regret later."

"Fine!" Aaron exclaimed, as a veil of silence and frustration filled the small yellow shotgun house.

CHAPTER 22

Posy Branch sat at her desk in the back room of French Tips, Juleps & Jazz, waiting for her next interviewee. With business booming, it was time to hire someone to replace Chiffon as hostess and to assist with managing the establishment. Posy had resisted for a while, mostly out of deference and respect to her beloved friend, but reality had settled in and Posy understood she could no longer handle the business with just Michael as a co-manager. French Tips was popular and lucrative so there was no paucity of qualified candidates applying for the position.

"I'm gonna fess up right here, sugar, I ain't that much into reading resumes," Posy confessed, "So let's just have ourselves a good old chat and see if we like each other."

"Sounds good to me. My name is Lawton Cavanaugh. I'm 32 years old, born and raised right here in New Orleans. I've worked in nail salons and in customer service management for 10 years. My prior nail salon experience was four years ago. I worked for Olivier Bellevue for a little under two years."

"Well, don't that beat all," Posy said with a devilish grin. "What did you do when you was with Olivier?"

"Floor manager for the most part. I took reservations, worked with the girls on scheduling and such, dealt with customer relations and complaints, and did pretty much whatever Mr. Bellevue didn't want to do.

Which at times could be substantial, including handling the business ledgers, bank runs, that sort of thing," Lawton replied.

"And did you like the work?" Posy inquired.

"Sure, I liked the work well enough, but I'm gonna be very frank, towards the end of my two years, I had some personal issues with Mr. Bellevue," Lawton stated.

"Can you tell me a little about them issues?"

"I guess, it was mostly a personality conflict. Mr. Bellevue didn't treat any of his employees very well. He was especially rough at times with the nail technicians. He would bully and yell at the girls. I never felt comfortable being around someone like that. But, it was a job and I got paid alright, so sometimes you just look the other way and hold your tongue," Lawton responded.

"Shoot! I wish someone done taught me how to hold my tongue. I ain't real politic when it comes to keeping my thoughts to myself," Posy laughed.

"That's the other thing. Mr. Bellevue was not always honest with his employees. He'd tell us one thing and then do the opposite. At times, he'd try to pit one of the nail technicians against another just to stir things up and create competition among the girls. It wasn't very nice and only caused tension and distrust," Lawton related.

"Well, we all one big happy family here," Posy announced. "I'm sorry you had a tough time with Olivier. I know exactly what you're talking about. Olivier ain't good people. He done shown his true colors to me. You're a nice looking boy, you present well to the clientele. You got a nice voice and a good smile. And you say that you good with numbers and accounting ledgers and such?" Posy asked.

"Yes, ma'am. I was real good at math in high school and I went to junior college for two years and had several accounting classes. I did real well. I can get you my transcripts," Lawton offered.

"I ain't sure that I need all that," Posy stated. "But what I do want is that I want you to go to the bar and sit and have a julep on the house. Have a chat with my bartender Michael. Michael is real good at judging folk and there ain't a soul on this here planet whose opinion I trust more. I've got a few more people I need to speak with. I'll give you a holla back in a day or two and let you know if you got the job."

"Thank you, thank you so much, Ms. Branch," Lawton said with a polite smile as he rose and shook Posy's hand.

"My mama is Mrs. Branch, honey, just call me Posy. I ain't one for formal this and that."

"Of course, thank you Posy. I'll go talk with Michael. And of course, thank you for the free julep," Lawton happily chirped.

"You in for a treat, son. Michael makes the best julep in the South. Ain't no brag, just fact," Posy chuckled. "I like you Lawton. I got a good feel about you. We'll be talking real soon now."

THE REPUBLICAN NATIONAL CONVENTION had been over for more than two weeks. President Andrew Cochran had prevailed against very strong odds. He had won over enough Independents and moderate Republicans to barely squeak out a first ballot victory against his former Vice-President Howard Mason. Howard Mason had garnered the majority of Jedediah Wilson's delegate support, after Wilson dropped out of the race. Virtually none of the Wilson delegates supported Cletus Sawyer, who wound up finishing a distant third. However, despite winning a narrow victory in the delegate race, the Conservative right-wing of the Party still was adamantly against the direction that President Cochran attempted to take the Party. And, though defeated at the Convention, Cletus Sawyer remained the voice of the opposition against the President in his own Party. In order to win the general election in November, Andrew Cochran and his campaign manager, Nathan Whitaker knew that there had to be some substantial fence-mending with the rabid, and annoyed, Party base. It wasn't going to be easy, but the task was essential for victory in the fall.

NATHAN WHITAKER SAT AT A TABLE at the Bourbon Steak restaurant in the Four Seasons Hotel in Washington, DC, waiting for his dinner companion, Senator Cletus Sawyer to arrive. Nathan glanced at his watch and smiled as he noticed that Senator Sawyer was over twenty minutes late. Nathan had been around politicians for most of his adult life. He understood the reality of political power gamesmanship. He was going to ask for a favor, and he was going to be made to wait for the opportunity. Finally, the opportunity arrived with the slumped shoulders and dour expression of a sore loser.

"Senator Sawyer, what a distinct honor and pleasure to see you again," Nathan insincerely gushed at Cletus Sawyer.

"Evening Nathan," Cletus curtly replied as he barely looked at Nathan Whitaker before taking his seat at the table.

"Can we get you a cocktail?" Nathan asked with a smile.

"Oh, you're gonna be getting me more than just a few cocktails," Cletus scowled in return. "Andrew Cochran is going to have to pay big, you understand?"

"I thought we'd have a cocktail or two, followed by a nice steak dinner, and then get to the matters at hand, but I'm fine with getting right down to brass tacks if you prefer, Senator," Nathan bluntly stated.

"Why should we waste our time playing pretend?" Cletus Sawyer asked with a smirk. "Look, I don't like you and your boss, and y'all think I'm some idiot uncle you can push to the kiddie table at Thanksgiving. No sense in building up phony pretenses. What are you offering?"

"Excuse me?" Nathan replied, well aware of what Cletus Sawyer was asking.

"Jesus H. Christ, Nathan!" Cletus growled. "I ain't in the mood to play. Secretary of State, yes or no?"

"The country has an outstanding Secretary of State in Secretary Lewis Mullen," Nathan coyly responded.

"Don't you be offering me Interior or the EPA or some crap like that," Cletus snapped. "I'll take Attorney General. Hell, I'm the ranking member of the Senate Judiciary Committee, that job is rightfully mine anyway. And if you dare tell me that the country has an outstanding Attorney General, I'll get up and walk out on you Nathan. But not before I take a $150 Kobe steak and a $200 bottle of bourbon to go!"

"Well, Potter Markbright is our current Attorney General," Nathan said playfully testing the waters.

"Potter Markbright hates Andrew Cochran even more than I do," Cletus loudly professed. "Y'all been biding your time trying to find a way to rid yourselves of that contentious old son-of-a-bitch. But, he was part of the bargain you paid to get to the White House in the first place. And then, when you had your little misunderstanding with the law Nathan, and when old Potter wouldn't raise a finger to help you, Cochran was livid. I ain't sure that they've had a civil word since."

"That's nothing more than rumor and speculation, Senator," Nathan replied.

"Don't bullshit a bullshitter, Nathan. I got eyes and ears. I know what time it is," Cletus responded. "I want Attorney General, plus I got some of my folks that need to be taken care of. Justice Department got plenty of jobs to go around, and I'm gonna get more than my share. And, don't feed me no crap about civil service and that non-partisan bullshit. I'm not interested in hearing it. You need the support of the Republican base to win in November. I still got a powerful voice with the Party's right-wing. We're playing poker now, Nathan, and I just laid down a straight flush, ace high."

"Of course, I'm not in a position to make any promises. I am only here as a representative for the Cochran campaign," Nathan stated.

"Blah, blah, blah," Cletus replied. "Look, ball is in your court, Nathan. I told you what I want, and I ain't taking nothing less."

"Thank you for your input, Senator. I can guarantee you that it will be given full consideration. I appreciate your frankness," Nathan said.

Moments later, the waiter approached the table.

"What's the most expensive bottle of bourbon you got here?" Cletus Sawyer asked the waiter while he stared at Nathan. Cletus had a huge mischievous grin on his face.

BESSIE COLLINS LOOKED OVER THE WEEKLY RECEIPTS for her voodoo shop business while shaking her head.

"We just doing well enough to keep afloat, pay the bills, and get us paid, but that's about it," Bessie lamented to Papa Levi.

"We do surely miss the business Esther done use to bring, ain't no denying that," Papa Levi responded.

"Yeah, well, you saw how Esther reacted when I went to apologize to her down at Jackson Square," Bessie said. "She barely looked me in the eye and would barely acknowledge that we was there. I tried to make amends, I said I was sorry and all, and nary a sign of any consideration or nothing."

"You think maybe if you start doing readings and the such again?" Papa Levi asked.

"No, I can't do it. I ain't gonna take folks good money for pretending. And the spirits don't talk to me like they do with Queen Rita and Esther. Though we sure did make good money when Esther be doing readings and séances. Folks was real happy," Bessie wistfully said.

"They is another mambo that I knows a bit. Her name is Countess Mariette Aubuchon. She mostly from Cajun country in Acadiana, but she been spending more time here in New Orleans lately," Papa Levi related to Bessie.

"Countess Mariette Aubuchon, that's a mouthful," Bessie said with a grin. "She a real Countess?"

"I don't rightly know, Miss Bessie. But them Cajun folk always given themselves titles and such," Papa Levi answered. "I done seen her do a sacrifice down by Lake Pontchartrain a piece ago. She had a big ol' crew with her. She reminded me a little of Queen Rita. Real theatric and all. But she had the respect of the others. She looked like she was for real."

"Where is she now?" Bessie inquired.

"Can't say for sure. She seems to move between Acadiana and here. She been around the Big Easy more lately, though I done never seen her down in Jackson Square. I think she do some work with the Marie Laveau folk now and then."

"Do you think that we should talk to her? See what's what?" Bessie asked.

"Ain't for me to say, Miss Bessie. It's up to you iffin' you want someone else working in your shop."

"Money was a lot better when we had Esther here regular," Bessie offered.

"You surely ain't lyin' about that," Papa Levi confirmed.

"Probably wouldn't hurt to talk to her. You know, just share a piece of pie and some sweet tea."

"I can spread the word that you want to speak with her, if you want?" Papa Levi asked.

"Talk don't hurt. See if we get along together. How old is she?"

"Can't rightly say, but she old. Late 70's maybe," Papa Levi answered.

"See if you can get word to her. Don't make no promises or nothing. Just have a sit down and visit for a spell."

"I'll see what I can do, Miss Bessie. I surely will."

CHAPTER 23

THE AUGUST HEAT OVERTOOK MUCH OF THE COUNTRY as the two political candidates, Senator Perry Douglas and President Andrew Cochran began campaigning against each other in earnest. Their respective campaigns began strategizing and plotting for any advantage they could find in attempting to sway the electorate. President Cochran met with Nathan Whitaker after a campaign stop in Denver, Colorado.

"Frankly Nathan, I'd rather drink more poison than make Cletus Sawyer my Attorney General," Andrew Cochran sighed while shaking his head.

"I certainly understand your point of view, but it's not like we have someone currently in the position that anyone particularly likes," Nathan countered.

"Ugh! That old stick in the mud, Potter Markbright was an election time compromise that I wish I had never made," Andrew stated. "But, I made that mistake once, I should not make it again if I am lucky enough to return to the White House. Won't Cletus take something else? I cringe at the thought of making the Justice Department a political bargaining chip yet again."

"Cletus wanted Secretary of State!" Nathan exclaimed with a chortle.

"Sure, of course. Let's make the top diplomatic face of my administration an inbred unsophisticated stupid ass who barely has the ability to string sentences together," Andrew Cochran spat back with a sarcastic sneer. "Lewis Mullen is possibly one of the only cabinet members that I am truly proud of. Several of the others are just glorified versions of Potter Markbright, nothing more than the result of political giveaways to curry favor with this group or that."

"It's all part of the game. And there may not be a second term of the Cochran administration if we don't solidify the base. We are running an uphill battle against Perry Douglas as it is," Nathan surmised.

"Douglas is a good man. There doesn't seem to be even a whiff of scandal or impropriety to him or his campaign," Andrew mentioned.

"We're digging into our opposition research now, and so far that seems to be the case. But everyone has some baggage. It's just a matter of uncovering it," Nathan responded.

"Damn, you're cynical, Nathan. Maybe he's just a good man, end of story," Andrew Cochran replied. "Some closets contain just clothes and not the skeletons of past indiscretions."

"Then we will have to manufacture something. The gay son has to have something we can exploit. He's a very talented campaigner for his father with a large following of his own. It would be advantageous to move him off the board with some scandal," Nathan stated with a sly grin.

"No, Nathan. We've already gone too far in some of the things we have done in the pursuit of preserving power. I won't smear innocent members of my opponent's family in order to retain my Presidency."

"It's politics. Everyone does it," Nathan added.

"I'm sorry I can't be that ruthless. At times, it's hard enough to sleep at night or look myself in the mirror," Andrew confessed.

"No worries, I'll take care of it. We won't step too far out of line. I've got a few ideas," Nathan said.

"I don't want to know. I want to keep this campaign civil and out of the gutter," Andrew reiterated.

"Understood," Nathan said while he glanced down at his cellphone. Another missed call from Jim Bob McCallum.

CAROLYN BARNES WAS IN CHAPEL HILL, North Carolina meeting with Helen Raymond's strategic advisor Riley Banks about coordinating the campaign strategy and travel itinerary for the Democratic Presidential and Vice-Presidential candidates.

"You do realize that I am more involved in Senator Raymond's strategic and policy team than in dealing with her scheduling right?" Riley asked Carolyn with a huge smile on his face. "That is more what campaign managers do, isn't it?"

"Would you rather that I speak to someone else?" Carolyn teasingly questioned.

"Oh no, I am happy to meet with you. Delighted even," Riley backtracked as the verbal gamesmanship continued.

"I thought that we came to a meeting of the minds in Philadelphia. That we forged an equally advantageous working relationship. However, if I'm mistaken about that, I am more than willing to speak with someone else who is more acquainted with strategic campaign planning for Senator Raymond," Carolyn sarcastically responded.

"You are absolutely correct. We are of one mind. Supple and explorative. A wholly intertwined and fully embraced political body," Riley grinned. "I'm very much in favor of continuing and expanding our relationship. As it pertains to the campaign, of course."

"Of course," Carolyn replied with a seductive smile.

RACE CASSERLY TOOK A LONG SIP OF HIS COCKTAIL as he sat in the boardroom of his oil company located in Houston, Texas. He stared out the window at the Houston skyline and sighed. He then turned toward his business associate and friend Carlisle Buchanan and displayed a sly grin.

"Now what?" Carlisle asked.

"We're not done yet," Race stated.

"I don't see how we're not," Carlisle replied. "Cochran won the Republican nomination. Barely, but he won. Howard Mason is relegated to the dust bin of history. He came within a handful of delegates of seizing the nomination from the incumbent President. But he's just another Vice-President who could never get beyond that status."

"Well, the game is not over, there are still pieces being moved around the board," Race explained. "Cletus Sawyer is pushing hard to be the next Attorney General if Cochran is elected. He aimed higher, but there was no way Cochran and Whitaker would promise him Secretary of State. In fact, I understand that Cochran is pushing back on Attorney General. And instead of sitting back and licking his wounds, Jim Bob

McCallum is attempting to get his old gang back together. As soon as he dropped Cletus Sawyer like a dead fish, he began angling to get back into the good graces of Cochran through Whitaker."

"How do you know this?" Carlisle asked a bit taken aback.

"Carlisle, please don't insult me," Race said shaking his head. "You know how much we spend every year on cyber intelligence, information gathering and political outreach. Ol' Jim Bob does the same thing. Ain't no secrets among Southern billionaires. It's not a matter of what each of us knows, it's only a matter of who gets there first."

"So, has Jim Bob convinced Whitaker to allow him back into the White House inner circle?"

"Not that I am aware. I only know that he is trying real hard," Race answered. "Thing is with Jim Bob, he's such an old and faithful dog, he's never willing to try any new tricks. Just keeps going back to the old playbook that he is accustomed to and comfortable with. I never got his fascination with that voodoo nonsense and poisons. Sure, it's relatively clean and cheap, but sometimes you've got to explore more innovative methods. Blood is a very heavy business expense, I get that. But, come on, it's the 21st Century, certainly we've progressed farther than 18th Century voodoo potions? Yet, then again, there is something to be said for the tried and true methods, especially when they've worked so successfully for you in the past. Save for a couple of silly witnesses and an over-eager prosecutor Jim Bob wouldn't have had to endure any embarrassment over his last escapade. But that turned out to be just a minor bump in the road for him."

"Howard Mason doesn't have the influence or backing to demand anything from Cochran. Cletus is lucky enough to have the knuckle-draggers on the far right of the Party that still pay attention to what he says. Cochran knows he needs them to have any chance at keeping the White House. Howard's only opportunity was at the convention. And as they say, close only counts in horseshoes and hand grenades," Carlisle stated. "Perhaps, in hindsight we should have had Howard retain his position as Vice-President while still challenging Cochran for the Party nomination. Then, in the event of a real and successful attempt on Cochran's life, Howard would have been President."

"I'm done with Howard. You're right there is nowhere else to go with him. Sometimes you don't get much return for your investments. Chalk it up as a loss and move on," Race summed up. "But there are other pieces left on the chess board. Right now Nathan Whitaker has taken on all of the attributes of a bishop. He's moving swiftly and diagonally all over the board. Nothing is simple, vertical or horizontal. He's moving across the lines. Problem is that Nathan can be erratic. Not every move he makes is fully thought out. His latest adventure in Cleveland is testament to that fact. Yet, he's the piece I covet. I always have. And, Jim Bob is attempting to move to claim him once again. That my friend, we cannot tolerate. For if you can't have what you covet, then it must not be had by anyone."

IT WAS AFTER 2:30 A.M. IN the morning. Michael had closed up French Tips, Juleps and Jazz about a half hour earlier. Still wound up from his work day, he walked down to Bourbon Pub to have a couple of cocktails before going home. It was a Friday night/Saturday morning in August, so there was still a very large crowd at the popular gay bar. Michael sipped on his vodka and soda as he watched the go-go boys gyrate and grind on the bar top, much like he did before Posy discovered him dancing at OZ. Michael never enjoyed his days as a stripper/male dancer. Being treated like a slab of beef was degrading and annoying. But, he was young and fairly new to New Orleans, and no one was giving him a job as a bartender. He stared at the large video screens, but out of the corner of his eye, he spotted a friendly face moving in his direction.

"Clay! Clay!" Michael called out attempting to be heard over the music and din from the crowd. Clay continued to move through the crowd seemingly oblivious to Michael's yelps. Michael watched as Clay stood at the edge of the bar, clearly enthralled by the fit body and well-packed thong of a very attractive dark haired dancer. Clay had made eye contact with the dancer and the two were sharing a few words before Clay took a couple of folded dollar bills and pulled back the dancers thong to insert the dollar bills and cop a lingering grope of the dancer's genitalia. It became clear that Clay was completely oblivious to Michael's presence and did not hear his shouts. Michael hesitated momentarily, but then decided to push his way through the crowd to Clay's location at the edge of the bar. He sidled up to Clay who was still enamored by the dancer.

"Hey you!" Michael shouted over the boisterous atmosphere. Clay turned in Michael's direction clearly stunned to see him at his side.

"Uh, hey Michael," Clay nervously said as he looked at Michael before quickly diverting his glance to the video screen.

"What brings you out tonight? Is Aaron here?" Michael asked with a broad smile, happy to see a friend.

"Yeah, uh no, Aaron isn't with me. He's at home sleeping. I was too wired to sleep so I decided to go out for a drink or two and try to relax," Clay allowed while fumbling his words.

"Yeah, nothing more relaxing than groping 8 inches of nylon thong," Michael kidded Clay with a laugh and a smile. Clay awkwardly grinned and shifted from foot to foot clearly uncomfortable to be caught in the act.

"Look, no worries. I don't judge. I used to dance across the street before Posy brought me to French Tips to bartend. There's nothing wrong with looking. There's also nothing wrong with a consensual $2 grope. We're gay men, I get it. It doesn't need to mean anything more than a little casual fun."

"Right, exactly," Clay responded as his demeanor rapidly changed from apprehensive to relaxed conversation with a friend.

"You want to walk down the street to Good Friends and have a drink?" Michael asked. "It's too loud in here to have much of a conversation."

"Sure, that would be great," Clay responded with a wink and a smile. The two friends proceeded out the door of Bourbon Pub and walked the very short block to another gay bar at the corner of St. Ann and Dauphine called Good Friends, which was far less noisy and raucous. The second floor balcony of Good Friends provided a lovely quiet atmosphere where one could actually have a conversation without screaming at your companion over the ear-splitting din.

"Does Aaron know you're out?" Michael asked.

"I don't know, probably not," Clay answered with a shrug of his shoulders. "He's a pretty heavy sleeper. That boy can sleep through anything. I laid in bed unable to fall asleep for a couple of hours. When I realized it was useless, I got dressed and came down here to get a drink."

"Does that happen often?" Michael inquired.

"I wouldn't say often, but it's been occurring more and more the last few months. I've got a lot on my mind, that I'm sorry I can't really talk about. It's about a potential new job. So, sometimes, I just go lay on the couch and read so as not to disturb Aaron. Other times, I might go for a run. And, then occasionally I come down here to be around other gay men who are just looking to have some fun and relax."

"Sure, I get it," Michael replied. "As long as that's all that it is, it's cool."

"See, you understand. Sometimes Aaron doesn't get me. In some respect, we're very different people. He is way more of a homebody than I am. Don't get me wrong, I love spending time at home just the two of us. But we're way too young to be doing just that. I want to go out more, be more adventurous, be a little reckless now and again. You know? That's not Aaron. He loves being at home. He cherishes stability. He's pushing me on this possible new job, and the responsibility of it would completely change our lives, my life."

"And you're not ready for that?"

"I don't know. Perhaps, I'm ready but I just don't really want it," Clay responded. "When I lived in Washington and worked as Chief of Staff to a very powerful Senator, during the day I played by all of the rules. I was professionalism personified. I was a very serious young man doing very serious work. But at night, when it was my time to relax, I was this lustful sexual animal. I couldn't get enough. I wanted to let loose and not care about the consequences. It was sort of this Dr. Jekyll and Mr. Hyde persona. And it was exciting. And I did a pretty good job of balancing the two sides. Stable and supremely responsible in the daytime, and reckless and risk-taking at night. Truthfully, there's still a part of me that longs for that double-life. That craves the excitement and thrill of it all."

"I know exactly what you're talking about," Michael agreed. "Of course, I've never had the responsibilities of a high powered job on Capitol Hill, but I understand the feeling. Does Aaron know about both sides of you?"

"Yes, to some extent. He knows I use to tramp around quite a bit when we were both working in DC. He never did it himself, that really wasn't his thing. But he knew. Perhaps, not to the full extent that I did it, but he knew some of it."

"And does he know that you still harbor some of those feelings?" Michael questioned.

"Well, that's where the rubber meets the road," Clay answered. "I love Aaron with all my heart. I was so happy when we got married. We have a very good sex life. But sometimes, it's just not enough for me. I'm not sure that I can explain it."

"So, you feel like you're being trapped. The potential new job with the increased responsibilities and conventional stability that Aaron deeply wants you to take, added to your own conflicted feelings about your sexual cravings and wanderlust is creating tension and anxiety within you," Michael summed up.

"Precisely!" Clay exclaimed. "I feel trapped, and I'm trying real hard not to overreact and do or say something really stupid and self-destructive. But it gets harder every day Michael, I swear its driving me crazy."

CHAPTER 24

Bessie Collins walked down Rampart Street towards her voodoo shop. A few feet away near the door of her shop she saw a small elderly woman standing patiently by the side of the entrance door. The women appeared to be swaying back and forth as she waited.

"Can I help you, ma'am?" Bessie asked as she approached the elderly woman who had gray braids that framed her dark weary and weathered face.

"I am looking for Bessie Collins," the woman stated with a raspy voice. "Is this her shop?"

"Yes, I'm Bessie and I am the proprietor of this shop," Bessie answered with a warm gentle smile.

"I am Countess Mariette Aubuchon, been told that you is looking to speak with me," the small elderly woman stated.

"Why yes, please come in," Bessie replied as she quickly unlocked the front door and turned on the lights. "We can sit in the back room and I'll put a tea kettle on in a moment. I've got some red Rooibos tea is that alright?"

"Yes, Rooibos is good for my weak bones," Mariette said while maneuvering herself over one of the wooden chairs in Bessie's back room. At just over five feet tall, Mariette was a frail woman who was slightly hunched over. Clearly she must suffer from osteoporosis, Bessie thought. Bessie placed the tea kettle on the small stove top and began to tidy up the table.

"Thank you for coming to see me," Bessie said. "I thought you might call first so that we could set up a time to meet. I hope I didn't keep you waiting."

"I do not have a cellphone," Mariette stated. "I am an old woman, I wake up early. These old bones won't let me rest for more than a few hours without stiffening up to the point of causing pain."

"I'm sorry to hear that," Bessie replied.

"It is what it is. At my age, pain is merely a reminder that you's still alive," Mariette said with a small chuckle. "Now what is it that you seek from me?"

"Well, this shop belonged to my auntie Queen Rita before she passed. She left it to me. I've been keeping it up and running in her memory. It is what she wanted," Bessie began.

"I knew Queen Rita. She was a very powerful mambo. But you are not a believer are you?" Mariette asked.

"Well, no not really," Bessie admitted. "I done kept the shop going with my friend Papa Levi. He helps me with stocking the shelves, ordering merchandise, cleaning the store, that sort of thing. He knows more about Haitian voodoo than I do, but neither of us truly practice it much."

"Who reads for the clients? Who do the sacrifices?"

"Up until a few months past, I had a mambo named Esther Francois doing readings and séances and the such," Bessie related to Mariette.

"You liked Esther, she done good by you?"

"We did some real good business together for a piece. The clients seemed to like her. But we had a falling out of sorts. It was my fault, but things ain't been the same since. Do you know Esther?" Bessie inquired.

"Oh yeah, I know Esther," Mariette said with her lips turned up as if she just ate something very sour. "Esther, she done practice in the dark arts. There is an evil juju to that woman."

"Really?" Bessie questioned. "I never got that sense from her. We got along right fine until that episode I mentioned."

"Even a serpent can act like a rabbit when it wants to. Best you be rid of her kind."

"The reason that I wanted to meet you was to ask if you would want to do some readings and the such here in my shop?" Bessie asked while pouring Mariette a cup of Rooibos red tea.

"Why you want to keep a voodoo shop iffin' you ain't practicing in the occult?" Mariette inquired before taking a long sip of tea.

"As I said before, I'm keeping it running in memory of my late auntie," Bessie responded.

"I ain't from around here, but I do spend me some time in New Orleans. I'm a bayou woman. So, I won't be around all the time."

"That would be fine," Bessie cheerfully replied. "We could do readings and séances by appointment only on whatever days that you're in town."

"You's a good woman Bessie Collins. I could tell from your aura when I first laid eyes on you. You trying to do right by Queen Rita, I admire that. Let me think on it a spell and let you know in a day or two," Mariette offered.

"Yes, of course, that would be real good," Bessie replied. "Just let me know when you can."

"This here is some nice tea," Mariette said as she smiled with the cup up to her lips.

IT HAD BEEN EIGHT MONTHS SINCE Stanford Winchester had retired from the Federal bench. He spent the first four months doing everything that he never had the time or opportunity to do when he was a judge. He travelled some. He became a tourist in his own town. He took in the Mardi Gras parades and all its frivolity for the first time in decades. He took long walks through Audubon Park and the Audubon Zoo. But, Stanford found himself lacking a day-to-day purpose in life. He was getting bored in the afternoons as he eagerly awaited Whitlee's return from work. He spent a good deal of time at Fritzel's chatting with his old retired friends. Especially, Calvin Putnam.

"I tell you true Calvin, I've got to find me something to fill the days that ain't gonna get me in trouble," Stanford admitted with a sly grin. "Drinking Sazerac's in the middle of the afternoon with you, while pleasant, isn't the proper way for a gentleman to conduct himself. I've never really had a problem with alcohol. It's been good to me over the years. Jack Daniels and I have been close friends. Now my friend is fixing on becoming a problem if I don't find something to occupy my time right proper."

"What about writing a book? You always used to talk about doing that when you were presiding over the Fifth Circuit and didn't have the time."

"Well, yes I did use to say that," Stanford confirmed. "And a couple of weeks ago I sat in front of my computer at home and stared at the blank screen of a new Word document. There are very few things in this world that are more terrifying than that damn blank screen. I'd write a sentence, read it back and then delete it. Back to the blank screen. I'd sit there for a half hour thinking. I'd write a paragraph, read it back and then delete it. Back to that evil blank screen. It was nerve-racking, I tell you."

"You were never at a loss for words when you were ruling over your courtroom like a dictatorial tyrant. There are plenty of attorneys in this here city that only wish you were at a loss for words back then. And, I ain't just blowing smoke up your skirt cause you're a friend of mine, but you wrote some of the most articulate well-reasoned opinions that I have ever read from any judge on any level. Truly Stanford, some of those opinions on major cases that you wrote were more poetic than prose. They were brilliant, and artful. Something the practice of law is lacking these days with this new generation who can't write a decent sentence to save their lives," Calvin complimented his friend.

"Them is very nice words to hear, Calvin, even though they may be slurred through an alcoholic haze," Stanford responded with a wink and a cackle. "But that was completely different. The topic was given to me in the way of the facts of the case and the presiding law to be applied. Writing fiction requires you to create something new from whole cloth. There's just that unholy blank screen staring you in the face."

"You are an excellent storyteller. You always have been. Maybe you just need an audience. Get yourself a secretary and just start telling her some of your stories," Calvin offered as a suggestion.

"I'm not sure there's enough money in this world to get someone to sit and listen to me ramble on while she types my worthless babble," Stanford quipped.

"No seriously, I think I'm on to something," Calvin argued.

"Calvin, the only thing you are on to is a bad hangover if you have one more drink," Stanford chortled.

Nathan Whitaker sat in his home office in front of his laptop computer. He was preparing a list of items that needed to be taken care of for the Re-Elect President Cochran campaign. He felt his cellphone buzz in his pants pocket. He fished out his phone to find a text message on the screen that read: "Call me or else. I'm done playing!" Nathan stared at the phone screen for a couple of minutes as various thoughts ran through his mind. He sighed deeply and began to search his contacts list for the number he had not used in well over two years.

"Hello Jim Bob, Nathan Whitaker here," Nathan stated into the phone in an unemotional monotone voice.

"Good evening Nathan, I see you received my message, not to mention my several missed calls," Jim Bob smarmily asserted. "We're old friends, you and me, Nathan. We go back a piece, and have a lot of shared history, you and me. And a number of secrets we share together, like any other two old friends."

"What can I do for you Jim Bob?" Nathan asked with an irritated pique in his voice.

"Come on now Nathan, is that how old friends talk to one another?" The ever wheedling Jim Bob asked.

"Jim Bob, if this is about a cabinet position for Cletus Sawyer, I've already spoken to Cletus and heard his request. I've transmitted that request to the President who is currently taking it under advisement. I've really got nothing to add at this moment," Nathan bluntly stated.

"Oh fuck me with a splintered rake!" Jim Bob exclaimed. "Did you think that I was calling you because I give a rat's ass what that Alabama hillbilly Cletus is asking for in the way of a cabinet position? He thinks he still speaks for them Tea Party idiots. Maybe he does, but if that's the case them fools are dumber than I thought if they is still taking their cues from that ignorant loser."

"Well, if that's not the case, then I'm not quite sure why you've been calling me," Nathan replied.

"See now, you're just being coy with me. You're a smart man Nathan, it's why I've always liked and respected you," Jim Bob responded. "You know damn well that I put that dumb dog down the minute he screwed up the nominating convention with that Wilson debacle. Talk about fucking up a one car funeral! You just playin' cuz you seen this move comin' for some time now. My guess is that you tried to casually run this by Andrew and see how it went. And good old choir boy Andrew shot you down, so you been avoiding me. Just admit that I'm right and we can talk about fixing this problem for both of us."

"For the sake of argument, let's assume that your supposition has a modicum of merit," Nathan began before being interrupted by Jim Bob.

"There you go. I like that smart boy talk. Now we on to something. Supposition on, Nathan."

"Look Jim Bob, President Cochran was adamant. I don't see how this can work," Nathan stated.

"I do declare, I can't recall the last time someone told me, 'Please Jim Bob don't give me your tens of millions of dollars or utilize all of your power and influence on my behalf,'" Jim Bob chided Nathan with a wicked laugh.

"It's not my call on this one," Nathan answered.

"Now, you're just bald-faced lying to me, Nathan. And good old friends don't lie to one another, especially when they both know the color of the sky. You can sit there and tell me that it's green even though I'm staring right at that bright blue sky. Where does that get either one of us? If I got to spell it out, I surely will. Here is why the sky is blue. It's because there is only one person on this earth, by the way, it's covered by that brilliant blue sky, that Andrew Cochran trusts more than himself. Always and forever. And I just happen to be speaking to him right here and now. And you and I know some things. Some things that should never see the light of day under that bright blue sky. And I bet you surely would like to keep it that way. So, let's stop calling up down and the blue sky green, shall we?" Jim Bob asked.

"What is it that you want?" Nathan inquired.

"I want to give Andrew Cochran bushel baskets of my money. I want to utilize every asset and whatever clout I may have to make sure that he is re-elected President of these United States. But most importantly, I want you and me to be real good friends again. As in always and forever, just like you and Andy. That's all I want. So, think about that Nathan. Try to rack your brain and figure out a downside to that proposition. I'll give you a little time. But next time I call, you best answer Nathan, you hear?"

CHAPTER 25

Posy Branch sat on a barstool at French Tips, Juleps & Jazz just staring at her bartender Michael's muscular shaven chest.

"You know Michael, I've never realized it before but you've got a number of freckles under your left nipple that if we connected them with a sharpie it would look like a small cat," Posy said with a playful grin.

"There's something wrong with you," Michael responded with a smile.

"No seriously sugar, it would be a cute little cat. Let me go get a sharpie from the office and I'll prove it to you," Posy persisted.

"Ain't happening, crazy lady, and stop staring at my chest! Michael demanded with a laugh. "And for the love of God, why can't I wear a shirt every now and then?"

"Baby, look in the mirror. You work real hard at the gym developing them big pecs and those lovely abs, why would you want to cover it up? We'd probably lose 20% of our female clientele if you started wearing a shirt. And we'd absolutely lose all of our gay customers."

"You've got a great body why don't you go topless?" Michael smirked in return.

"First of all, there is something to be said for a clingy blouse and a push-up bra. And secondly, and more importantly I'm an old woman. Trust me, my girls ain't what they use to be when I was back in my beauty pageant days," Posy laughed and snorted as she looked down at her own cleavage. "Mother Nature is a bitch, and gravity don't help a middle-aged woman either."

"That is just silly talk, you are a gorgeous woman, Posy Branch. Any man would kill to spend some time with you," Michael responded. "Especially a certain officer of the law," Michael responded with a devilish grin.

"So, you boys been talking have you?" Posy asked. "Norris is a real good man, Michael. I can understand why the two of you are friends. You both solid, reliable, truly nice people."

"He thinks the world of you. He can't stop talking about you. Other night we were playing cards with a couple other boys and Norris would not shut up. Posy said this and Posy did that. I had to tell him, 'Hey, I'm with the woman 10-12 hours a day, I don't need to hear about her the other 12 hours too!" Michael grinned and winked.

"Thank you sugar, you always got my back," Posy replied. "Speaking of business, so what you think of that Lawton Cavanaugh boy from the other day?"

"He seems like a good guy. We had a nice chat over a julep. He's got the experience. And he sure don't have many good things to say about Olivier," Michael answered.

"Who do?" Posy responded with a laugh and a snort. "You think we should bring him on?"

"He's the best candidate we've seen so far. I liked him, he seems like good people. I think he'd fit in well with everyone else around here. And besides, you and I could stand some time off every now and then. It's been rough doing double-shifts the last few months. I can't recall the last time you went on any kind of vacation. And Norris loves to go on little weekend excursions. He's been saying he wants to ask you to go with him, but you always telling him you're too busy. It's about time you make yourself a little less busy."

"I hear you sugar. It surely would be nice to take a little trip now and then. Dip my toes in the Gulf before summer is over. Well, that settles it. French Tips has a new host and co-manager. I'll give Lawton a call and let him know. Things are looking up. We gonna have some fun around here, but you still got a tiny cat under your nipple," Posy smiled and laughed.

"As Chantale use to say, "You is crazy, girl!"

PRESIDENT ANDREW COCHRAN SLUMPED IN HIS CHAIR in his private office in the upstairs residence at the White House. Sue Lynn Cochran walked over to the desk where her husband was sitting carrying a glass of bourbon on the rocks.

"I'm exhausted already and we haven't even begun the general election campaign," Andrew confessed.

"Battling your own Party for months on end has to take a toll, not to mention being seriously ill after an attempt on your life," Sue Lynn stated.

"I'm probably one major foreign crisis away from a nervous breakdown," Andrew admitted. "I think I'm doing the right thing. I try to convince myself of that every day. The Republican Party cannot continue moving to the right. We are becoming a fringe party. We've got to moderate to encompass more independent thinking voters. Yet, it's a fight. I'm not sure how I won the nomination at the convention."

"You had a lot of help, including Nathan who just wouldn't allow you to lose," Sue Lynn replied. "You've known how I feel about Nathan, Andy. I always had my doubts. But when you were in the hospital, he was there every single day. Then once you got better, he turned around the campaign. I have a new appreciation for him that I never had before."

"Yeah, Nathan. I owe him a lot. And you're right, without his guidance, assistance and his sheer will to win, I'd be a lame duck one term President watching a member of my own Party running in the general election," Andrew stated with a world weary voice. "But the thing about Nathan is that I don't think he understands that there have to be limits. That not everything is fair game. He doesn't want to just push the envelope he wants to tear it to shreds. We were meeting the other day, and some of the things coming out of his mouth, frankly scare me. I'm not Richard Nixon for Christ's sake."

"No, you're not. But you are President Andrew Cochran. You're in charge of your administration Andy, not Nathan. You set the limits and as a friend and a subjugate to your authority, he needs to abide by the limits you set."

"You know that is not as easy as it sounds when it comes to Nathan. He has a win at all costs mentality that I never had," Andrew admitted. "Don't get me wrong, I can never repay him for what he has done for me over the years. He is my brother and I love him dearly. I'm just not sure that I can control him anymore."

"I don't think that you are giving yourself enough credit Andy. Nathan loves you, he wouldn't do anything to harm you. If you clearly and distinctly set the limits, he won't violate your trust and do something behind your back," Sue Lynn reassured her husband.

"I hope you're right dear."

It was 3:00 a.m. as Aaron Rose groggily wiped the sleep from his eyes and realized that he was alone in his bed. He walked to the living room to see if his husband Clay was sleeping on the couch again. He was not. Nor was he anywhere to be found in their small yellow shotgun house. The occurrence of Clay being gone in the middle of the night was becoming more frequent. Aaron understood that Clay was becoming more anxious as the likelihood of Perry Douglas winning the Presidency was becoming closer to fruition. Yet, he also knew that that fact alone did not tell the whole story. He was witnessing the gradual reemergence of the old Clay Grover who he knew as a friend. The Clay Grover who existed prior to the two of them falling in love and getting married. Aaron was a gay man in his mid-thirties with a healthy sex drive. But he knew that Clay had a far greater appetite for sex than he had himself. He thought that once they committed to one another that that side of Clay would fade away. Now, he wasn't so sure.

CHAPTER 26

L ABOR DAY, THE UNOFFICIAL END OF SUMMER and the beginning of the Presidential general election season. It was the time of year when the American electorate started to pay attention to the upcoming election in earnest. The stakes were high. The Democrats hoped to keep their control of Congress and win back the White House. The Republicans hoped that they could piece together a splintered coalition and retain, at the minimum, one branch of the Federal government.

AARON ROSE BOUNDED UP THE SHORT STEPS up to his house and giddily strode through the front door. His husband, Clay Grover was in the kitchen preparing dinner for the two of them.

"Wow! That smells good. What are you making sweetie?" Aaron inquired.

"I'm trying my hand at gumbo, plus I attempted for the first time to make cornbread from scratch. And finally, I made strawberry shortcake," Clay answered. "We'll see. We could wind up grabbing burgers down the street if this turns into an unmitigated disaster."

"Have you been listening to the local news?" Aaron asked.

"Nope, I had some Billie Holiday on earlier. It seemed like good cooking music. What's up? Why are you so giddy?"

"Senator Douglas is making a campaign appearance at Tulane in two weeks," Aaron joyfully announced.

"Really?" Clay asked with astonishment. "He's got zero chance of winning Louisiana. Why waste the time here?"

"Sounds like it's to support the down ballot Democratic candidates, the Governor and Samuel Marvin," Aaron said.

"That's cool."

"So, we're going right?" Aaron questioned.

"Sure," Clay responded. "But calm down Aaron. Let's just go and hear him speak, and let's leave the Chief of Staff business out of it. Alright?"

"Don't you want to get backstage and see him personally?" Aaron questioned with a sadness etched across his face. "I do."

"And you have every right to. You worked with him for years. You two had a wonderful relationship. I respect that, and the fact that you would want to say 'hello.' But I don't need to be a part of that."

"But won't it seem weird if I go backstage to greet him and my husband isn't there with me? The man attended our wedding, Clay," Aaron beseeched.

"Look, let's not argue about this now. It's two weeks away. Maybe, I'll change my mind by then," Clay answered. "I just don't want to be boxed into anything right now."

"Do you know how that sounds?" Aaron asked a bit peeved.

"I'm guessing not good, from the look on your face and the tone in your voice," Clay stated. "I respect your wishes to want to see him, I do, and you should. But similarly, you should respect my wish not to be a part of that if I so choose."

"Sometimes I don't understand you at all," Aaron huffed.

"Come on, don't be like that. I made this wonderful or perhaps godawful dinner, let's change the topic and just enjoy our evening together, ok?"

"Are we going to be together the entire evening?" Aaron challenged.

"Yes, of course," Clay responded.

"Even at 3:00 a.m.?" Aaron pushed.

"Aaron don't, please don't. I planned on making things up to you by trying to make us a nice meal and being attentive to your needs. Why do you have to ruin it with your attitude?"

"And why do you have to sneak out of our bed at 3:00 a.m. and go wherever it is that you go?" Aaron demanded.

"Listen to yourself. You're answering your own question," Clay responded as he turned off the stove and briskly walked out of the house.

FIFTEEN MINUTES LATER, CLAY GROVER WAS PERCHED on a barstool at French Tips, Juleps & Jazz ordering a scotch and water from Michael.

"Everything use to be so easy. No conflicts or arguments. Just a lot of fun, good times, and great sex," Clay lamented. "Now everything is a battle with him. I don't understand why he can't get it that I really don't want to be pressured into taking this new job if it comes to fruition. And that's a big 'if.' Nothing is set in stone, yet I'm supposed to be overjoyed at the prospect of accepting something that is still so nebulous."

"Have you told him that the prospect of this new job, whatever it is, is causing you anxiety, and that you'd rather not discuss it?" Michael asked.

"Yes. Every time he brings it up," Clay said while shaking his head. "It's complicated. I wish I could tell you what this is all about, but I promised someone that I wouldn't mention it. It's a very important position. And it would require us moving fairly soon. In a few months. Thing is, I didn't seek out the job. It was offered to me. And though it was very flattering to be asked, I have mixed feelings about accepting the job. It would be very high pressure and very high exposure. And as of today, no one is even sure if the job would be available to me."

"That's some job," Michael replied with a grin. "Someone offered you a job that may not be available to you?"

"I told you, it's complicated," Clay repeated.

"So, why is Aaron pressuring you to take a job that may not actually be available, that makes no sense?"

"It does and it doesn't," Clay replied. "He's not wrong for thinking that it may be there for me. That prospect seems to be increasing daily. But it's not for sure, not yet."

"Is it a good job? Is it a job that someone with your background would want? Is it something that you would wish for Aaron, if the shoe was on the other foot?" Michael questioned.

"Yes, to all those things," Clay replied.

"Then I'm confused," Michael confessed. "And the problems that you and Aaron are having are solely focused on this potential job? It has nothing to do with what we've talked about before, your sexual wanderlust or at least curiosity?" Michael bluntly asked. Clay sat there for a few moments and downed his drink.

"To be completely honest, it's both. I suppose I'm just focusing on the job aspect of it, because I feel guilty about not being satisfied with only having Aaron in my life sexually. That's not his problem. We have great times in bed. It's on me. That's my issue not his. So, I guess I'm just using the job thing to deflect from my own feelings of guilt and shame about wanting something else."

"Do you still love him? Do you still want to spend your life with Aaron?" Michael inquired.

"Yes, absolutely," Clay replied.

"Then go home Clay. Get off that barstool and go back home. You understand that this is not about Aaron's issues, it's about yours. If you want to save your relationship with him, go back home now," Michael firmly stated. Clay sat for a few moments taking in everything that Michael had said.

"You're right. You're so right. I've been putting this on him, when it's my problem that I haven't wanted to confront. Aaron is not pressuring me to take the job, he is encouraging me to seize an opportunity that few people are ever given. I would absolutely want the same thing for him. Thanks man, you've been a great friend to both of us." Clay stood up and walked out the door of French Tips. He did not walk home. He ran home.

CLAY ENTERED THAT ADORABLE LITTLE YELLOW shotgun house that they both fell in love with when they first moved to New Orleans. Aaron was sitting on the couch in total silence staring off into space, deep in thought.

"Aaron," Clay said barely above a whisper. "I am so sorry, please forgive me. I've been acting like an idiot because it was easier to do that than confront the truth. I've got a lot to tell you, and I am ashamed of all of it. I've got a problem. But I hope that you will listen to me and that we can work this through. I love you, and right now that is all you need to know." Aaron looked up at his husband and smiled.

"Sit down next to me Clay. Let's talk and work this out. We can do this together," Aaron replied as he took Clay's hand and pulled him down to the couch next to him.

By mornings light, they awoke, their bodies intertwined together in the same bed, still very much a couple in love.

CHAPTER 27

PRESIDENT ANDREW COCHRAN AND NATHAN WHITAKER sat in a hotel suite in Cincinnati, Ohio talking together as they awaited the commencement of a Town Hall meeting with residents of Cincinnati that would take place in the hotel's convention center.

"Where's Cindy appearing tonight?" Andrew asked his campaign manager.

"Congresswoman Bridgman is in Denver giving a speech at a rally in a couple of hours," Nathan responded.

"How has she been doing on the campaign trail?" Andrew inquired.

"She's been great. Cindy is a real pro. She comes across as very natural and caring. The crowds seem to love her," Nathan advised.

"Then she's turned out to be the right choice, just as you had recommended," Andrew replied with a smile. "And your relationship with her?"

"Neither of us have any time, and we are seldom in the same state, so there's nothing going on between us other than a healthy friendship."

"Ok, old chum, I believe you. It's hard for Cupid to work long distance, I get it," Andrew said with a wink of an eye.

"She's helping in the polls as well," Nathan added. "Douglas got a nice bounce after the Democratic Convention, but his lead seems to be dissipating as the voters begin to understand the moderate course we are charting for the country. We're only three points down. But of course, it's very early."

"That's not half bad for a candidate that just went to war with half of his Party," Andrew commented. "What about our fundraising efforts?"

"We're good for the rest of September. We've got enough cash on hand for us to fully spend in the battleground states that we've focused our attention on, but past say the first week of October, we've got to start raising more money. We've got a decent grassroots funding mechanism beginning to bring in some cash, but it's nothing compared to the Democrats. And of course, we lost some of our big dollar donors when we went to war with the Conservative right-wing of the Party," Nathan stated before taking a pause. "Which brings us back to a conversation you don't want to have. Jim Bob McCallum."

"Not happening, Nathan, don't waste your breath," Andrew emphatically responded.

"Andy, he's offering to fund your campaign with up to $100 million dollars. Additionally, he will actively pressure some of the well-healed Southern Conservatives that we lost with our move to the center to get back on board with our campaign. Not only with their votes, but with their wallets as well," Nathan encouraged.

"I don't care," Andrew replied. "I've never felt comfortable taking money or advice from that man. He was a necessary evil in my first campaign for the Presidency, but now that he is no longer part of our key donor group I want to keep it that way."

"It will make our efforts that much harder without him. He is eager to give us anything we need with respect to our financing issues. Without him, we're going to have to scrape by with what we have and forage for new donors," Nathan reiterated.

"I'm sorry Nathan, my mind is made up on this issue. We will not accept one penny from Jim Bob McCallum. We'll have to make do without his money and influence. If that costs me the election, so be it. That's a price I'm willing to pay to not be under that man's influence and beholden to his agenda," Andrew resolutely replied.

"Ok, I got it. But, if you don't accept Jim Bob's offer of friendship, in his mind, that makes you his enemy," Nathan cautioned.

"I'll take that chance."

LATER THAT NIGHT, PRESIDENT COCHRAN was taking questions from the assembled audience at the townhall meeting in Cincinnati that was a part of his Ohio campaign stop. The President shared light-hearted stories with the audience and intently listened to their expressions of concern for themselves and the country, as he attempted to answer their questions.

"Yes, next question, over here, you sir," President Cochran stated motioning to a middle-aged man in the third row.

"My name is Alex Broomfield, Mister President, and my question is about what you plan to do to bring good manufacturing jobs back to Ohio and other Midwestern states?"

"Thank you for your question, Alex. That is a very important and also complex question. During the primaries, a number of my opponents were quick to say that they would ensure that American companies will no longer send jobs to foreign countries. They also promised to reinstate jobs in industries that are no longer viable in the 21st century. So, I think we need to start this discussion with the realization that some of the jobs lost are never coming back. I understand that that is not something that people want to hear, but it is simply the truth of the matter. We now live in a highly technical and efficient society where robots can do the jobs that required manual laborers thirty or forty years ago. Technology has replaced the human element with a far more cost-efficient substitute. Those jobs are never returning. What we need to do is to provide retraining to the individuals that use to have those jobs in new more modern technologies so that they can return to a more vibrant and effective workforce. We also need to provide tax incentives for companies so that they want to open up new manufacturing facilities in this country instead of in China, India, or Mexico. That is of course, just the first steps that we need to take. And I hope to show you what American workers can look forward to in a second term of a Cochran administration."

"Yes, ma'am, right here in the first row," President Cochran stated pointing to an elderly woman in front of his low platform.

"Good evening President Cochran, my name is Sadie Swift, though everyone calls me Grandma Sadie. I am a practicing Buddhist and a life-long Democrat. I am here tonight because I am curious about you," the elderly woman bluntly stated.

"Welcome Grandma Sadie, I'm pleased to have all people of various religious and political affiliations at my campaign events," Andrew

Cochran responded. "Tell me, how can I assist you with your curiosity about me?"

"I'm trying to figure out who you are?" Grandma Sadie questioned. "Are you the right-wing bigoted jackaloon who campaigned as a staunch Conservative four years ago and won the White House promising deeply disturbing social policies or are you the middle-of-the-road moderate that you are portraying yourself as now? Which one is a fraud, and which one is the real Andrew Cochran?" A few 'boos' were shouted by a handful of members of the audience.

"No, please. Everyone is free to express their opinions here. It is a fair question. I can understand the confusion and concern. Admittedly, there has been a fairly severe shift in my rhetoric and especially in my policies as President since I was last elected four years ago. But before I answer your question, let me thank you for your choice of words. I love the term 'jackaloon.' For those of you who are unaware, it is the polite way of calling someone a 'jackass.' We will make that our word of the day. Now, to the substance of your question," Andrew Cochran began, but not before briefly taking a sip of water.

"No one who runs for President is ever fully prepared to take on the duties of the Presidency. All the campaign rhetoric in the world doesn't amount to a hill of beans once you assume the office. Mario Cuomo, the former Governor of New York, a good man and a liberal crusader, who I'm sure you knew of Grandma Sadie, once said, 'You campaign in poetry. You govern in prose.' What he meant was that despite all of the fancy and eloquent speeches and promises that you might make while campaigning for an office, once you assume that office you are faced with the real and daunting facts of the matters at hand. Serious problems cannot be solved by flowery rhetoric. You have to adjust to the circumstances. Partly, that is what I did after I took office as President of the United States. You are no longer serving your own constituency, you are serving all of the American people whether they voted for you or not. So, ideology is quickly replaced by reality. Added to that a scandal that rocked my administration very early in my first year caused me to move more swiftly to a moderate centrist approach to governing the nation than even I had anticipated. Once in office, I quickly discovered that 'compromise' is not a four letter word. Though there are some in my Party that would argue strenuously with that assessment. So, to sum up, I believe that I am a moderate Republican who believes in being fiscally responsible but who tries very hard to be accepting and open-minded when it comes to social issues. Does that answer your question, Grandma Sadie?"

"I'm not sure I'm buying it, but it will do," Grandma Sadie grudgingly responded with a grin on her face.

"Well then, that's good enough for me," President Cochran smiled and nodded. "Next question?"

POSY BRANCH WAS VERY FREQUENTLY WEARING a big smile as she talked to her customers at French Tips, Juleps & Jazz. The business was doing very well. A steady flow of customers during the weekdays and enormous crowds on the weekends. She was dating a good man who loved and respected her. And, with the hire of Lawton Cavanaugh as the new host and co-manager of the establishment, Posy had the ability to take a little more time off to enjoy herself.

"Lawton, sugar, you fittin' in real good," Posy said to her newest employee. "Customers are real happy with the way you been treating everyone, and the nail gals want to eat you with a spoon you so sweet to them."

"That's nice to hear," Lawton said with a satisfied grin. "I'm just treating folks like I would want to be treated. Show some respect and listen to any complaints without getting all defensive about it."

"Well, you do what you do, boy, cuz it's workin'," Posy replied. As Lawton greeted a couple of new customers entering the door, Posy walked over to the bar and began chatting with Michael.

"That boy is a natural charmer, he got a nice smooth easy way about him, don't he?" Posy asked Michael while watching Lawton talk with the new customers.

"Yeah, he's working out just fine," Michael agreed. "I know it's only been a few weeks since he started, but it's like he's been here for years. He gets along with everyone. He's always on time. He doesn't mind working double shifts or staying late to close up, he's been great so far. And, I hear tell that you're putting your extra time off to good use," Michael said with a sly grin.

"You boys talk too much. Y'all's worse off than a couple of cackling hens," Posy admonished, followed by, "What did Norris say?"

"Not much, just that the two of you are very much enjoying each other's company," Michael answered while raising his eyebrows and smiling from ear-to-ear.

"I ain't gonna lie to you Michael, that is one special man. He treats me like a queen. He listens to everything I say without judging or telling me that I'm wrong or stupid. I know that don't seem like much, but given how I was treated when I was Nathan's wife, it's night and day, sugar."

"I'm just glad that you're both happy. That makes me feel good, because you're both special people and you both deserve to be treated well," Michael said. "So, are things getting serious?" Michael asked. Posy paused for a few moments prior to responding.

"It's still a little too early to say 'serious' but things are surely moving in that direction. Norris is someone who I feel so comfortable with and he makes me laugh. I tell you true, if a man treats me with respect and makes me laugh, that's usually case closed. Folks take themselves way too serious. You gotta have fun in life. I'm a goof, you know that. I love to sing, and dance and have me a good time. I'm having some real good times with Norris. We like the same kind of music. He ain't afraid to get out on a dance floor and shake his money-maker. And, as I say, he likes to laugh and have fun."

"Oh, I know that. Sometimes when we're playing cards, Norris will tell a joke or say something and we're all laughing so hard, we're almost peeing on ourselves," Michael added.

"So, yeah, I'm real happy and I ain't afraid to show it. What about you, sugar? You got someone special on the side who makes you happy?" Posy asked.

"I'm good. I'm having my share of fun. You know me, I ain't the kind to get real serious with anyone. At least not at this stage in my life. Plus, I don't think I'm the marrying kind," Michael allowed.

"Speaking of the marrying kind, I saw Clay Grover sitting at the bar talking real serious with you a couple of times recently. He and Aaron doing ok?" Posy questioned with concern.

"I don't know," Michael acknowledged. "They're having some problems. Clay is going through some stuff right now, and he doesn't seem to want to talk to Aaron about it. I tried to persuade him to just sit down and talk about it with him, but ultimately it's up to them to work it out."

"Well, I hope they can get through whatever it is. They's such a sweet couple of boys, and they seem so right together. I hope they can make it work," Posy stated sincerely.

"I hope so too," Michael confirmed.

BESSIE COLLINS WAS IN THE BACKROOM OF HER SHOP carefully examining her ledger sheets for her business income for the past two weeks. Papa Levi sat on one of the wooden chairs opposite her small desk.

"If I did my ciphers correct, the last two weeks been the best weeks we done had since the Mardi Gras crowds come into the city in February," Bessie proudly declared. "Some of our old customers coming back and taking a shine to Mariette. They like her easy manner and she real good with folk."

"That surely is good news," Papa Levi said with a wide smile. "I watched one of her sessions with customers the other day. She nice and polite. Ask a lot of questions and done give a good reading. She ain't as dramatic as Esther was, but I think people like Mariette's approach better. Even when she do a séance, ain't all that shaking and moaning like Esther do. She just connect with the spirit world and give folk the answers they seek."

"I hear you good," Bessie added. "Esther brought in good money, they ain't no denying that fact. But Esther sure did bring her own baggage. With Mariette, it way more relaxed and comfortable in here. Money ain't quite like it was with Esther, but it's still early. Come the holidays, I bet we gonna be doin' just fine."

"Yeah you right, Miss Bessie. Once them holidays come on us, we gonna be living in the high cotton. We certain the Countess gonna be staying around the Big Easy come then?"

"I surely did ask her that very question just the other day," Bessie replied. "She done told me that she be looking for a more permanent place to stay around here. She is happy with the way things is working out. She still got kin in Cajun country she need to see every now and then, but she trying to get herself more situated here in New Orleans. She an old woman, she looking to stay more in one place. And she liking it here with us, so far."

"I got me a friend who is looking to take on a boarder, I can talk to him see what's what," Papa Levi offered.

"Oh, that'd be real nice. I think once she have a nice place to stay she be more willin' to put in more time here at the shop," Bessie said with a nod.

"Let me ask, and as soon as I know what my friend is looking for money-wise, I'll let you know and we can tell the Countess," Papa Levi related.

"That would be right fine. Now, let me count this here money one more time," Bessie said with a happy giggle.

CHAPTER 28

STANFORD WINCHESTER WALKED INTO ARNAUD'S RESTAURANT with a happy grin on his face. He surveyed the large formal dining room attempting to catch a glance of his dear old friend. Then, moments later he spotted Lucius Collins with his back to Stanford placing a drink order at the bar. Stanford walked over to the bar until he was just a couple of feet behind Lucius, who had no idea Stanford was standing directly behind him.

"You best tell Arnold to put in an order for a Sazerac," Stanford said in a deep bellowing voice. Lucius' body shook as he spun around on his heels in complete surprise.

"Oh, Lordy me, Stanford!" Lucius exclaimed. "I almost jumped right out of my own skin."

"I'm sorry my old friend. I saw you standing here and the childish imp inside me wanted to sneak up behind you and surprise you," Stanford said with a laugh.

"Oh, you surely did that," Lucius said as his rattled nerves began to relax. "Now that I done caught my breath, it is a lovely, if unexpected surprise to see you. Is Miss Whitlee in your company?"

"No, I'm afraid not. There is an evening event at the Fifth Circuit that she is attending tonight. A conference and dinner for a visiting judge from Great Britain or some such thing," Stanford related.

"Why don't you get yourself situated at your table, I see it's open and

I'll have a word with the maitre'd and let him know that that table is booked for the next two hours. And I'll get to having Arnold fix you a Sazerac just the way you like it right quick."

"Sounds like an outstanding plan," Stanford agreed. A few minutes later, Lucius appeared at Stanford's usual table with a well-crafted Sazerac.

"Have you been enjoying retirement?" Lucius asked as he placed the cocktail on the table in front of Stanford.

"Why yes, for the most part. I've been spending way too much time at Fritzel's in the middle of the afternoon getting into trouble with Calvin Putnam. But yes, it's nice not to have to worry about everything going on at court every day," Stanford stated.

"I saw on the news this morning that Presidential candidate Senator Douglas is coming to our fine city to give a speech in about ten days. There's gonna be lots of influential folks there. You thinking about going to see that? Rub shoulders and talk with some folks?" Lucius inquired.

"Well, most of the people that will be there still view me as an irascible old Republican, so I ain't so sure that they want their shoulders anywhere near mine," Stanford answered with a chuckle. "But back when I was nominated for the Supreme Court, Senator Douglas was the Judiciary Committee chair and he treated me with great respect. I met him at a funeral for his friend a few years later for a few brief moments. He's a good man. I've been listening to some of his speeches on the campaign trail. He is a man that I do admire, even though I may not agree with some of his political stances. It might be nice to see him speak in person. We don't get many Democratic candidates for President speaking down here in Louisiana. The more I think about it, that is an outstanding idea, Lucius. I believe that I will take that in."

"Very good sir, keep you and Mr. Putnam out of trouble for at least one afternoon," Lucius laughed. "Now, what can I get you for dinner?"

"Yet another good question," Stanford smiled.

NATHAN WHITAKER LOOKED AT THE SCREEN of his iPhone, and a slight shudder moved across his being. This was not the call he wanted after a good day on the campaign trail with President Cochran.

"Good evening Jim Bob," Nathan stated into his phone.

"Hello there Nathan. I see your boy is moving up in the polls. He's within spitting distance of that good for nothing Perry Douglas. Now, if you only had millions of dollars to get your message across to them stupid sheep, y'all call voters," Jim Bob responded with an oily tone in his voice.

"President Cochran is doing well given the fractured nature of the Republican Party. He's got a strong message for Independent voters who are pleased with the bi-partisan bills that have been passed by Congress and signed into law by the President that are moving this country forward," Nathan responded.

"I ain't one of your sheep, Nathan. You can save that candied-ass bullshit for them. Time is up. I need to know if your boy is going to accept my magnanimous gesture of friendship or is he going to do something self-destructive and politically stupid?" Jim Bob asked.

"After thoughtful contemplation, President Cochran thanks you for your generous offer of campaign support, however, he has asked me to inform you that he is going to decline your offer, with all due respect, of course," Nathan stated in a monotone voice with little emotion.

"Oh Nathan, that ain't good. And you know in your heart that ain't good. Either you're not trying hard enough boy or you done lost your magical spell over that wooden puppet you call your friend," Jim Bob scolded.

"I'm sorry, the President has made up his mind on this issue," Nathan added.

"Andrew Cochran ain't got a thought in his head unless you put it there Nathan. That's been true since the two of you were college punks chasing sorority skirts. So, all I can assume is that it's you that don't want to dance with me no more. And, as you damn know, that ain't sitting well with me. Four years ago I was the one who brung you and your puppet to the big dance. He don't smell the White House without my money and influence. And when you had your little misunderstanding with law enforcement, it was my money that bought you the best defense attorney money could buy. Now, you want me to go sit in the corner by myself, I don't think so," Jim Bob spat into the phone his voice raising with every word.

"Truly Jim Bob, this is the President's decision. To some extent, I agree with you. We will need money to push our message forward in

October. But, he is insistent, there is nothing that I can do to convince him otherwise," Nathan stated.

"Well then, seems like you've lost your magic touch, Nathan. Your wooden puppet thinks he's a real man and that's a dangerous situation for both of us," Jim Bob snarled.

"There's nothing more I can do. I'm sorry. Goodbye Jim Bob," Nathan said into the phone.

"We'll see about that," Jim Bob replied before throwing his cellphone against a wall.

THE DOUGLAS AND RAYMOND FAMILIES GATHERED backstage before they were all to make a campaign appearance together in Raleigh, North Carolina. Perry Douglas was accompanied by his wife Katherine and his son Robert. Hellen Raymond was flanked by her husband Malcolm and their children. Carolyn Barnes and Riley Banks stood off to the side as the candidates and their families posed for group photographs.

"They look good together. They all seem to like one another. It seems natural and not staged," Carolyn whispered to Riley.

"Yeah, but what does that really get you? Voters have become so jaded and cynical. They don't believe in sincerity or frankly care about likability anymore. Gone are the days of 'Camelot' when a good-looking young candidate and his sophisticated French-speaking wife could woo the world with their charming appeal and grace," Riley replied.

"I'm not sure that I buy that completely," Carolyn stated. "I think it's still important to have a candidate that people like and respect. Who they believe will fight for their interests when they get elected."

"Wow, you really are a liberal!" Riley exclaimed. "Voters will choose someone who will do what they think they want. Problem is, they've got no clue as to what they truly want that is in their best interest. People will claim to be Libertarians and want government out of their lives, just as long as they still get their Medicaid benefits and Social Security checks on time. There is little consistency to what they truly believe. It's all about perception. It's the qualities that they project on to a candidate as opposed to knowing the actual qualities of that candidate. Television creates reality it doesn't project what is real. You can run a pathological liar for public office. However, if television portrays him as telling the truth, then they believe that that person is truthful."

"How did a nice woman like Hellen Raymond get involved with such a cynical skeptic?" Carolyn asked with a grin.

"Senator Raymond knew that I was a Political Science professor. She wanted someone on her advisory staff she could count on to deliver her factual truth as opposed to parroting to her what she wanted to hear. Sycophants are a dime a dozen, truth tellers come at a much higher price," Riley smiled in response.

"Oh, so that's what we're calling ourselves these days, truth tellers, eh?" Carolyn chided back.

"Brilliant scholar or sage philosopher king aren't bad, if they are still available," Riley joked.

"I didn't realize that they cultivate such enormous egos at Chapel Hill?" Carolyn glibly retorted.

"Nothing but. Would you like to see my enormous ego? I don't live too far from here," Riley seductively inquired.

"Behave yourself," Carolyn stated, only to find Robert Douglas standing over her shoulder.

"Oh my, is someone other than me misbehaving?" Robert asked with salacious interest.

"We were just talking about my enormous ego," Riley answered with a crooked smile.

"You two degenerates can dazzle each other with the size of your egos. I've got a job to do," Carolyn sighed and shook her head as she left Riley and Robert standing off to the side. She swiftly walked towards the two candidates and their families.

"I'll show you mine if you show me yours?" Robert playfully asked.

OUTSIDE THE ENTRANCE DOOR TO FRENCH TIPS, Juleps & Jazz, Posy spotted a person lurking in the shadows outside on the street. It was late at night and the streetlights could only illuminate so much. Clearly the shadowy figure was peering inside of the establishment with great interest.

"Michael, you see that man outside shifting back and forth trying to see what's going on in here?" Posy asked her friend.

"Yeah, he's been there for about a half hour. I think it might be Olivier," Michael answered. "He keeps himself in the shadows so I can't say for sure."

"That's just creepy the way he darts from one corner of the building to the next. It seems like he's keeping an eye on Lawton," Posy stated.

"I think you're right," Michael replied.

"Well, only one way to know for sure," Posy said as she began to walk out the door of her salon and into the street.

"Hold up!" Michael called as he quickly reached for the baseball bat he kept behind the bar and raced to her side.

"Olivier Bellevue, is that you?" Posy called out as she approached the person.

"What business is it of yours bitch?" Oliver answered.

"Because this is my business and you been prowling around it," Posy angrily answered.

"I'm on a public street, minding my own business. You got no call to come out here and harass me," Olivier barked in return.

"No. You is minding my business and I want to know why?" Posy pressed.

"Is that Lawton Cavanaugh up in there?" Olivier inquired.

"Yeah. And he's working for me now, so you best leave that boy be," Posy responded.

"Why that traitorous little guttersnipe! I hired that boy when no one would touch him with a ten-foot pole. I taught him everything he knows about the nail business. I treated him like a younger brother. And now, he goes and works for a no account whore like you?" Olivier vehemently pronounced.

"Watch your mouth, Olivier," Michael warned.

"Or what? You gonna hit me with your bat. I'm on a public street, you got no cause for threatening me," Olivier responded.

"What do you want, Olivier?" Posy questioned. "You ain't welcome inside."

"Oh, y'all gonna find out what I want. You don't toss Olivier Bellevue out like some piece of trash and not pay the consequences. As they say, revenge is a dish best served cold."

"You best get on, or I'm gonna call the police," Posy stated. "They know all about you."

"I ain't done nothing wrong. But someday I just might," Olivier said as he walked off into the shadows.

CHAPTER 29

"**T**HAT WAS AMAZING!" CLAY GROVER EXCLAIMED in the exhilaration and exhaustion of the post tumescence of sex with his husband.

"If that is all it takes to keep you home at 3am, then I think we have this problem licked," Aaron proudly proclaimed.

"That was wonderful, breath-taking, and wholly satisfying, but the problem goes deeper than just having really great sex with you," Clay replied. "But it's my problem and I need to solve it myself."

"I can't help?" Aaron asked.

"Oh, don't get me wrong, that helped immensely. But us having sex together has never been part of my problem. I've never had sex with anyone else that has ever gratified me more than when I'm with you. The issue, my issue is that despite an experience just like this, that I still have cravings to have sex with other men. I know in my heart and in my head that it can never be this good with anyone else, but that doesn't forego me having the desire," Clay explained.

"So, now what?" Aaron questioned.

"I've got my first appointment with a sex therapist on Thursday," Clay stated. "Her name is Dr. Samantha Crawford. Her office is in the CBD."

"Does she want to see both of us?" Aaron inquired.

"Not at first. At some point during my therapy, she will probably want to do joint sessions with both of us. But to start, she only wants to see me. I need to figure out what drives my sexual urges to go outside our marriage. Once I understand the impetus, I might be better able to control my response and actions."

"Why a woman doctor?"

"She comes very highly recommended. She has had great success with treating sexual addictions. And frankly, I think I'd feel more comfortable talking to a woman than a straight man," Clay confessed.

"Aren't there any gay doctors who treat sexual addiction?

"Probably. But in my mind, seeing a gay doctor is probably not the best idea right now," Clay said with a sheepish grin.

"Oh yeah, that's probably a wise choice," Aaron responded.

"Changing the topic at least for the moment, I've been giving it a lot of thought and I think that we should both go to see Senator Douglas speak at Tulane together next week," Clay stated. "Furthermore, if we are given the opportunity we should both go backstage to extend our greetings and say hello."

"Are you sure?"

"Absolutely. Senator Perry offered me a position if he wins the election. How rude would it be of me not to go see his speech and then talk to him afterwards when he is right here in our hometown? I was raised better than that. I know better than that," Clay said with a wink.

"And you won't feel the pressure or anxiety you've been experiencing by doing that?" Aaron asked.

"Right this minute, no. When I'm there, I don't know yet. But if I can't handle that pressure, then there is no way in hell I should even consider taking the position of White House Chief of Staff. Plus, you never know, it's been several months since he and I spoke, he may have changed his mind or even forgot that he asked me at all," Clay responded.

"I doubt that that's the case, but you're right, you never know," Aaron acknowledged.

"I've spent far too much time agonizing over something that may never happen. I've never been afraid of a challenge before, I'm not sure how or why I've become such a stupid wimp these last few months. Even if the job was offered to me and I accepted it, I'd find out real fast if I could do the job or not. Henry Fitzsimmons would have kicked my butt up and down the Capitol Hill steps if he ever heard me whine and whimper the way I've been carrying on lately. All I've done is discredit his belief in me and embarrassed myself. But, we're burying that self-doubting mess of a Clay Grover. Let the real Clay Grover, the one who was Chief of Staff to one of the most influential, powerful and beloved Senators in this country's history draw breath again. The Clay Grover that was smart enough and courageous enough to pursue Aaron Rose because he understood that he couldn't possibly find a better lover and husband in the entire world. We're resurrecting that Clay Grover right here and now. The other one can go to hell!"

"Hallelujah!" Aaron exclaimed. "That's the Clay Grover I fell in love with!"

"I love you, Aaron. Thank you for not walking out on me. Trust me, I deserved it. Though right now, we need to stop talking in third person, it's starting to creep me out," Clay said with a hearty laugh.

"THAT WAS AMAZING!" NORRIS COALTREE SAID as he laid next to Posy Branch in his bed after an evening of amorous adventure.

"Yeah, that was real nice," Posy responded with a satisfied smile.

"Posy Branch, you rock my world," Norris stated sincerely. "I've never met anyone quite like you. You're by far the most beautiful woman I've ever dated. You're a very successful businesswoman, and you are great fun to be around. You're just amazing."

"Well, them is real nice words to hear, Norris. But don't be putting me on a pedestal, I get nervous with heights," Posy replied with a smile.

"I'll be there to catch you if you fall," Norris responded.

"Too soon to be making promises like that Norris. We just getting comfortable with one another. I ain't going nowhere. Big Easy is my home now. Let's just take it nice and easy, and we'll get there in time," Posy stated with a wink and a smile.

"It's just that I don't want to lose you," Norris countered.

"No worries sugar, I'm right here. I know a good man when I find one. But, I rushed once, I ain't gonna do that again. I jumped at the chance to marry a good-looking powerful man when I was a young girl. All that got me was being treated like a pretty lamp that you stick in a corner. And told that my bulb was too dim to associate with smart proper folk. Once bit best forget. One mistake better cake, my mama use to always tell me," Posy said.

"Alright, I heard ya and I understand," Norris nodded. "Different topic, how are things going at French Tips?"

"Oh, things are just fine. Michael probably done told you that we hired a new host and co-manager. His name is Lawton Cavanaugh. Sweet boy with a real nice disposition. He's giving Michael and I a chance to take some time off for ourselves. Customers love him, he's a fine addition to our little family. Only thing is that he used to work for Olivier Bellevue and Olivier been nosing around to see what's what. Did Michael tell you?" Posy asked.

"No, he sure didn't. I don't like the sound of that. When did this happen?"

"A couple of days ago. It really wasn't a big deal. Michael saw someone hiding in the shadows out on the street just looking inside. We thought it might be Olivier. So, I went out to the street and sure enough it was him," Posy answered.

"Posy, you shouldn't be doing things like that. Just going out to the street and confronting a possibly dangerous man," Norris scolded.

"Shoot, it was nothing. Besides, Michael was right by my side with his bat. Nothing was gonna happen. I just wanted to ask him what he was doing snooping around French Tips."

"And what did he say?" Norris questioned Posy.

"Nothing really. He was clearly upset that Lawton was now working for me, but that's about it. He went slithering away when Michael threatened to call the cops," Posy matter-of-factly responded.

"Did he make any threats to you or Michael?"

"He said something about not doing anything wrong, but he might. Something like that. I didn't pay it much attention," Posy answered.

"Posy, honey, you got to be careful. I told you we looked at him for Chiffon's murder, and he had an airtight alibi. But he's one disturbed man. He consorts with some criminal types. We're still keeping an eye on him. You got to promise me that you won't do nothing like that again. If you see him hanging around again, you call me. You hear?" Norris emphatically said.

"Yes, Sergeant Coaltree, I hear and I obey," Posy said seductively as she reached under the bed covers. "But for right now, let's get back to a few gun tricks."

"THAT WAS AMAZING!" PERRY DOUGLAS SAID as he exited the stage of the large auditorium in Richmond, Virginia where he had just participated in the first Presidential debate of the election campaign. "I'm pumped.

It was a smart, issue-oriented debate without any rancor or animosity."

"That was one of the better Presidential debates in decades," Carolyn Barnes added. "You both had a really good evening. No knockout blows were delivered, but the American people got to see and hear the differences between the candidates on substantive policy issues."

"Yes, I think we both represented ourselves and our viewpoints admirably," Perry continued. "I'm glad that it came down to the President and I, instead of say Cletus Sawyer or Jedediah Wilson. That would have been a whole different kettle of fish, that's for sure."

"Well, that wasn't the case tonight. There were times when it was hard to discern who the Republican candidate was and who the Democrat was," Carolyn responded.

"Andrew Cochran has come a very long way in his thinking and his rhetoric since he was elected as a firebrand Conservative four years ago. That's good for the country as a whole, but it does make it a little harder for me in this campaign to draw some distinctions. To say that he has moderated his stance would be to put it mildly. Four years ago, he was all for privatizing Social Security, now he seems to believe that government control is just fine."

"There are still many differences in your policy positions, and I think you did a nice job drawing the distinctions, but yes, it is a different campaign than he ran in the last election," Carolyn observed.

"Is there any snapshot data available as to who won?" Perry inquired.

"Yeah, some," Carolyn stated as she looked at her iPad. "You appear to be leading in the voter focus group data, but by a slight margin. For all intents and purposes, it seems more like a draw."

"I'll take that for my first Presidential debate against the incumbent President," Perry said with a grin.

"You should," Carolyn agreed. "It was a good night."

THE NEXT MORNING, THE POLLS REFLECTED the tightness of the race. Perry Douglas was leading some of the national polls by a margin of 3 points. A few polls had the race as basically a dead heat. The American voters seemed to like and be impressed with both candidates. In the dog-eat-dog world of power politics that was a win-win situation.

CHAPTER 30

Stanford Winchester stood in front of the mirror in his Royal Street home bathroom carefully adjusting his blue and green bowtie. What had been an everyday ritual was now a once in a great while exercise in donning proper attire. No longer a prestigious judge on a prominent Federal Circuit Court, Stanford in his retirement was more accustomed to wearing an open collar shirt and khaki slacks in the daytime instead of a custommade suit and tie. However, that day he was going to his alma mater, Tulane University to watch Senator Perry Douglas speak to a large crowd of students, supporters, politicians, and other New Orleans dignitaries. He was looking forward to the opportunity. Stanford put on his suit coat, once more adjusted the tilt of his bowtie, and smiled in the mirror. He was ready to return to the world of politics, if only for one day.

Clay Grover and Aaron Rose shared bathroom space in their small shotgun house as they both prepared themselves to attend the afternoon speech of Senator Douglas at Tulane University. Both men shared a common excitement as they readied themselves for their foray back into the world of Washington power politics.

"You good?" Aaron asked his husband, Clay.

"Absolutely," Clay replied.

"No anxiety or apprehension?" Aaron inquired.

"Nope, not at all," Clay answered. "I'm just looking forward to seeing Senator Douglas and some of his staff, it's been a while."

"Good, me too," Aaron agreed. "There are times I really miss some of the folks I used to work with. We were always like a very close-knit family. Plus, the Senator's son Robert is going to be at the rally as well. I haven't seen Robert since he was in his early 20's and still in college."

"I understand that Robert's been knocking them dead on the campaign trail doing the get-out-the-vote rallies on college campuses," Clay stated.

"Yeah, the boy has always been pretty well-spoken and charismatic. He's a great kid, I mean young man," Aaron responded.

"He's not that much younger than you, old man," Clay teased.

"Seven or eight years, I believe. He's turned into quite the advocate for gay rights," Aaron said with a smile.

"Did you know he was gay when you were working with his father?" Clay questioned.

"Officially, no. I mean, Senator Douglas never mentioned it to me, but then again, I'm not sure he would have even if he knew at the time. And Robert didn't say anything. Though we would give each other these knowing glances. You know, the hey, I'm a member of the band are you?"

"Ah, yes, you boys in the band," Clay grinned in return.

"You still good with going backstage after the speech and saying hello to the Senator, Robert, and the rest?" Aaron inquired.

"Sure. My bet is that the Senator doesn't even recall that he offered me the position," Clay replied.

"I'll take that bet, how much?" Aaron asked.

"Fifty bucks."

"What if the topic isn't raised or we don't get to speak to him?"

"Then it's a draw, no money exchanges hands," Clay stated.

"You're on," Aaron agreed.

"Speaking of on, put your suit coat on. We don't want to be late," Clay said while donning his own suit coat.

"My how things have changed. You've gone from not sure that you wanted to go at all, to now wanting to make sure that we're not late," Aaron kidded.

"Shut up and walk!" Clay commanded with a laugh as the couple headed towards the door.

BESSIE COLLINS WATCHED FROM THE SIDE of the beaded curtain into her backroom as Countess Mariette Aubuchon was in the midst of conducting a séance with two customers. The elderly woman gently swayed from side to side as she moaned slightly. Then, she began to take questions from the couple who were seeking answers about the unexpected death of their teenage son. Mariette listened intently and answered the questions in her own voice. Twenty minutes later, the couple emerged from the small room, thanked Bessie profusely and were on their way satisfied with what they had been told. After they left, Bessie walked into the backroom to find Mariette slumped over in her wooden chair.

"Mariette, Mariette, you ok?" Bessie asked with concern in her voice. Mariette raised up her body from the table and looked at Bessie.

"I'm fine, child. Just that I'm old and séances take more out of me than they used to," Mariette said wearily.

"How did you know all that stuff you done told them folks?" Bessie inquired.

"Bessie, folks tell me about their dearly departed. They show me a picture. I take what they give me, and the spirits tell me the rest. Most part, I'm trying to give folks comfort for their loss. Folks hear what they want to hear. Hopefully, I can help put their minds to rest just a little," Mariette explained.

"That couple sure was pleased with what you told them. They couldn't stop thanking me on their way out," Bessie stated.

"I do the best I can," Mariette replied. "But séances are rough on me now. I can't do but a few a month. Tarot cards, palm readings, tea leaves, that don't affect me much."

"How you liking the place that Papa Levi set you up in?" Bessie questioned.

"It's real nice. Good-sized room, comfortable bed, nice folks. I'm very appreciative of Papa Levi putting in a good word with his friend for me," Mariette answered. "I like it here. You both treat me fine."

"We're glad to have you here. You is real easy to get along with and the customers seem right pleased with the service you provide them."

"That surely is nice to hear. Sometimes folk don't give old people the time of day, but it ain't so here," Mariette said with a smile.

"So, you gonna stay with us for a piece?" Bessie asked.

"You know I got to get back to my kin in the bayou a couple of times a month, but other than that yeah. You is good people," Mariette replied with a soft smile.

"I'm surely glad to hear that," Bessie said happily.

SENATOR PERRY DOUGLAS HAD JUST FINISHED a rousing campaign speech at Devlin Fieldhouse on the campus of Tulane University. He was escorted to a large room where he was meeting and greeting with New Orleans politicians, dignitaries and some old friends. Patiently standing in line to greet Senator Perry was Stanford Winchester.

"Justice Winchester, what a delightful surprise and extraordinary honor," Perry Douglas stated as he extended his hand in friendship.

"Good afternoon, Senator Douglas, what a wonderful and passionate speech you gave. It was crafted brilliantly, and it was a joy to partake," Stanford Winchester responded with a warm smile.

"Thank you, Justice Winchester, I appreciate the kind words. I am so pleased to see you. Unfortunately, our paths have not crossed since Henry Fitzsimmons' funeral. And, may I say, it was so incredibly thoughtful of you to travel all that way to attend his memorial service. Henry would have been pleased and proud to have you there. Though we may have had our contentious moments, and disagreements on policy views, Henry and I thought very highly of you. You handled yourself with such dignity and grace at the Judiciary Committee hearings during what must have been a very trying time for you. You have my deepest respect and admiration," Perry said quite sincerely.

"Well, thank you Senator Douglas, that means the world to me. And please, call me Stanford. I retired from the bench at the end of last year. I am no longer a judge, I am but a proud citizen," Stanford stated.

"Yes, I heard about your retirement. It saddened me that you were no longer on the federal bench. I hope that you are enjoying a very well-earned retirement," Perry replied.

"I'm getting into some trouble in the afternoons from time to time. New Orleans can be a dangerous place for a man with too much time on his hands," Stanford responded with a chortle. "But, yes, I am enjoying my leisure time. Fortunately, I married a wonderful woman who keeps me in my place."

"Indeed. I understand that you are married to Judge Hammond. I've heard wonderful things about her professionally," Perry allowed. "By chance is she with you today?"

"Unfortunately, not. She had an oral argument scheduled for this afternoon, so she was unable to attend. I am truly blessed. She is a remarkable judge and an exceptional person. I still have no idea what she ever saw in the likes of me?" Stanford laughed.

"No doubt she saw a brilliant jurist and a very good and decent man," Perry answered. "I apologize they are waving me over for a short press conference. May I trouble you for your contact information? I'd love to continue our conversation in the very near future, if you would be so kind."

"Absolutely, that would delight me no end," Stanford eagerly replied. "I'll jot down my information and give it to your aide."

"Thank you so much. There is so much I'd like to talk to you about. I'd relish getting your insights on a number of topics that I've been thinking about lately," Perry said.

"It would be my honor and pleasure," Stanford stated. "Good luck to you Senator Douglas, it was a wonderful speech and I very much look forward to speaking to you anytime."

Stanford watched as Senator Douglas was quickly escorted to a location where the local press waited for a brief Q&A session with the candidate. He smiled, happy to have had the opportunity to share a few words with an old foe and a new friend.

AARON ROSE AND CLAY GROVER MILLED ABOUT in the large meet and greet room waiting for Senator Douglas to finish his press availability. As they waited, Aaron spied Robert Douglas out of the corner of his eye.

"Robert, Robert!" Aaron exclaimed attempting to gain Robert's attention.

"Hey Aaron," Robert replied as he turned and walked towards Aaron. "Great to see you!"

"Look at you, all grown up," Aaron stated. "You were just a scruffy college kid last time I saw you hanging out in your dad's Senate office."

"Yeah, I've put on a few pounds, shaved that nonsense off my face, and can afford a decent haircut now," Robert admitted.

"Oh, Robert, I'd like to introduce you to my husband, Clay Grover," Aaron said by way of introduction.

"Very nice to meet you Clay," Robert said as he extended his hand to Clay. Clay and Robert shook hands as Robert looked over at Aaron.

"My mom and dad had told me that you were married. They loved attending your wedding, but they didn't tell me about Clay. Good work Aaron! He's absolutely gorgeous."

"I'm right here," Clay kidded while blushing.

"I'm sorry," Robert apologized and turned to Clay. "You're absolutely gorgeous!" Robert said directly to Clay with a big smile on his face. Clay blushed a little harder.

"Thanks," Clay replied. "I did pretty good for myself, as well," he smiled while putting his arm around Aaron.

"Oh, you sure did," Robert agreed. "The two of you should be models for the little plastic figures they put on wedding cakes. You are the perfect gay couple. And as to Aaron, when I first met that one, my young body shivered. I thought good work dad, you're hiring gay Abercrombie boys now. If you'll recall, Aaron, the first time I met you, my dad's secretary basically had to drag me out of his office so that the two of you could get some work done."

"I do remember that," Aaron laughed. "I thought that you were just being a defiant teenager."

"Oh no. I was smitten. She had to drag me out of there. I just wanted to be around you. You just confirmed how gay I was for me." Aaron began to blush at Robert's frankness.

"Anything for the cause," Aaron said with a grin. "And speaking of causes, what a wonderful job that you're doing, Robert, on behalf of your father. You are a rock star out there on the campaign trail. You are drawing large college crowds at the get out the vote events and getting a lot of young people involved with the campaign."

"As you said, anything for the cause," Robert responded with a wink and a smile. "It's pretty crazy. I never had any desire to be involved in politics. But when dad announced his intentions to run for President, well, I knew I had to help any way I could. So, they put me out there doing college campuses and I really took to it. I'm proud of who I am and I'm not afraid to talk about it to anyone who is willing to listen. And, of course, I'm so proud of my dad, and was more than willing to talk about him and his plans for this country. It really wasn't anything big, just me talking to people. But, I have to tell you, when you get in front of a large crowd and they're cheering and chanting and sharing the love with you, it's intoxicating. I love it. There's such a rush of adrenaline right before you go on stage. It's almost sexual. Sometimes, I have to check myself, you know?"

"OK, we might be straddling the line of TMI here, too much information," Aaron laughed. "Oh yeah," Robert uttered. "I feel so comfortable talking with you guys. Just chalk that one up to a little girl talk."

"No worries," Clay grinned.

"I take it you guys are hanging around to say 'hi' to dad, right?" Robert asked.

"Yes, but if he's too busy . . ." Aaron replied before Robert took Aaron by the hand.

"Come with me boys, we're going to the boss lady." Robert led Aaron and Clay through the tight packed crowd moving towards Carolyn Barnes.

"Carolyn, you remember Aaron," Robert said by way of introduction.

"Of course," Carolyn replied with a big grin. "How are you, Aaron?"

"I'm great, thanks. It's so nice to see you," Aaron stated enthusiastically. "I'd like to introduce you to my husband, Clay Grover."

"Nice to meet you Clay," Carolyn said. Clay nodded and repeated the sentiment.

"Carolyn was the Senator's communications director when I was working as an aide," Aaron related to Clay. "And now she is the successful campaign manager for the next President of the United States."

"We'll see about that," Carolyn chuckled. "There's still a long way to go."

"My darling, these scrumptious men would like to speak with papa," Robert stated in a very effected English boy accent. "Could you end that intolerable press engagement?"

"You see what I have to put up with from this one?" Carolyn said to Aaron and Clay nodding in Robert's direction. "I love the boy, and he's one of our most popular and successful campaign surrogates, but some days . . ." she laughed.

FIVE MINUTES LATER, AARON AND CLAY HAD BEEN TAKEN by Carolyn to a quiet office room away from the meet and greet crowd, where they were soon joined by Senator Douglas.

"Aaron and Clay, how wonderful to see you," Senator Douglas said as he entered the room with his hand extended toward Aaron.

"It's a distinct honor to see you sir," Aaron replied with a smile. "Your speech was uplifting. It was truly excellent."

"A pleasure to see you Senator," Clay offered. "And I wholeheartedly agree with Aaron's assessment, it was a great speech."

"Thank you, gentleman. I'm so pleased that you could find the time to take in some of my political babble," Senator Douglas replied with a laugh. "I try to keep honing my speeches and shorten the time it takes to deliver them, but Carolyn informs me that I'm doing a miserable job and that they tend to meander a bit too much and for far too long."

"I didn't think so," Clay responded. "I thought it was right on point and delivered with poise and alacrity."

"I am so pleased to see both of you. Unfortunately, I don't have a lot of time to visit. Carolyn has booked another appearance for me in Baton Rouge. The campaign bus leaves in a few minutes, or so I've been told. But, Clay, I'd like to follow up on the conversation we had in Chicago several months ago," Senator Douglas said as Aaron glanced at Clay with a grin on his face.

"I can have Robert show me around the campaign bus," Aaron offered as a way of giving Clay and the Senator the room for a private conversation.

"No, please stay Aaron, this concerns you as well," Senator Douglas replied. "It's still two months away and it is a very tight race, but what I said several months ago still holds true, Clay. If I happen to be lucky enough to persuade the American people to elect me as their next President, I would very much like for you to be my White House Chief of Staff. I don't need an answer today of course, but will you seriously consider it?"

"That is a great honor sir, one that I'm not fully certain that I deserve," Clay responded. "But of course, I will give it deep thought and reflection, Senator Douglas."

"Excellent," Senator Douglas remarked. "And Aaron, if I am elected President, it would please me if you would consent to being on my White House counsel staff. Would you please consider it?" Aaron was shocked by the invitation. He took a few moments to settle himself.

"Yes, of course, Senator Douglas. Like Clay, I'm not sure that I'm deserving of such an honor, but I certainly will give it serious consideration," Aaron gushed.

"Well, very good, that pleases me no end. Though, it is all up to me now to win," Senator Douglas chuckled. "There's Carolyn giving me the two-minute warning. I must be off, but I'll be in touch with both of you in the very near future. It's was wonderful to see both of you again. And, if I don't screw this up perhaps we will all be working together again just like old times."

"Thank you, Senator. Good luck," Aaron wished Senator Douglas as he left the room. Clay took his wallet out of his back pocket and counted out fifty dollars2 and handed it to Aaron with a sheepish grin on his face.

"Easiest fifty dollars I ever made," Aaron stated while putting the money in his pocket. "You and me working in the White House together!" Aaron exclaimed.

"Wow, that was surreal!" Was all Clay could answer.

CHAPTER 31

SEPTEMBER SLIPPED INTO OCTOBER AS THE RACE for President became more intense, yet the two candidates Senator Perry Douglas and President Andrew Cochran maintained a sense of civility and decorum in campaigning against one another. Each candidate demonstrated the differences they had in policy positions, but the rhetoric remained without vindictiveness, false insinuations, and ugly partisanship. However, that did not mean that there wasn't a burning will to win on behalf of both camps. Surrogates pushed the fundamental differences, and the strategic campaign planners were invested in opposition research and attempting to exploit any and all real or perceived weaknesses of the opposition.

NATHAN WHITAKER LOOKED AT THE TELEPHONE NUMBER on his cell phone, he did not recognize the caller, though he was aware of the fact that it was a Houston, Texas area code. Normally, he would not answer and allow the caller to leave a voice mail message, but this time Nathan decided to take the phone call.

"Hello," Nathan intoned into the phone.

"Is this Nathan Whitaker?" The booming voice with a Texas accent inquired.

"Yes, this is he. Who am I speaking with, please?" Nathan asked.

"Nathan, this is Race Casserly. We've met a couple times on the political rubber chicken circuit in Houston."

"Yes, Mr. Casserly, I recall," Nathan confirmed.

"Nathan, please call me Race. I ain't one for needless formality. Besides, I like to think of us as friends," Race responded.

"Alright Race, what can I do for you?" Nathan bluntly asked.

"Oh, it ain't what you can do for me Nathan, it's what I can do for you," Race replied. "You see Nathan, I'd like to ensure that Andrew Cochran remains President of the United States. I'm not a big fan of Perry Douglas and his tax and regulations way. I'd rather see a practical Republican who understands the needs of big business to be the caretaker of our nation's economy. Someone who doesn't despise oil companies with all his heart. I do believe Andrew Cochran to be that man, and I just want to offer him my support."

"Thank you, Race, the President is grateful for all the support he receives, however, he is not in a position to make any promises at this time," Nathan explained.

"I ain't looking for promises, Nathan, I only request careful and thoughtful reflection and consideration for a very few policy positions, nothing more," Race stated.

"You mentioned something about your support?" Nathan queried.

"Yes of course, I am willing to support President Cochran's re-election campaign to the tune of fifty million dollars."

"That's a very generous offer," Nathan said after a brief hesitation at the magnitude of the donation. "However, all I can do is make the President aware of your proposed contribution to his campaign."

"Of course, please do make the President aware of my offer, however, let's not play games here, Nathan," Race said slowly and with conviction. "I am well aware that your campaign is strapped for money. Some of your big money donors from the right-wing of the party have abandoned you. And, President Cochran will not allow himself to be sullied by Jim Bob McCallum's money and demands. You need to finish off October with a bang. You desperately need this money to move the campaign forward."

"How do you know about Jim Bob McCallum?" Nathan asked stunned that Race was aware of that situation.

"Nathan, I'm a businessman. The old adage that 'knowledge is power' could not be more true. I have an intelligence gathering arm of my company that would make the CIA blush with envy. Hell, some of my boys taught the Russians how to hack computer infrastructures when we were closing an Arctic Circle oil drilling deal with the powers that be in Moscow. I know a good deal about a good many things, Nathan. And that includes a good many secrets, that y'all would love to keep as secrets. But that is neither here nor there, because we're friends and friends zealously protect the secrets of other friends. This phone call is merely to extend a little financial support to my choice for President, that's all."

"I'll have to discuss this with the President," Nathan said flatly, his head reeling from all of the implications in Race's last statement.

"Of course you do Nathan, of course you do. Take a few days and think about it. I'll be back in touch soon. Goodbye, my friend," Race stated before ending the call.

Nathan felt a shiver traverse his spine. The big dogs were running the street and he knew that staying on the porch was no longer an option.

POSY BRANCH SAT IN HER BACK OFFICE at French Tips, Juleps & Jazz reviewing the previous month's financial records when her co-manager Lawton Cavanaugh entered the small room.

"How's it going?" Posy asked with a happy smile.

"We've got a real nice crowd for a Wednesday afternoon," Lawton reported. "All the nail technicians are busy, and we've got a half dozen clients waiting for appointments drinking at the bar and chatting with Michael."

"He certainly pleases the women, ain't no debating that point," Posy stated.

"Well, visually and with his fun-loving personality," Lawton added with a grin.

"That's true, and the girls can only hope," Posy chuckled. "So, what's your story, Lawton? I mean, I don't want to get too personal, and you can just tell me to mind my own business."

"No, that's alright, I don't mind talking about it," Lawton responded.

"So, you got a girlfriend?"

"Nope. I'm single and ain't rightly looking to be tied down just now," Lawton stated. "I've been through some stuff. Only been the last couple of years that I figured out who I was and what I wanted."

"How so?" Posy questioned.

"I've been a bit confused about my sexuality for a few years. Or rather, let's just say that I was keeping my options open. I've had a couple of boyfriends and a few girlfriends. I experimented in my twenties and wasn't really sure what I wanted. Though, I haven't been with a man for a couple of years now, and my last experience was pretty bad. I'm pretty convinced that I am happier both psychologically and physically with women."

"I'm sorry to hear that you had a bad experience, but we all do at one time or another. I had a bad marriage that lasted way too long," Posy related.

"Michael told me that Olivier Bellevue was prowling around a bit ago," Lawton stated.

"Yeah, he's an odd bird. He's just trying to rile up Michael and me," Posy replied.

"I think he was trying to find out how I was fitting in here," Lawton allowed with a shake of his head. "You see, Olivier was the bad relationship that I was talking about. When I first started working for him, I was still into dating boys. Olivier took a liking to me. He wasn't really my type, but one thing led to another at work. He was always flirting with me, trying to push the limits. And one night, after way too many drinks, he and I got together. It was interesting. He was so much different than some of the young boys I had been with. So, we continued on for a while. Then Olivier, started to get serious. He told me that he loved me and wanted to spend his life with me. I was having fun, but I sure didn't want to get serious with him. For me, it was just sex. Well, he kept pushing me and I kept resisting. Then the sex started to get too rough for me. Olivier was into things that I didn't want to do. It's when he threatened my job if I didn't stay his boyfriend that I knew I had to get out of that situation. And, it wasn't easy, but I finally left him."

"That sure explains a lot," Posy stated. "I couldn't understand why he was snooping around. He knows he don't scare Michael or me. I get it now. Well, don't you worry about a thing Lawton. We're gonna take care of you. If Olivier tries to approach you, you just let me know. My boyfriend is a police sergeant, so we can take care of things if Olivier gets out of line."

"Thank you, Posy, that's good to know. I don't think he wants to hurt me, he's just curious as to what's going on," Lawton replied. "But as you said, he's a strange bird."

ROBERT DOUGLAS WAS NOT PART OF THE TRAVELING Douglas campaign that went on to Baton Rouge and then headed to Orlando. Instead, he stayed in New Orleans for a couple of days. He attended another get out the vote event at Loyola University of New Orleans. He informed the college crowd that he decided to remain in New Orleans instead of moving on to Baton Rouge with his father because he understood that "Jesuits really like to party." After his appearance at Loyola, Robert decided to put that statement to the test by taking in the festivities in the French Quarter. After dining at Root on Magazine Street, Robert headed to the gay bars on Bourbon Street for a lively night of entertainment. Robert kept an eye on the Bruno Mars video at Bourbon Pub while he scoped out the crowd. He was in a festive mood after a successful appearance before another adoring college crowd. After a couple of hours at Bourbon Pub, Robert went to Good Friends and Lafitte's before ending his evening at the gay bar OZ around 2:00 a.m. Robert sat on a stool underneath the gyrating buttocks of a go-go boy perched above him dancing on the bar. A tall muscular, very attractive man soon occupied the stool to Robert's right. Robert tried to discreetly check out the attractive stranger while slipping a dollar bill in the dancer's thong.

"Pretty nice bubble butt," Robert said to the stranger to his right while nodding in the dancer's direction.

"It's not bad, but he needs to firm it up," the stranger replied.

"Looks pretty tight to me, but then again, I'm not a dancer," Robert responded.

"I was, right here at this bar a couple years ago," the stranger stated very matter-of-factly while running his hand through his long blonde hair.

"I'm Robert, nice to meet you."

"My name is Michael. Are you from around here?"

"No, I'm just in town for a couple of days. I was here . . ." Robert began before stopping himself, thinking that he didn't want to reveal his identity or his purpose in town. "I was visiting a friend that goes to Loyola."

"That's cool," Michael answered.

"And you, what do you do now that you're not a dancer?" Robert asked.

"I'm a bartender, manager, and jack-of-all trades at a nail salon, bar, jazz club in the French Market area called French Tips, Juleps & Jazz."

"You like it there?"

"I absolutely love it. I work for a friend of mine who is an absolute hoot. She has so much energy and she's such a fun person to be around. Every day is a little Mardi Gras with her," Michael related to Robert.

"Sounds wonderful. It's so great if you can have fun and be relaxed at work," Robert said with a smile.

"Where you from, what do you do?" Michael asked.

"Chicago. I'm a curator at an art gallery in the River West neighborhood of Chicago."

"You like what you do?" Michael inquired.

"I do, though I've been away from it for a bit. I'm helping a friend," Robert white-lied.

"Welcome to the Big Easy, Robert. We're all friends here. Can I buy you a drink?" Michael asked.

"Absolutely!" Robert exclaimed, hopeful for a great end to a very good day in New Orleans.

CHAPTER 32

Stanford Winchester fished his cell phone out of his pants pocket as he sat in his parlor at home reading a newspaper. He looked at the screen and did not recognize the caller other than it was a Washington, D.C. area code. Stanford slid the bar of his iPhone.

"Hello?" Stanford intoned.

"Justice Winchester, this is Thomas Jacobs, I am an aide to Senator Douglas. The Senator would like to speak with you, may I connect you?"

"Of course," Stanford answered

"Justice Winchester, this is Perry Douglas, how are you sir?" Senator Douglas asked.

"Why, Senator Douglas, this is a distinct honor, sir. I am well," Stanford responded.

"Excellent! Justice Winchester I was hoping to take advantage of your generous offer to speak with me about a number of issues that I would very much like to get your opinions about, sir," Perry Douglas began.

"I am pleased to assist any way I can, Senator, but I am but a private citizen with little useful knowledge outside of my career in law," Stanford stated.

"Well, it is your lifelong knowledge of the law and its practical applicability that I would like to draw from," Perry Douglas answered. "The gist of my call is due to the fact that I have been working on my policy positions on law enforcement reform and I would like to get your feedback on a number of issues, if you would be so kind. For example, I am going to call for the repeal of minimum sentencing guidelines. Too many of our citizens are sitting in prison for victimless drug dealing or possession crimes. I am also against the privatization of prisons. I find imprisoning people for profit a slippery slope that can easily lead to quotas and systemic abuse. I'd also appreciate your views about the tort reform legislation currently wallowing in Congress."

"That is an impressive list of topics, Senator. I'd be pleased to give you my thoughts for what little they are worth. But I am not a scholar or political operative, all I can offer to you are my opinions," Stanford replied.

"That is exactly what I'm looking for Justice Winchester, your opinions and your passion about the law," Perry Douglas responded.

"In that case, I'm all yours, ask away," Stanford said with pride.

"Wonderful. Thank you so much for your time and invaluable insights. Let's begin with sentencing guidelines, shall we?"

NATHAN WHITAKER WAS ABOARD AIR FORCE ONE as President Cochran traveled to Ohio for a campaign rally in Toledo. Nathan waited in the main cabin as the President concluded a phone call with his National Security Advisor.

"Nathan, I'm sorry, have you been waiting long?" President Cochran asked his campaign manager and old friend.

"No sir, just staring out the window while sipping on some bourbon," Nathan explained.

"Sounds like a good plan, the bourbon that is," Andrew Cochran replied with a grin. "So, you want to talk campaign finances I'm told?"

"Yes sir. I believe we have a big money donor who would like to assist with financing our campaign as we come down to the wire," Nathan stated.

"And who is this angel come from heaven?" Andrew asked with a smirk.

"Race Casserly," Nathan bluntly said.

"The Houston oil billionaire?"

"One in the same."

"I thought he was the money man behind Howard Mason's primary campaign?" Andrew Cochran questioned.

"He was, and now he'd like to help you get re-elected," Nathan answered.

"Let's start with the obvious, what does he want?" Andrew inquired.

"We haven't discussed specifics yet, but I'm sure the list includes loosening EPA regulations for gas emissions, granting drilling rights to government held wilderness areas, ending the ban on oil drilling in the Arctic Circle, and the other usual demands from oil concerns," Nathan stated.

"And what is the neighborhood of his contribution to our campaign?"

"Possibly, up to fifty million dollars," Nathan replied without flinching.

"That's a damn nice neighborhood," Andrew said with a chuckle. "What's the catch?"

"I'm not sure, I'm trying to figure it out," Nathan reported.

"It's a lot of money for EPA regulations," Andrew countered. "Find out what all of the attached strings constitute. I'm not going to accept his money unless I know precisely what it is that he wants from my administration. Also, let's look into his background as well. All I truly know is that he is third generation oil money, and that he is a bit of an odd recluse."

"Yes sir. This could be just what we need, a fresh infusion of cash for the last month of the campaign," Nathan offered.

"Not without knowing all of the conditions attached to that cash, Nathan," Andrew declared.

"I'm on it," Nathan assured his friend.

"HOW IS THERAPY GOING?" AARON ROSE ASKED his husband Clay as the two sat down for dinner together at their Marigny neighborhood home.

"Well, I've only had three sessions, but I feel like we're making some progress," Clay responded.

"Any clues as to where the issue may have started?"

"The fact that I repressed my sexuality for so many years when I was growing up and then even as a young adult probably didn't help matters, but that doesn't tell the whole story. Some people are just more sexually curious. Some act upon it, and some don't," Clay explained.

"You like your therapist?" Aaron inquired.

"I do, though I'm still learning to trust her and trust myself, which isn't that easy for me," Clay stated.

"Is there a connection between the promiscuous behavior and the stress of possibly becoming a very powerful and influential person?" Aaron asked.

"That was more of an excuse than something that had a causal effect, I think," Clay answered.

"Speaking of . . ." Aaron began before stopping himself.

"It's all right, you can ask me if I've been thinking about it," Clay told Aaron. "And yes, I have been giving it a lot of thought. I haven't made up my mind yet, but I am certainly more open to the idea of returning to Washington than I was before. And what about you? Do you want to go back into politics and return to DC?"

"I'm not sure either, but it's hard to not want to be part of the White House Counsel's office if you're an attorney. Just two years on one's resume could open a lot of doors," Aaron stated. "Don't get me wrong, I love our life here and the work we do is rewarding, but ultimately I'm not sure I would want to do this for the rest of my life. This is a once in a lifetime opportunity."

"Yeah, that's what I've been thinking. It would probably only be for four years, and probably less. Chief of Staff is not a position that one stays in for very long. But what an experience it could be," Clay said wistfully.

"So, we're going back to Washington?" Aaron asked.

THERE IS A PHRASE WHOSE ROOTS CAN BE TRACED back to the 14th Century and Geoffrey Chaucer. "Mighty oaks from little acorns grow." Early October and the acorns had fallen from the tree. The lucky acorns that do not get devoured by hungry squirrels, deer, or an assortment of other woodland creatures claim their territory by sending an embryonic root down into the soil to anchor the plant and search for water. In Washington, DC and in New Orleans the embryonic roots were being planted. Now, it was just a matter of them being allowed to grow.

CHAPTER 33

NATHAN WHITAKER PACED BACK AND FORTH with his cell phone securely held in his hand. He looked down at the screen of his phone before glancing back up and around the room. Then he glanced back down to the screen. This was the portrait of indecisiveness. Finally, Nathan scrolled through his contacts and selected a name. The phone rang as Nathan took a deep breath.

"Nathan Whitaker," Race Casserly answered his phone. "My guess is that you are calling with good news."

"Well, I can tell you that President Cochran has a level of interest in your magnanimous offer of campaign funding support," Nathan reported.

"But he wants to be sure he knows what I want in return," Race quickly asserted.

"I guess that is one way to put it," Nathan responded.

"I'd rather view it as friends helping friends," Race stated. "Andrew Cochran is a good man who I personally believe will better represent this country than Senator Douglas. I want him to retain the White House and I will do whatever I can to see that that happens. Conversely, if I ever need a little help with a regulatory agency or with diplomatic assistance on a foreign business deal, I would assume that my friends Nathan Whitaker and Andrew Cochran would afford me and my interests all due consideration and reasonable accommodation. This is about friendship, Nathan."

"I understand, however it is the President's position that . . ." Nathan began before being interrupted by Race.

"Nathan, Nathan, you're looking at this all wrong. What part of friendship do you not understand?" Race asked with an unctuous tone in his deep voice. "Do not ask today for a grocery list of things that may not be required from the local market for over a year or longer from now. Some days you may need a standing rib roast, other days you only require peanut butter. Lists are only snapshots of a moment's desire, they should not be seen as definitive or all inclusive. You get my meaning?"

"I understand, but of course, there have to be limitations. There is a big difference between Russian caviar and canned tuna fish," Nathan offered in response extending the grocery list analogy.

"Friends don't take advantage of friends. They help each other to the best of their ability. Isn't that right, Nathan?" Race questioned.

"Yes, that is true, but even in the best friendships there must be boundaries that exist and are adhered to in order to preserve and protect the mutual advantages of the friendship," Nathan countered.

"You see there, I do believe that you are talking about small accommodations made to acquaintances, not the strong bond of dear and reliable friends," Race challenged. "I want us to be excellent friends who trust and respect one another, Nathan. Friends who will do anything to foster and promote the best interests of their friends. But this is a dance of semantics that I would rather not participate in with friends. I am putting forth my money, influence and unswerving devotion to aid my friends in the final critical month of campaigning. Do you really want to define our friendship now in any other terms?"

"I see your point," Nathan conceded after a few moments of deliberation before responding. "President Cochran and I welcome your friendship."

"Excellent, Nathan, simply excellent. And have no fears, I don't take advantage of my friends, I only assume to have their full support. Once we end this conversation, I will have the first installment of my devotion wired to your campaign office. I can only hope that you are as happy about our mutual commitment to each other as I," Race stated.

"Of course."

LAWTON CAVANAUGH WALKED SWIFTLY THROUGH the French Market neighborhood of New Orleans on his way to work at French Tips, Juleps & Jazz. He politely smiled at local merchants as he traversed the streets of the French Quarter. Lawton enjoyed the atmosphere at French Tips, and he certainly enjoyed the friendship extended to him by Posy, Michael and the other employees as well. Posy had been right. They treated each other as a tight knit and happy family. Even the newcomer. Lawton continued his sojourn to French Tips until he felt someone tugging on the back of his jacket. He quickly spun around on his heels to see who was behind him.

"What's up, Lawton?" A smiling Olivier Bellevue asked.

"Hello Olivier," Lawton blankly responded. "Not much, I'm on my way to work."

"Yes, I heard that you're working for that stupid cunt, Posy Branch," Olivier challenged.

"Please don't refer to her like that. She's a friend of mine," Lawton hastily corrected.

"She ain't your friend. She don't give two shits about you, Lawton. She only cares about what she can get from you. And once she's done with you she will kick you to the curb just like she does with everyone else," Olivier protested. "I speak from first-hand experience. She's a traitorous bitch, I'm here to tell you."

"That's not the sense that I get from her. Posy and the rest of the staff have treated me real well. I'm happy with them," Lawton countered.

"She's just stringing you along for the ride, you'll see. When she's done with you and you ain't important to them anymore, she won't be so friendly. I know what I'm talking about," Olivier persisted.

"If and when that happens, I'll deal with it, but it sure ain't the case now," Lawton responded.

"That woman don't care about no one but herself. She is an ice bitch with a cold heart. She won't love you like I did," Olivier confessed. "We had something real nice going on. I admit that I may have come on a little too strong and you were young and I may have scared you off, but I've learned from that mistake."

"It's over," Lawton confirmed. "I was young and didn't know better. I don't hold no grudges against you. It was what it was at that time, but that seems like ancient history to me now."

"Don't feel like that to me," Olivier replied. "I could still be real good for you."

"I'm sorry, that just ain't where I'm at in my life. I'm more inclined to women, I think," Lawton offered with a sheepish grin.

"She just got you all confused. You ain't thinking straight," Olivier responded unaware of the inadvertent pun.

"It don't have nothing to do with Posy. I met a girl at French Tips named Virginia. She's a regular customer. We get along real fine," Lawton stated.

"Nobody loved you better," Olivier demanded clearly becoming irritated by the direction of the conversation.

"Look, I'm sorry Olivier. I didn't mean to upset you. I truly didn't, but it's never gone be like it was with you and me again. I've got to go now. I don't want to be late for work."

"Yeah, go on then. You didn't hurt me, boy. But you won't be able to say the same about that lying manipulative bitch. You'll see," Olivier threatened. "You'll see!"

BESSIE COLLINS WAS HUMMING TO HERSELF as she busily went about making a peach pie in her kitchen. It had been a while since Bessie had baked a pie. In fact, it was her first pie since she had locked herself up in her house and did nothing but make pies after the poisoning attempt on President Cochran several months earlier. At that time, Bessie was making amends for what she had perceived as her possible role in the assassination attempt, only to discover that she had been wrong. This was much different. This was a happy Bessie making a pie for a friend, like she had done for so many years.

"Oooh girl, something smells good up in here," Lucius Collins said as he entered the kitchen after his lunch time shift at Arnaud's. "That is the smell of love and I almost forgot how good it done smell."

"Before you be getting yourself all worked up, this pie ain't for you," Bessie giggled as she informed a dejected Lucius.

"You ain't teasing is you?" Lucius asked with a disappointed tone.

"Tomorrow is the Countess' birthday, me and Papa Levi gonna have a little party for her down at the shop," Bessie stated.

"That surely is nice. You is a good woman, Bessie Collins. But you know it don't hurt nobody to spread a little of that sweet sugar around,"

Lucius kidded his wife. "Sounds like you and Mariette get along real good."

"She's a real sweet older woman. She been through some stuff, but she nice and polite to everyone and gives folks what they want. It surely is nice having her around," Bessie admitted. "Papa Levi done took to her as well."

"Well, that's good cuz I ain't sure that I can be chasing after you down the street running off to Jackson Square every time something go wrong," Lucius poked fun at Bessie.

"Hush your mouth, you old fool," Bessie laughed in return. "I had good cause for thinking what I did. What with all that went on with Queen Rita and the such. And besides, I never done really trusted Esther. She always had something going on. Ain't like that at all with Mariette."

"Course I never spent that much time around either, but from what I do know, you is right about that," Lucius agreed. "There was something dark about Esther, I ain't getting that same feeling with Mariette. She very much who she present herself to be. I guess she deserves a nice pie unlike the rest of us."

"Oh, for lands sake, stop sulking around like a forlorn child," Bessie laughingly scolded her husband. "I done said this here peach pie is for Mariette, but I'm making a pecan pie for you, Lucius." Lucius smiled broadly and took his wife into his arms for a good long squeeze.

"You is a good woman Bessie Collins. You surely is."

POSY BRANCH GOT OUT OF BED and sat in a chair in the corner of the bedroom as she watched Norris Coaltree sleep. She found herself doing this same thing every now and then. It was as if she needed to remove herself from the scene in order to believe that she had finally found a man who she could fully be herself with. A man who understood and appreciated every quirky aspect of her vibrant personality. It was her way of pinching herself and reminding herself to live in the moment. Times were good and only getting better. She had a thriving business, the respect of the New Orleans business community, and the love of a good stable man who only wanted her to be herself. She sat quietly and observed carefully afraid that any false move could change everything. All she wanted was to preserve that moment for as long as she could. She so desperately wanted this acorn to secure its roots and blossom into a sturdy and everlasting oak tree.

CHAPTER 34

PRESIDENT ANDREW COCHRAN PACED BACK AND FORTH in his hotel suite prior to a fundraising event in New York City. His campaign coffers had very recently been replenished with a substantial contribution from Race Casserly, a Texas billionaire who he only knew in passing. The fact that he was now indebted to someone he barely knew was not sitting that well with him.

"Nathan, are we clear on the level of commitment and the amount of institutional assistance that we are willing to provide Race Casserly?" Andrew Cochran asked his campaign manager.

"To an extent," Nathan replied. "I made it clear to Race that his contributions to this campaign does not entitle him to a blank check when it comes to what favors he can curry from a Cochran administration."

"What specifically is he looking for?" Andrew questioned.

"In general terms, allowances and protections associated with domestic oil exploration and oil production and administrative assistance involving his new business dealings in foreign markets," Nathan responded.

"Is that it?" Andrew persisted.

"Race is an international businessman, what he wants today may not fully equate to what he wants tomorrow. His responses to specific questions can be as slippery, as well, oil," Nathan stated with a grin.

"Why am I not feeling satisfied with the terms of this relationship, Nathan?" Andrew asked.

"We need his monetary support to finish this campaign. Other than Jim Bob McCallum no other big money donors are rushing to provide us with additional funding. We've already turned down Jim Bob's overtures and have very possibly turned him into an enemy. We are running out of options, and frankly we are in no position to strictly dictate terms. Trust me, I have not sold out this administration for fifty pieces of silver. I've only done what I believed needed to be done in order to preserve this administration's chances of retaining a second term," Nathan said bluntly and slightly agitated.

"Ok, Nathan, calm down. I didn't mean to rile you. And you know I trust you implicitly. You are my brother. I wouldn't even be in the position of being a month away from the general election and fighting for a second term without you. I'm just a little apprehensive about climbing into bed with billionaire donors without knowing what they expect in return for their support," Andrew calmly reassured his friend.

"I understand Andy, and to some extent I share those apprehensions, but I'm doing the best I can to get us the money we need without selling out the ranch to a slick Texas billionaire," Nathan explained in a more friendly and relaxed tone. "I've made no promises. I've only stated that we will give all due consideration to the requests of all of our friends and supporters. That's it."

"Fair enough. I'm satisfied because I know how strenuously you fight for this administration, how much you fight for me," Andrew replied with a gentle smile. "Now, let's go out there and shake some money out of the Big Apple tree."

"WELL SENATOR, NOW YOU'VE HIT ON A TOPIC where I tend to differ with many of my Conservative colleagues. I do not advocate for tort reform. I am against most of the proposed changes in the civil justice system that I have seen that aim to reduce the ability of victims to bring tort litigation or to reduce damages that they can receive. Nothing that these old eyes have viewed seems fair or equitable. Corporations enjoy enough benefits in the practice of law. I do not propose that we give them any further advantages. There are other remedies for dealing with frivolous lawsuits," Stanford Winchester stated into the telephone.

"I must admit that I am very pleasantly surprised to hear your views on the topic," Senator Perry Douglas responded. "We seem to be of one mind on this issue."

"Oh, I can give you several other points of disagreement," Stanford chuckled.

"Of that I have no doubt," Perry Douglas replied with a laugh. "But seriously, these discussions that we've had have been an immense help to me. It's often very enlightening to probe the ideas on the other side of the aisle."

"But I'm currently straddling the aisle," Stanford acknowledged. "You see, not long ago I changed my party affiliation. I am now an Independent voter."

"My word, I had no idea," Perry stated with surprise. "Would it be horribly rude of me to ask why?"

"No, not at all," Stanford responded. "I must admit that the Republican primaries made me sick to my stomach. I could no longer countenance the destructive manner in which President Cochran's opponents viciously attacked not his policies but the man himself and his morality. It was simply appalling. Politics is rough and tumble, I get that. However, when we stoop to blatantly false personal attacks on the character of a candidate instead of focusing on differences on policy issues, we descend to schoolyard bullying and name calling. That is not appropriate behavior for selecting the President of the United States in the greatest country on earth. Unfortunately, the Republican campaign turned into a ridiculous free for all that made me rethink my party affiliation."

"There is another option, you know," Perry Douglas joked.

"Baby steps, Senator, baby steps. I'm an old man who may no longer have the agility to move that robustly," Stanford kidded in return. "Though I must commend Senator Raymond and yourself for running an admirable campaign without vitriol or falsehoods. It was a pleasure viewing grown-ups acting accordingly."

"Thank you, I appreciate the kind words. Senator Raymond is a gentile woman of the South who truly believes in honesty, integrity, and mutual respect. I am pleased and honored to have her as my running mate," Perry stated.

"Indeed," Stanford concurred.

"Well, I've taken up enough of your time, but I want to thank you once again for indulging me and providing me with your invaluable insights and wisdom about tort litigation and judicial reform," Perry said.

"It is my pleasure, Senator. It's helpful to me to answer your inquiries and keep this old fossilized brain of mine somewhat active," Stanford chuckled. "Next topic?"

"I'd love to get your input on protecting voter's rights through the courts," Perry answered. "Next Tuesday around 10am?"

"I would be delighted. I'll give that some thought and try to come up with some practical perspectives to share with you," Stanford replied.

"Excellent, simply excellent."

AARON ROSE AND CLAY GROVER WERE PLAYFULLY KIDDING with one another at work in front of their co-worker Emily Dubois. The two were involved in silly word games and one-upmanship.

"What's with you two, you are practically giddy?" Emily asked with a smile.

"Just having a little fun, being playful," Aaron replied.

"Well, good!" Emily exclaimed. "That's what's been missing around here the last few months. Before it seemed like the two of you didn't want to have anything to do with one another. It was kinda a drag being around both of you at the same time. This is more like it. My happy boys just having a good time."

"Yeah, sorry about all of that, it was my fault," Clay quickly asserted. "I was letting things weigh on me and bringing everyone else down because of it. But we've disposed of that Clay."

"Ok, the way you just put that is a little creepy, but sure, ok," Emily chuckled.

"I was a bit of a nag as well. Sometimes, I let my own excitement take over a situation," Aaron added.

"Let's not turn this into who was more to blame and just focus on being the happy boys, shall we?" Emily admonished with a grin.

"You're right. Let's focus on the fact that we need to have fun around this place. It can't be all work all the time," Aaron said.

"That's correct and it's why I'm going to miss you two knuckleheads. You've been a great addition to the office," Emily stated.

"What do you mean?" Clay asked with a perplexed look on his face.

"Guys, this is an old building, these walls are paper thin. I heard you a couple of weeks ago talking, rather loudly may I add, about whether Clay should take a job in Perry Douglas' administration and move back to Washington," Emily bluntly responded.

"Ooops! That was my fault, we shouldn't have been talking about that here at the office," Aaron sheepishly replied.

"Try using your library voice next time," Emily joked. "But no worries my lips are sealed. It's not my business, so I certainly won't mention it to Caleb or anyone else."

"Thank you for that," Clay sincerely said. "We're still sorting things out, and of course, the election is tight so who knows if the opportunity will even present itself."

"Well, if it does, I will miss you both madly. And we will have to stage a going away party that will put Mardi Gras to shame," Emily gleefully chirped.

"That's what makes it a hard decision. We both love it here. The firm, our clients, the city, and the way of life in the Big Easy. It would be hard to give all of this up. But we'll cross that bridge when we come to it. Nothing is getting decided today," Clay remarked.

"Let's all go to French Tips and get wasted on Michael's juleps after work tonight," Aaron happily suggested.

"Sounds awesome to me," Emily giggled.

"Look who the cat dragged in?" Michael bellowed from behind the bar as he spotted Clay, Aaron, and Emily walk through the front door of French Tips, Juleps & Jazz.

"Peach and ginger juleps and plenty of them," Emily shouted in response.

"Hello gorgeous," Michael seductively offered.

"Why thank you Michael, always the considerate gentleman," Emily said in her best Southern belle voice.

"Actually, I was referring to Clay," Michael heartily laughed.

"Always the bridesmaid never the bride," Emily lamented with mock scorn. "I'm surrounded by wildly handsome gay men and I might as well be a lamp in the corner."

"Not necessarily," Michael responded. "You know, we have a new host and co-manager. His name is Lawton Cavanaugh. He's that cute young thing over there," Michael said while gesturing with his head. "And he's straight."

"Do tell," Emily cooed. "He is cute, and Lawton Cavanaugh is a wonderful Southern name. Is he from around here?"

"Born and bred in New Orleans. He's a great guy. He gets along with everyone here, and Posy is treating him like he's her son."

"Truly, you say," Emily nearly moaned.

"Come on Emily, let me introduce you to him," Clay chuckled as he took Emily by the hand and led her over to where Lawton was standing. Meanwhile, Aaron took a seat at the bar and watched as Michael prepared the juleps.

"What you been up to?" Aaron asked Michael.

"Not much buddy. Just work, having some fun," Michael responded before changing the topic. "Hey Aaron, you use to work with Senator Douglas when you were in Washington, right?"

"Sure did, why?"

"Well, I saw that he and his son were in town a week or so ago."

"Yes, they were at a campaign rally at Tulane. Clay and I went and met with the Senator afterwards," Aaron said.

"Do you know Robert Douglas?" Michael inquired.

"Sure, of course. I knew Robert when he was a young college scamp. And here he is all grown up now and knocking them dead on the campaign trail," Aaron acknowledged.

"Is he a good guy?" Michael pressed the line of questioning.

"Yeah, Robert's great. He's funny, clever, pretty easy going. He's very comfortable in his own skin," Aaron replied. "Why do you ask?"

"Nothing, just curious," Michael answered with a bowed head as he prepared the juleps and smiled.

CHAPTER 35

IT WAS THE MIDDLE OF OCTOBER, just a little over three weeks until Election Day, and the Presidential race was tightening. A new infusion of money into the Re-Elect President Cochran campaign had allowed the President's team to inundate the air waves with campaign ads in most of the battleground states. The national polls showed the President pulling within two points of Senator Douglas. Two popular candidates were providing the nation with a choice. The temperatures were beginning to dip across the country but the race for the Presidency was red hot.

STANFORD WINCHESTER WALKED THROUGH THE DOOR of Fritzel's only to find his old friend Calvin Putnam in his usual spot at the bar.

"I can only assume that you've sold your house Calvin since you seem to be living here at Fritzel's now," Stanford chuckled as he patted his friend on the back.

"The only way you would know that, you old horse thief, is because you're in here nearly as much as I am," Calvin joshed.

"Name calling will get you nowhere, Calvin. On the other hand, buying me a Sazerac will get you the pleasure of my company for about thirty minutes. That's when Whitlee should be returning from court," Stanford said with a wink.

"Sit yourself down, always happy to support your alcoholism," Calvin uttered with a wicked cackle. "What you been up to ol' boy?" Calvin asked.

"Well, since you asked, I've been having some very interesting conversations with Senator Douglas," Stanford replied.

"Who?" Calvin questioned, unsure that he had heard Stanford correctly.

"Senator Perry Douglas of Illinois. One of the two men running for President," Stanford repeated in an exaggerated slow manner.

"I ain't that drunk yet. Stop pulling my leg," Calvin insisted.

"First off, you probably are. You smell to high heaven of bourbon. And secondly, I'm not joking," Stanford responded.

"Why in blue blazes would a Northern liberal like Perry Douglas want to talk to a Southern Conservative Republican like yourself?" Calvin questioned.

"Independent, Calvin, Independent," Stanford corrected. "As you would know if you ever bothered to venture out of bars and into the illuminating sunlight of reality, Senator Douglas was at Tulane giving a fine speech a few weeks ago. I attended because it seemed like a better expenditure of time than sitting here knocking down bourbon with you. I met with him afterwards at a meet and greet and we struck up a conversation about judicial reform. Something that I know a tad about. Senator Douglas asked if he could call me from time to time to pick what is left of my brain, and there you have it. We've had three phone conversations since which have been absolutely delightful. He's a very learned man, with great curiosity. He is open to hearing alternative viewpoints. He wants to get the best ideas possible, regardless of the political affiliation of the source. He is not, like many others, rooted in myopic partisanship."

"Sounds like you want to marry him?" Calvin jokingly snarled.

"No, but I may very well vote for him," Stanford offered.

"Stanford Winchester is going to vote for a Northern liberal Democrat!" Calvin exclaimed. "Your pappy just died all over again!"

"Go ahead, have your fun. But, he is a serious, honorable man and a voice of good judgment and reason. What more would you want in a President?"

"A Republican that ain't gonna tax my pants off and give my money to some Northern big city welfare queens," Calvin answered while shaking his head.

"Sometimes I wonder why we are friends," Stanford stated with a grin and a chuckle. "I know that you are a more educated and reasonable man than that, Calvin. So, I'm going to chalk that comment up to double digit cocktails and let it be. I like Senator Douglas. I am thoroughly enjoying our conversations. He is challenging me and I him. It's stimulating intellectual problem solving. He presents an issue, and then we discuss the various approaches to attempting to solve that issue. I need this type of mental exercise to keep my brain from atrophying. I am having the time of my life. I anxiously look forward to our next call."

"You're enjoying the attention from a man who very well may be President in less than a month. You like being important and the center of attention, Stanford, you always have," Calvin muttered and slurred as his alcohol consumption that afternoon was now showing visible signs.

"I'm going to get you a cab, and you're going to go home and sleep it off, my friend," Stanford said as he attempted to get Calvin on this feet and off the bar stool. Once outside, Stanford poured Calvin into a cab and gave the cab driver $20 and Calvin's address.

"You're a good man, Stanford," Calvin muttered while slouched over in the back seat of the taxicab.

"You are too old chum. You are too."

BESSIE COLLINS SAT ON A WOODEN STOOL behind the counter at her voodoo shop on Rampart Street. Papa Levi, as was his wont, was sweeping the floor and humming to himself.

"What's that song you is humming? It surely sounds familiar," Bessie asked.

"Done heard it on the radio this morning and it's stuck in my head," Papa Levi explained. "The fella on the radio said that it was Jose Feliciano doing 'Light My Fire'. Pretty little song and that boy sure can play guitar."

"Yeah, I know that song. It goes something like, '"Come on baby light my fire. Come on baby light my fire. Try to set the night on fire,'" Bessie sing-said to Papa Levi.

"Yeah, that be it," Papa Levi agreed. "Real nice song, real smooth and such."

"I need to bring a radio in here. We should be listening to music all day long. After all this is the Big Easy. Home to Louis Armstrong," Bessie proclaimed.

"That there is a fine idea," Papa Levi smiled. "Though we'd have to turn it off when the Countess is doing her séances and readings."

"Well, of course," Bessie chided. "I know that. But there is so much other time when it's just me and you and the customers and we should have some fine music playing like they do in the department stores."

"Speaking of the Countess, she surely was so surprised and happy when you brought her that pie for her birthday and we had ourselves a little party," Papa Levi said with a wide smile.

"Yeah, she sure did like it. She kept going on about how happy we made her feel and she had a little tear in her eye. I could see before she wiped it away. Makes your heart feel so good, when you make someone happy like that, don't it?"

"It surely do, Miss Bessie, it surely do," Papa Levi answered. "When is the Countess returning?"

"Next week, she said. She down in the bayou with her kin this week," Bessie replied. "I do like her, she is good people."

"I done saw Esther the other day," Papa Levi offered. "She was coming out of Marie Laveau's. I seen her and she seen me. I waved and smiled real friendly like, and she just put her head down and walked away. Not nary a smile or gesture in return."

"We best off that she ain't around here no more," Bessie said with a shake of her head. "She done made us some good money, so I'll always be grateful for that, but she just wasn't a friendly sort. And she been practicing in them dark arts. Mariette done told me that."

"Then you is right. We don't need that black magic around here. We surely don't," Papa Levi affirmed as he continued sweeping the same space of floor with his old broom.

NATHAN WHITAKER STARED AT THE POLLING NUMBERS with a smile crossing his face. The increased spending on television commercials in the battleground states was having an effect. Nathan owed Race Casserly a return call. He wanted to be able to report good news with respect to the additional campaign funding, and he was not disappointed.

"Race, Nathan Whitaker here, I'm returning your call from yester-day," Nathan enthusiastically said into the phone.

"Nathan, you sound happy. My money must be having its desired effect," Race replied in his deep baritone voice.

"Yes, thank you again. We've closed the gap by two points nationally and we might have a chance of pulling off come from behind wins in

Florida and Iowa," Nathan responded.

"Excellent, I am so pleased to be part of the Cochran campaign. My only regret was that I didn't get involved sooner four years ago," Race confided to Nathan.

"We're very happy to have your support," Nathan stated. "Now, what can I do for you?"

"Oh, yesterday's call, that's right. It's really a very minor thing," Race began. "As you might remember there is a medical research center being constructed in Baton Rouge, Louisiana. It is being funded by the state and federal government. I have an aunt on my father's side, who I am very close with. Her name is Hellen Casserly. She is 91 years old and she has Alzheimer's disease. If at all possible, I'd like to have my aunt considered when it comes to naming the research facility. Without delay, I plan to make a very generous contribution to the research institute in my aunt's name."

"Is that the same medical research institute that Jim Bob McCallum wanted to have named for his wife, Mabel?" Nathan questioned.

"Why, now that you mention it, I believe that you are correct. That had completely slipped my mind. Unfortunate, that that whole double murder indictment had the effect of removing his wife's name from being considered for the institute," Race smarmily replied.

"I have to admit I have very little knowledge of how these things are decided when it comes to naming federal projects. But, I'll make some inquiries and see what I can tell you," Nathan offered.

"That's all I can ask for. Of course, it would be so nice if my aunt could see that a mental research institute was named after her, Hellen G. Casserly, while she is still with us. God love and protect her," Race said.

"Let me look into it. I can't make any promises, but the Cochran administration is certainly in your debt, and if at all possible, we'd like to make your wishes come true," Nathan offered.

"Isn't that what true friendship is truly all about?" Race stated in an unctuous manner.

"I suppose so," Nathan hesitantly agreed. "Was there anything else?"

"Heavens no," Race quickly replied. "Just the simple satisfaction of knowing that you will make inquiries so pleases me, Nathan."

"Well, then, I should let you go. I've got a campaign to run. I'll get back to you in a few days with respect to your request. Good-bye Race."

"Good-bye Nathan," Race intoned with a wicked smile.

ESTHER FRANCOIS STOOD IN FRONT OF THE LARGE MANSION in the Garden District of New Orleans. She carried a well-worn brown leather satchel in her right hand. Esther rang the front doorbell and waited a couple of minutes. A male servant opened the door and stared directly at Esther and shrugged.

"Please come around to the back kitchen entrance," the servant in a white waist coat instructed. Esther slowly ambled around to the back of the large house and was met at the rear door by the male servant.

"Is your master home?" Esther inquired.

"Not presently, but he has made me well aware of the arrangements. You can give the package to me and provide me with the information regarding your request," the male servant stated. Esther reached into her satchel and retrieved a small box wrapped in brown paper and tied with hemp. She handed the box to the male servant. She then took a folded piece of paper out of her coat pocket.

"There is a name on this paper. There is an address on this paper," Esther said slowly and clearly.

"I understand," the male servant responded. "Is there anything else?"

"No, I've lived up to my end of the bargain . . ." Esther confirmed as her voice trailed off and her eyes closed briefly. When she reopened her eyes the kitchen door of the large mansion had been closed.

OLIVIER BELLEVUE GOT OUT OF HIS CAR and stood on the side of the road, waiting. He was on a back road just outside of Lafayette, Louisiana. A black pick-up truck pulled up alongside of Olivier's car. A man exited the pick-up truck and walked towards Olivier.

"You looking real nice tonight," the pick-up truck driver said as he surveyed Olivier from head to foot.

"That's not happening, let's just get on with it. Here it is," Olivier offered, as he handed an envelope to the pick-up truck driver. "Also, here's a piece of paper that has a name and address. Got it?"

"Yeah, I got it," the driver responded while grasping the folded paper. "Though it seems like a waste of a nice night and a full moon. Hell, I even washed the blanket I keep in the back of the pick-up."

"Not tonight," Olivier said, as he turned and walked to his car.

CHAPTER 36

CAROLYN BARNES HAD AN EXPRESSION OF CONCERN on her face as she reviewed the latest polling results from a handful of hotly contested battleground states. The Douglas campaign's five-point lead was now down to two points or less. Independent suburban women were gravitating to the moderate views being expressed by President Cochran. Florida, Iowa, and Colorado all thought a few weeks ago to be relatively safe states for Senator Douglas were now all up for grabs. The dynamic was shifting and Carolyn knew that it was her job to figure out how to stem the tide and reestablish a foothold among skittish Independent voters. Additionally, excitement for the Douglas campaign among the 18-25 year-old demographic appeared to be waning. It was time to get Robert Douglas back out on the campaign trail in key states.

PRESIDENT ANDREW COCHRAN AND FIRST LADY Sue Lynn Cochran sat together on a white couch on Air Force One holding hands as their plane prepared to touch down in Orlando, Florida. The couple were scheduled to make a campaign appearance together later that evening.

"You might still pull this remarkable comeback off," Sue Lynn said to her husband. "To think a few months ago, most people didn't give you a chance to win the Republican Party nomination."

"I'm still trailing, but yeah, I'd have to agree even I'm a bit surprised by it," Andrew Cochran conceded.

"The American people understand that you're working for them and not the fat cat Republicans on the far right," Sue Lynn added.

"Well, that's in part because I was eschewed out of that club, when I didn't continue to espouse their viewpoint," Andrew smiled. "But I firmly believed that the Republican Party needed to get back to its more reasonable and socially moderate beliefs. There is nothing wrong with being a Rockefeller Republican."

"Actually, that was quite a savvy move. Instead of being yet another yammering Conservative ideologue you pivoted back to the days of more centrist Republicanism," Sue Lynn agreed.

"Nathan's legal issues had a lot to do with that," Andrew conceded. "I had to save my nascent administration from scandal. But then when that was all behind him, Nathan got on board and helped craft a very approachable message and campaign strategy that has brought us this far. His suggestion of a moderate New Englander for Vice-President was a masterstroke. And, Cindy has turned out to be an articulate and savvy campaigner. I owe a great deal of our success to Nathan. But, at the same time, I must admit that he takes too many risky chances. My campaign, this last month, is being funded by a Texas billionaire that I barely know. Of course, Nathan tells me that everything is under control, yet I can't help but feel I've made a deal with the devil and have no clue what the price tag is for his contributions."

"Andy, you're the President of the United States. Nathan cannot make promises on your behalf, especially if you have no idea what those promises entail. Race Casserly can believe what he wants to believe, but only you can decide the price for his play in the game of power politics," Sue Lynn responded.

"Someone has been watching too many episodes of 'House of Cards,'" Andrew chuckled as he smiled at his wife.

CLAY GROVER WALKED INTO HIS HOUSE and was warmly greeted by his husband, Aaron.

"How did your therapy session go today?" Aaron inquired.

"Good. I think that we are making some real inroads into why I have addictive tendencies when it comes to sex," Clay responded.

"That's great," Aaron stated. "Anything you'd care to share?"

"Not now," Clay replied. "We're working through some things, and I'd rather not talk about them at this moment. For now, I'd like for it to be something I discuss just with my therapist until I get a better handle on the cause for my impulses."

"Got it, no worries, new topic. The election is getting rather tight as we get down to the final days," Aaron broached.

"It is, but I think Senator Douglas will still pull it out," Clay stated.

"Is that wishful thinking or sage political observation?" Aaron kidded his husband.

"A little of both, I guess," Clay answered.

"So, are we now rooting for White House Chief of Staff?" Aaron asked with a grin.

"I wouldn't necessarily say rooting, but things changed when Senator Douglas offered you a position on his White House Counsel staff. It would be pretty cool if we were both working in the White House. An opportunity that very few people are ever offered," Clay replied.

"Yeah, that would be interesting," Aaron concurred. "So, in other words we're rooting for jobs in the White House?" Aaron heartily laughed.

"Yes Aaron, we're rooting for our jobs in the White House," Clay begrudgingly acquiesced with a broad smile.

RACE CASSERLY PUSHED HIS BOOTS AGAINST HIS OFFICE DESK as he smiled at his associate, Carlisle Buchanan. Race stared at his iPhone and dialed a number he had not dialed in years.

"I'm going to enjoy this," Race said as he winked at Carlisle.

"Is this Jim Bob McCallum?" Race asked in his deep baritone voice. "Race Casserly here. How the hell are you Jim Bob?"

"I'm doing alright, I guess," Jim Bob hesitantly responded.

"It's been too long, we don't talk much anymore," Race said.

"We never talk," Jim Bob corrected. "So, why are we talking now?"

"Well, I figured you were going to find out anyway, so I thought it was the right thing for me to tell you direct," Race answered.

"Tell me what?" Jim Bob bluntly inquired.

"As you may have noticed Andrew Cochran is picking up speed and may still win this here election," Race began. "He got an infusion of new money into his campaign and they been running ads all over the television in the key battleground states."

"What's that got to do with me?" Jim Bob curtly asked.

"That's just the point, Jim Bob, it ain't got nothing to do with you. You see, it's my money that is funding the Cochran campaign now. Your old running buddy Nathan Whitaker was pleased as punch to receive my very generous contributions. That Nathan, he's a smart man. I just thought you'd like to know that we share personal acquaintances. I know how close you were to Nathan, what with you paying for his legal bills and all. Oh, and the plots you two done hatched, absolutely brilliant. Justice Martin had to go, and you two wily fellas was smart enough to see that fact and act upon it. My hats off to you. And you pulled it off without nary one day behind bars. Well, and that love-sick clerk, she's what we call collateral damage, ain't that right?"

"You just talking through your hat. That's nothing but foolish talk," Jim Bob snapped back.

"Oh, I know a good many things Jim Bob. I got me an intelligence network that makes the boys at the Pentagon green with envy. I know what's what, and so do you. That's why we got so much in common," Race said with a smarmy tone.

"We ain't got nothing in common. I made billions on my own without my pappy leaving me an oil company. I built my company from scratch, you ain't built shit. You were given everything you own," Jim Bob said angrily.

"You're sorta right there, Jim Bob. I have been given a lot. But I've also done a lot with what I've been given. For example, I made a very sizable donation to this new medical research institute that is being built with federal funding in Baton Rouge. Maybe you've heard about it? Then, in talking with my new good friend Nathan Whitaker, it appears that that institute might very well be named after my beloved aunt, Hellen Casserly. Now, wouldn't that be something, a brand new medical research center bearing the Casserly name," Race gloated.

"Fuck you!" Jim Bob ranted. "That ain't never going to happen!"

"I don't know about that, you should probably talk to your friend Nathan. He seemed to think that it was pretty much a done deal if Andrew Cochran wins the election," Race calmly responded.

"Nathan Whitaker is no friend of mine," Jim Bob fumed.

"Now, I'm so sorry to hear that after how close the two of you been over the years. You got his best friend elected President and all. And then you done taught them boys how to effectively use poison to get what they want in this world. You're kinda a real life Agatha Christie!" Race happily exclaimed. "And Nathan and his friend Andrew sure took to your lessons real good. Some would say them lessons is why Andrew Cochran is within striking distance of winning the election instead of being a wildly disappointing one term President who was ousted during the primaries by his own Party. Yeah, them boys took to your lessons, that is for sure."

"I ain't got time for your rumors and gossip. In fact, I don't have time for you," Jim Bob huffed.

"Oh, I can substantiate all of it," Race claimed. "I got some tapes of conversations that would make a two-bit whore blush. Richard Nixon ain't got nothing on me. As I told you, information gathering is imperative to my business. Just ask the Prince of Dubai. I got me a real good oil deal out of that one."

"You done wasted enough of my time with your lies and mind games. Lose this number if you know what's best for you," Jim Bob threatened.

"Please give my best to your wife Mabel," Race chirped as Jim Bob ended the call. Race put his phone on the desk and smiled at Carlisle.

"I can't remember the last time I had that much fun," Race laughed.

CHAPTER 37

A LATE OCTOBER CHILL BEGAN TO SET IN across the country. In the north, the leaves on the trees were in full autumnal colors in a resplendent prelude to their annual demise. In the south, a seasonal cool filled the air as fall winds rattled tree branches in a wooden symphonic prelude to the days of winter. It was less than two weeks before Election Day and the candidates were crisscrossing the country attempting to squeeze the last few votes out of the electorate. Most voters had already made up their minds, but some were still deciding which candidate they preferred and which direction they wanted to see the country head. But before that would all be decided, it was days away from Halloween. New Orleans prepared for the influx into the city of visitor ghosts and goblins over the holiday weekend. And, Washington too, was becoming a very spooky place.

NORRIS COALTREE REACHED DOWN AND PICKED HIS SHIRT off the bedroom floor. He brushed it off and attempted to smooth out the wrinkles before slipping his arms through the sleeves. Posy Branch walked into her bedroom with two cups of steaming coffee in each of her hands. Posy handed one of the cups of coffee to Norris and smiled.

"I keep telling you that you should hang your shirt up right proper in my closet, then it wouldn't be so wrinkled when you put it back on," Posy admonished with a grin.

"Posy, my love, when I'm pulling this shirt off in your bedroom at night and dropping it to the floor, I ain't exactly thinking about how wrinkled it's going to be the next morning. I tend to have other things on my mind," Norris chuckled in response.

"Oh, I know what's on your mind, and sugar, I'm all on board. I'm just saying it wouldn't take much more time or effort to hang it up before we get busy," Posy replied with a twinkle in her eyes.

"Maybe next time," Norris halfheartedly promised.

"I'll believe it when I see it."

"Oh shoot, I almost forgot, I got something for you," Norris said as he fished a small box out of his pants pocket. Posy stared at the small black box.

"Norris, we had this conversation, right?" Posy said with trepidation in her voice.

"Oh no, it ain't that," Norris laughed. "Trust me, there ain't no diamonds on this," he stated handing the box to Posy. Posy opened the box and looked at the small object inside totally bewildered.

"What is it? I ain't got a clue," Posy offered with a perplexed expression on her pretty face.

"It's an alert device. You know, like the device you see old folks wear and use when they 'fallen and can't get up,'" Norris explained.

"I ain't quite at that stage yet," Posy responded. "As you might recall from last night, I'm still pretty limber and can still get up and down real good."

"No, it ain't for medical alert, it's like that but this one goes directly to the Police Department hotline," Norris explained.

"What do I need this for?" Posy questioned still somewhat confused.

"Look, Halloween is just days away. We get a lot of folks coming into the city. Most are here to just have fun, but you always get a few that is trying to take advantage of the situation. I want you to be safe. If you press the button, it alerts the police department directly that you are having some trouble. It's also got a tiny GPS device in it, so if you're at home or on the street or at French Tips, we'd be able to track you down and come quick," Norris said.

"I know you are just trying to look after me, and I love you for it. But I really don't think I need something like this," Posy sweetly replied.

"Posy darling, please do this for me. It's real small so it don't take up much space. You can wear it around your neck, or put it in your pocket or purse," Norris pleaded.

"Alright, my sweet man. I can see how much this means to you. How much I must mean to you. So, I'll keep it, but I ain't wearing it around my neck," Posy said with a laugh.

"That's fine with me, just as long as you keep it and use it if some rough necks are giving you trouble at the bar," Norris answered.

"Yes sir, Sergeant Coaltree," Posy giggled as she gave Norris a big hug and a deep long loving kiss.

BESSIE COLLINS WAS STANDING BEHIND THE GLASS COUNTER at her shop helping a customer with an amulet from her display case when Papa Levi came huffing and puffing through the front door. Bessie excused herself from her customer, and she helped Papa Levi into the backroom of the shop and gave him a cool glass of water. Papa Levi took a long sip and attempted to calm down and regulate his labored breathing.

"You is in such a state," Bessie proclaimed. "What's wrong?"

"It's the Countess," Papa Levi responded. "My friend who owns the home where she is a boarder, done found her dead in bed this morning. She didn't come down for breakfast the way she normally do, so he went to check on her, and found that she had passed."

"Oh no, that's terrible!" Bessie exclaimed. "How did she die?"

"They don't rightly know yet. The police came and took away the body this morning. They also took some things they found in her room. She was an old woman, so real possible that her heart just gave out," Papa Levi replied. "Police is trying to locate her kin in bayou country. One strange thing. They found a small voodoo structure outside of the boarding house on the steps. Police ain't sure what to make of it."

"I can't believe that Mariette is gone. I surely am going to miss her and her gentle ways," Bessie said sadly.

"Death come for all of us, just a matter of when and where," Papa Levi solemnly stated.

"Do the police think that someone may have done something to Mariette?" Bessie inquired.

"Nothing that I done heard, Miss Bessie. But I'm sure that they'll look at everything."

"It's just a shame in this here world," Bessie intoned. "Such a shame."

STANFORD WINCHESTER HAD JUST ENDED A CALL with Senator Douglas when his wife Whitlee walked into his home office with a cup of tea.

"I cannot lie, I'm going to miss these phone calls with Senator Douglas. We have such stimulating conversations about the law and the judicial system. The Senator says that he is picking my brain, but the truth of the matter is that it is a robust give and take on issues of grave concern for the country and the preservation of Constitutional values," Stanford told Whitlee before taking a sip of hot tea.

"Well, all I can say is that you light up like a Christmas tree right before one of your planned calls and immediately thereafter. You are positively glowing Stanford!" Whitlee proclaimed.

"It's an intense mental exercise in rational problem solving. At times the Senator provides a point of view that I had not fully considered before, and at times it is vice versa. We enjoy each other's company and the discussions are both factual and philosophical but never rancorous or argumentative. It is truly how Washington should go about solving the nation's problems," Stanford elaborated.

"And that was the last of them before the election?" Whitlee inquired.

"Yes, I do believe so. The Senator will be campaigning from now until Election Day. He basically said that this was our last session. And as I said, I will miss them dearly. These conversations allowed me to analyze issues and present potential solutions. I had to think things through and parse my words carefully. I've not been asked to do that since my retirement," Stanford answered.

"Does this mean that you miss being on the bench?"

"Yes and no. I miss the intellectual challenges, but I surely don't miss the day-to-day functions of the court. After I became Chief of the Circuit, I found myself practicing law less and becoming more of an administrative overseer," Stanford replied.

"Is there a way to indulge in one without being bound to the other?" Whitlee challenged.

"Not as a Chief Judge, I don't believe," Stanford responded. "But perhaps in a different position and in a different venue."

"Perhaps we need to explore ways to afford you that opportunity?" Whitlee said.

"No, my dear. This was a once in a lifetime opportunity. Somehow, I was able to convince Senator Douglas that I had something worthwhile to offer. I don't see this situation ever presenting itself again. I'm an old man, few have interest in anything that I have to say," Stanford lamented.

"Clearly Senator Douglas did. You have much to offer. You are a sage and reasoned man, Stanford Winchester," Whitlee proudly stated.

"Bless you my love, but I am well aware of my status in retirement. I am the old pair of shoes in the very back of the closet. I still function, and I served my time well. But there are other newer, shinier shoes that are in the front rows. Seldom does one rummage so far back in the closet when newer pairs are at the ready and are in far better shape."

"You mark my words, there is a need and demand for the wisdom of Stanford Winchester. The fact that you are still in the closet and not in the Salvation Army bin is only testament to that fact," Whitlee countered with a loving smile.

JIM BOB MCCALLUM COULD NOT GET HIS CONVERSATION with Race Casserly out of his head. He thought about it often and it was driving him into a mighty rage. In rational moments, he convinced himself that they were only words and wild unsubstantiated speculation. Yet, he also knew that much of what Race had talked about rang of some truth. He was not completely wrong. It almost seemed like Race had heard some of the exact conversation that Jim Bob had with Nathan Whitaker. And that fact alone drove Jim Bob insane. Jim Bob had reached for his phone several times over the course of the subsequent days after Race's call, but then thought better of it. However, one evening he watched an interview with Nathan Whitaker on a cable news program, and when Nathan praised recent fundraising efforts as a reason for the President's rising poll numbers, Jim Bob snapped.

Nathan Whitaker stared at his ringing cell phone and the name on the caller screen. He hesitated for a few moments, but ultimately decided to answer.

"Hello," Nathan intoned.

'Ain't you a busy and important man these days," Jim Bob harshly stated into the phone.

"Good evening Jim Bob," Nathan answered.

"You got time for old friends Nathan, or are you too busy with your new ones?" Jim Bob asked.

"I'm not sure I know what you are referring to?" Nathan questioned.

"New friends, Nathan, it's a simple concept," Jim Bob repeated. "I understand that you are cozying up with Race Casserly now that he is funding your boyfriend's campaign."

"I'm not sure where you are getting your information," Nathan countered.

"I'm getting my information from that no account son of a bitch himself," Jim Bob ranted into the phone. "Race Casserly called me to tell me that he is now funding Cochran's campaign. He also mentioned that you been making him some promises."

"Oh, I see," Nathan demurely responded.

"Oh, now you see! Now you see!" Jim Bob shouted. "My money wasn't good enough for the suddenly pious Andrew Cochran. He didn't want to be tarnished by my stank. But he crawls into bed with that deceitful criminal, Race Casserly. There's been more dead bodies dropped into his open oil wells than Carter has pills. I'm a regular choir boy compared to that thieving liar. Yet, you choose his support over mine!"

"Calm down Jim Bob, it isn't like that at all," Nathan said attempting to quiet the tempest on the other end of the phone.

"You telling me that Race Casserly is lying to me, that Cochran's campaign is not accepting his money?" Jim Bob loudly inquired.

"I didn't say that," Nathan replied.

"Are you taking Race's money or not? It's a simple question, Nathan."

"The campaign to Re-Elect has received support from a good many people. Race Casserly is just one of thousands," Nathan said in a diplomatic fashion.

"But Jim Bob McCallum ain't one of those thousands is he Nathan?" Jim Bob huffed in an accusatorial tone.

"Now, Jim Bob . . ." Nathan began before being quickly interrupted by Jim Bob.

"No, you listen to me, Nathan," Jim Bob snapped. "You and Cochran don't smell the White House without my connections and money four years ago. You and I took care of matters and put that pathetic puppet in the White House. Then a little trouble comes our way, and that whimpering coward cuts and runs. Leaving you and me high and dry. Well, my money bought us the verdicts we deserved. Guilty, innocent, it's all a bunch of nonsense. Either you can buy yourself out of trouble or you can't. I could and I did for both of us. Then when you get back into the good graces of puppet-boy, I come around as an old dear friend, offering my money and all of my connections and clout to help you keep the White House, and what do I get in return? A kick in the ass and shoved out of the picture. Not as much as a thank you for all you've done for us."

"Then let me rectify that and thank you very much for everything that you've done for the Cochran administration," Nathan sweetly stated.

"Shut the fuck up, Nathan!" Jim Bob yelled into the phone. "It's way way too late for that now. Not only did you intentionally snub me, you went over and begged for Race Casserly's money. The man who I have been battling for power with for over two decades and that is who you go to bed with? My mortal enemy! There couldn't have been a better way for you to hurt and betray me if you had drawn it up on a god damn chalk board! So, let me tell you how I am going to exact my righteous retribution for the egregious wrong that you have conspired and perpetrated against me. I am going to destroy you and your best friend, Andrew Cochran. I can promise you that that man will never win a second term. You know all about October surprises during election years, don't you Nathan? Well, you ain't seen nothing yet!"

"Jim Bob let me explain," Nathan began before he heard the dial tone. Nathan physically shook as he stared at the phone screen.

"Call ended."

CHAPTER 38

COUNTESS MARIETTE AUBUCHON'S BODY WAS IDENTIFIED and claimed by her next of kin. Because of her advanced age and the peaceful manner in which she passed, her family elected not to have an autopsy done on her body. The Police lacking any clear evidence that foul play was involved acquiesced to the family's wishes. Mariette's family took control of her body and arranged to have her buried in a small mausoleum in New Orleans. It had been Mariette's wishes to be interned in New Orleans. Bessie and Lucius Collins and Papa Levi were the only non-family in attendance at the grave site.

"I'm glad that she went real peaceful like," Bessie said to Lucius and Papa Levi as they walked out of the gates of the cemetery.

"That's all any of us can ask for as we depart this here earth," Papa Levi confirmed. "Sure is sad though. She was making a nice life for herself here in the Big Easy. Customers all liked her and she was making friends and such."

"She wasn't from here, I wonder why she wanted to buried here in New Orleans instead of in Cajun country?" Bessie asked.

"Lots of mambos in mausoleums in St. Louis cemetery. Same like Queen Rita. Mambos believe in the afterlife. They don't want to be cremated or buried. They want to rise up and walk out of their tomb like Jesus," Papa Levi explained.

"That don't make no practical sense," Lucius interjected dismissively.

"Maybe you and I don't believe it, but it real to them," Papa Levi responded.

"You two show some respect for the dearly departed. Don't matter none what either of you believe," Bessie scolded.

"Now what?" Lucius asked. "You goin' back to the shop and openin' up for the rest of the afternoon?"

"Not today," Bessie answered. "I thought we'd go have a nice hot lunch and toast to the memory of Mariette."

"That sounds like a fine idea," Papa Levi agreed.

"Yeah, I'm hungry, I could surely go for a nice plate of something," Lucius added with a grin.

THE FOLLOWING DAY WAS HALLOWEEN AND the crowds began to fill the French Quarter as the festivities ramped up. Michael had opened French Tips, Juleps & Jazz in the morning. Posy Branch was not due to arrive until noon. Posy and Lawton Cavanaugh would be managing the afternoon and night shifts until closing at 2:00 a.m. On a busy day like Halloween, it was all hands on deck.

"What's up good looking?" Posy greeted Michael as she entered her establishment.

"Been busy this morning. Lots of women coming in and getting their nails done to match their costumes for this evening," Michael answered. "Speaking of, what will you be wearing tonight?"

"I wasn't feeling real creative this year so I dug my old witches costume out of the closet," Posy responded.

"At least you get a choice," Michael countered. "Since you never let me wear a shirt, I'm stuck with the same old flashing devil horns on my head, and that tired old devil's tail coming out of my jeans."

"Sugar, there ain't nothing old or tired about your tail. It's tight and perfectly round," Posy laughed.

"Bet you say that to all of the boys," Michael joked.

"Where is my boy Lawton?" Posy asked.

"He's in the back going through last night's receipts," Michael answered. "I'm heading back there, you want me to tell him that you'd like to talk to him?"

"Yeah, that would be real nice," Posy stated as Michael walked from the bar to the back room of French Tips. Moments after Michael left, his cell phone, which he had left on the bar top began to ring. Posy looked at the name on the screen, "Robert Douglas." Posy picked up the phone and answered.

"Hello, Michael is not available at the moment may I take a message?" Posy answered and asked in a playful manner.

"Yes, hi. Could you please let Michael know that Robert was calling to wish him a Happy Halloween? Nothing important, just thinking about him," Robert responded.

"Ain't that sweet. I'll be sure to let him know, darling," Posy replied. "You a local boy, Robert?"

"No, not exactly. I'm from Chicago, but I'm currently in Maine," Robert said.

"If it ain't rude of me to ask, then how do you know my Michael?" Posy inquired.

"We spent a couple of days together when I was visiting New Orleans a little while ago," Robert stated. "We became friends fairly quickly."

"Michael is real easy to get to know and like. That's my heart, right there," Posy gushed.

"Yes, he is," Robert confirmed. "He's a very natural and sweet guy."

"I'll let him know that you called Robert," Posy said. "Your last name is Douglas, like the Presidential candidate, huh? Bet you get asked if you is related all the time."

"Well, yeah. I'm his son," Robert explained.

"Get out!" Posy exclaimed. "True? You ain't kidding?"

"Nope, I'm his son. In fact, I'm about to go on stage at a campaign event at the University of Maine, so I should get going. Please let Michael know that I called to say, hey."

"I surely will. Happy Halloween to you Robert," Posy said as the call ended. Posy put Michael's phone back on the bar top and smiled wide as Michael approached accompanied by Lawton.

"Michael, you handsome devil! You sure is living in the high cotton now, child. You in the real high cotton!" Posy gleefully shouted. Michael shrugged with a perplexed look on his face as he approached the bar.

JIM BOB MCCALLUM SAT QUIETLY IN A CHAIR in the corner of his wife Mabel's bedroom. The elegant and ornate large room had been transformed into the home equivalent of a hospital room. Monitors, a drug cabinet, and oxygen tanks took over the space once occupied by expensive antique Louis the Fourteenth furniture. The doctor concluded his examination of Mabel and turned and walked towards Jim Bob.

"Her time is coming. There isn't much time left. Her breathing is becoming rather shallow and her pulse is becoming faint. A few days, maybe a week or two at the very most," the doctor solemnly stated in a hushed voice.

"There ain't nothing else that you can do, doc?" Jim Bob asked. The desperation and anguish in his voice was palpable.

"I'm so sorry. The disease has made its progression to the final stage, there's really nothing else that can be done. You've taken Herculean steps to extend your wife's life as long as possible. The rest now is in God's hands," the doctor replied. The doctor left the room, as Jim Bob moved to Mabel's bedside.

"My precious girl, don't you worry one bit," Jim Bob whispered. "I'll be right here beside you. You ain't going nowhere without me. I've got a few matters that I need to take care of, but then darling, we going home together. I promise you this with all my heart. My heart has been broken to bits. I cannot envision life without you, my sweet. Don't be afraid. I'm gonna be right by your side."

AARON ROSE AND CLAY GROVER DRESSED IN THEIR SAME court jester costumes from last year entered French Tips and were warmly greeted by Posy Branch and Lawton Cavanaugh.

"Look how cute you boys are," Posy said admiring their costumes. "Those are fine looking costumes!"

"Indeed," Lawton chimed in. "Did you buy those at the theatrical costume shop on Magazine Street?"

"Sure did," Aaron confirmed. "If you're going to get a costume, might as well get something that looks relatively authentic."

"Well, they look great on both of you, nice work," Lawton praised.

"You two gorgeous men go get yourself a drink on the house," Posy said with a grin. "You just won the first door prize for the evening with them costumes."

"Why, thank you Posy. We will certainly take you up on that generous offer and make our way through the crowd to Michael's bar," Aaron replied.

"Alright then, I'll see you boys in a little bit. Got more customers to get seated," Posy chirped while moving towards her newly arrived guests.

"See, what did I tell you," Aaron boasted. "Posy loved our costumes, they got us two free drinks. And she never noticed or mentioned that we were in the same costumes last year." The guys walked up to the bar and greeted Michael.

"Hey guys," Michael greeted his friends, followed by, "Wow, same costumes as last year. I guess some gay men have no shame," he said with a mischievous grin.

"There you go! We're going to be a laughingstock at OZ and Bourbon Pub," Clay kiddingly exclaimed.

"Wait a minute," Aaron protested. "This is coming from the same guy who is wearing the same flashing devil horns, and sorry devil's tail hanging out of his jeans as last year."

"I, my friend, have no choice. Since Posy won't let me wear a shirt my options are limited," Michael explained in his own defense.

"I think Michael has a very nice tail," Clay added with a devilish smile. Meanwhile, Posy had circled back to the bar area and put her arms around her two court jesters.

"What y'all been jibber-jabbering about?" Posy inquired.

"Proper gay etiquette and how some are completely oblivious to it," Clay quickly replied sarcastically.

"Well, I don't know nothing about that, but did Michael mention who he's been carrying on with lately?" Posy asked.

"No, he hasn't, but please do tell?" Aaron curiously questioned. Michael shifted uncomfortably from side to side while staring directly at Posy.

"You know Michael is a modest type, he don't go tooting his own horn much, but he's been having a long distance relationship with sort of a celebrity," Posy said building up the tension.

"Now you have to tell us," Clay enthusiastically demanded.

"In fact, the guy just called Michael earlier today just to tell him that he was thinking about him," Posy added.

"OK, c'mon who is it?" Aaron questioned. "You've built up the suspense long enough."

"Well, you boys know about that Democratic Senator who's running for President. It's his son Robert Douglas," Posy proudly announced.

"What?!?!?" Aaron screamed at the top of his lungs. Michael could only stand there with an embarrassed grin on his face.

FIVE HOURS LATER, POSY BRANCH WAS MAKING HER LAST CALL for alcohol announcement as she was preparing to close up for the night. The crowd began to dissipate, but the cash registers were brimming with a very large Halloween day take. Business had been as good as ever, but Posy was ready to call it a night. Her boyfriend, Norris Coaltree was working the night shift, so she would retire to her home alone, accompanied by only a nice bottle of pinot noir.

"That sure was a good evening. Folks had plenty of fun," Posy commented to Michael.

"Yeah, it was a nice chill crowd. No troublemakers or no one having too much to drink and getting out of hand," Michael added.

"That's right, I noticed that myself. Sometimes Halloween can be a real shit-show with unruly drunks and such, but tonight was pretty easy going," Posy acknowledged. "But poor Aaron, I thought he was going to stroke out after I told him about you and Robert Douglas! I didn't remember that Aaron worked for his pappy and knew Robert real well."

"Yes, he was shocked to say the least," Michael agreed.

"So, what is going on with you two?" Posy asked.

"Nothing really. We spent a couple of days having fun together when he was down here in the Big Easy for that campaign rally with this father. We had a nice time. We exchanged info and have kept in touch over the phone. But it's really nothing more than that. He's a nice guy. Real funny and smart. We like to talk to each other, but he lives in Chicago, and I'm here. So, that is about as much as there will be to that," Michael confessed.

"It ain't necessarily so," Posy sarcastically responded. "You see they got these things called airplanes."

"I'm not much of the boyfriend type to begin with and when you factor in long distance. It just wouldn't work," Michael concluded.

"It's your life, sugar. I done made enough mistakes of my own in the past. Just hope you don't let Mr. Right get away. They ain't many of them out there," Posy counseled her friend.

"Yes, Mama Posy," Michael replied affectionately. "I'm listening, trust me. But for now, time for us to jet. I'll get the lights and lock the back room. You get the front and I'll meet you at the door." Michael and Posy locked up and were outside on the street by 2:30 a.m.

"I'll walk you home," Michael insisted.

"No baby, thank you, but there's still plenty of people on the street. I'm good. Just gonna go home open this bottle of pinot noir, and soak in a hot tub for an hour. That always makes me sleep like a baby," Posy said with a chuckle. "And besides it's just getting good down at OZ. If you ain't gonna pursue Mr. Right, then you can at least go and find Mr. Right Now."

"You sure?" Michael questioned.

"Sugar, I'm dressed like a witch, carrying a lethal weapon. Who is going to mess with this crazy lady?"

"What lethal weapon?" Michael asked puzzled.

"Oh, it's this here bottle of wine. My intent is to kill it dead," Posy laughed as she hugged Michael and kissed him on the cheek, before walking down the French Quarter streets headed home.

POSY BRANCH WAS WITHIN STEPS OF HER HOUSE when a black van pulled up next to her. Two men wearing Halloween masks attempted to grab her off the street and wrestle her into the back of the van. Posy struggled mightily as the two men got her close to the open sliding door of the van. Once inside, one man pinned her down to the floor, but she used all of her strength and agility to free her hands.

"Get the damn chloroform rag over her nose and mouth," one of the men demanded of the other. Instead of using her freed hands to scratch and gouge her assailants, Posy pushed her right hand into her pocket. Her other hand was seized, as a sweet-smelling rag was pushed over her nose and mouth. Posy felt herself blacking out. Moments later, everything was as dark as the early morning hours of All Saints Day. The black van drove swiftly down the streets of New Orleans brushing the long hanging branches of a few poplar trees, headed towards the southbound freeway.

CHAPTER 39

THE MOSS LADEN CYPRUS TREES GLINTED in the Louisiana moonlight as alligators slithered from the swampy shores into the thick green water. The smell of a cypress swamp is distinctive. If you are from the south it is as familiar a smell as the Southern Magnolia trees in the spring. Posy Branch groggily regained conscience to the smell of a cypress swamp. The black van was about five miles outside of LaFayette, Louisiana heading deep into Cajun country.

"Where are we?" Posy slurred as she asked one of her captors.

"You'll be finding out soon enough. You surely are one good looking woman," the second man stated while leering at Posy who was tied up on the floor of the van.

"Why are you doing this?" Posy challenged.

"Oh, you know why. You done crossed the wrong man," one of the masked men said. "You should have known better than to come into New Orleans and put Olivier Bellevue out on the street. Cher, that is where you made your bed. Olivier don't take kindly to being embarrassed and taken advantage of. That stupid black boy-girl paid the price for challenging him, now it's your turn. The swamp gators gonna enjoy you but not before we do. We gonna take turns and rip you up real good. Give the gators some blood to smell in the water."

"Where is that coward Olivier? If he wants revenge, why ain't he here?" Posy demanded.

"He's in Florida, Cher. He can't be around when these things go down. Just like he was out of town when our brothers hung that freak show whore from a tree."

The black van pulled over to the side of the road in a swampy area. One of the men tore at Posy's clothes as she was tied by her hands and feet.

"We should flip to see who gets to fuck this stupid cunt first," one of the men said loudly. Posy tensed up her body and closed her eyes, as she attempted to keep her knees securely together. She could hear the cypress tree branches scrapping across the roof of the van as the late fall breeze swirled through the swamp. She felt a rough hand grab her by the neck. The smell of stale liquor was on the breath of her attacker. She kicked at the man with all the force she could muster in a last attempt at thwarting the inevitable.

And then, through the front windows of the van, blue strobing light filled the back cabin of the van. The screeching of car tires sounded like the most beautiful symphony possible as sirens and shouts from outside the van filled the early morning air. Within seconds, the Lafayette municipal police, Louisiana State police officers, and New Orleans police officers encircled the van and forced the men out into the cool swamp air. They were outmanned by dozens of law enforcement officers and quickly surrendered to save their own lives. Posy Branch was lifted from the van by a police officer and covered with a blanket.

"Thank God, you were able to activate the security monitor in your pocket, Ms. Branch," the officer stated. Posy could not speak. She was in shock. But she knew that she was safe, and for the moment, that was all that mattered.

THREE HOURS LATER, POSY BRANCH WAS BACK in New Orleans, sitting in a chair in the New Orleans police building in the French Quarter. Sergeant Norris Coaltree entered the room and Posy broke down and cried in his arms.

"It's alright now, you're safe, sugar. Everything is going to be alright," Norris whispered as Posy sobbed. Moments later, Michael entered the room and tears began to well-up in his eyes as he watched Posy clutch onto Norris' strong arms and weep.

"This is all my fault," Michael stated loudly. "If I would have just followed through and walked her home none of this would ever have happened."

"That's not true, Michael. You can't blame yourself," Norris countered. "She's alright now. It's over. The half-wits we arrested are singing like birds to save their own necks. We've got enough on Olivier Bellevue to put him away for a very long time. He was arrested by the Panama City police about thirty minutes ago. They're working out extradition back to Louisiana as we speak."

"I can't help but feel responsible. I'm supposed to protect her and I failed," Michael lamented, clearly very shaken. Posy raised her head from Norris' shoulder. She stared at Michael and provided a small smile.

"We're gonna be fine, my sweet boy. We gonna be just fine. You didn't let me down. You couldn't. It was my decision to go home alone. Please don't blame yourself. I don't. I love you, Michael, you're my heart," Posy quietly said.

Michael smiled in return. There wasn't anything else that needed to be said.

NEWS OF POSY'S ORDEAL TRAVELLED QUICKLY. The next morning, Clay Grover and Aaron Rose raced to the police station when they heard of the news. Not long thereafter, Stanford Winchester and his wife Whitlee arrived at the police station offering their support and their assistance in any way possible. Many of the merchants of the French Quarter sent flowers and cards to French Tips, Juleps & Jazz. The onslaught of support and well wishes was almost overwhelming. Neighborhood watch groups were formed and instituted quickly. Posy was made to feel loved and protected. The healing process was well underway.

A FEW DAYS LATER IT WAS THE FRIDAY before the Presidential election, and the national polls had the race for President as basically a dead heat. Senator Perry Douglas clung to a razor thin one-point lead. However, late Friday night ushered in an enormous October surprise. In politics, an October surprise is a news event deliberately planned or created to have an impact on the Presidential race. This one had enormous implications just three days from Election Day.

Several news agencies were fed written reports and numerous audio tapes that were damning and damaging to President Cochran's campaign. A number of audio tapes appeared to have conversations with the President's campaign manager, Nathan Whitaker, in which Whitaker was asking a New Orleans mambo about the amount of digitalis poison a healthy 180 pound male could safely ingest without causing permanent damage to vital organs, but would cause some temporary, yet serious health concerns. Since the attempt on the President's life involving digitalis poisoning was never solved and a perpetrator was never revealed, a few had questioned the legitimacy of the poisoning attempt. A very few had called it a political stunt to curry favor from the public. That story was never widely covered by the mainstream press but always lingered in the shadows of fake and highly partisan news outlets. The internet would have spurts of popularity over the topic, but ultimately the story often faded into the background of political news. Not now. The rumors now had the voice of the President's campaign manager associated with the story.

Many of the traditional new agencies withheld the news story attempting to verify the voice as that of Nathan Whitaker and the authenticity of the audio tapes. But some less traditional news venues pounced on the story and it soon became inflamed internet fodder. There were also reports of Nathan Whitaker with a prostitute, and allegations that Whitaker's mild poisoning was also self-induced to substantiate the administration's claim that some nefarious individual or group were committed to attacking and killing Cochran and his top aide. If true, this new evidence would point to the fact that it was all an elaborate ruse concocted to garner sympathy from the American public at large, and Republican primary voters specifically.

The Cochran administration went into full-fledged damage control. First, the White House attempted to fully discredit the story and blame it on some liberal Democrats foisting fake news on the American people in an effort to discredit the President on the eve of the election. But once further details surfaced it became increasingly harder to reference the story as nothing more than dirty tricks partisan politics. The second response of the Cochran administration was to remove Nathan Whitaker as a prominent surrogate for the President. He was swiftly replaced as campaign manager by Sam Brainard, the White House Chief of Staff. At least for the final two days before Election Day.

Many people around the President attempted to tamp down the fires of controversy and scandal days away from the election. But once some news agencies and private audio identification companies began to verify the voice on the audio tape as Nathan Whitaker's, the fire began to burn out of control. Nathan was removed from all official and political roles almost immediately.

SATURDAY MORNING, NATHAN WHITAKER was in the Washington DC area in his car, while he attempted to call his life-long friend, Andrew Cochran, on the telephone. Andrew Cochran was making a weekend appearance in Iowa before flying to Florida that night for two additional campaign appearances. Nathan made several attempts to connect with the President without success. He refused to leave a voicemail message, and instead kept re-dialing the number. After a number of tries, Nathan was successful. However, the call was answered by an aide to President Cochran, not Andrew himself.

"This is not a good time, Nathan," the aide said simply, coldly, before ending the call.

Nathan was distraught and overwhelmed with emotion as he continued to drive towards Frederick, Maryland. A little over an hour later Nathan was at his destination. He took a big swig from a bottle of Bulleit Bourbon and shook his head. He took his smart phone out of his pants pocket and began to draft an email addressed to Andrew Cochran's private email. It read as follows:

> Dear Andy,
>
> First and foremost old friend, you must know how much I love you. My heart is broken. I've ruined everything for you when my only intent was to do everything I could possibly do to support and love you. I have no life without you. This has been the unmistakable truth that soon became evident to me after we met our freshman year at Vanderbilt. I am most happy when I am with you. I understand that is no longer possible for reasons of my own doing.
>
> You always tried to steer me in the right direction. Even back in college you warned me about being too reckless and ambitious. You always told me, 'Nathan, stop trying to jump off cliffs without looking, you don't know how hard the landing is.' You were right, Andy. You always tended to be right about these things. You were always the responsible brake to my wild tendencies to

put the pedal to the metal. I thank you for that. You looked after me and cared for me more than any other person on this earth.

I am writing to you from a place that we visited together during our summer break after completing our junior year of college. Remember that summer we decided to pack up my car and head to the battle fields of the Civil War in the eastern theater. We went to Antietam, Gettysburg, Fredericksburg, Bull Run and many more battlefields in the region. I'm now at Harpers Ferry. I know you'll remember that this site changed hands 14 times during the Civil War. It was vitally important to both sides. It's also where Abolitionist John Brown assembled a small army in Harpers Ferry and made a valiant last stand against the federal troops. It's a beautiful setting with the river running through the gorge at Maryland Heights.

It is here, my friend, that I am going to say goodbye to you. There are no more last stands left in me. I've done enough damage to your life and complicated things beyond comprehension and repair. I love you too much, I cannot bear what I've done to you. So, farewell old chum, there's just one more cliff to jump. And I am well-aware of the landing.

I love you, Andy. Always and forever. Nathan.

A HOWL OF DESPERATION AND ANGUISHED PAIN filled the cabin of Air Force One, as President Andrew Cochran read the email from Nathan Whitaker several minutes after boarding the plane. The tortured cries and intense sobbing were unbearably heartbreaking for anyone to hear.

Two hours later, State and Federal police were at the bottom of the 400 foot cliff of Maryland Heights. They carefully removed the human remains from the rocky sides of the gorge. The early November wind gusts rattled the leafless limbs of the chestnut oak trees that are found on the northern slope of the mountain. The old trees banged and moaned their wooden requiem in haunting unison.

CHAPTER 40

Election Day. President Cochran eschewed all of the previous plans to be in his home state of Georgia for Election Day in order to remain in Washington DC with the body of his best friend, Nathan Whitaker who was to be buried in a small private ceremony the following day in a cemetery in Virginia. At that moment, the Presidency and the election meant absolutely nothing to him. In his most candid moments with only a very few trusted friends and close aides would he admit that he actually hoped that he would lose the election. The loss of Nathan Whitaker had left him tortured and hollow. He blamed himself for Nathan's suicide. The joy and pleasure that often could be seen in his gleaming blue eyes were gone.

Chicago was all abuzz as it prepared for the possible acceptance speech from the next President of the United States. The Douglas for President Campaign office was packed with volunteers and well-wishers. The crowd was cautiously optimistic yet very enthusiastic. The last national polls taken the previous day indicated that Senator Douglas was leading President Cochran by three and a half points. A good lead, but still within the margin of error. Furthermore, several battleground states were still too close to call for either candidate.

Carolyn Barnes met with a team of pollsters in her office at the campaign headquarters in downtown Chicago. There was nothing left to poll, the election was now in the hands of the voters. Turnout appeared to be strong, but it was still early in the afternoon. Carolyn turned in her chair and saw two smiling faces standing in the doorway to her office.

"There you are!" Carolyn exclaimed as she rose to her feet and walked over to give Aaron Rose and Clay Grover a big hug.

"We just got in from the airport, we haven't even gone to the hotel yet," Aaron explained.

"How was your flight?" Carolyn asked.

"It was great, first class," Clay offered. "They actually feed you in first class."

"As always, my husband's only concern is eating," Aaron said playfully. "Please thank Senator Douglas for providing the first-class airfare and the hotel room," Aaron added.

"I believe we've put you up at the Palmer House, and you can thank the Senator yourself when you see him this evening," Carolyn responded. "If everything goes according to plan, he wanted to have his White House Chief of Staff and Assistant White House counsel present this evening for the festivities and available to start building the new administration tomorrow morning."

"Sounds great!" Clay replied. "And how are things looking so far?"

"Pretty good, I think. President Cochran was coming on strong the last two weeks and was certainly closing the gap. That is until this whole unfortunate incident with the information being fed to the press and the horrible tragedy involving Nathan Whitaker. From Friday to Monday, it appears we may have picked up as much as two to three points with the remaining undecided voters," Carolyn stated confidently.

"It is terrible," Aaron confirmed. "The Whitaker suicide just gives more credence to the material leaked to the press. It is harder to argue that it is nothing but unsubstantiated lies and rumors if your campaign manager commits suicide over the leaked information."

"Any inside information on where the leaked materials came from?" Clay inquired.

"Well, I can tell you unequivocally that it didn't come from this campaign, the DNC, or any Democratic political operatives that we are aware of. If we win, this is not how any of us wanted to do it. Which leads us to think that it came from either inside the Republican Party or someone closely connected to the Party and the candidate," Carolyn surmised.

"Cletus Sawyer?" Aaron questioned. "I understand that he is still upset about how he was treated by the President."

"Perhaps, but I doubt it. Cletus Sawyer was never close with Nathan Whitaker and some of the information released must have been gained by someone who was at least at one time a friend of Nathan Whitaker," Clay stated.

"Secrets don't remain secrets for very long in Washington politics. I'm sure we will become aware of the source of the leaked materials soon enough," Carolyn added.

"What's soon enough, boss lady?" Robert Douglas asked as he popped his head into Carolyn's office doorway hearing only the last few words of Carolyn's explanation.

"The monumental stress that you give me won't dissipate soon enough after this election is over is what I was telling the guys," Carolyn jokingly responded.

"Ah, my gaydar had sensed that there were handsome gay men nearby," Robert announced as he threw himself into Clay's arms, and then into Aaron's. "How are my scrumptious NOLA boys?"

"We're good, we just arrived from the airport a few minutes ago," Clay answered. "Carolyn was filling us in on some things."

"But before we veer off topic, speaking of NOLA boys, I understand that there may be something going on with you and yet another NOLA boy," Aaron said with a huge smirk on his face.

"This is why there are so few gay men working for the CIA. They just can't keep a secret to save their lives," Robert flamboyantly lamented while tossing his head back.

"It's not Michael's fault," Clay quickly interjected. "Posy was the one who spilled the beans."

"Oh, that's right. I spoke with her on the phone and asked her to relay a message to gorgeous Michael," Robert admitted.

"So, you're the one who blew your own cover," Carolyn loudly announced with great pleasure.

"Don't you have voters to bribe or something?" Robert responded with a dramatic huff as he turned and walked away.

"Never a dull moment," Clay gleefully added.

"Oh, never, ever," Carolyn confirmed with a sigh.

IT WAS 9:17 P.M. IN CHICAGO ON ELECTION DAY. The west coast states' polls had closed just minutes earlier. With the addition of the electoral votes being added from the bedrock Democratic states of Washington, Oregon, California, and in this case Nevada, several news agencies proclaimed Senator Perry Douglas as the President Elect. The people in the grand ballroom at the Palmer House Hotel as well as the hundreds of thousands of people who filled Grant Park in Chicago waiting to hear the victory speech of the next President of the United States exploded with cheers and screams of happiness.

Less than twenty minutes later, Senator Perry Douglas received a very sincere concession call from President Andrew Cochran. With that the President Elect and his family boarded several limousines and with the Secret Service highly apparent, they drove the short distance from the hotel campaign headquarters to Grant Park, where Perry Douglas would deliver his victory speech live in front of a quarter million of his fellow citizens and supporters. Carolyn, Aaron, and Clay stood at the far side of the stage locked arm in arm as they awaited the arrival of the future First Family.

President Elect Douglas gave one of the best speeches of his political career. He promised to unite the country and move forward on a progressive agenda to solve the nation's many problems. Perry Douglas graciously thanked and praised President Andrew Cochran. He commented favorably on the fair and civil manner in which both campaigns conducted themselves during the general election. He promised on continuing the achievements made by President Cochran with respect to bipartisan compromise and consensus building. And finally, Perry Douglas asked for a moment of silence in tribute to President Cochran's former White House Chief of Staff, campaign manager, and beloved lifelong friend, Nathan Whitaker.

ONE DAY LATER, ANDREW COCHRAN WAS STANDING with his wife at the internment ceremony for his best friend at a cemetery in Northern Virginia. He had just lost an election for the first time in his political career. He had just lost his Presidency. And he could not have cared less. In fact, he was relieved that in two months' time he would no longer be in the public spotlight. That he could return to his native Georgia and hopefully fade into obscurity. At least as much as a former President could ever become obscure. There was no fight left in him. There never would be again. He had lost his fight. He had lost Nathan.

TWO DAYS AFTER THE ELECTION OF PERRY DOUGLAS, Stanford Winchester was digging deep into his trousers' front pocket to retrieve his smart phone. Stanford glanced at the screen of his phone and smiled.

"Good afternoon Mr. President-Elect," Stanford happily intoned.

Fifty-five minutes later, Stanford said, "Goodbye, sir." He sat quietly in his rocking chair, not moving an inch or a muscle. Shortly thereafter, his wife Whitlee walked into the room and stared at her motionless husband for a few long moments.

"What is it Stanford, what's wrong?" Whitlee questioned after Stanford appeared almost comatose. The sound of her voice quickly shook Stanford from his stupor.

"That was one peculiar call," Stanford finally slowly uttered.

"Who was it? How so?" Whitlee challenged.

"I'm not exactly sure, but I may have just talked my way into being nominated by President-Elect Douglas as his Attorney General, by spending over forty-five minutes explaining to the President-Elect why I am not suited to be Attorney General," Stanford said unsure of what he was saying.

"I don't understand," Whitlee replied.

"My dear, neither do I," Stanford admitted.

"Well, what transpired? What was said?" Whitlee asked.

"I answered the call and congratulated the President-Elect on his hard-fought victory. He then thanked me for my willingness to thrash out with him some judicial reform ideas over the phone the last few weeks. I told him how much I had enjoyed our conversations and how much I will miss them. He then explained to me that I wouldn't have to miss them and in fact they could become far more regular if I consented to being his choice for Attorney General of the United States. I must have spent forty-five minutes elaborating on my short comings, how I was ill-suited for the position, that I was old and retired, that I had never served in law enforcement. That my career was judicial not prosecutorial. Whitlee, honestly, I went on and on about my failings and why I would not be a good choice for that or any cabinet position."

"And then what did he say?" Whitlee inquired.

"He told me that I had just listed all of the reasons why he wanted me for the position. He doesn't want someone from law enforcement, he wants someone who has seen both sides of the law from the bench to be his Attorney General. He then went on to say some very flattering things about my intellect and my fair and honest judgment, and my agreeable temperament. He informed me that he wanted to fill his cabinet with not only Democrats, but also some Republicans and Independents. When I protested again about being happily retired, he challenged me. He said that the highly intelligent and informative conversations that he had had with me, were with a person who was far from being retiring or retired. He told me that he sensed my zest for judicial problem solving. He was very gracious and complimentary. He then asked me to seriously consider the position. He told me that he was looking for only a two-year commitment. To help him set the tone for his new administration and to bring to the Justice Department the same discipline and decorum that I had brought to the Fifth Circuit," Stanford answered.

"What did you say?" Whitlee eagerly questioned her husband.

"What could I say?" Stanford began. "I thanked him for the honor of being considered for the cabinet position and also for his high praise of me. I told him that I would have to discuss this with you. I again reiterated, in brief, why I was not a qualified candidate, and finally, as any citizen being asked to do something by the President-Elect would do, I informed him that I would give great thought and deliberation to his request."

"Now what?" Whitlee asked.

"My dear, I don't have a clue."

CHAPTER 41

B Y SUNDAY MORNING, TWO DAYS AFTER President-Elect Douglas'
conversation with Stanford Winchester, Stanford's name was being
bandied about all of the morning political talk shows as being Perry
Douglas' first choice to be the next Attorney General of the United States.
Stanford sat on the couch in his living room next to his wife Whitlee.
They both sipped their coffee and were mesmerized by the conversations
from the various political talking heads on the television.

"This ain't real helpful from the perspective of easily being able to say,
'no,'" Stanford aptly summed up.

"No, my dear, if that is going to be your answer, it won't be easy at all,"
Whitlee agreed.

"Well surely you agree that that should be my answer," Stanford said.
"I mean, we have a wonderful life right here in New Orleans. We both
love it here. We are immensely happy here. Your highly important and
successful career is here. Right?"

"Yes, of course we are very happy here, my love. But we can be happy
anywhere. Our love for each other provides us comfort wherever we
would go," Whitlee responded.

"That's not quite the definitive response that I was seeking, coun-
selor," Stanford replied with his dry wit showing. "A tad too much gray
introduced into my black and white facts."

"I love you too much to lie to you Stanford. When I came home from work after you had one of your two hour afternoon conversations with Senator Douglas, you were absolutely glowing. You were so full of life having bantered about ideas that you had had about judicial reform for decades. And for days thereafter, there was little else that you wanted to talk about. You were having the time of your life. And Senator Douglas, in his infinite wisdom realized the goldmine of knowledge and intellect that he had tapped into and he kept on digging. Now, as the President-Elect he wants to keep on digging. And can you blame him? Stanford, you have so much to offer this President and this nation. You're not mentally ready for retirement. If you were, you wouldn't have been so immensely happy and proud to carry on with Perry Douglas for weeks on end. You can be a very political man when you want to be. You would have figured out some gracious way to push aside his inquiries and not participate. But you did the exact opposite. You begged for more. You both calendared the next date like school kids looking forward to their next field trip. Giddy with excitement to escape your home room and explore the expansive universe of what if?"

"I always did like 'what if' questions. Speculating about what one would do if you had access to such power," Stanford whimsically replied.

"Think long and hard before you give an answer that you reflexively think you are supposed to give," Whitlee counseled her husband.

"Thank goodness I married a smart woman," Stanford replied with a wink and a loving grin.

ON MONDAY MORNING STANFORD'S SMART PHONE began to ring. He was not expecting a call from the President-Elect so soon. He was informed that he could take his time. That no decision needed to be made until after the Thanksgiving holiday. Stanford turned his phone over, and slightly trembled when he saw the name of the caller, Jim Bob McCallum.

"Hello," Stanford hesitantly offered into the phone.

"Hello Stanford, Jim Bob McCallum here. How are you?"

"I'm well, Jim Bob, thank you for asking," Stanford answered feeling somewhat odd.

"I bet you're sitting there wondering why in tarnation is Jim Bob McCallum calling me after all these years and some less than cordial comments?

"Well, I'm not sure I would put it that way," Stanford responded diplomatically.

"Truth is Stanford, I was watching some TV yesterday morning, and them moderators on them shows was talking about the fact that the President Elect wants you as his Attorney General. I could have been knocked over with a feather hearing such a thing. But I think that it is plum wonderful. Congratulations! And I hope you accept. Washington could use a good ol' boy from New Orleans to clean things up in that white marble cesspool," Jim Bob stated enthusiastically.

"Thank you, Jim Bob. But it's all talk and speculation at this point," Stanford mentioned.

"Other thing that I wanted you to know, is that my darling girl Mabel ain't long for this world. She fought the good fight and lasted longer than any of them doctors thought she would. But even I know the end is near. We were once great friends. You and LeeAnn and me and Mabel. We was the center of the social world down here. So, as an old friend, I thought you would like to know," Jim Bob said with a deep sadness in his tone.

"I'm so sorry to hear that," Stanford solemnly replied. "Mabel is a wonderful woman, and she was such a supportive and loving friend to both LeeAnn and myself. I'm truly heartbroken to hear that it has to come to this. Alzheimer's is such an insidious and destructive disease. If there is anything that I can do, please let me know."

"Actually, there is one thing that I think that we can both do to honor Mabel," Jim Bob answered. "I'd like to bury the hatchet between us. As I said, we all had been such good friends for so long. It bothered Mabel no end when we fell out four years ago. She rightfully blamed me for poisoning our relationship. I tell you true, Stanford, she would get so upset with me for not being a better friend to you. Sometimes, I think some of the bad blood between us did her health no good. No good at all."

"It does no good to think like that. Sometimes even good friends drift apart. We don't need to get into specifics," Stanford allowed.

"So, what do you say? Will you join me for a drink in honor of my beloved Mabel? Let her leave this earth knowing that you and I could at least share a cocktail together for a few minutes?" Jim Bob offered. There was a pronounced silence on the line as Stanford carefully considered Jim Bob's conciliatory gesture.

"Sure," Stanford responded. "Where and when?"

"Wednesday at 1:00 p.m. at the Columns Hotel. I hope you don't mind, but I don't want to be more than a couple of blocks from home in case something happens," Jim Bob explained.

"Of course, I wholly understand. See you then," Stanford replied. He glanced back at his phone before slowly letting it descend deep into his pants pocket.

THE NEXT DAY, STANFORD WINCHESTER DECIDED to pay a visit to another old friend. He stopped in to say 'hi' to Bessie Collins at her voodoo shop on North Rampart. The small bell above the entrance door proclaimed Stanford's arrival.

"Well, ain't this just a wonderful surprise," Bessie gushed. Bessie scampered from behind the glass counter to give Stanford a big hug.

"I should stop by more frequently, that was a lovely warm welcome," Stanford said with a smile.

"Is it alright to hug an Attorney General?" Bessie chuckled.

"Easy there now, Bessie. Nothing's been decided. Though folks sure seem like they're in a hurry to get me packed up and on my way to Washington," Stanford joked in return.

"Nothing could be farther from the truth. We know that we can't be thinking just about ourselves. If we got to share you with the rest of the country for a little while so be it. We can't claim all of the good fortune for ourselves," Bessie boasted about her friend. "Lucius gonna be tickled pink when he hear that you come by to see me. I wish I had known you was coming I would have baked a real nice pie."

"You've spent way too many years fussing over the likes of me. Surely, I do not know what I ever did to deserve such wonderful friends," Stanford happily said. "I also don't know why I deserve such a wonderful woman like Whitlee as my wife. I am truly blessed. And while I'm here I'd like to purchase one of those lovely necklaces you have in the display case for her."

"Oh, you mean the amulets," Bessie corrected. "They all have specific meanings and purposes. What were you thinking about?"

"How about one for love?" Stanford asked.

"Well, for love, how about this one here?" Bessie suggested as she held up a lovely gold chain with a ruby amulet.

"That one is perfect," Stanford said tenderly. "I'm all about love and reconciliation these days. In fact, tomorrow afternoon at 1:00 p.m., I'm going to the Columns Hotel to share a cocktail with Jim Bob McCallum," Stanford announced.

"Oh goodness, Stanford, you sure you want to do that?" Bessie nervously asked. "After all that man said about you and did to them poor folks?"

"Now Bessie, Jim Bob was fairly tried and acquitted by a jury of his peers. Being a former judge, that's good enough for me. The rest is just gossip and unsubstantiated innuendo. As for what he said about me, that's in the past. Jim Bob seems sincere about mending fences. His poor wife Mabel is in very grave health. She's not long for this world, and Jim Bob wants to honor her and her memory by making amends with those he believes he has wronged in the past. That's an honorable sentiment," Stanford responded.

"I don't got a good feeling about this," Bessie said with a concerned look on her pretty face. "I know the Good Lord preached to us about forgiveness and all, but some folk are beyond redemption. Some folk are just plain no good."

"I don't think that you have anything to worry about," Stanford said to ease Bessie's mind. "It's the middle of the day, we will be in a public place. And I will be very mindful, trust me."

"Don't drink nothing that man offers to you from his own hand," Bessie cautioned.

"No worries, Bessie, my dear friend. I will be fine," Stanford answered with a cheerful smile.

THE NEXT MORNING, BESSIE WOKE UP and baked a fresh pecan pie for her friend Stanford. She didn't have time to allow it to cool properly before she needed to make her way to the shop, so she left the pie on her kitchen counter and would return to fetch it at lunchtime. She would bring it to the shop with her after lunch and then stop by Stanford and Whitlee's home with the pie after she closed up her shop for the evening.

As the noon hour approached, Bessie looked over at Papa Levi who was asleep in his wooden chair in the corner of the shop.

"Papa Levi wake up. I need you to watch after the store while I go home and fetch the pecan pie I made this morning," Bessie said.

"I ain't sleeping," Papa Levi protested. "I'm just resting my eyes."

"You snore while you is resting your eyes?" Bessie questioned with a smirk.

"Pecan pie, you say," Papa Levi responded, attempting to change the topic.

"I'm sorry it ain't for you. I made it for Stanford. But I'll make you a pie tomorrow, ok?" Bessie asked.

"Sounds good to me," Papa Levi replied with his eyes wide open. "How long you gonna be?"

"About an hour and a half. I got me an errand I got to run. And I was going to have a nice hot lunch at home for a change. You want me to bring you a bowl of jambalaya?"

"That surely would be nice, thank you kindly," Papa Levi gratefully stated. "Go on now, my eyes is open and I'll take care of any customers that come in while you is gone."

"Alright then. I'll see you in a bit."

STANFORD WINCHESTER DIDN'T WANT TO TAKE A CHANCE on driving his car if he was going to have a couple of cocktails so he walked to Canal Street, the dividing street between the Central Business District and the French Quarter. There, he would catch the St. Charles Streetcar Line which would drop him off steps from the Columns Hotel, where he was to meet Jim Bob McCallum.

Stanford sat in the back of the streetcar taking in the sights and sounds of the city that he loved so much. His mind filled with thoughts of leaving the Big Easy, if only for a couple of years. He was a tad apprehensive about his meeting with Jim Bob, yet, Stanford also believed that it was commendable for Jim Bob to want to honor his wife by putting aside past grievances. That is, if his intentions were sincere.

Stanford walked into the hotel and proceeded straight into the Victorian Lounge. It was the dark wooded ornate bar room where he had had a conversation with Jim Bob almost four years ago. Jim Bob sat in the same red upholstered wing back chair that he sat in the last time Stanford was there. Next to the chair was a small side table with a cherry wood box sitting to Jim Bob's right. An Asian rug covered a part of the gorgeous wood floors. A second wing backed chair was to the side and about five or six feet from the chair occupied by Jim Bob. The bar and the lobby of the hotel were empty with the exception of

Stanford, Jim Bob, and a bartender, who was busily crafting a pair of Sazeracs.

"Greetings Stanford," Jim Bob bellowed as he stood up and extended his hand to an old friend and more recent foe.

"Hello Jim Bob," Stanford stated as he took Jim Bob's hand into his own.

"I am so pleased that you decided to join me today. I told Mabel where I was going, and I swear I saw her face light up," Jim Bob said.

"How is Mabel doing?" Stanford asked with a concerned voice.

"Not well, not well at all. She's confined to her bed and she breathes with the aid of an oxygen mask. Her pulse is weak, and her pallor is an ashen hue. I love her so much Stanford, it's so hard to see her go like this. But that is precisely why I am glad that you are here to toast her with me and let bygones be bygones."

"I know it's a Wednesday afternoon in early November, but the hotel seems almost vacant except for you, me and the bartender," Stanford observed.

"That's because it is," Jim Bob replied. "I bought out the entire hotel for the day. I gave the owners one million dollars to cancel reservations for today and have the place vacant for 24 hours."

"Why?" Stanford questioned, now beginning to feel uneasy about the situation.

"Because I didn't want to be interrupted. Because I know that since the Sunday morning talk shows, you've probably had some reporters sneaking around you for an interview or some kind of story. Because I thought a meeting of this magnitude deserved the utmost privacy. Well, and because one million dollars is frankly lunch money to me," Jim Bob responded with a chortle and the wink of an eye.

"Well, I have spied a couple of reporters in front of my house on Royal after the news broke on Sunday," Stanford confirmed. "But this is quite over the top, renting out a hotel for a day."

"I'm happy to do it if it means that we can have a pleasant conversation," Jim Bob said with a smile. "And here comes our cocktails." A tuxedoed bartender carried a tray with two Sazeracs over to the far corner of the lounge where Jim Bob and Stanford were seated. Each took a cocktail off of the silver serving tray. Stanford looked a bit askance at his drink. Jim Bob quickly picked up on Stanford's hesitation.

"Oh, hell Stanford, I ain't gonna have Jimmy poison you. A Southern gentleman don't poison his friends. Well, I guess unless you're Andrew Cochran and Nathan Whitaker. But hell, them power hungry boys didn't poison each other they just drank poison themselves to get all kinds of sympathy, news coverage, and most importantly, votes. And hell if it didn't work! Concocted quite a scam that turned around Andrew's failing primary campaign and had the country whispering about all sorts of fake conspiracies against the President and his top aide. Kind of brilliant, actually. Except poor old Nathan didn't realize that the mambo he was asking for advice about poison was recording the phone call. Real smart boy, just got careless from time to time," Jim Bob explained.

"How do you know that? Or is that just your own speculation?" Stanford asked a bit taken aback by the information.

"C'mon now Stanford, you know better than to ask me that question. I'll answer anything you wanna ask me in the spirit of friendship, but don't ask nothing you don't wanna know," Jim Bob warned. Jim Bob then changed the topic quickly, "You want another Sazerac?"

"I've barely touched this one, no thank you," Stanford responded.

"Alright then. Thank you, Jimmy, you can go. And please lock the front door on your way out," Jim Bob stated as he addressed the bartender. Jimmy walked towards the lobby of the hotel and exited the front door locking it from the outside.

"Is that really necessary?" Stanford asked.

"Well, you never know when some curious tourist gonna be poking their head in, so best to lock the door so that we are undisturbed. Plus, if you're going to ask me questions like that, Jimmy don't need to hear them answers," Jim Bob replied.

"May I ask what is in the lovely wooden box at your side?" Stanford inquired.

"Something for later, but also a little memorabilia," Jim Bob explained as he opened the box slightly and took out a few photographs. He handed Stanford three old and age worn photos. "That first one is of LeeAnn and me at high school graduation. That was taken before you entered the picture and swept LeeAnn away from me. The second one is from my wedding day to Mabel. There we are all four of us, so young and full of life. And that last photo is once again of the four of us at your swearing in ceremony when you were appointed to the Fifth Circuit. We all did surely spend some nice times together."

"Yes, fond memories," Stanford agreed before taking another sip of his cocktail.

"Most more fond for you than me," Jim Bob said as his tone turned darker and less friendly.

BESSIE WALKED THROUGH THE STREETS of the French Quarter from her home heading towards her voodoo shop on North Rampart Street. She carried a small shopping bag containing Stanford's pecan pie and a container of homemade jambalaya and a piece of cornbread for Papa Levi. It was about 1:30 in the afternoon. As she turned onto Rampart Street she saw billows of thick black smoke rising into the blue sky. Moments later, Bessie heard sirens from fire trucks headed into the direction of the smoke. Bessie quickened her pace until she realized that the smoke was coming from the vicinity of her shop.

Bessie broke into a full out sprint as she raced towards her business establishment. When she was one block away, she realized that her small old wooden shop was engulfed in flames. The fire and police department vehicles arrived about the same time that Bessie reached the scene. Bessie struggled to get closer but she was restrained by police officers who were attempting to set up a fire perimeter for the safety of the public.

"Let me go!" Bessie shouted. "That's my shop! My friend is in there!"

The police officer apologized, but informed Bessie that he could not allow her any closer. A small woman wearing a Mardi Gras mask approached Bessie from behind. She stood just behind Bessie's right shoulder.

"He ain't in there," the masked woman said in a deep voice.

"Who are you? What do you know?" Bessie demanded as she turned towards the woman.

"Papa Levi ain't in the building. Ain't that all you need to know right now?" the masked woman asked.

"How do you know that?" Bessie questioned clearly agitated and upset.

"He ran off out the back door when he saw trouble coming," the woman calmly stated. "Ain't got no beef with that sad old man."

"Who are you? Who doesn't have a beef with Papa Levi?" Bessie asked with tears streaming from her eyes.

"Bessie, you done messed with the wrong mambo. Esther Francois is a powerful Haitian mambo. Yet you turned her out, humiliated her in public, showed yourself to be a greedy bitch with no concern for anyone but yourself. Then, when you went and brought in that Cajun pretender and treated her like the false royalty she claimed herself to be, you went too far. Esther done threw Mariette out of this town years ago with the help of your auntie, Queen Rita. Mariette wasn't Haitian, she was just a fake mambo from the swamps. The true mambos chased her from the Quarter. She went back to Cajun country and hid there for years. Then gradual like after the Queen's death, Mariette started to sneak back into the Big Easy and take over some of Esther's customers. Well, Esther don't forget, and now Mariette just another pretender taken by the foxglove."

"Esther is not going to get away with this. She will be arrested and spend the rest of her life in prison!" Bessie exclaimed to the masked woman.

"Cher, Esther ain't nowhere she can be found. Her wealthy friend and benefactor flew Esther out of New Orleans early this morning on his private jet plane. By now, she be landed in Haiti and gone up into the mountains. Nobody gonna find you if you lose yourself in them mountains," the masked woman related in a gentler tone. "Esther is gone for good."

Bessie listened to the woman while watching her business burn to the ground. She began to process everything that the woman had said. When she turned around to confront the woman, she was gone. Lost in the crowd that had gathered to watch the fire department attempt to extinguish the flames. Bessie authoritatively grabbed a police officer by the arm and shouted her plea for assistance with urgent resolve and anguish.

STANFORD WINCHESTER TOOK ONE LAST SIP of his Sazerac finishing off the cocktail. He turned towards Jim Bob and smiled pleasantly.

"That was a well-made drink. Please give my compliments to Jimmy when you see him next," Stanford said.

"Today is the last time I will see Jimmy the bartender," Jim Bob solemnly stated, his mood now completely changed from the convivial spirit that he greeted Stanford with when he arrived. "I won't be seeing anyone else ever again."

"I don't understand," Stanford replied, confused by Jim Bob's words and dark demeanor.

"Well, then let me enlighten you," Jim Bob began. "One way or another I am leaving this world today. There are two options. The first resides in this here wooden box, the second awaits me at my house." Jim Bob then proceeded to take the wooden box into his lap and turn it towards Stanford as he opened the hinged lid.

"These are two of the finest antique Constable Saw Handle Precision Dueling Pistols that money can buy. They are .50 Caliber and were made in Philadelphia circa 1830. Look at that gorgeous walnut handle stock and unfinished Belgium steel. Looks like they were made yesterday, don't it? I know that you are a history buff, Stanford, so you should enjoy this fact. A very similar version of these Constable pistols were used by Alexander Hamilton and Aaron Burr when they dueled each other leading to Hamilton's death. Of course, those pistols preceded these by about 30 years, so these are a bit more technically advanced in craft and workmanship."

"Why are you telling me this?" Stanford asked now clearly agitated.

"Because we are both gentlemen of the South, and I plan to end this lifelong grudge that I've had with you, you smarmy son of a bitch, with honor and dignity," Jim Bob calmly responded. "The pistols are both loaded and cocked. Since I am the challenger, you may have first choice of weapon."

"This is preposterous!" Stanford shouted. "I'm not going to duel you, Jim Bob. You're out of your mind!"

"You have no choice, Stanford, don't you see that?" Jim Bob questioned with a sardonic grin. "If you win, you get to walk out that door and you are done with me forever. However, if I win, I will have the pleasure of watching you suffer for a few happily pleasing moments. I will then take that short stroll through the Garden District to my home. I have a vial of a rare and powerful poison that was given to me by my good friend Esther Francois. Haitian mambos truly have an affinity and skill with poisons. I will mix that poison into a glass of water. I will give Mabel several sips, before I take a few sips myself, and then I will lay in bed next to my dying wife. So, you see old chum, I plan to die today, and

I am wholly at peace with it. I've promised Mabel that we will enter the afterlife together, and that is precisely what we will do. So, my advice to you, is choose your weapon. We will pace off and may the better shot and the best man win."

"There is no way that I will perpetrate this ridiculous farce with you," Stanford angrily said as he raised up from his chair and briefly looked directly at Jim Bob. "If you want to kill yourself, have at it, but it will not be by my hand." Stanford turned and proceeded to walk towards the lobby and the front door.

Moments later a shot rang out and a small amount of smoke billowed out from the barrel of the antique pistol. The shot hit Stanford in the small of the back, as he crumbled to the floor. Jim Bob walked over to the fallen Stanford, as he stood and looked over his rival.

"You had to have it your way, didn't you? It's always has been that way ever since I first laid eyes on you as you stole the love of my life away from me. The high and mighty Stanford Winchester always got precisely what he wanted and if it wasn't to his liking everyone would suffer. You could have just played along and been a Justice on the Supreme Court. But no, you had to make a fuss and refuse the nomination because you didn't get it the way that you wanted it. Nathan and I paid a substantial price for your little prima donna moment, you pompous ass! Then you married another woman and defiled the memory of my sweet LeeAnn. No, you don't get to do that. And when I heard the news about you possibly becoming the next Attorney General of this nation. Enough! It was more than I could stand. You don't get to win all of the time, Stanford. So now, I have won. I get the righteous retribution against you that I justly deserve," Jim Bob spat out vindictively.

Stanford fighting against the shock from the fact that he had been shot in the back, began to put his hand in his pocket to grasp his cellphone. His limbs began to twitch and he felt paralysis begin to set in.

"Oh, one other thing that I should mention before I leave you to bleed out on this lovely rug. I told you a little white lie. Earlier I mentioned that I would not poison you. And of course, there was no poison in the Sazerac that you certainly enjoyed. However, the shell of the ball fired from the pistol was soaked in curare. It is a paralyzing poison that was used by Amazonian Indians when they hunted their prey. It causes weakness of the skeletal muscles and can cause eventual death by asphyxiation due to the paralysis of the diaphragm. It was another gift from my friend Esther Francois, who I transported back to Haiti this morning on one of my private jets. I understand that she had a special surprise for your friend Bessie Collins as well. So, you see Stanford, you are unable to crawl or move or even call for help. You will either bleed to death or you will die from asphyxiation. Either way you lose. But, I need to be off now. Mabel and I have a long journey ahead of us. Goodbye Stanford Winchester."

Jim Bob McCallum opened the front door of the hotel and departed with a cynical and overly demonstrative wave. Stanford fought to gain control of his limbs and mobility without success. The blood oozed from the small-bore hole in his back staining the lovely rug beneath him.

THE LEAFLESS CHESTNUT OAK TREES ON THE NORTH SLOPE of Maryland Heights shook in the November gusty winds. While the weeping willow and cypress trees swayed and heaved in the temperate breezes in the Garden District of New Orleans. The trees of life can grow and flourish for many years, but ultimately fall and decay in the unforgiving forest. Nature can be cruel.

RESTORATION

Y ES, NATURE CAN BE CRUEL but it can also be forgiving. For many decades, conservation organizations warned that, once destroyed, tropical forests could never be restored. However, thirty years of restoration research, since the early 1980's, now challenges this formerly widely held belief. In fact, it is quite apparent that natural regeneration is possible. Some forests that were subject to fires or other calamities, either natural or caused by humans, can undergo wondrous restorations.

Merriam-Webster defines restoration as "the act or process of returning something to its original condition." Additionally, restoration is "the act of returning something that was stolen or taken." Though at times, it seems quite the contrary, human beings are very capable of being restorative. And when humans intervene to restore something, whether it be assisting with forest restoration or returning something taken, it can be a healing and joyous event.

BESSIE COLLINS ARRIVED AT THE COLUMNS HOTEL in a New Orleans municipal police car. Bessie and the police officer raced into the lobby of the hotel to find Stanford Winchester on the floor lying in a pool of his own blood. Moments later an EMT van arrived and the emergency technicians took all steps possible to save the life of Bessie's beloved friend. Stanford was barely alive. He had lost a significant amount of blood, and the curare poison had inhibited his ability to draw in oxygen. Bessie sobbed as she stood helplessly while Stanford was loaded into the EMT van and transported the short distance to St. Charles General Hospital.

TWO MONTHS LATER, IT WAS JANUARY 20TH. It was a mild day in Washington, D.C. for mid-January. The temperature was around 42 degrees and the sun shone brightly in the Democratic blue sky. Dignitaries and guests awaited the swearing in ceremony for the next President of the United States, Perry Douglas. A huge crowd assembled at the foot of the Capitol Building. President Cochran and the First Lady graciously welcomed President Elect Douglas and Katherine Douglas to the White House earlier that morning.

While the Douglas' were being welcomed by the Cochran's, Clay Grover and Aaron Rose sat at a table at Pete's Diner on Capitol Hill. They were flanked by their longtime friend, Ben Carrol, who still worked in Washington, the President Elect's son Robert Douglas, and Robert's invited guest for the Inaugural festivities.

"Best breakfast on Capitol Hill bar none," Clay Grover said to his breakfast companions.

"Clay is known for excessive adulation when it comes to food, but in this case, he's not exaggerating," Aaron confirmed his husband's claim.

"Honestly, for all of the years that my dad was a Senator, not once did he ever take me here for breakfast," Robert stated.

"Well, today we rectify that unfathomable wrong," Clay announced with a chuckle.

"I'm not the breakfast food fanatic that Clay is, but they serve a great cup of coffee," Ben added. "Usually in the past when I'd come here with Clay before work, he'd have a 4 egg omelet, a side of bacon and a short stack of pancakes covered in maple syrup and butter. I'd have a cup of coffee, and maybe a plain bagel."

"How on earth can you eat like that and stay so fit and healthy?" Robert asked in amazement.

"I know! Right?" Aaron exclaimed and pleaded. "He eats everything and he doesn't gain a pound. It's wonderful and mind boggling. And also frustrating, because I'm eating a salad and he's eating a triple cheese-burger. And I'm the one who gains weight!"

"What can I tell ya boys, Mother Nature likes some of us more than she likes others," Clay boasted.

"Oh, shut up!" Aaron jokingly admonished. "No one wants to hear it."

"The only breakfast food that I've had the pleasure of watching you eat were a few beignets," Robert said to his guest. "Well, other than me."

"He's incorrigible," Michael said with a sheepish grin. "But I guess when you're the son of the President of the United States, you can get away with a lot of things."

"Not true," Robert protested. "Now that I will be visiting the White House from time to time I've been lectured about needing to be on my best behavior until I'm blue in the face."

"By whom, your mom?" Michael sweetly asked.

"Oh no, by boss lady. Or rather the new White House Director of Communications," Robert responded with rolled eyes.

"Yeah, I can attest to that," Clay added with a laugh. "I heard Carolyn lay into him pretty good the other day."

"Well, in three days I'll be back in Chicago, so she can say whatever she wants now," Robert said.

"And where will you be in three days, Michael?" Aaron asked.

"Behind the bar at French Tips, Juleps & Jazz, of course," Michael answered. "But the big change is that Posy is now allowing me and the other male servers to wear black t-shirts with a French Tips embossed emblem on them. We don't have to be bare-chested all the time anymore."

"Tis a pity, if you ask me," Robert interjected. "Who doesn't enjoy a muscular shaved chest?"

"Try it every day for three years and get back to me," Michael laughed.

"How is Posy?" Aaron inquired. "We saw her right before we relocated back to Washington, and she seemed fine, but that was right before Christmas."

"She's great. Back to being Posy. It's almost like she's wiped that whole ordeal from her memory. She's loud and crazy and great fun. But she is a little more careful these days. We all are, I suppose. Are you coming back to New Orleans for her and Norris Coaltree's wedding in June?" Michael asked.

"You bet," Clay answered enthusiastically. "In fact, she got us in a bear hug and wouldn't let go of either Aaron or I until we promised to return for the wedding."

"Excellent! It will be great fun. It has to be, it's Posy!" Michael exclaimed.

"Everybody ready to order? I'm starving," Clay asked.

"Some things never change, you're always hungry," Aaron chided his husband with a big smile.

BESSIE AND LUCIUS COLLINS HELD HANDS as they stood in front of the mausoleum in St. Louis Cemetery #1 in New Orleans. Established in the late 1700's, it is the oldest existent cemetery in New Orleans. It is the final resting place of many prominent New Orleans families. Bessie placed a bouquet of white flowers at the foot of the vault. She said a prayer, wiped a few tears from her eyes, and gently squeezed her husband's hand. The Collins made their way through the cemetery gates and walked through the French Quarter towards the French Market. They were the invited guests of Posy Branch and her fiancé Norris Coaltree for a get-together at French Tips, Juleps & Jazz to watch the Presidential Inauguration on big screen televisions. They arrived a little after 10:00 a.m., with the official swearing in ceremonies commencing at 11:00 a.m. Central Time, noon in Washington, D.C.

French Tips was decorated in red, white, and blue bunting with small American flags adorning the floral arrangements on each table. The house jazz band was playing patriotic music as the crowd began to file in and take their seats. Posy had arranged for a local caterer to supply Lucky Dog hot dogs, and other food stuffs for her guests. She had also commissioned Bessie to bake two dozen pies for the event. Something that Bessie was not only happy and proud to do, she relished the fact that so many people would be able to sample her pies.

Posy spotted Lucius and Bessie entering her establishment and quickly made her way through the crowd to greet them.

"Welcome, welcome!" Posy exclaimed as she threw her arms around Bessie and squeezed her good. It caught Bessie a bit off guard, but Bessie just giggled happy to be shown so much loving attention.

"My, this place looks simply wonderful!" Bessie enthused. "All the lovely red, white and blue colors and sashes. Makes me feel like I'm right there in Washington at the Inauguration."

"That was what I was going for," Posy explained. "I wanted folks to feel like they was part of all them festivities and such. After all, not all of us can be the invited guest of the son of the President of the United States."

"What am I, chopped liver?" Norris asked with a big grin.

"Oh no, sugar, you is U.S. Prime beef center cut, ain't no doubt about that," Posy laughed and snorted. "I'm just so proud of my Michael. Right there, rubbing shoulders with all them Washington muckety mucks. I just want to bust my buttons thinking about what a wonderful experience he must be having. My only regret is that he ain't here to make some nice juleps for y'all. But truth be told, my other bartender Jerome ain't half bad himself. I got a special table right up front for y'all." Posy escorted Bessie and Lucius to a table for six in the front of the bar, in a prime spot near one of the large television screens.

"Lawton, Lawton!" Posy yelled out from across the room, have Jerome make a couple of extra fine mint juleps for Bessie and Lucius, will ya?"

"You got it," Lawton shouted in return.

"Hey, you got somebody on lookout? Does the band know the cue?" Posy yelled in return.

"Yeah, everybody knows. Pete's got a lookout," Lawton loudly responded.

There were only twenty more minutes until the Inauguration ceremonies were about to commence in Washington. Posy's establishment was packed with friends and loyal customers. She couldn't contain her broad smile as she looked around the crowded room of people who cared so dearly for her.

"Almost here," Pete yelled from outside of the bar while standing on the street. A hush fell over the previously raucous crowd as the jazz band began to play the opening notes of the New Orleans classic song, "When the Saints Go Marching In." Pete quickly and gently took control as he pushed the wheelchair over the entry way and into French Tips. Everyone in the bar stood and cheered. Stanford Winchester and his wife had just arrived. They were followed by Calvin and Lucille Putnam.

Stanford was overwhelmed as he surveyed the many smiling faces of his friends filling the large establishment. He squeezed Whitlee's hand as he dabbed tears from his eyes. It had been a long and arduous road to recovery, but this moment had made it all worthwhile. Pete pushed Stanford's wheelchair up to the table where Bessie and Lucius were seated. Stanford sat right next to Bessie with Whitlee on his other side. Calvin and Lucile Putnam rounded out the table of honor. The gathered assemblage would not sit down or stop applauding Stanford. A few, including Calvin, began chanting, "Stanford, Stanford," until the entire room was doing it. Stanford tentatively raised his right hand to acknowledge the loving tribute. The band continued to play as Posy wept with joy.

A half hour later, everyone had settled down and had a few drinks and something to eat as they watched the swearing in ceremony for President Perry Douglas. More importantly, Stanford's friends were able to talk with him and offer their love and support.

"This is more than any one man deserves," Stanford said to Lucius and Bessie. "I'm overcome with emotion."

"Folks love you Stanford, they love you so much," Bessie said affectionately. "Sometimes you don't understand it, until something happens and they almost lose you. This morning, Lucius and I visited the grave site of my friend Mariette. As I stood there, I mourned for her, but I was also so grateful that I didn't lose you as well."

"The only reason that I'm here today is because of you, Bessie. I owe you my life. If you hadn't shown up when you did, well . . ." Stanford softly said before he began to choke up with tears streaming from his eyes.

"You is surely here now, and that's all that matters," Bessie replied. "Now, you just need to keep getting better and keep getting stronger."

"Well, on that account, I'm certainly making progress. My physical therapist says that I might be out of this infernal contraption and walking on my own with a cane in a couple of months. Whitlee is a real task master at home and doesn't allow me to skip any of my exercise therapy sessions."

"Are you sad that you ain't Attorney General?" Bessie hesitantly asked.

"Not at all, not at all. This is where I belong. President Douglas has been so incredibly kind and supportive. He asked when I feel up to it, if I would consider being a Special Advisor to the President for Judicial Reform. I could do most of my work here in New Orleans, and visit Washington once or twice a year. That is perfect for me," Stanford explained. "But enough about me how are you doing, Bessie?"

"Real good. The insurance company came through with the money from the fire. And between that and the generous loan that you done give me, we broke ground on the new structure last week. This one gonna be made of brick, with four big commercial ovens. I ain't exactly sure what I'm gonna call it yet, but I'm leaning towards, 'Bessie's Best Pies.' Tell you true, sometimes I gotta pinch myself when I realize that I'm gonna own my own bake shop. Making pies for folks is always what I dreamed of. Don't seem possible that it's coming true."

"I couldn't be happier for you. And I know you will be a big success. And that there is a fine name, 'Bessie's Best Pies.'" Stanford said proudly.

Lucius nodded his head in total agreement. Then he looked over at Whitlee with a sense of anticipation.

"Is it alright, Miss Whitlee?" Lucius asked.

"Yes Lucius, one is fine. He's off that certain medication now," Whitlee replied. With that, Lucius stood up and placed a white bar towel over his left arm. Standing proudly in front of his longtime friend, Lucius asked Stanford, "May I get the distinguished gentleman a cocktail?" Stanford laughed at, but also enjoyed the theatrics.

"Do birds have beaks?" Stanford responded on cue.

"Oh, they surely do, sir, they surely do," Lucius said as he laughed heartily. Lucius made his way to the bar and a few minutes later he returned with a Sazerac for Stanford.

"Made just the way you like it sir. I asked Jerome to add an extra dash of Peychaud's Bitters." Stanford took a good long sip. The last Sazerac he had was the afternoon at the Columns Hotel bar.

"Nicely done, nicely done indeed," Stanford stated with the wink of an eye.

A few minutes later, Bessie left the table for a couple of minutes and returned with an extra-large slice of her homemade pecan pie. She set the plate and a fork in front of Stanford and giggled like an excited schoolgirl.

Stanford picked up the fork and scooped a large portion of pie into his mouth. The buttery richness of the pecan filling and the perfect crust made his lips curl into a satisfied smile.

"This surely is fine pie," Stanford proclaimed, wholly contented. "This surely is."

It was mid-January, but it felt more like spring to all of those attending the Presidential Inauguration on Capitol Hill in Washington, and all of those assembled to honor Stanford Winchester in New Orleans. April was less than three months away and with it comes nature's resplendent restoration in all its vivid living colors.

Photo by Molly Johnson

Mr. Catalano resides in Chicago, IL. He has Bachelor of Arts and Master of Arts degrees in Political Science. He has melded his life-long fascination and love of politics with numerous years of working in the legal profession, into his first love, that of writing fiction.